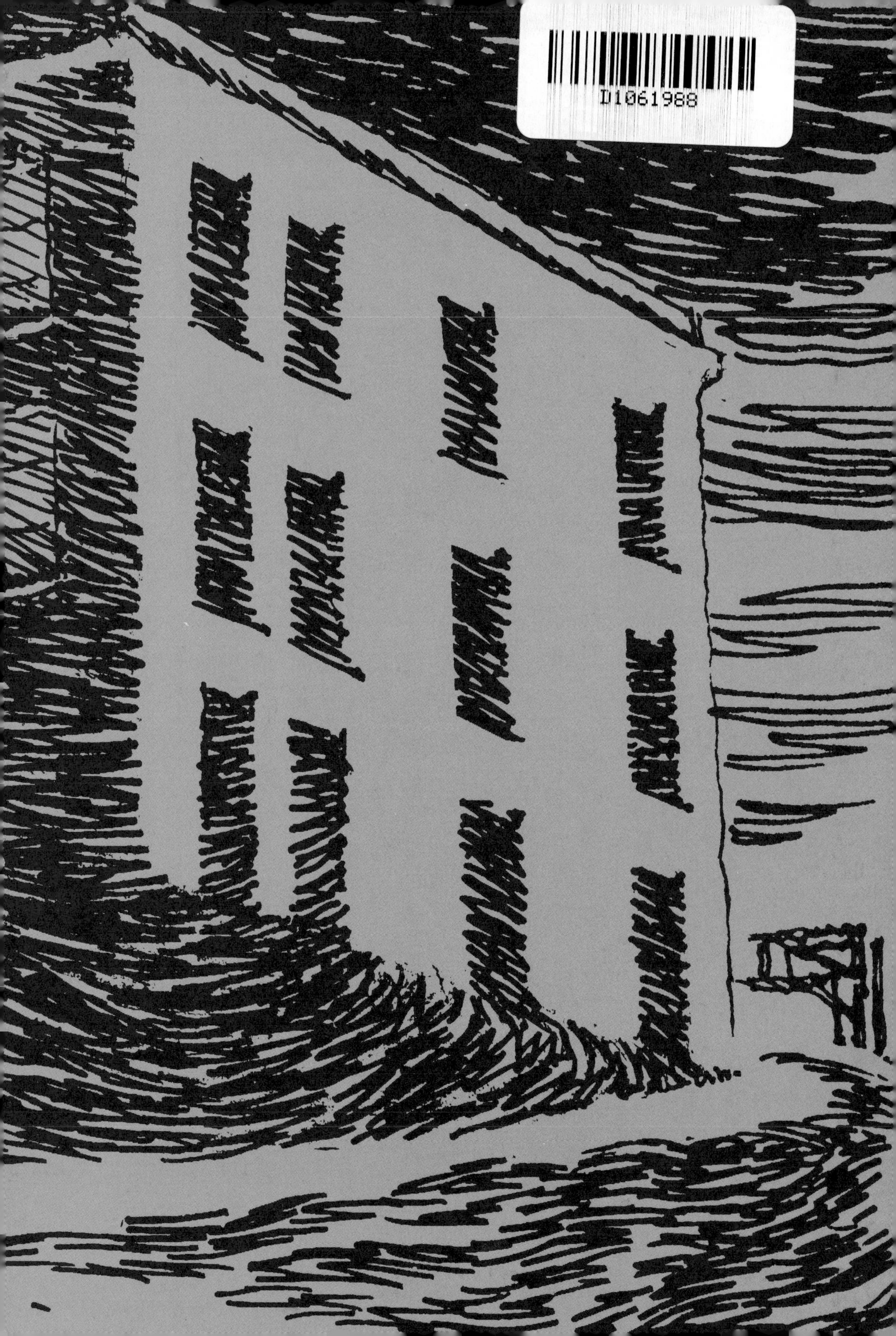

HAIR SHIRT

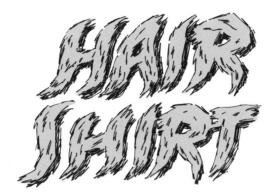

Patrick McEown

Coloured by Liz Artinan

SELF
MADE
HERO

First published in English in 2011
by SelfMadeHero
5 Upper Wimpole Street
London WIG 6BP
www.selfmadehero.com

English edition © 2011 SelfMadeHero

Written and Illustrated by: Patrick McEown
Colourist: Liz Artinan
Editorial and Production Assistant: Lizzie Kaye
Publishing Director: Emma Hayley
With thanks to: Doug Wallace and Jane Laporte

First published in French by Gallimard in 2010
© Gallimard 2010

A CIP record for this book is available from the British Library

ISBN: 978-1-906838-27-0

10 9 8 7 6 5 4 3 2

Printed and bound in China

TO EVERYONE WHO PLAYED A PART.

DAVE COOPER AND KAREN MESSER,
IN PARTICULAR.

- PATRICK McEOWN

Hairshirt: literally, "a shirt made of hair", used in some religious traditions to induce a degree of discomfort or pain as a sign of repentance and atonement.

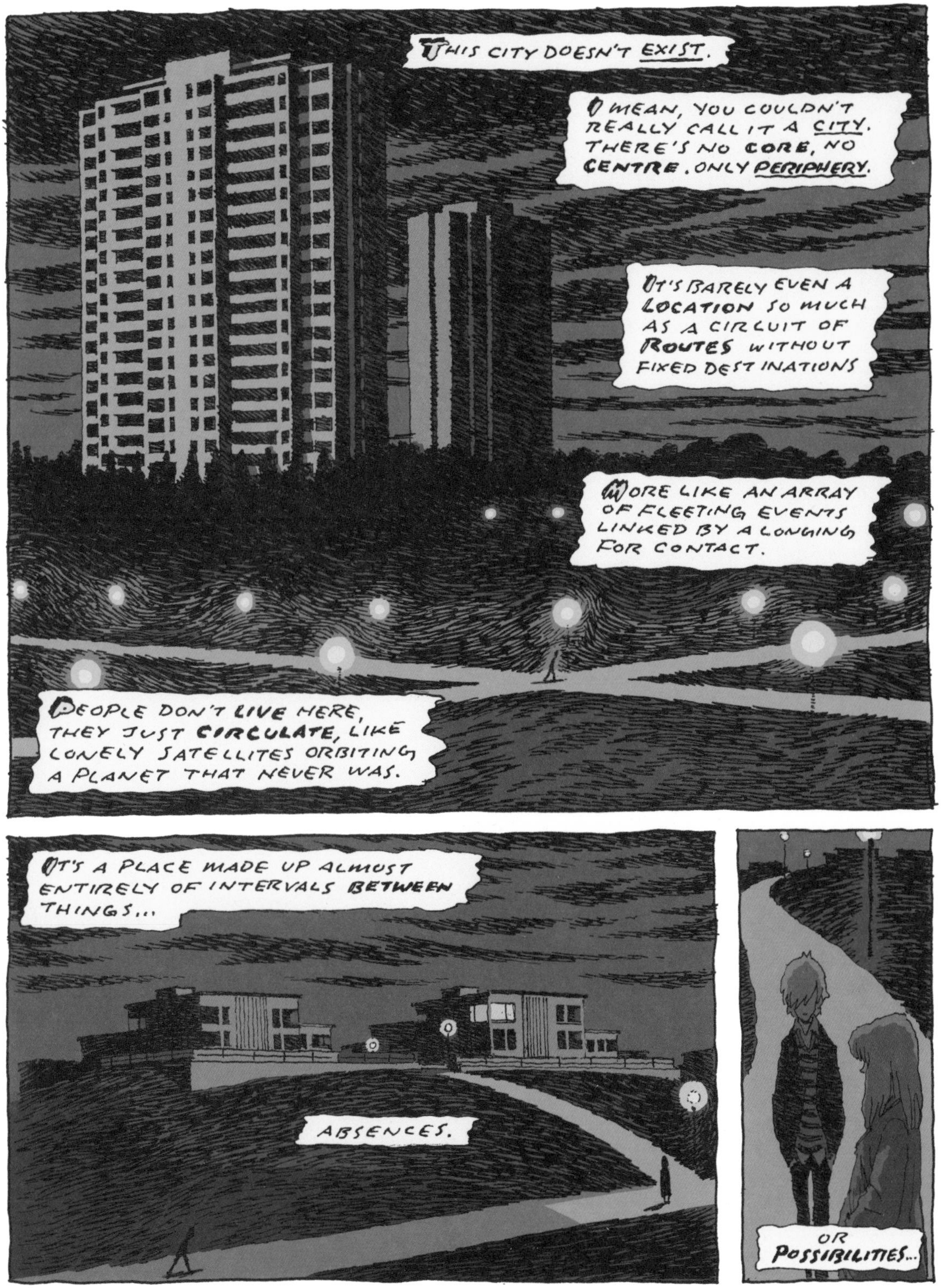
THIS CITY DOESN'T EXIST.
I MEAN, YOU COULDN'T REALLY CALL IT A CITY. THERE'S NO CORE, NO CENTRE. ONLY PERIPHERY.
IT'S BARELY EVEN A LOCATION SO MUCH AS A CIRCUIT OF ROUTES WITHOUT FIXED DESTINATIONS
MORE LIKE AN ARRAY OF FLEETING EVENTS LINKED BY A LONGING FOR CONTACT.
PEOPLE DON'T LIVE HERE, THEY JUST CIRCULATE, LIKE LONELY SATELLITES ORBITING A PLANET THAT NEVER WAS.
IT'S A PLACE MADE UP ALMOST ENTIRELY OF INTERVALS BETWEEN THINGS...
ABSENCES.
OR POSSIBILITIES...

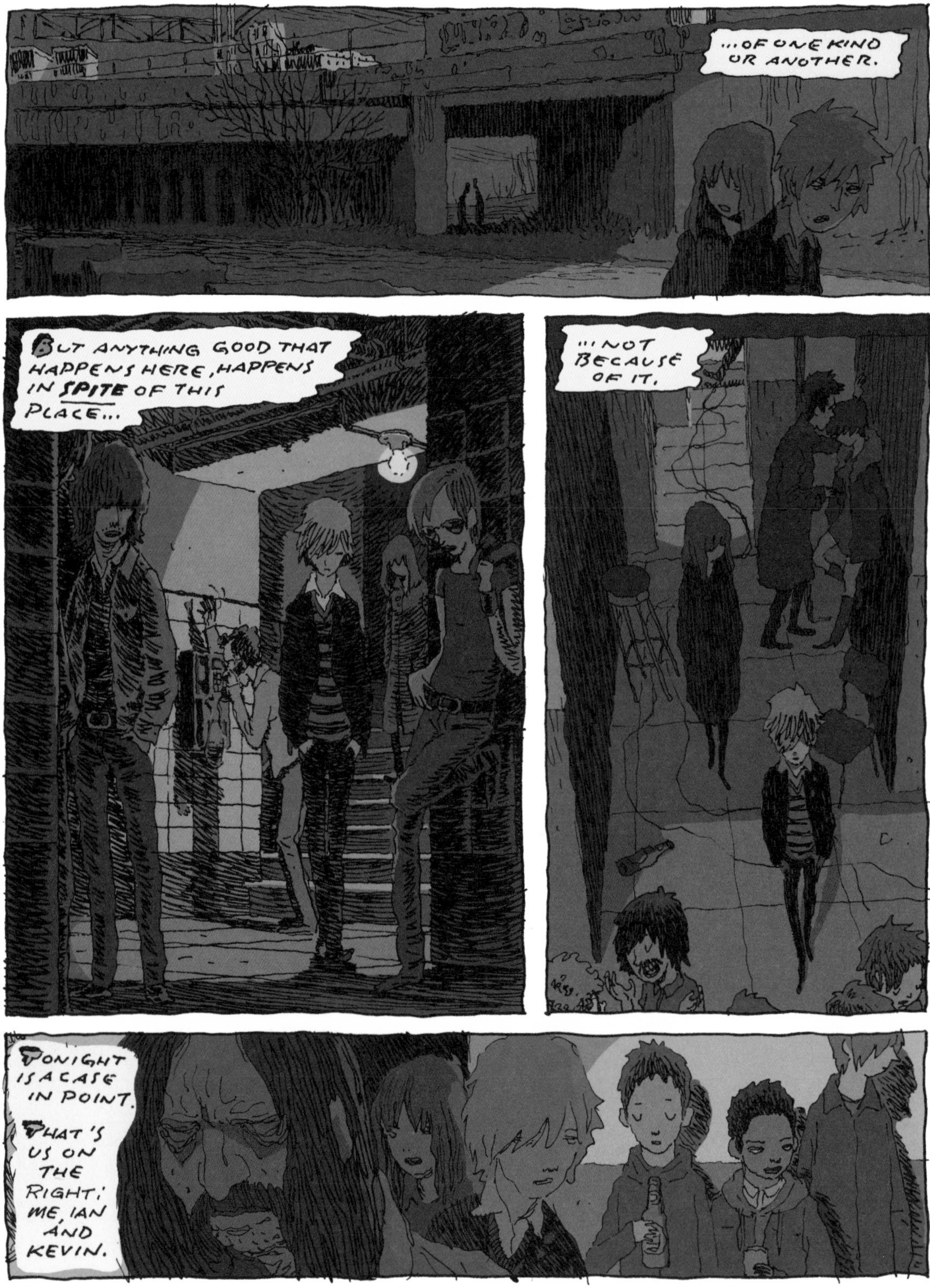
...OF ONE KIND OR ANOTHER.
BUT ANYTHING GOOD THAT HAPPENS HERE, HAPPENS IN SPITE OF THIS PLACE...
...NOT BECAUSE OF IT.
TONIGHT IS A CASE IN POINT.
THAT'S US ON THE RIGHT; ME, IAN AND KEVIN.

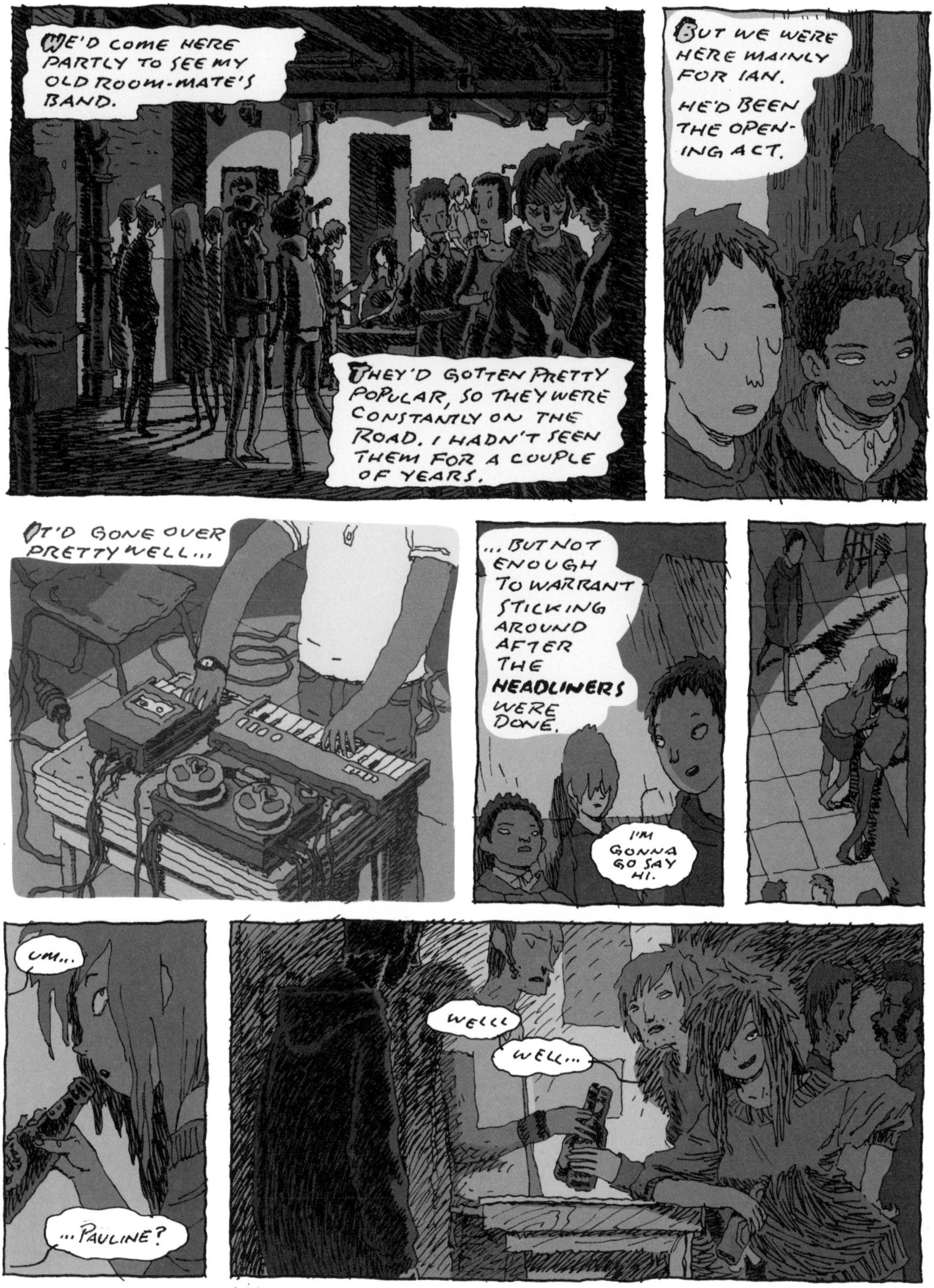
WE'D COME HERE PARTLY TO SEE MY OLD ROOM-MATE'S BAND.
THEY'D GOTTEN PRETTY POPULAR, SO THEY WERE CONSTANTLY ON THE ROAD. I HADN'T SEEN THEM FOR A COUPLE OF YEARS.
BUT WE WERE HERE MAINLY FOR IAN.
HE'D BEEN THE OPENING ACT.
IT'D GONE OVER PRETTY WELL...
...BUT NOT ENOUGH TO WARRANT STICKING AROUND AFTER THE **HEADLINERS** WERE DONE.
I'M GONNA GO SAY HI.
UM...
...PAULINE?
WELLL
WELL...

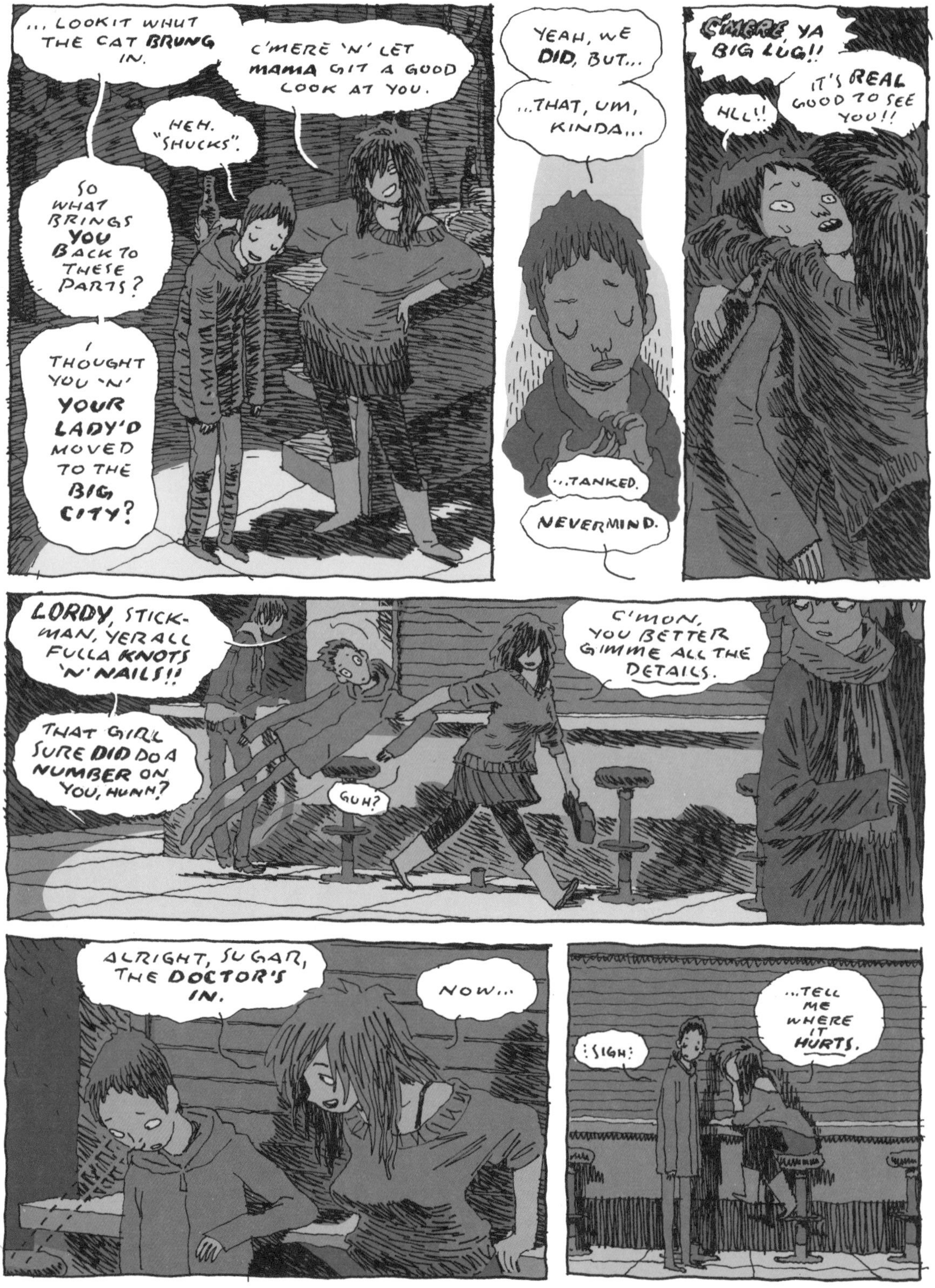
...LOOKIT WHUT THE CAT BRUNG IN.
C'MERE 'N' LET MAMA GIT A GOOD LOOK AT YOU.
HEH. "SHUCKS".
SO WHAT BRINGS YOU BACK TO THESE PARTS?
I THOUGHT YOU 'N' YOUR LADY'D MOVED TO THE BIG CITY?
YEAH, WE DID, BUT...
...THAT, UM, KINDA...
...TANKED.
NEVERMIND.
C'MERE YA BIG LUG!!
HLL!!
IT'S REAL GOOD TO SEE YOU!!
LORDY, STICK-MAN, YER ALL FULLA KNOTS 'N' NAILS!!
THAT GIRL SURE DID DO A NUMBER ON YOU, HUNH?
GUH?
C'MON, YOU BETTER GIMME ALL THE DETAILS.
ALRIGHT, SUGAR, THE DOCTOR'S IN.
NOW...
:SIGH:
...TELL ME WHERE IT HURTS.

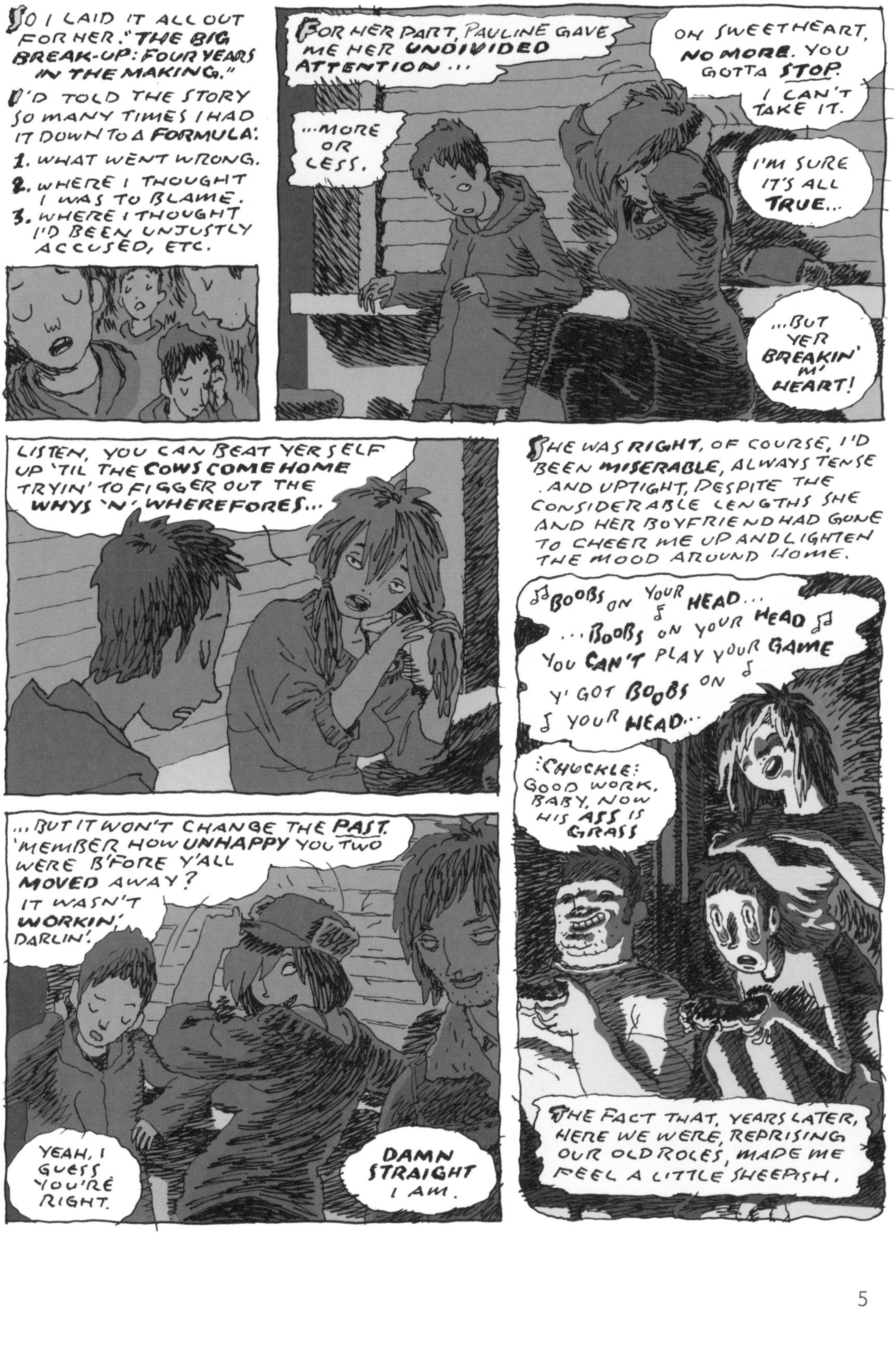
SO I LAID IT ALL OUT FOR HER: "THE BIG BREAK-UP: FOUR YEARS IN THE MAKING."
I'D TOLD THE STORY SO MANY TIMES I HAD IT DOWN TO A FORMULA:
1. WHAT WENT WRONG.
2. WHERE I THOUGHT I WAS TO BLAME.
3. WHERE I THOUGHT I'D BEEN UNJUSTLY ACCUSED, ETC.
FOR HER PART, PAULINE GAVE ME HER UNDIVIDED ATTENTION ...
...MORE OR LESS.
OH SWEETHEART, NO MORE. YOU GOTTA STOP. I CAN'T TAKE IT.
I'M SURE IT'S ALL TRUE...
...BUT YER BREAKIN' M' HEART!
LISTEN, YOU CAN BEAT YERSELF UP 'TIL THE COWS COME HOME TRYIN' TO FIGGER OUT THE WHYS 'N' WHEREFORES...
...BUT IT WON'T CHANGE THE PAST. 'MEMBER HOW UNHAPPY YOU TWO WERE B'FORE Y'ALL MOVED AWAY? IT WASN'T WORKIN', DARLIN'.
YEAH, I GUESS YOU'RE RIGHT.
DAMN STRAIGHT I AM.
SHE WAS RIGHT, OF COURSE, I'D BEEN MISERABLE, ALWAYS TENSE AND UPTIGHT, DESPITE THE CONSIDERABLE LENGTHS SHE AND HER BOYFRIEND HAD GONE TO CHEER ME UP AND LIGHTEN THE MOOD AROUND HOME.
BOOBS ON YOUR HEAD... ...BOOBS ON YOUR HEAD YOU CAN'T PLAY YOUR GAME Y' GOT BOOBS ON YOUR HEAD...
:CHUCKLE: GOOD WORK, BABY, NOW HIS ASS IS GRASS
THE FACT THAT, YEARS LATER, HERE WE WERE, REPRISING OUR OLD ROLES, MADE ME FEEL A LITTLE SHEEPISH.

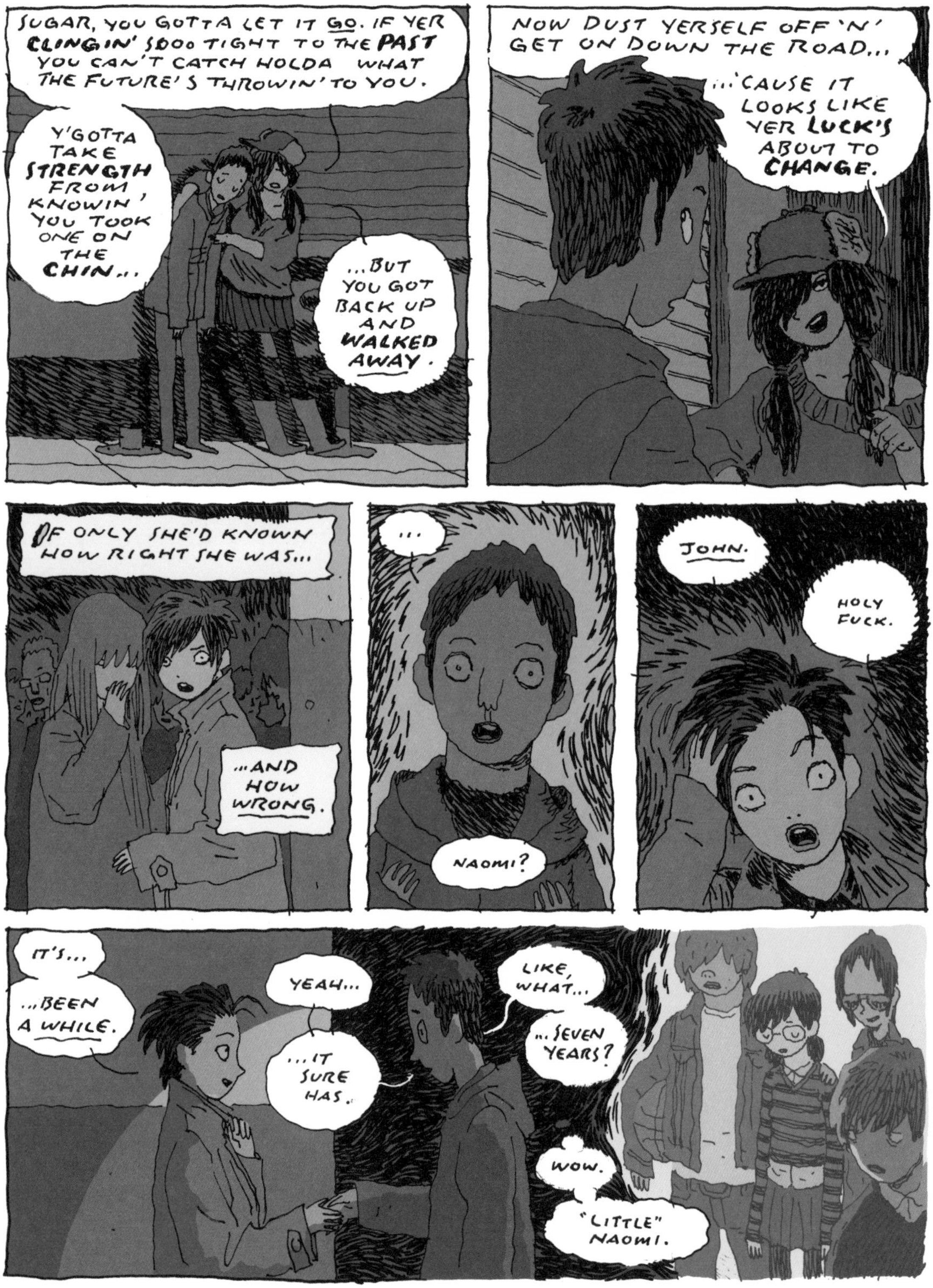
SUGAR, YOU GOTTA LET IT GO. IF YER CLINGIN' SOOO TIGHT TO THE PAST YOU CAN'T CATCH HOLDA WHAT THE FUTURE'S THROWIN' TO YOU.
Y'GOTTA TAKE STRENGTH FROM KNOWIN' YOU TOOK ONE ON THE CHIN...
...BUT YOU GOT BACK UP AND WALKED AWAY.
NOW DUST YERSELF OFF 'N' GET ON DOWN THE ROAD...
...'CAUSE IT LOOKS LIKE YER LUCK'S ABOUT TO CHANGE.
IF ONLY SHE'D KNOWN HOW RIGHT SHE WAS...
...AND HOW WRONG.
...
NAOMI?
JOHN.
HOLY FUCK.
IT'S...
...BEEN A WHILE.
YEAH...
...IT SURE HAS.
LIKE, WHAT...
...SEVEN YEARS?
WOW.
"LITTLE" NAOMI.

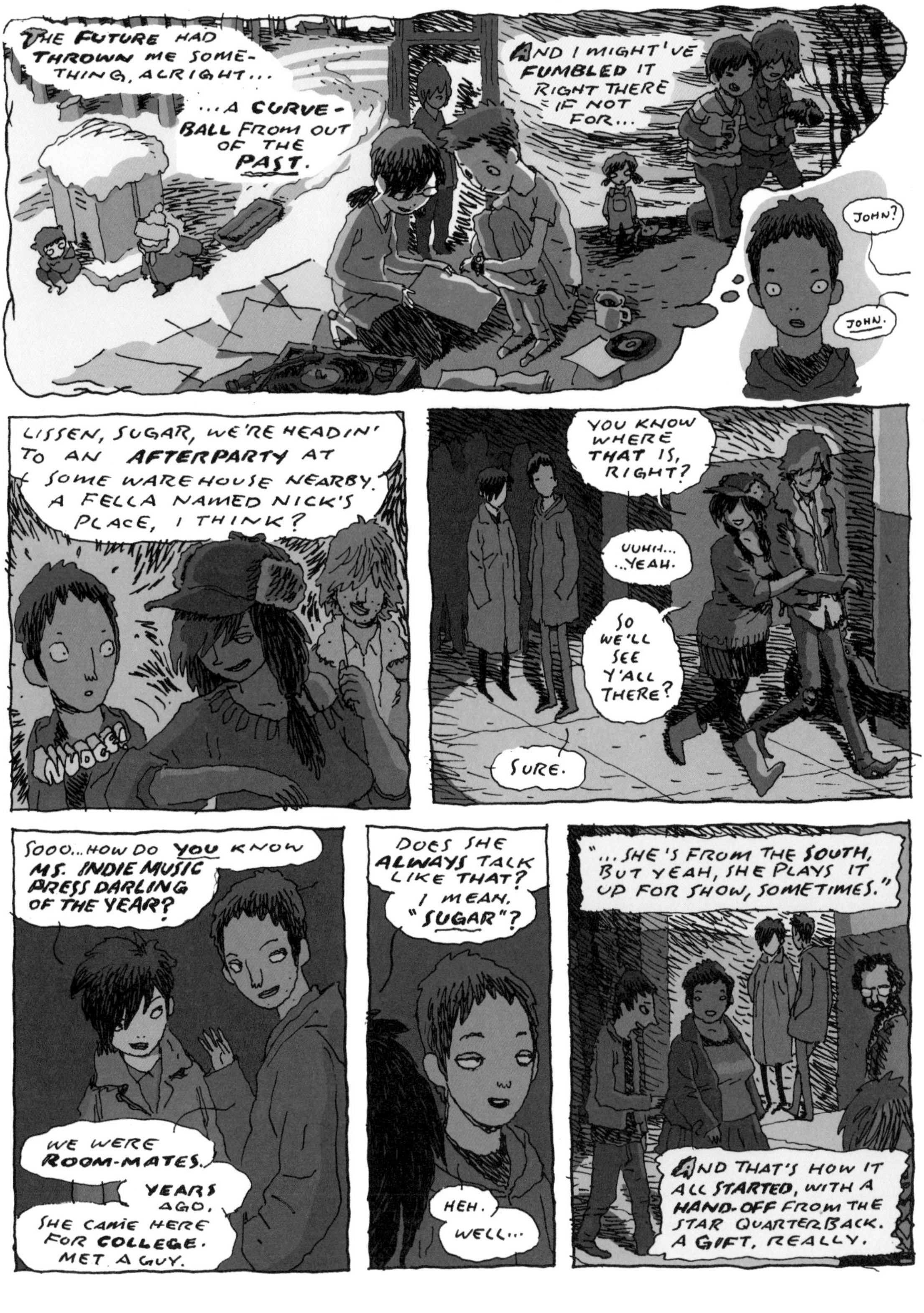

THE FUTURE HAD THROWN ME SOMETHING, ALRIGHT...
...A CURVE-BALL FROM OUT OF THE PAST.
AND I MIGHT'VE FUMBLED IT RIGHT THERE IF NOT FOR...
JOHN?
JOHN.
LISSEN, SUGAR, WE'RE HEADIN' TO AN AFTERPARTY AT SOME WAREHOUSE NEARBY. A FELLA NAMED NICK'S PLACE, I THINK?
NUDGE!
YOU KNOW WHERE THAT IS, RIGHT?
UUHH... ...YEAH.
SO WE'LL SEE Y'ALL THERE?
SURE.
SOOO... HOW DO YOU KNOW MS. INDIE MUSIC PRESS DARLING OF THE YEAR?
WE WERE ROOM-MATES.
YEARS AGO.
SHE CAME HERE FOR COLLEGE. MET A GUY.
DOES SHE ALWAYS TALK LIKE THAT? I MEAN, "SUGAR"?
HEH.
WELL...
"...SHE'S FROM THE SOUTH, BUT YEAH, SHE PLAYS IT UP FOR SHOW, SOMETIMES."
AND THAT'S HOW IT ALL STARTED, WITH A HAND-OFF FROM THE STAR QUARTERBACK. A GIFT, REALLY.

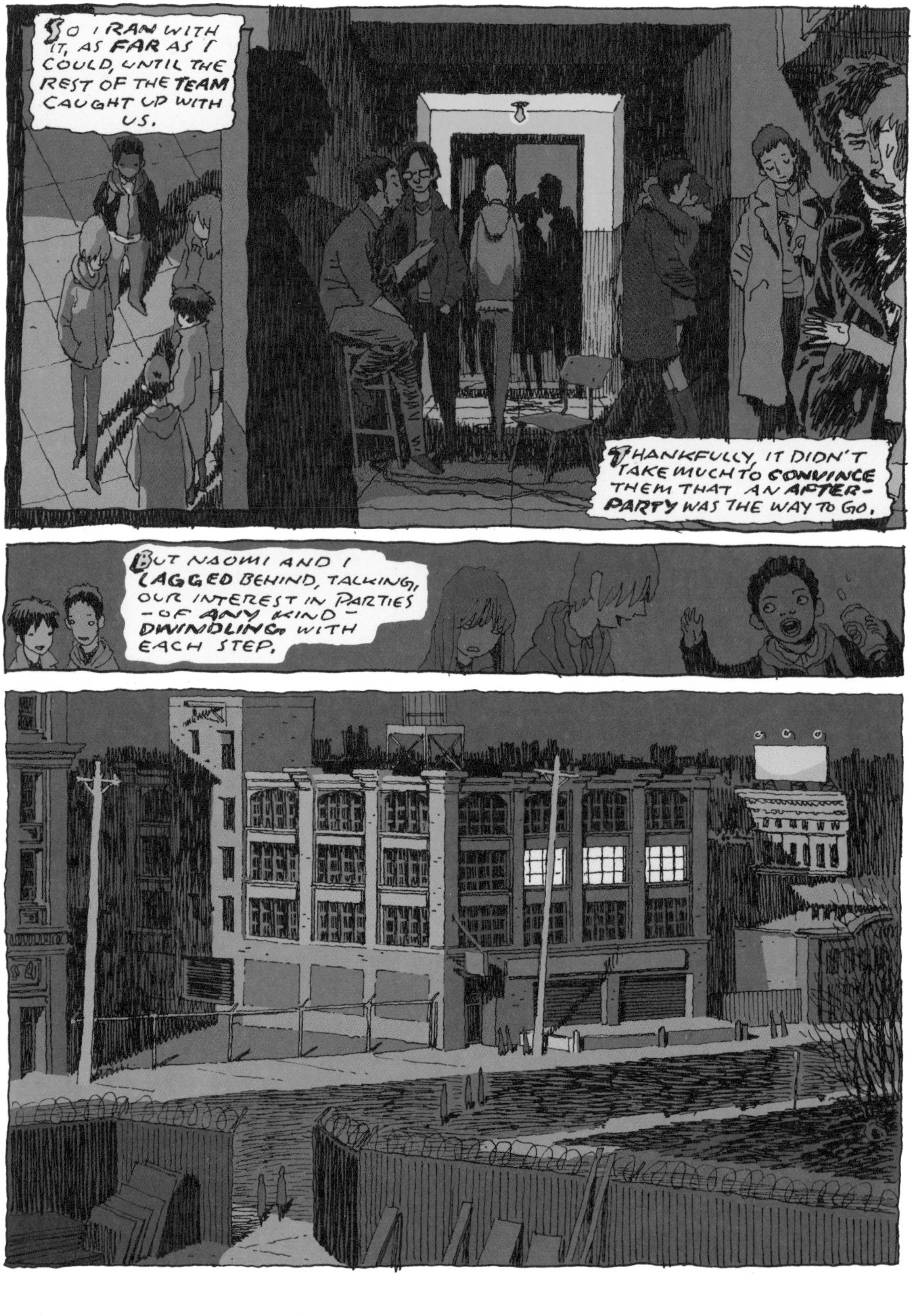
SO I RAN WITH IT, AS FAR AS I COULD, UNTIL THE REST OF THE TEAM CAUGHT UP WITH US.
THANKFULLY, IT DIDN'T TAKE MUCH TO CONVINCE THEM THAT AN AFTER-PARTY WAS THE WAY TO GO.
BUT NAOMI AND I LAGGED BEHIND, TALKING, OUR INTEREST IN PARTIES - OF ANY KIND - DWINDLING WITH EACH STEP.

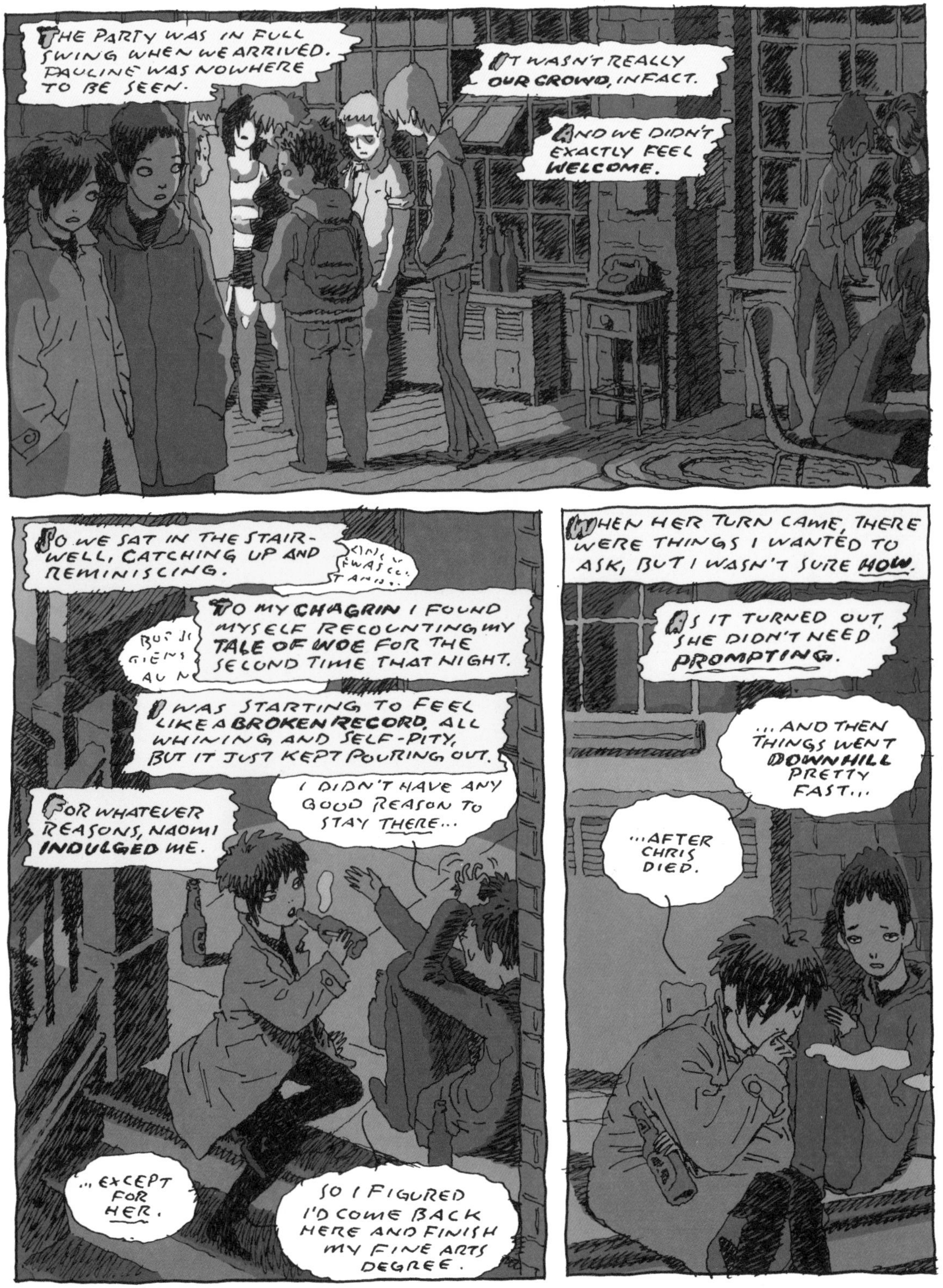
THE PARTY WAS IN FULL SWING WHEN WE ARRIVED. PAULINE WAS NOWHERE TO BE SEEN.
IT WASN'T REALLY OUR CROWD, IN FACT.
AND WE DIDN'T EXACTLY FEEL WELCOME.
SO WE SAT IN THE STAIRWELL, CATCHING UP AND REMINISCING.
TO MY CHAGRIN I FOUND MYSELF RECOUNTING MY TALE OF WOE FOR THE SECOND TIME THAT NIGHT.
I WAS STARTING TO FEEL LIKE A BROKEN RECORD, ALL WHINING AND SELF-PITY, BUT IT JUST KEPT POURING OUT.
FOR WHATEVER REASONS, NAOMI INDULGED ME.
I DIDN'T HAVE ANY GOOD REASON TO STAY THERE...
...EXCEPT FOR HER.
SO I FIGURED I'D COME BACK HERE AND FINISH MY FINE ARTS DEGREE.
WHEN HER TURN CAME, THERE WERE THINGS I WANTED TO ASK, BUT I WASN'T SURE HOW.
AS IT TURNED OUT, SHE DIDN'T NEED PROMPTING.
...AND THEN THINGS WENT DOWNHILL PRETTY FAST...
...AFTER CHRIS DIED.

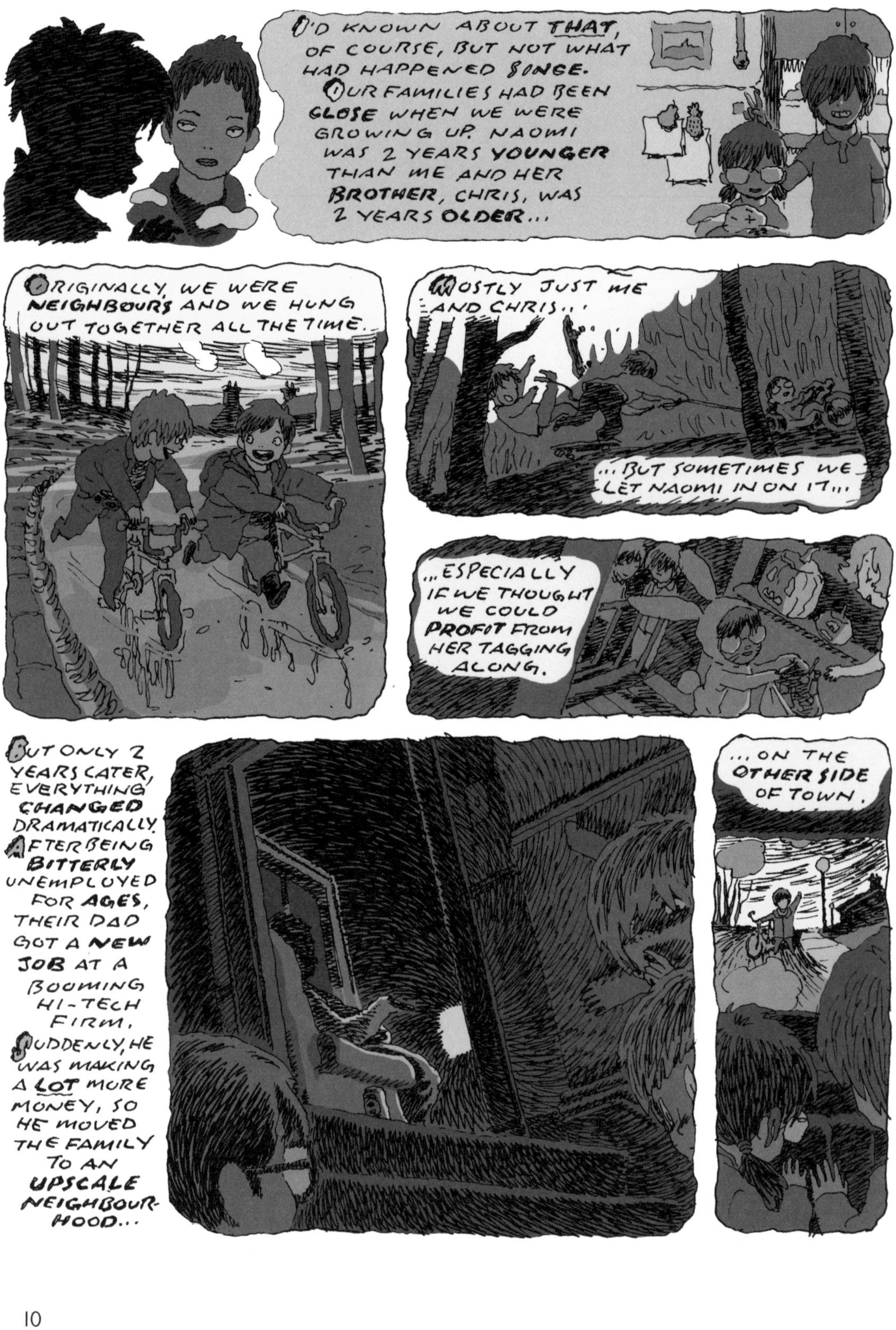
I'D KNOWN ABOUT THAT, OF COURSE, BUT NOT WHAT HAD HAPPENED SINCE. OUR FAMILIES HAD BEEN CLOSE WHEN WE WERE GROWING UP. NAOMI WAS 2 YEARS YOUNGER THAN ME AND HER BROTHER, CHRIS, WAS 2 YEARS OLDER...
ORIGINALLY, WE WERE NEIGHBOURS AND WE HUNG OUT TOGETHER ALL THE TIME.
MOSTLY JUST ME AND CHRIS...
...BUT SOMETIMES WE LET NAOMI IN ON IT...
...ESPECIALLY IF WE THOUGHT WE COULD PROFIT FROM HER TAGGING ALONG.
BUT ONLY 2 YEARS LATER, EVERYTHING CHANGED DRAMATICALLY. AFTER BEING BITTERLY UNEMPLOYED FOR AGES, THEIR DAD GOT A NEW JOB AT A BOOMING HI-TECH FIRM. SUDDENLY, HE WAS MAKING A LOT MORE MONEY, SO HE MOVED THE FAMILY TO AN UPSCALE NEIGHBOURHOOD...
...ON THE OTHER SIDE OF TOWN.

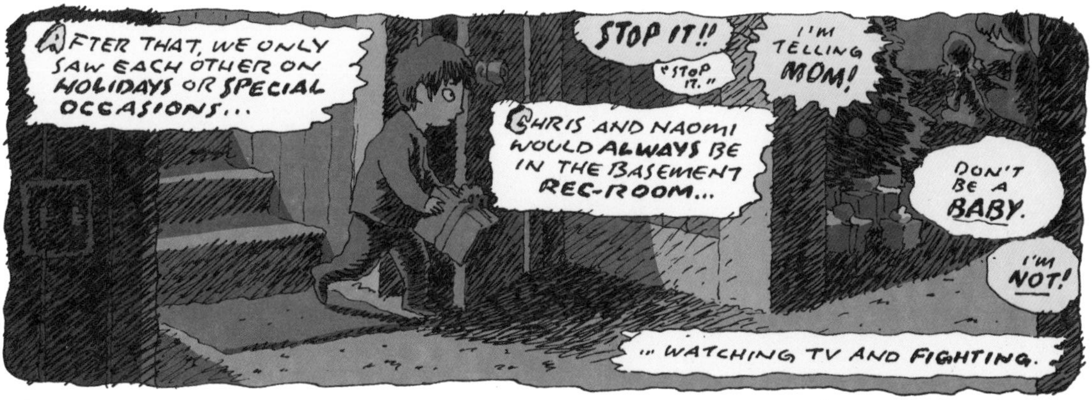
AFTER THAT, WE ONLY SAW EACH OTHER ON **HOLIDAYS** OR **SPECIAL OCCASIONS**...
CHRIS AND NAOMI WOULD **ALWAYS** BE IN THE BASEMENT **REC-ROOM**...
STOP IT!!
"STOP IT."
I'M TELLING MOM!
DON'T BE A BABY.
I'M NOT!
... WATCHING TV AND **FIGHTING**.

BY THE TIME I WAS 16, THE SAME YEAR CHRIS WOULD BE KILLED IN A **CAR ACCIDENT**, HE AND I HAD LONG SINCE **GROWN APART**. IT WAS PARTLY DUE TO THE **AGE DIFFERENCE** AND PARTLY DUE TO LIVING AT **OPPOSITE ENDS** OF TOWN, BUT MOSTLY IT WAS JUST **PERSONALITY**.

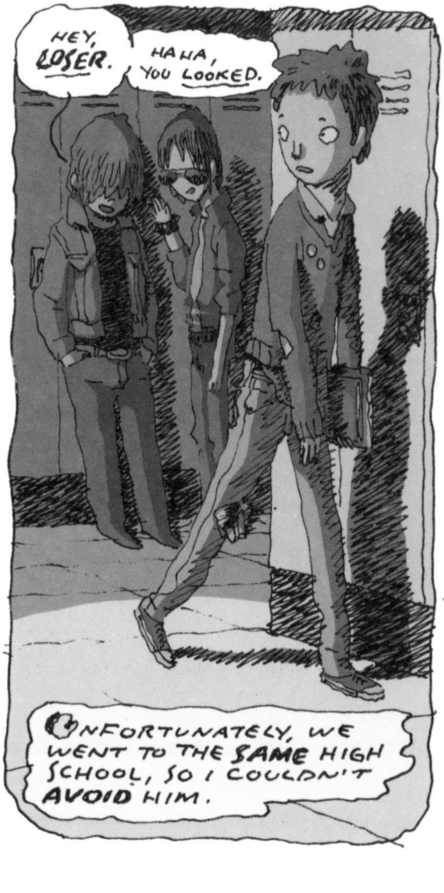
HEY, LOSER.
HAHA, YOU LOOKED.
UNFORTUNATELY, WE WENT TO THE **SAME** HIGH SCHOOL, SO I COULDN'T **AVOID** HIM.

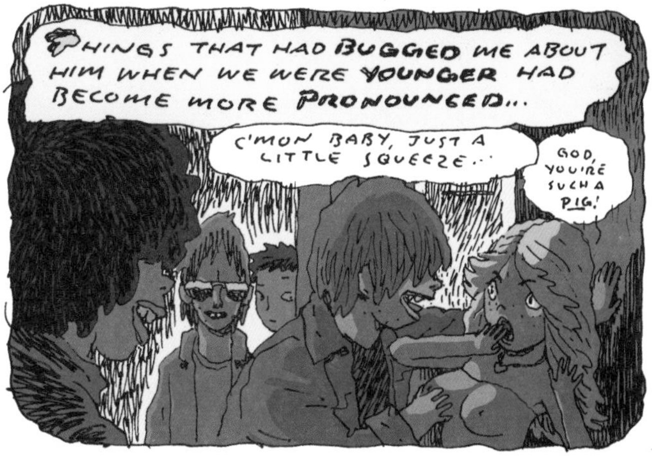
THINGS THAT HAD **BUGGED** ME ABOUT HIM WHEN WE WERE **YOUNGER** HAD BECOME MORE **PRONOUNCED**...
C'MON BABY, JUST A LITTLE SQUEEZE...
GOD, YOU'RE SUCH A PIG!

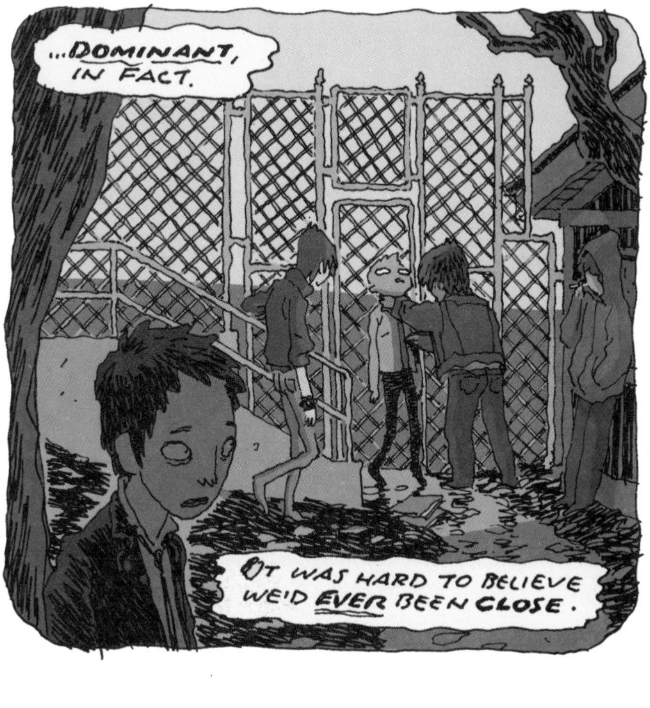
...DOMINANT, IN FACT.
IT WAS HARD TO BELIEVE WE'D EVER BEEN **CLOSE**.

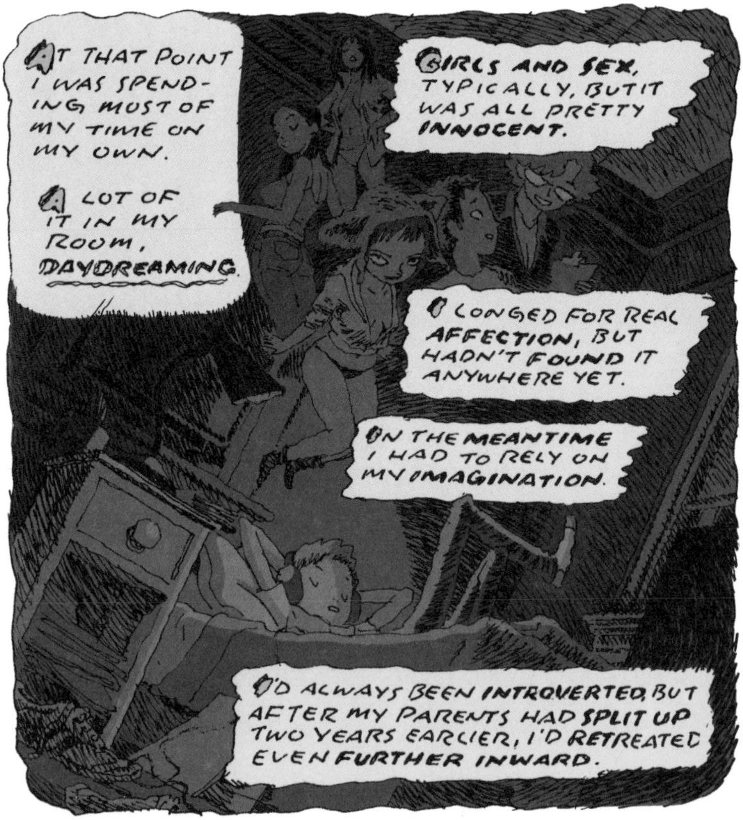
AT THAT POINT I WAS SPENDING MOST OF MY TIME ON MY OWN.
A LOT OF IT IN MY ROOM, DAYDREAMING.
GIRLS AND SEX, TYPICALLY, BUT IT WAS ALL PRETTY INNOCENT.
I LONGED FOR REAL AFFECTION, BUT HADN'T FOUND IT ANYWHERE YET.
IN THE MEANTIME I HAD TO RELY ON MY IMAGINATION.
I'D ALWAYS BEEN INTROVERTED, BUT AFTER MY PARENTS HAD SPLIT UP TWO YEARS EARLIER, I'D RETREATED EVEN FURTHER INWARD.

BY CONTRAST, CHRIS HAD GONE IN THE TOTAL OPPOSITE DIRECTION.
HE WAS ALWAYS MORE RECKLESS AND SELF-ASSURED. AS A KID, I ADMIRED THAT, BUT AS I GOT OLDER I WAS REPULSED BY WHAT HAD BECOME ARROGANCE AND CRUELTY.

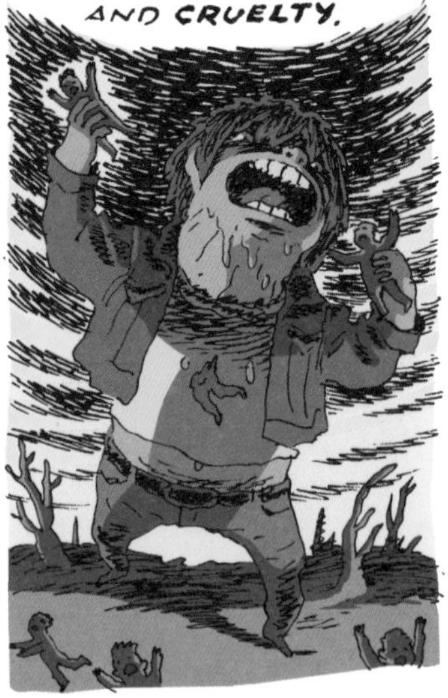

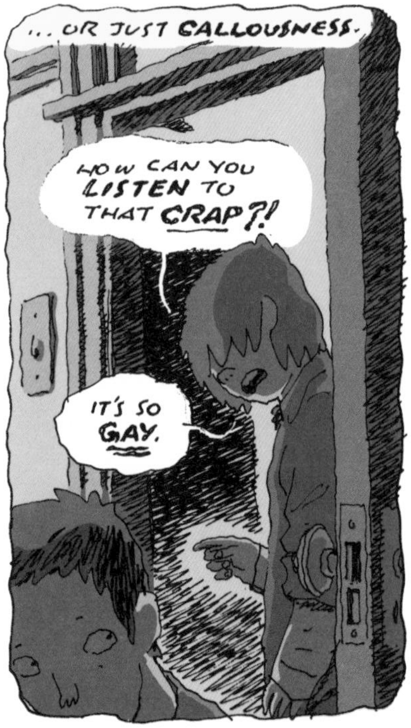
... OR JUST CALLOUSNESS.
HOW CAN YOU LISTEN TO THAT CRAP?!
IT'S SO GAY.

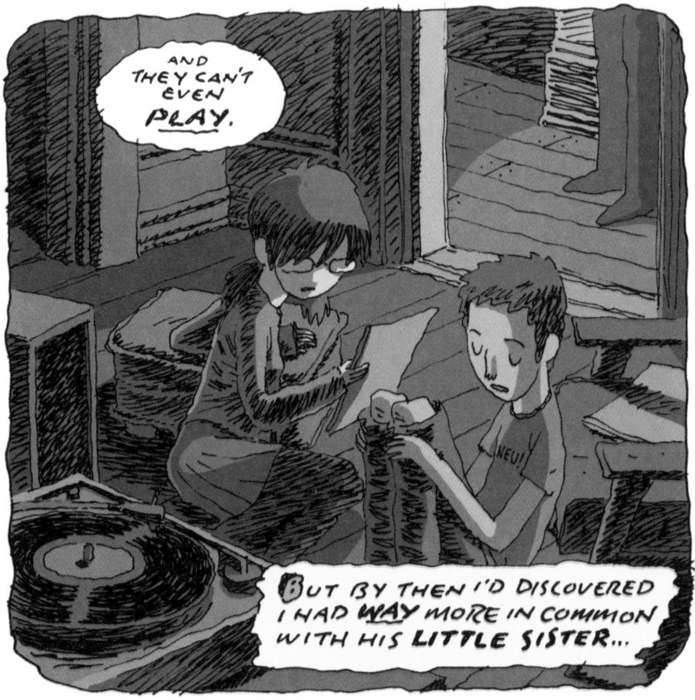
AND THEY CAN'T EVEN PLAY.
NEU!
BUT BY THEN I'D DISCOVERED I HAD WAY MORE IN COMMON WITH HIS LITTLE SISTER...

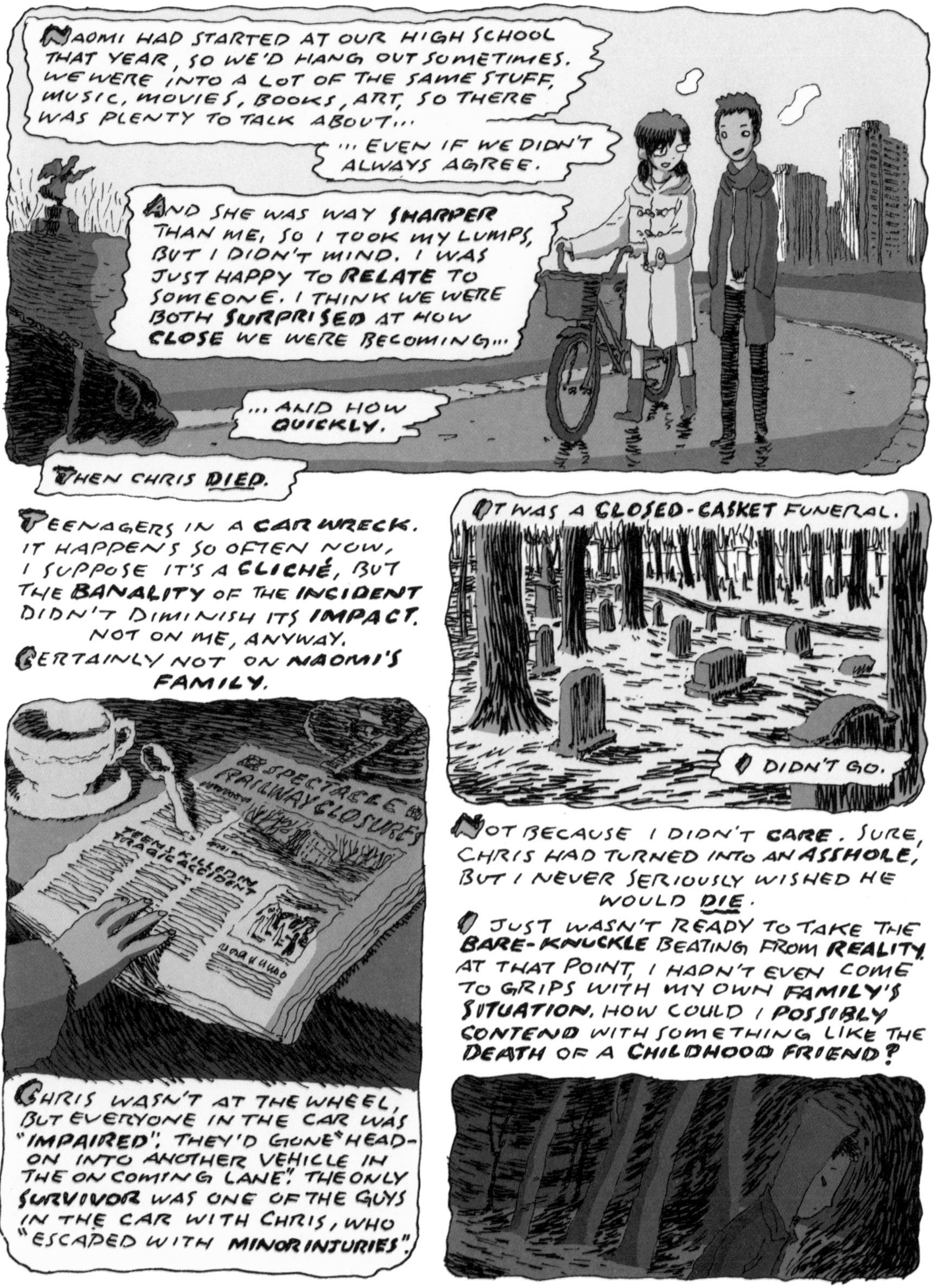
NAOMI HAD STARTED AT OUR HIGH SCHOOL THAT YEAR, SO WE'D HANG OUT SOMETIMES. WE WERE INTO A LOT OF THE SAME STUFF, MUSIC, MOVIES, BOOKS, ART, SO THERE WAS PLENTY TO TALK ABOUT...
... EVEN IF WE DIDN'T ALWAYS AGREE.
AND SHE WAS WAY SHARPER THAN ME, SO I TOOK MY LUMPS, BUT I DIDN'T MIND. I WAS JUST HAPPY TO RELATE TO SOMEONE. I THINK WE WERE BOTH SURPRISED AT HOW CLOSE WE WERE BECOMING...
... AND HOW QUICKLY.
THEN CHRIS DIED.
TEENAGERS IN A CAR WRECK. IT HAPPENS SO OFTEN NOW, I SUPPOSE IT'S A CLICHÉ, BUT THE BANALITY OF THE INCIDENT DIDN'T DIMINISH ITS IMPACT. NOT ON ME, ANYWAY.
CERTAINLY NOT ON NAOMI'S FAMILY.
SPECTACLE
RAILWAY CLOSURES
TEENS KILLED IN TRAGIC ACCIDENT
CHRIS WASN'T AT THE WHEEL, BUT EVERYONE IN THE CAR WAS "IMPAIRED". THEY'D GONE "HEAD-ON INTO ANOTHER VEHICLE IN THE ONCOMING LANE". THE ONLY SURVIVOR WAS ONE OF THE GUYS IN THE CAR WITH CHRIS, WHO "ESCAPED WITH MINOR INJURIES".
IT WAS A CLOSED-CASKET FUNERAL.
I DIDN'T GO.
NOT BECAUSE I DIDN'T CARE. SURE, CHRIS HAD TURNED INTO AN ASSHOLE, BUT I NEVER SERIOUSLY WISHED HE WOULD DIE.
I JUST WASN'T READY TO TAKE THE BARE-KNUCKLE BEATING FROM REALITY. AT THAT POINT, I HADN'T EVEN COME TO GRIPS WITH MY OWN FAMILY'S SITUATION. HOW COULD I POSSIBLY CONTEND WITH SOMETHING LIKE THE DEATH OF A CHILDHOOD FRIEND?

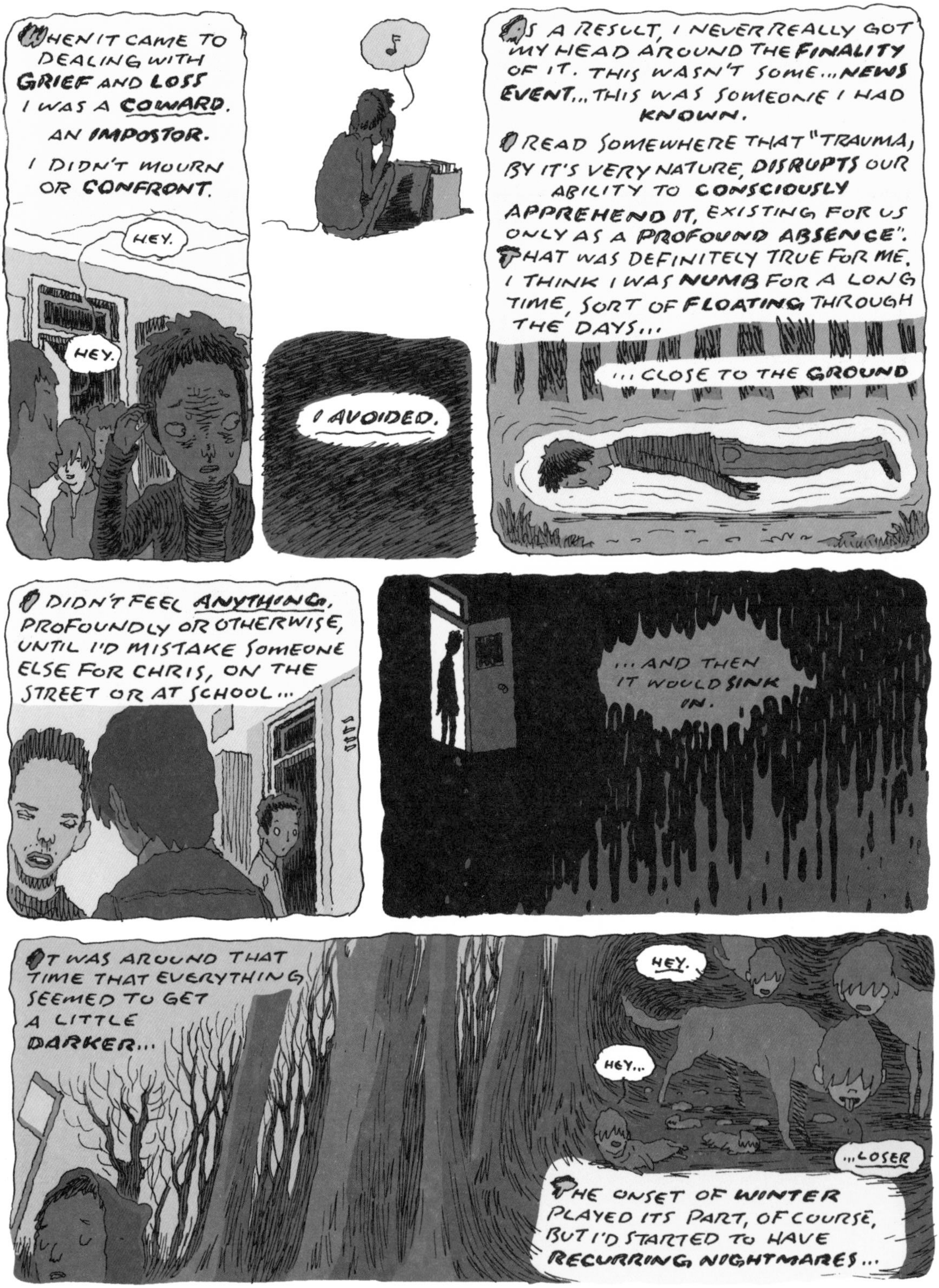
WHEN IT CAME TO DEALING WITH GRIEF AND LOSS I WAS A COWARD.
AN IMPOSTOR.
I DIDN'T MOURN OR CONFRONT.
HEY.
HEY.
I AVOIDED.
AS A RESULT, I NEVER REALLY GOT MY HEAD AROUND THE FINALITY OF IT. THIS WASN'T SOME... NEWS EVENT... THIS WAS SOMEONE I HAD KNOWN.
I READ SOMEWHERE THAT "TRAUMA, BY IT'S VERY NATURE, DISRUPTS OUR ABILITY TO CONSCIOUSLY APPREHEND IT, EXISTING FOR US ONLY AS A PROFOUND ABSENCE".
THAT WAS DEFINITELY TRUE FOR ME. I THINK I WAS NUMB FOR A LONG TIME, SORT OF FLOATING THROUGH THE DAYS...
... CLOSE TO THE GROUND
I DIDN'T FEEL ANYTHING, PROFOUNDLY OR OTHERWISE, UNTIL I'D MISTAKE SOMEONE ELSE FOR CHRIS, ON THE STREET OR AT SCHOOL...
... AND THEN IT WOULD SINK IN.
IT WAS AROUND THAT TIME THAT EVERYTHING SEEMED TO GET A LITTLE DARKER...
HEY.
HEY...
...LOSER
THE ONSET OF WINTER PLAYED ITS PART, OF COURSE, BUT I'D STARTED TO HAVE RECURRING NIGHTMARES...

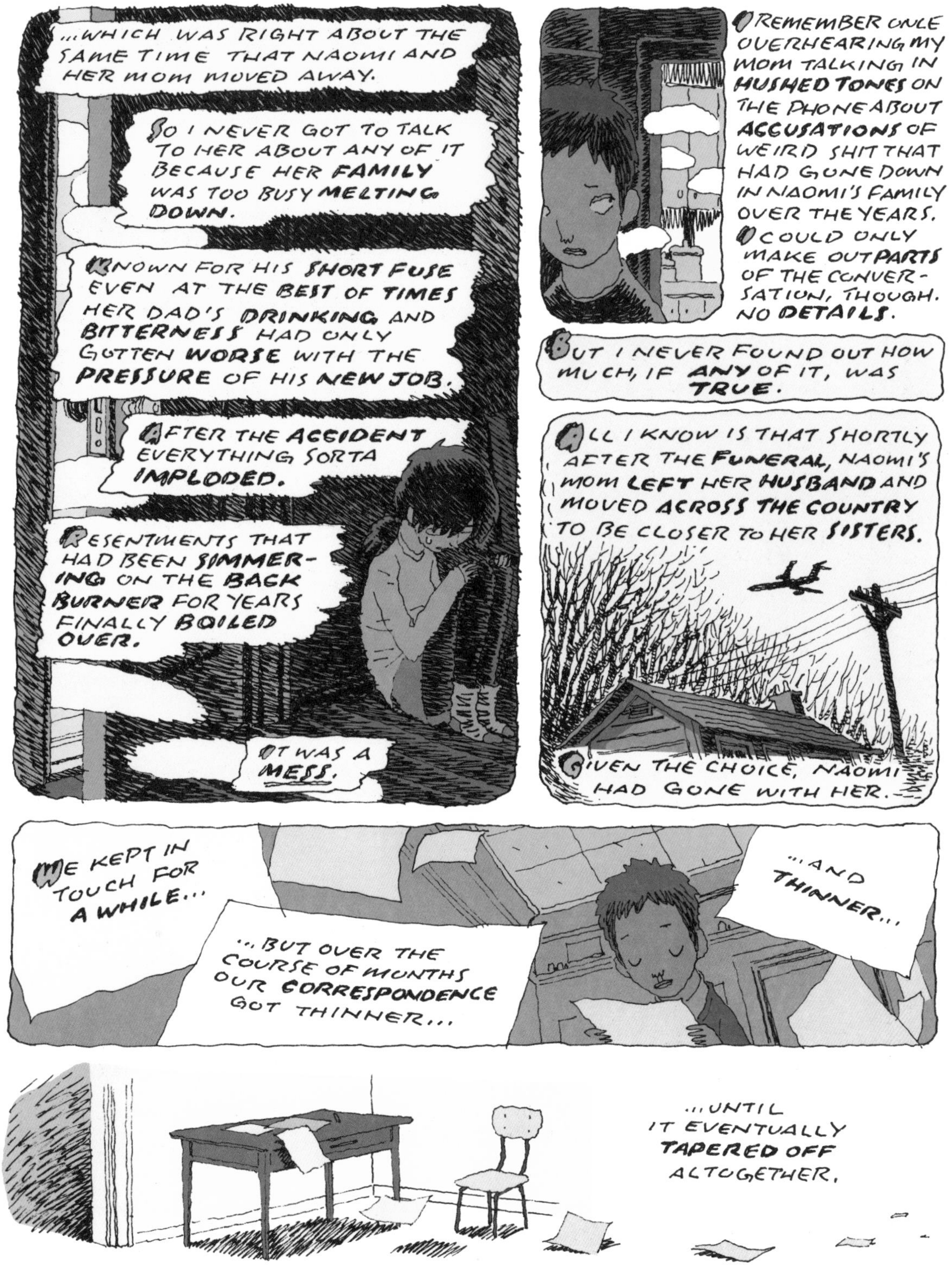
...WHICH WAS RIGHT ABOUT THE SAME TIME THAT NAOMI AND HER MOM MOVED AWAY.
SO I NEVER GOT TO TALK TO HER ABOUT ANY OF IT BECAUSE HER FAMILY WAS TOO BUSY MELTING DOWN.
KNOWN FOR HIS SHORT FUSE EVEN AT THE BEST OF TIMES HER DAD'S DRINKING AND BITTERNESS HAD ONLY GOTTEN WORSE WITH THE PRESSURE OF HIS NEW JOB.
AFTER THE ACCIDENT EVERYTHING SORTA IMPLODED.
RESENTMENTS THAT HAD BEEN SIMMERING ON THE BACK BURNER FOR YEARS FINALLY BOILED OVER.
IT WAS A MESS.
I REMEMBER ONCE OVERHEARING MY MOM TALKING IN HUSHED TONES ON THE PHONE ABOUT ACCUSATIONS OF WEIRD SHIT THAT HAD GONE DOWN IN NAOMI'S FAMILY OVER THE YEARS.
I COULD ONLY MAKE OUT PARTS OF THE CONVERSATION, THOUGH. NO DETAILS.
BUT I NEVER FOUND OUT HOW MUCH, IF ANY OF IT, WAS TRUE.
ALL I KNOW IS THAT SHORTLY AFTER THE FUNERAL, NAOMI'S MOM LEFT HER HUSBAND AND MOVED ACROSS THE COUNTRY TO BE CLOSER TO HER SISTERS.
GIVEN THE CHOICE, NAOMI HAD GONE WITH HER.
WE KEPT IN TOUCH FOR A WHILE...
...BUT OVER THE COURSE OF MONTHS OUR CORRESPONDENCE GOT THINNER...
...AND THINNER...
...UNTIL IT EVENTUALLY TAPERED OFF ALTOGETHER.

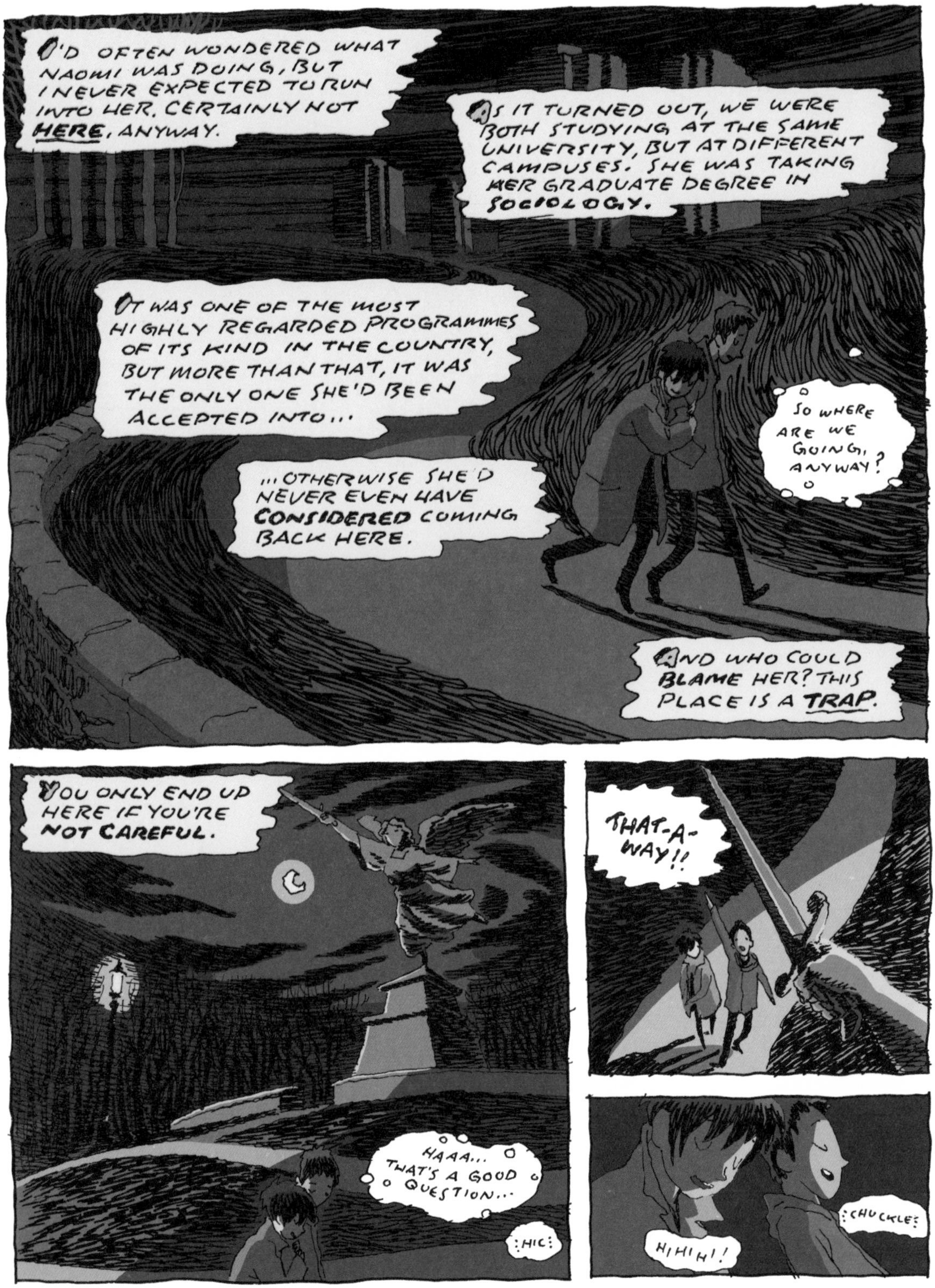
I'D OFTEN WONDERED WHAT NAOMI WAS DOING, BUT I NEVER EXPECTED TO RUN INTO HER. CERTAINLY NOT HERE, ANYWAY.
AS IT TURNED OUT, WE WERE BOTH STUDYING AT THE SAME UNIVERSITY, BUT AT DIFFERENT CAMPUSES. SHE WAS TAKING HER GRADUATE DEGREE IN SOCIOLOGY.
IT WAS ONE OF THE MOST HIGHLY REGARDED PROGRAMMES OF ITS KIND IN THE COUNTRY, BUT MORE THAN THAT, IT WAS THE ONLY ONE SHE'D BEEN ACCEPTED INTO...
SO WHERE ARE WE GOING, ANYWAY?
...OTHERWISE SHE'D NEVER EVEN HAVE CONSIDERED COMING BACK HERE.
AND WHO COULD BLAME HER? THIS PLACE IS A TRAP.
YOU ONLY END UP HERE IF YOU'RE NOT CAREFUL.
HAAA... THAT'S A GOOD QUESTION...
HIC
THAT-A-WAY!!
CHUCKLE
HIHIHI!

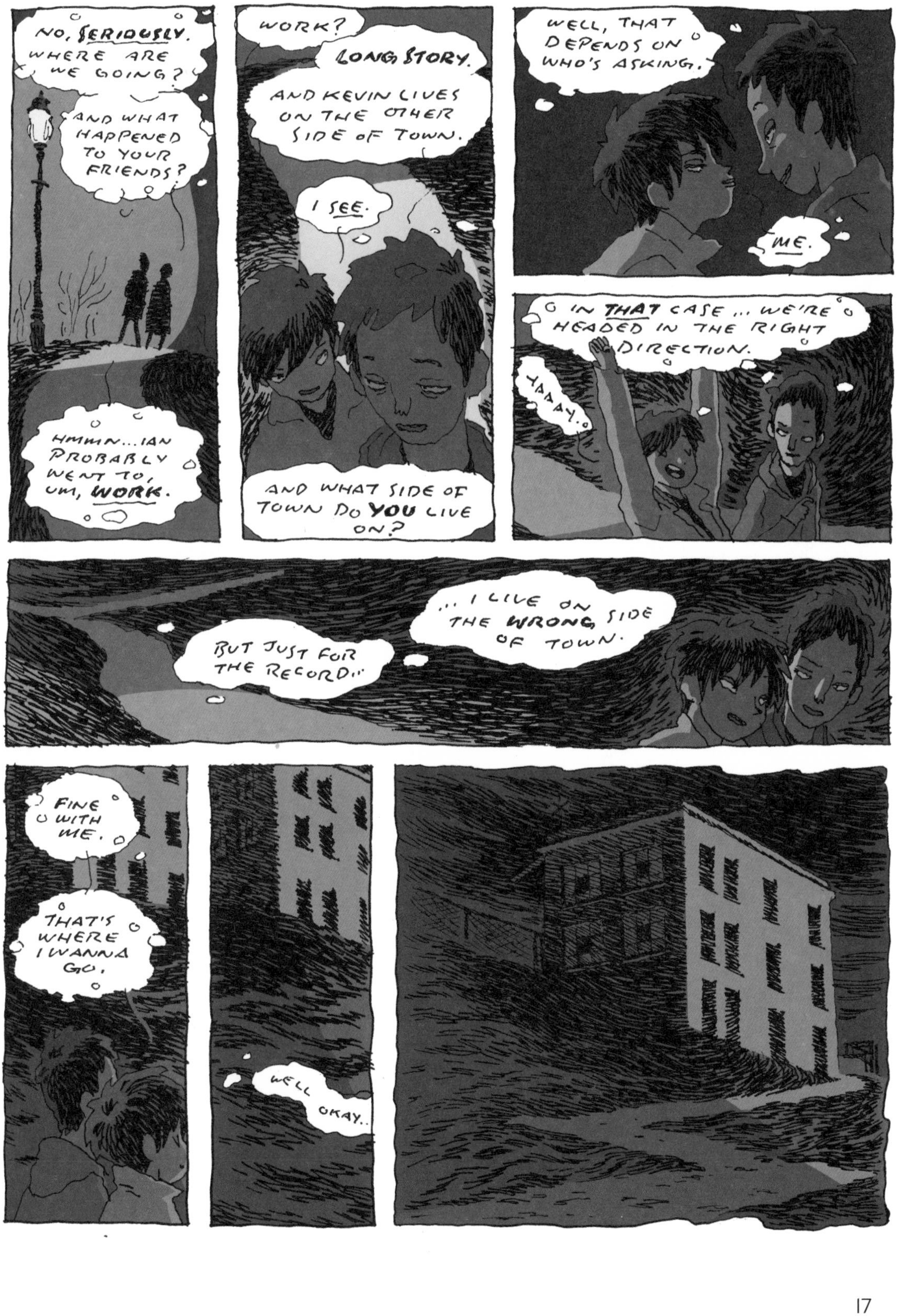
NO, SERIOUSLY. WHERE ARE WE GOING?
AND WHAT HAPPENED TO YOUR FRIENDS?
HMMM... IAN PROBABLY WENT TO, UM, WORK.
WORK?
LONG STORY.
AND KEVIN LIVES ON THE OTHER SIDE OF TOWN.
I SEE.
AND WHAT SIDE OF TOWN DO YOU LIVE ON?
WELL, THAT DEPENDS ON WHO'S ASKING.
ME.
IN THAT CASE... WE'RE HEADED IN THE RIGHT DIRECTION.
YAAAY..
BUT JUST FOR THE RECORD...
... I LIVE ON THE WRONG SIDE OF TOWN.
FINE WITH ME.
THAT'S WHERE I WANNA GO.
WELL OKAY..

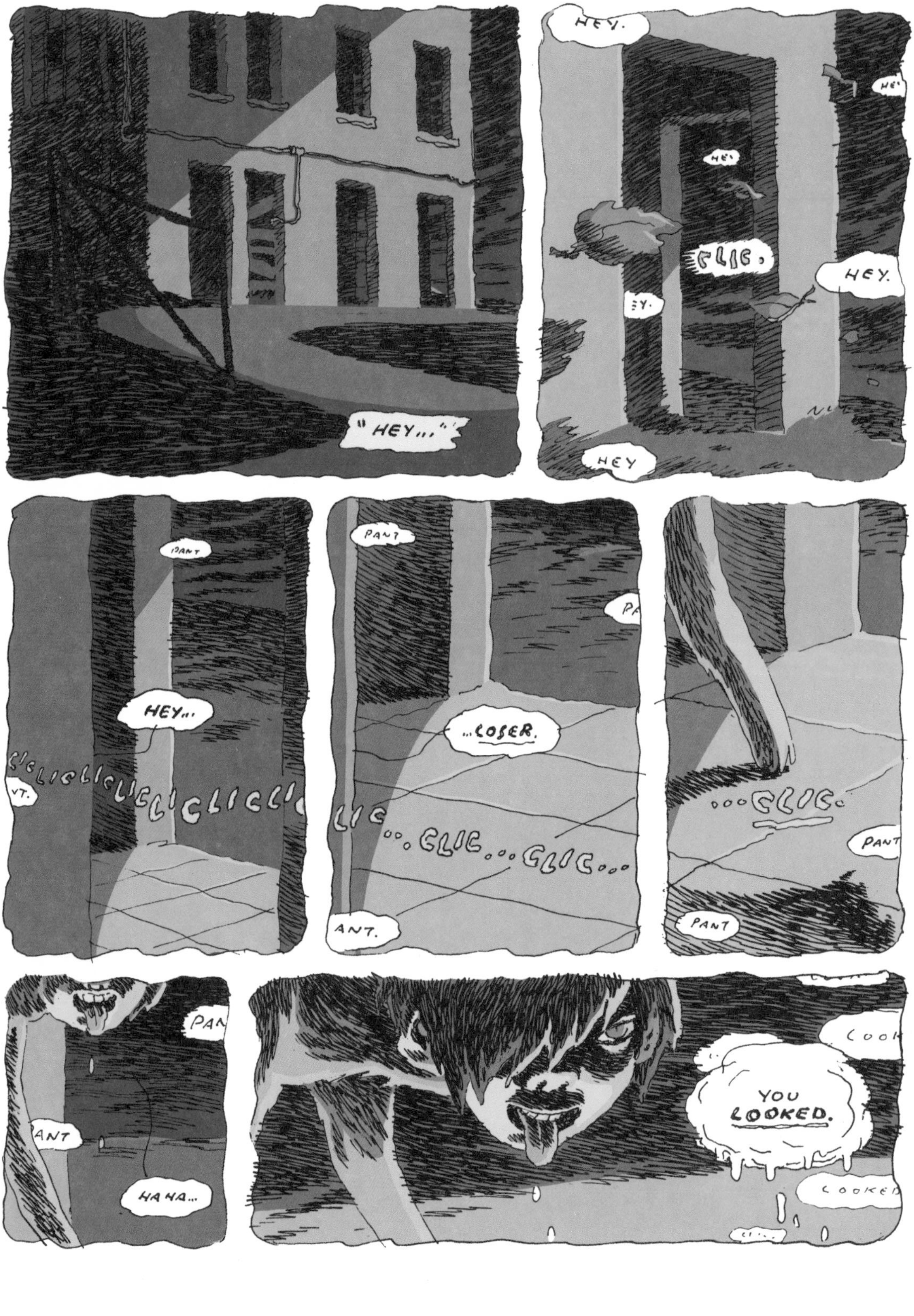
"HEY..."
HEY.
HEY
HEY
CLIC.
HEY.
EY.
HEY
PANT
HEY...
VT.
CLICLICLICLICLICLICLICLIC
PANT
PA
...LOSER.
CLIC... CLIC... CLIC...
ANT.
...CLIC.
PANT
PANT
PAN
ANT
HA HA...
LOOK
YOU LOOKED.
LOOKED

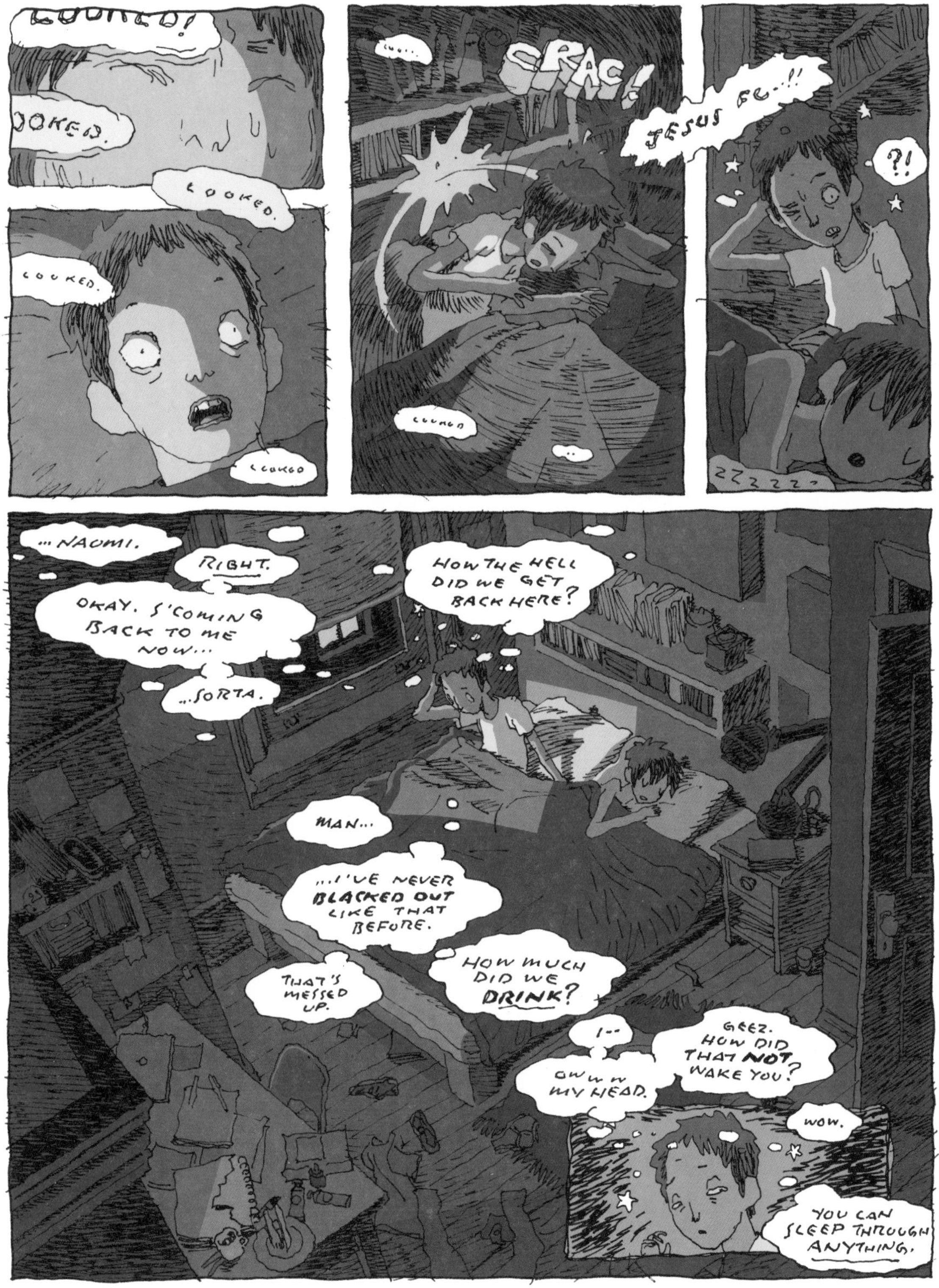

LOOKED.
LOOKED.
CRAC!
JESUS FU..!!
?!
ZZZZZZ
...NAOMI.
RIGHT.
OKAY. S'COMING BACK TO ME NOW...
...SORTA.
HOW THE HELL DID WE GET BACK HERE?
MAN...
...I'VE NEVER BLACKED OUT LIKE THAT BEFORE.
THAT'S MESSED UP.
HOW MUCH DID WE DRINK?
I--
OWWW MY HEAD.
GEEZ. HOW DID THAT NOT WAKE YOU?
WOW.
YOU CAN SLEEP THROUGH ANYTHING.

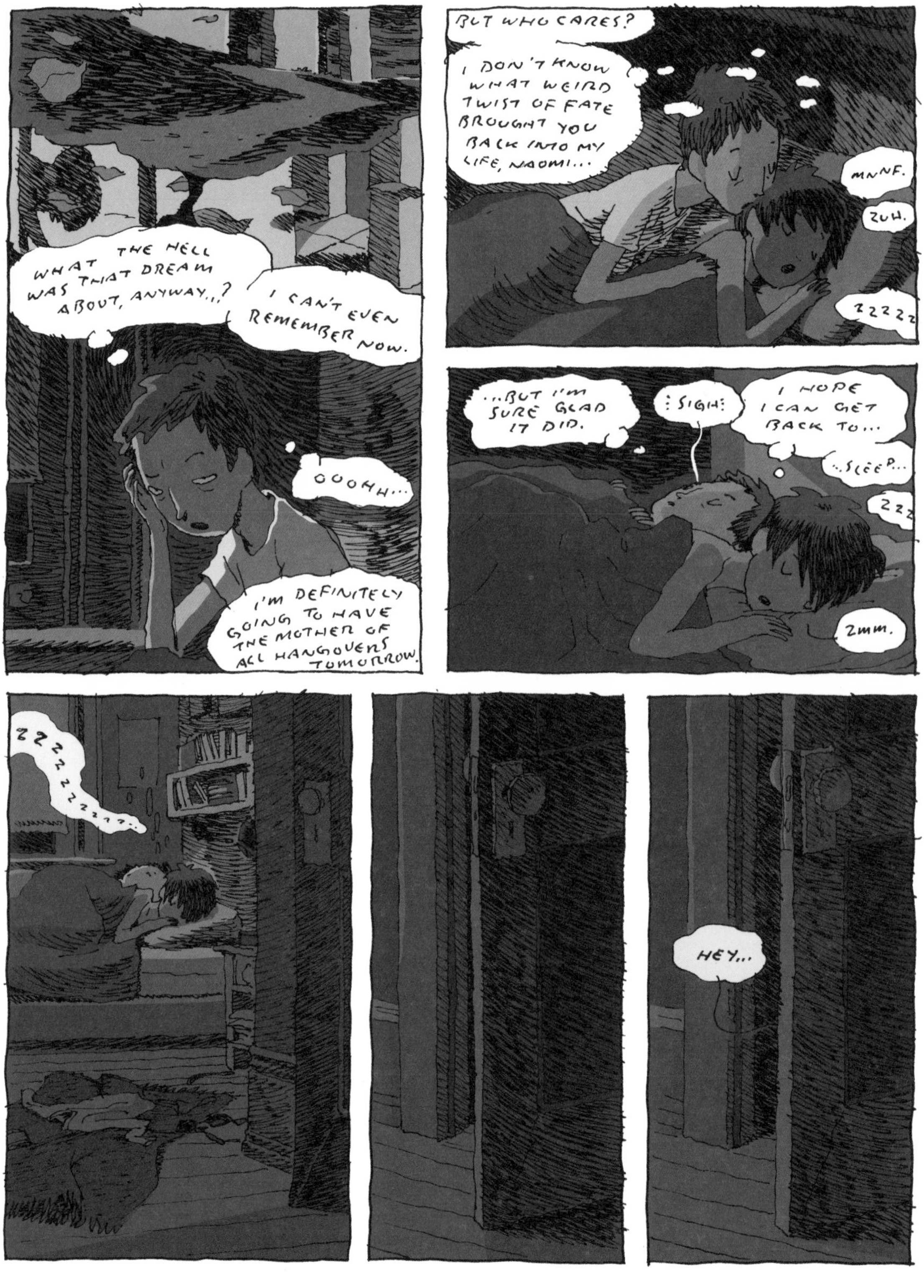
WHAT THE HELL WAS THAT DREAM ABOUT, ANYWAY...?
I CAN'T EVEN REMEMBER NOW.
OOOHH...
I'M DEFINITELY GOING TO HAVE THE MOTHER OF ALL HANGOVERS TOMORROW.
BUT WHO CARES?
I DON'T KNOW WHAT WEIRD TWIST OF FATE BROUGHT YOU BACK INTO MY LIFE, NAOMI...
MNNF.
ZUH.
ZZZZZ
...BUT I'M SURE GLAD IT DID.
:SIGH:
I HOPE I CAN GET BACK TO...
...SLEEP...
ZZZ
ZMM.
ZZZZZZZZZ...
HEY...

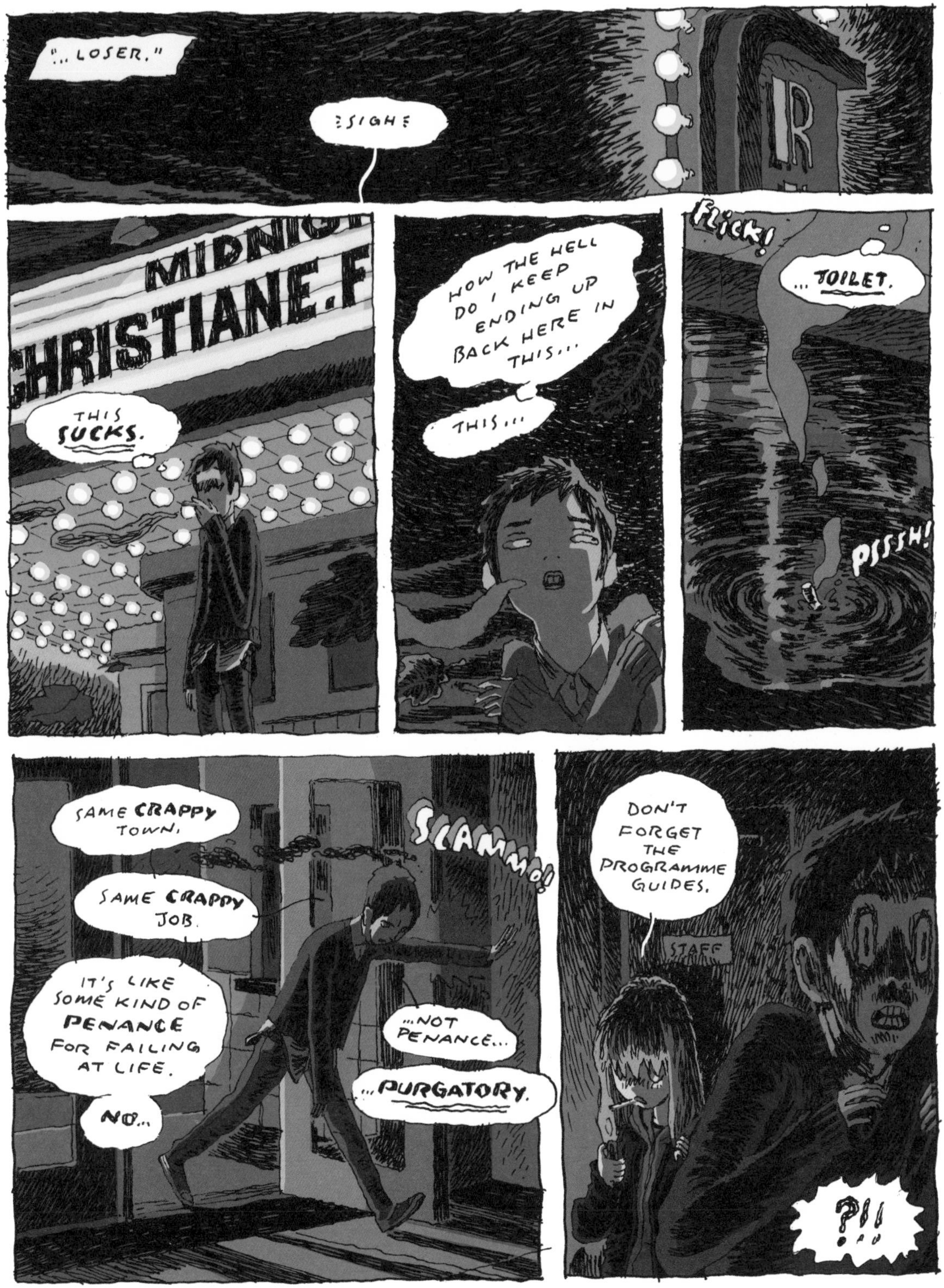
"...LOSER."
ƎSIGHƎ
MIDNIGHT
CHRISTIANE.F
THIS SUCKS.
HOW THE HELL DO I KEEP ENDING UP BACK HERE IN THIS...
THIS...
FLICK!
...TOILET.
PSSSH!
SAME CRAPPY TOWN.
SAME CRAPPY JOB.
IT'S LIKE SOME KIND OF PENANCE FOR FAILING AT LIFE.
NO...
SLAMM!!
...NOT PENANCE...
...PURGATORY.
DON'T FORGET THE PROGRAMME GUIDES.
STAFF
?!!

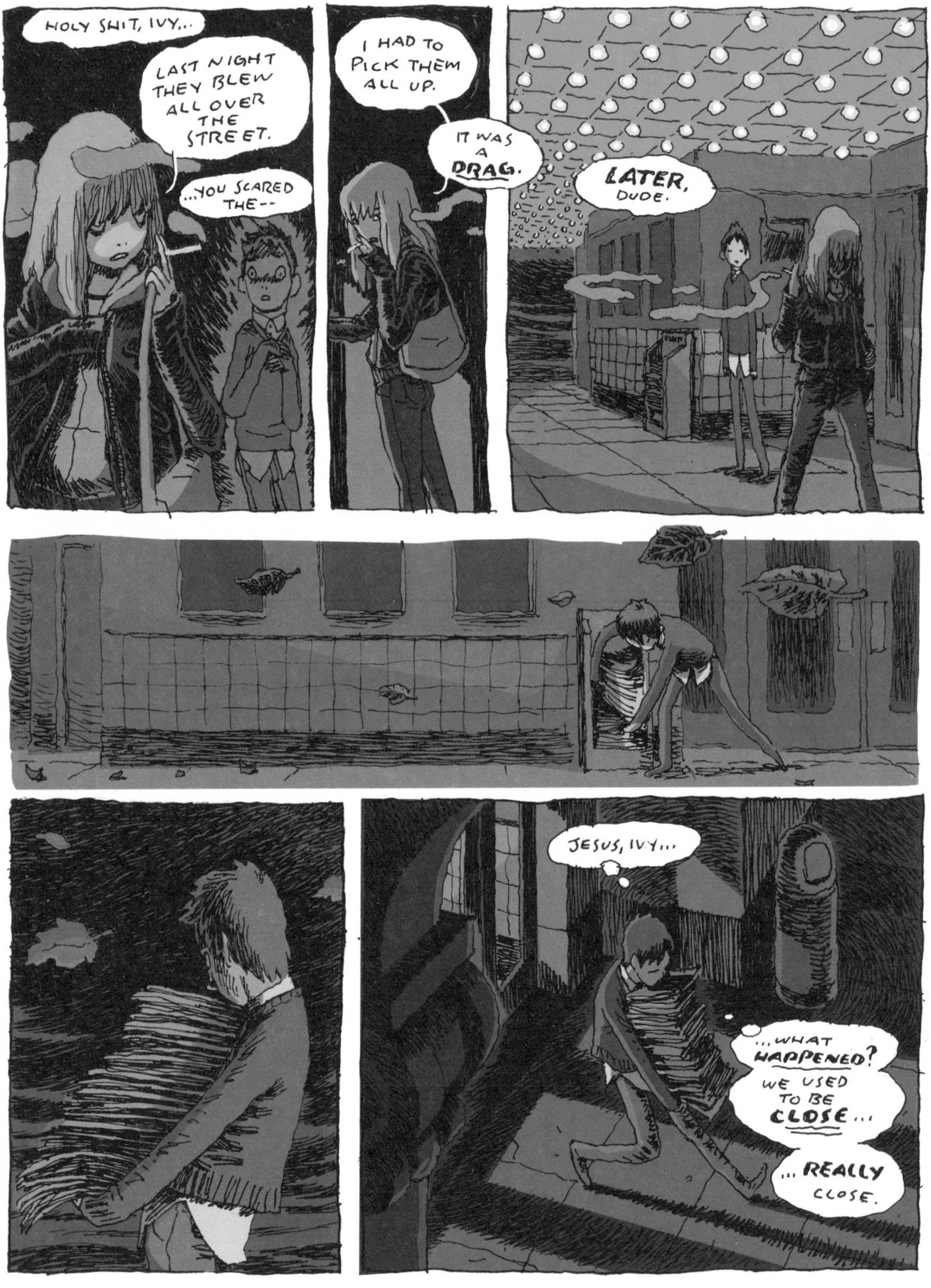
HOLY SHIT, IVY...
LAST NIGHT THEY BLEW ALL OVER THE STREET.
...YOU SCARED THE--
I HAD TO PICK THEM ALL UP.
IT WAS A DRAG.
LATER, DUDE.
JESUS, IVY...
...WHAT HAPPENED?
WE USED TO BE CLOSE...
...REALLY CLOSE.

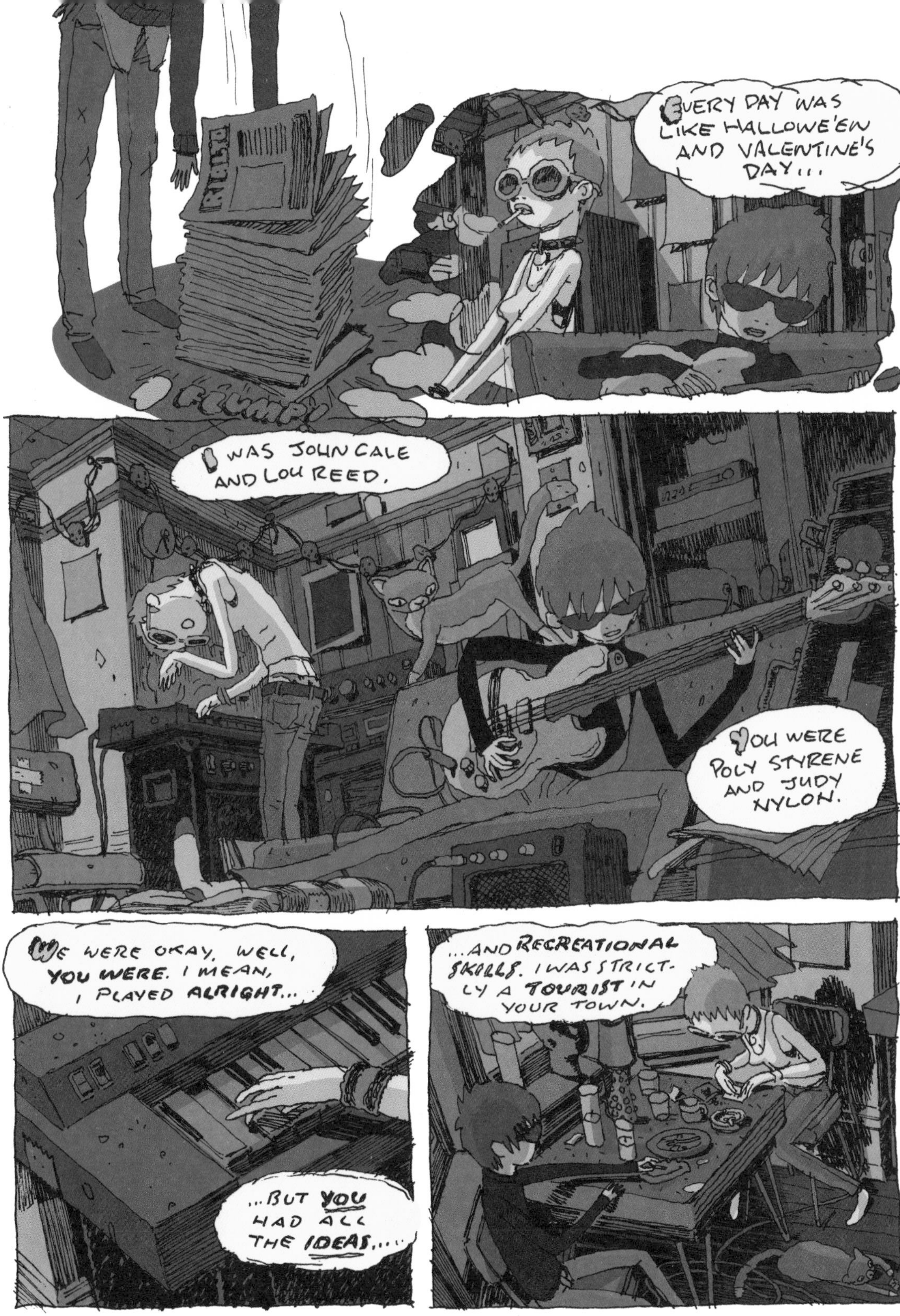
EVERY DAY WAS LIKE HALLOWE'EN AND VALENTINE'S DAY...
FLUMP!
I WAS JOHN CALE AND LOU REED.
YOU WERE POLY STYRENE AND JUDY NYLON.
WE WERE OKAY. WELL, YOU WERE. I MEAN, I PLAYED ALRIGHT...
...BUT YOU HAD ALL THE IDEAS....
...AND RECREATIONAL SKILLS. I WAS STRICTLY A TOURIST IN YOUR TOWN.

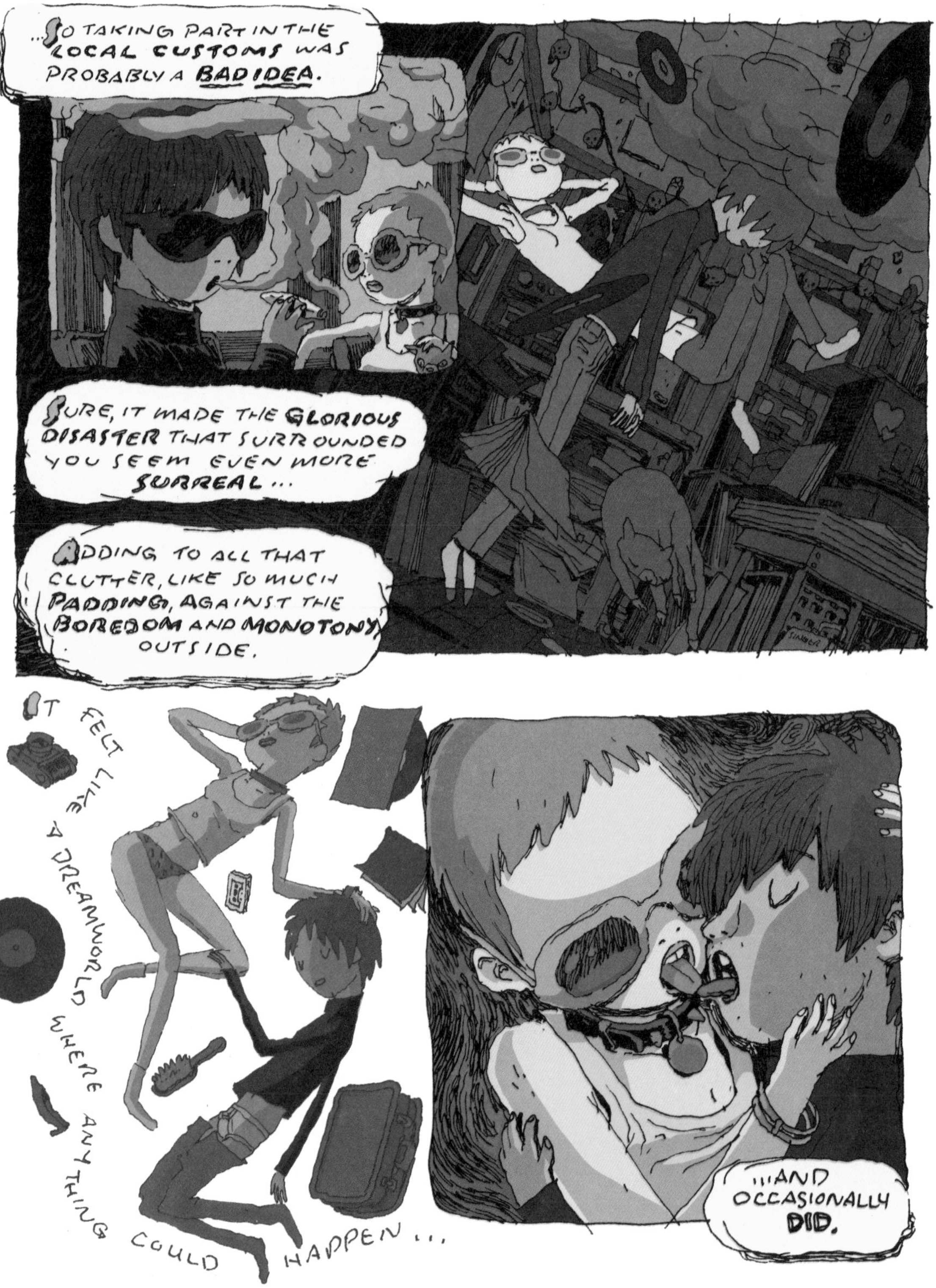
...SO TAKING PART IN THE LOCAL CUSTOMS WAS PROBABLY A BAD IDEA.
SURE, IT MADE THE GLORIOUS DISASTER THAT SURROUNDED YOU SEEM EVEN MORE SURREAL...
ADDING TO ALL THAT CLUTTER, LIKE SO MUCH PADDING, AGAINST THE BOREDOM AND MONOTONY OUTSIDE.
IT FELT LIKE A DREAMWORLD WHERE ANYTHING COULD HAPPEN...
...AND OCCASIONALLY DID.

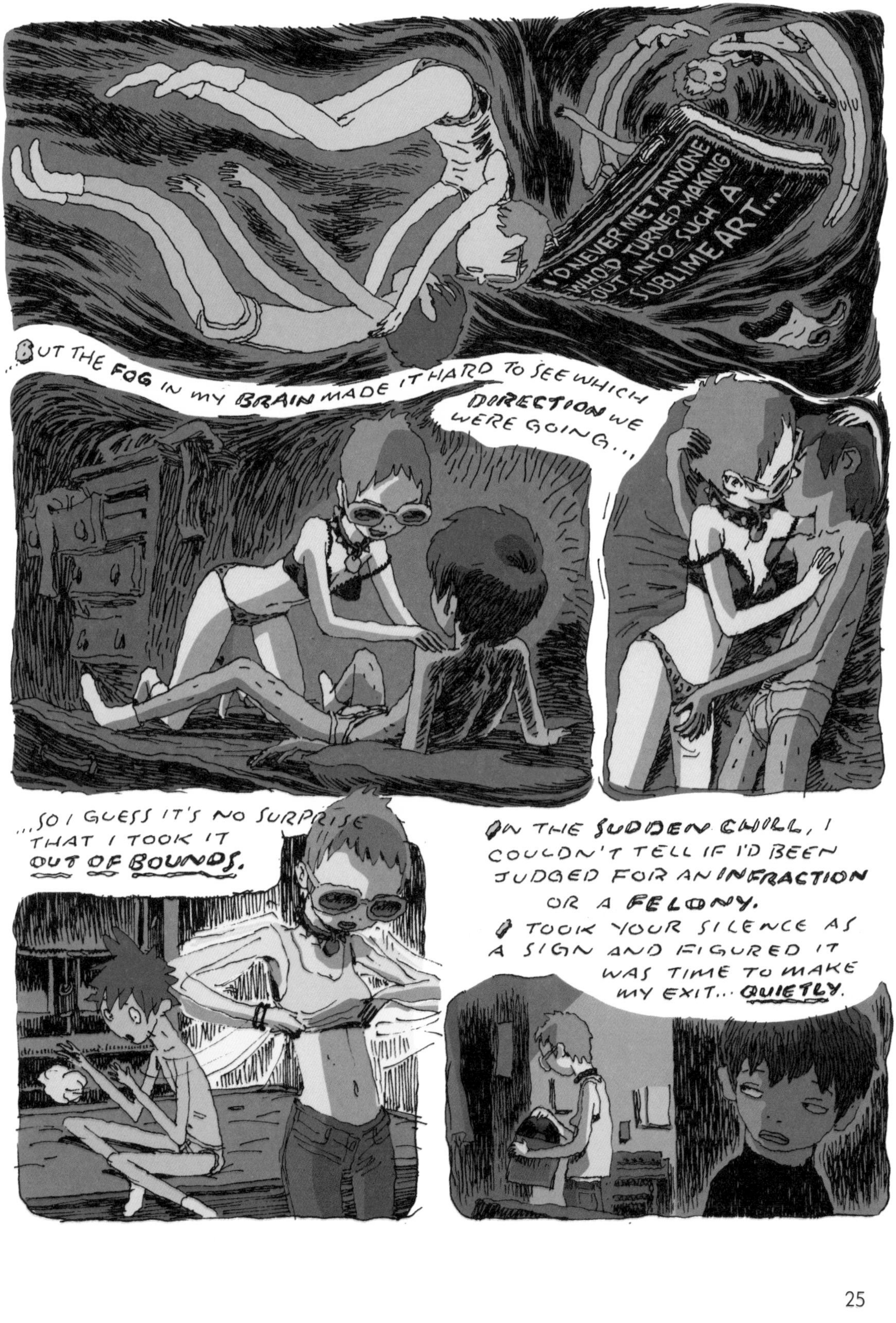
I'D NEVER MET ANYONE WHO'D TURNED MAKING OUT INTO SUCH A SUBLIME ART...
...BUT THE FOG IN MY BRAIN MADE IT HARD TO SEE WHICH DIRECTION WE WERE GOING...
...SO I GUESS IT'S NO SURPRISE THAT I TOOK IT OUT OF BOUNDS.
IN THE SUDDEN CHILL, I COULDN'T TELL IF I'D BEEN JUDGED FOR AN INFRACTION OR A FELONY.
I TOOK YOUR SILENCE AS A SIGN AND FIGURED IT WAS TIME TO MAKE MY EXIT... QUIETLY.

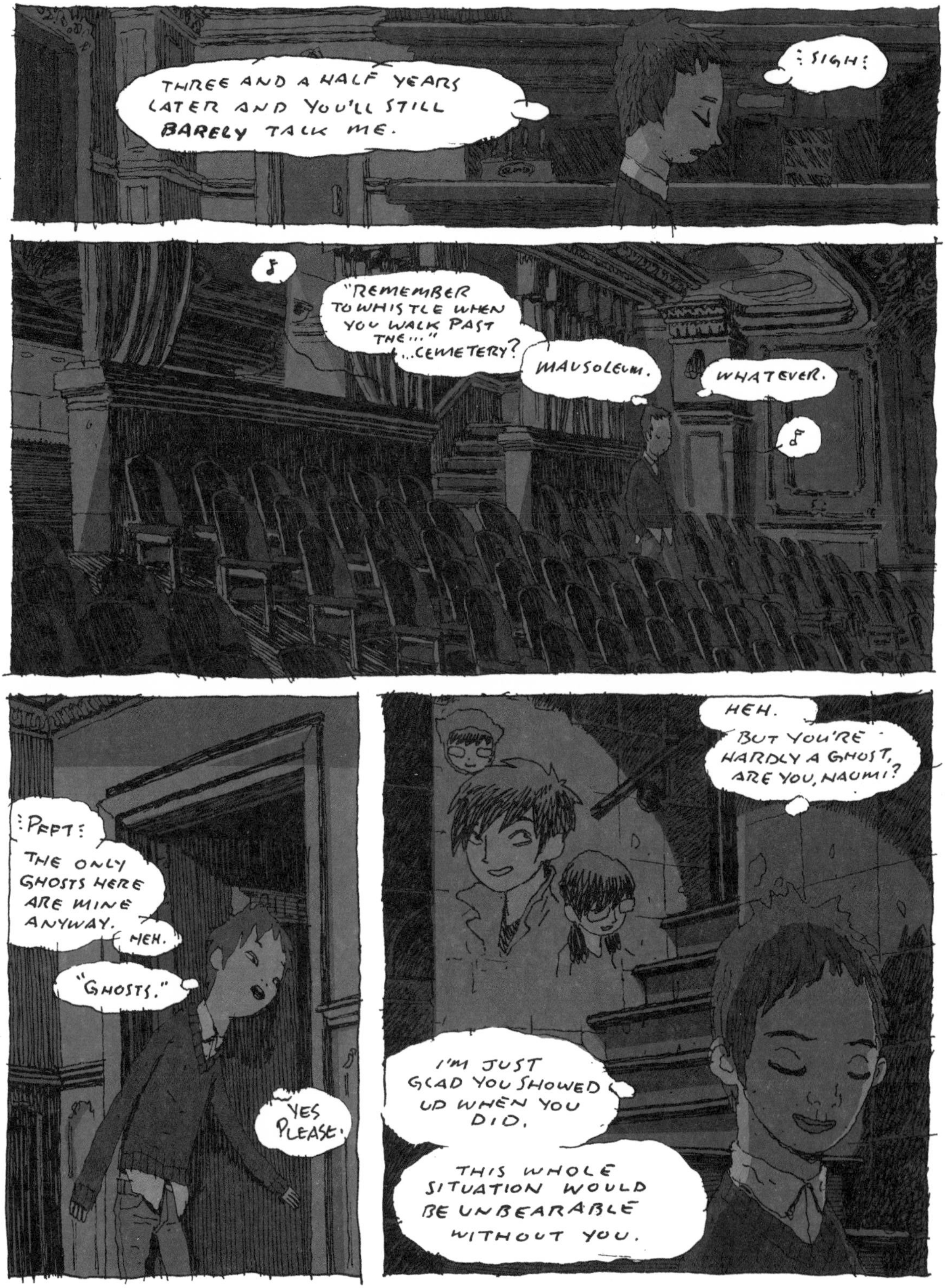
THREE AND A HALF YEARS LATER AND YOU'LL STILL BARELY TALK ME.
SIGH
"REMEMBER TO WHISTLE WHEN YOU WALK PAST THE..."
...CEMETERY?
MAUSOLEUM.
WHATEVER.
PFFT
THE ONLY GHOSTS HERE ARE MINE ANYWAY.
HEH.
"GHOSTS."
YES PLEASE.
HEH.
BUT YOU'RE HARDLY A GHOST, ARE YOU, NAOMI?
I'M JUST GLAD YOU SHOWED UP WHEN YOU DID.
THIS WHOLE SITUATION WOULD BE UNBEARABLE WITHOUT YOU.

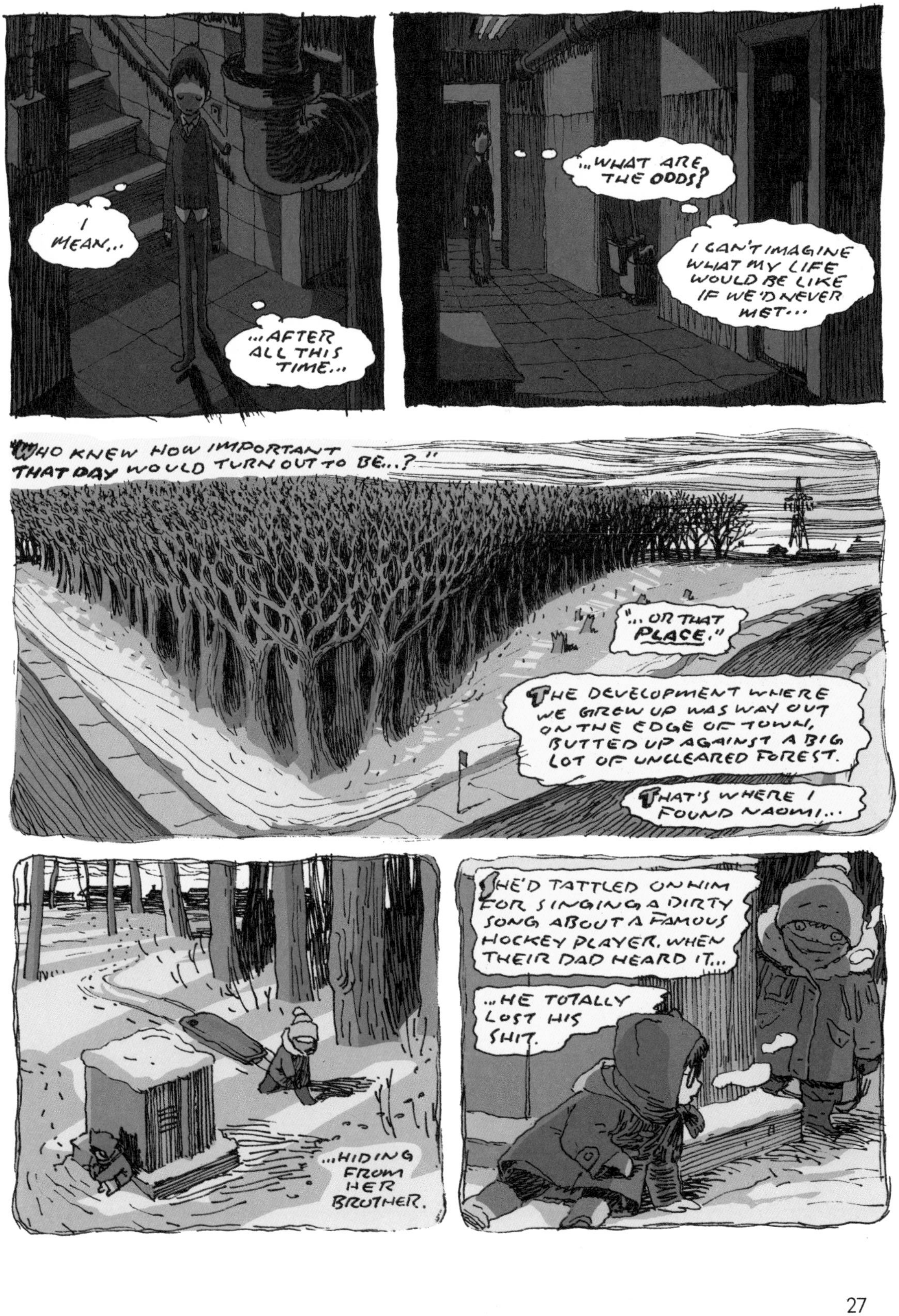
I MEAN...
...AFTER ALL THIS TIME...
...WHAT ARE THE ODDS?
I CAN'T IMAGINE WHAT MY LIFE WOULD BE LIKE IF WE'D NEVER MET...
"WHO KNEW HOW IMPORTANT THAT DAY WOULD TURN OUT TO BE...?"
"...OR THAT PLACE."
THE DEVELOPMENT WHERE WE GREW UP WAS WAY OUT ON THE EDGE OF TOWN, BUTTED UP AGAINST A BIG LOT OF UNCLEARED FOREST.
THAT'S WHERE I FOUND NAOMI...
...HIDING FROM HER BROTHER.
SHE'D TATTLED ON HIM FOR SINGING A DIRTY SONG ABOUT A FAMOUS HOCKEY PLAYER. WHEN THEIR DAD HEARD IT...
...HE TOTALLY LOST HIS SHIT.

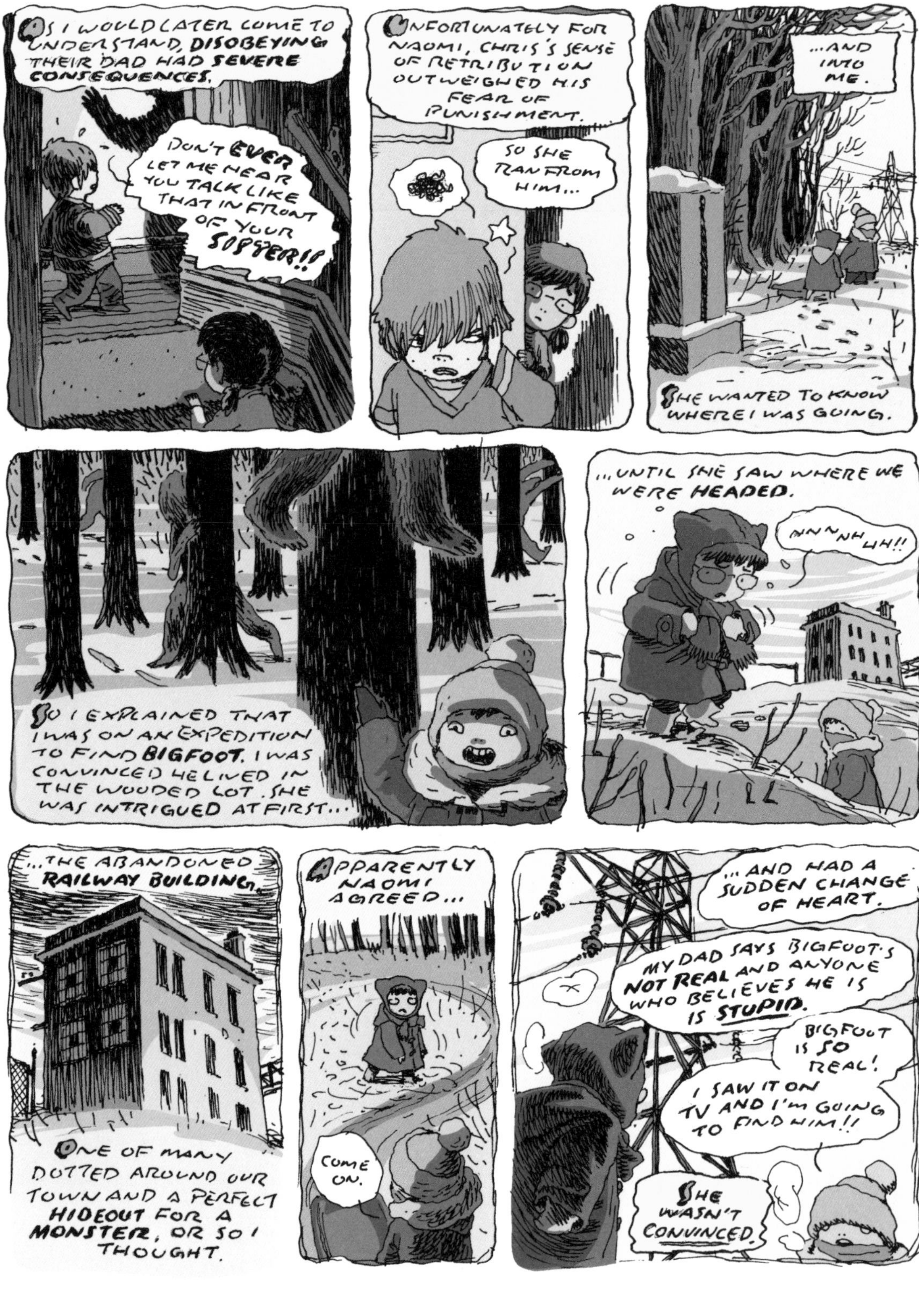
AS I WOULD LATER COME TO UNDERSTAND, DISOBEYING THEIR DAD HAD SEVERE CONSEQUENCES.
DON'T EVER LET ME HEAR YOU TALK LIKE THAT IN FRONT OF YOUR SISTER!!
UNFORTUNATELY FOR NAOMI, CHRIS'S SENSE OF RETRIBUTION OUTWEIGHED HIS FEAR OF PUNISHMENT.
SO SHE RAN FROM HIM...
...AND INTO ME.
SHE WANTED TO KNOW WHERE I WAS GOING.
SO I EXPLAINED THAT I WAS ON AN EXPEDITION TO FIND BIGFOOT. I WAS CONVINCED HE LIVED IN THE WOODED LOT. SHE WAS INTRIGUED AT FIRST...
...UNTIL SHE SAW WHERE WE WERE HEADED.
NNNNH UH!!
...THE ABANDONED RAILWAY BUILDING...
ONE OF MANY DOTTED AROUND OUR TOWN AND A PERFECT HIDEOUT FOR A MONSTER, OR SO I THOUGHT.
APPARENTLY NAOMI AGREED...
COME ON.
...AND HAD A SUDDEN CHANGE OF HEART.
MY DAD SAYS BIGFOOT'S NOT REAL AND ANYONE WHO BELIEVES HE IS IS STUPID.
BIGFOOT IS SO REAL! I SAW IT ON TV AND I'M GOING TO FIND HIM!!
SHE WASN'T CONVINCED.

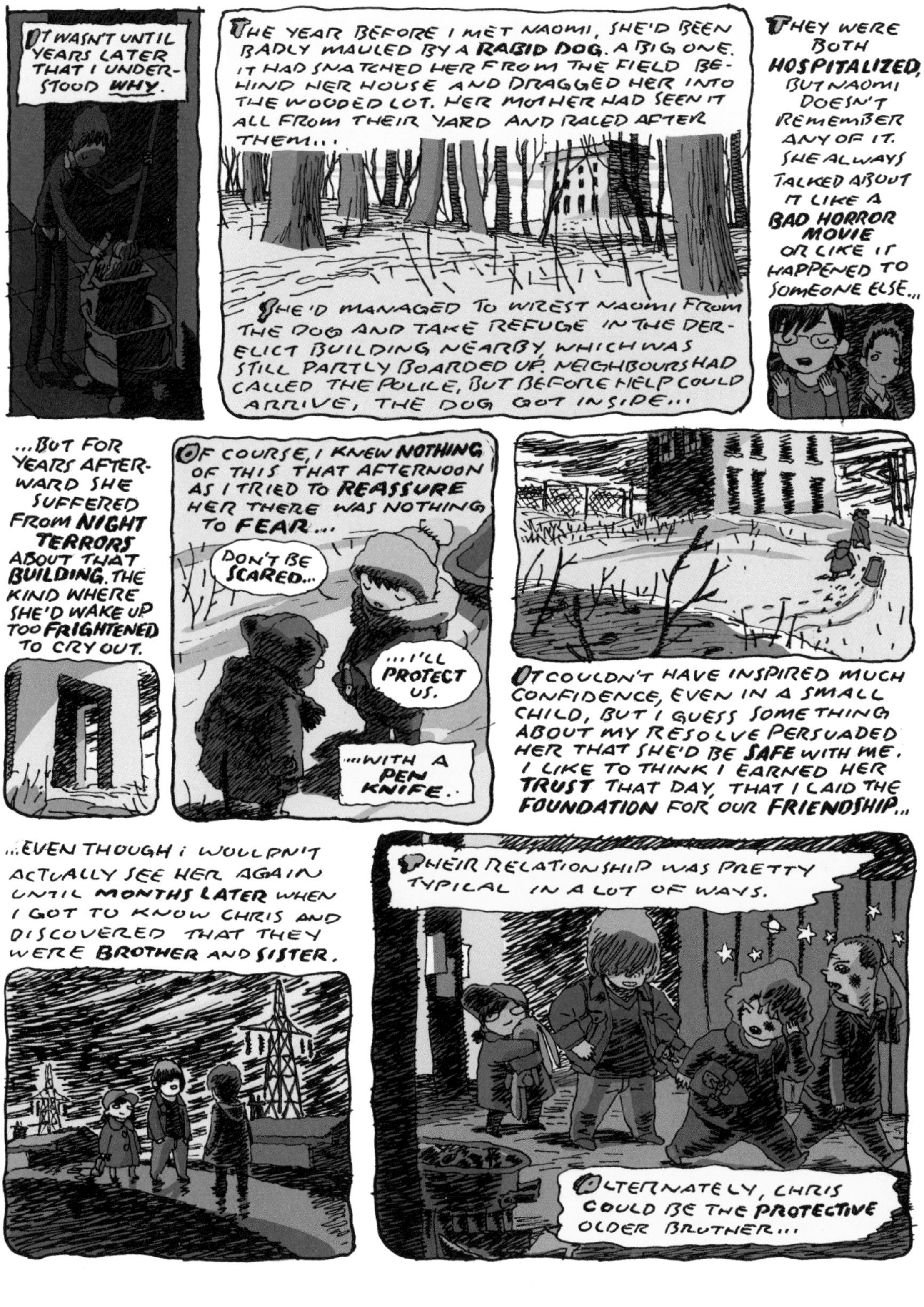
It wasn't until years later that I understood WHY.
The year before I met Naomi, she'd been badly mauled by a RABID DOG. A big one. It had snatched her from the field behind her house and dragged her into the wooded lot. Her mother had seen it all from their yard and raced after them...
She'd managed to wrest Naomi from the dog and take refuge in the derelict building nearby, which was still partly boarded up. Neighbours had called the police, but before help could arrive, the dog got inside...
They were both HOSPITALIZED, but Naomi doesn't remember any of it. She always talked about it like a BAD HORROR MOVIE or like it happened to someone else...
...But for years afterward she suffered from NIGHT TERRORS about that BUILDING. The kind where she'd wake up too FRIGHTENED to cry out.
Of course, I knew NOTHING of this that afternoon as I tried to REASSURE her there was nothing to FEAR...
DON'T BE SCARED...
...I'LL PROTECT US.
...WITH A PEN KNIFE.
It couldn't have inspired much confidence, even in a small child, but I guess something about my resolve persuaded her that she'd be SAFE with me. I like to think I earned her TRUST that day, that I laid the FOUNDATION for our FRIENDSHIP...
...Even though I wouldn't actually see her again until MONTHS LATER when I got to know Chris and discovered that they were BROTHER and SISTER.
Their relationship was pretty typical in a lot of ways.
Alternately, Chris could be the PROTECTIVE older brother...

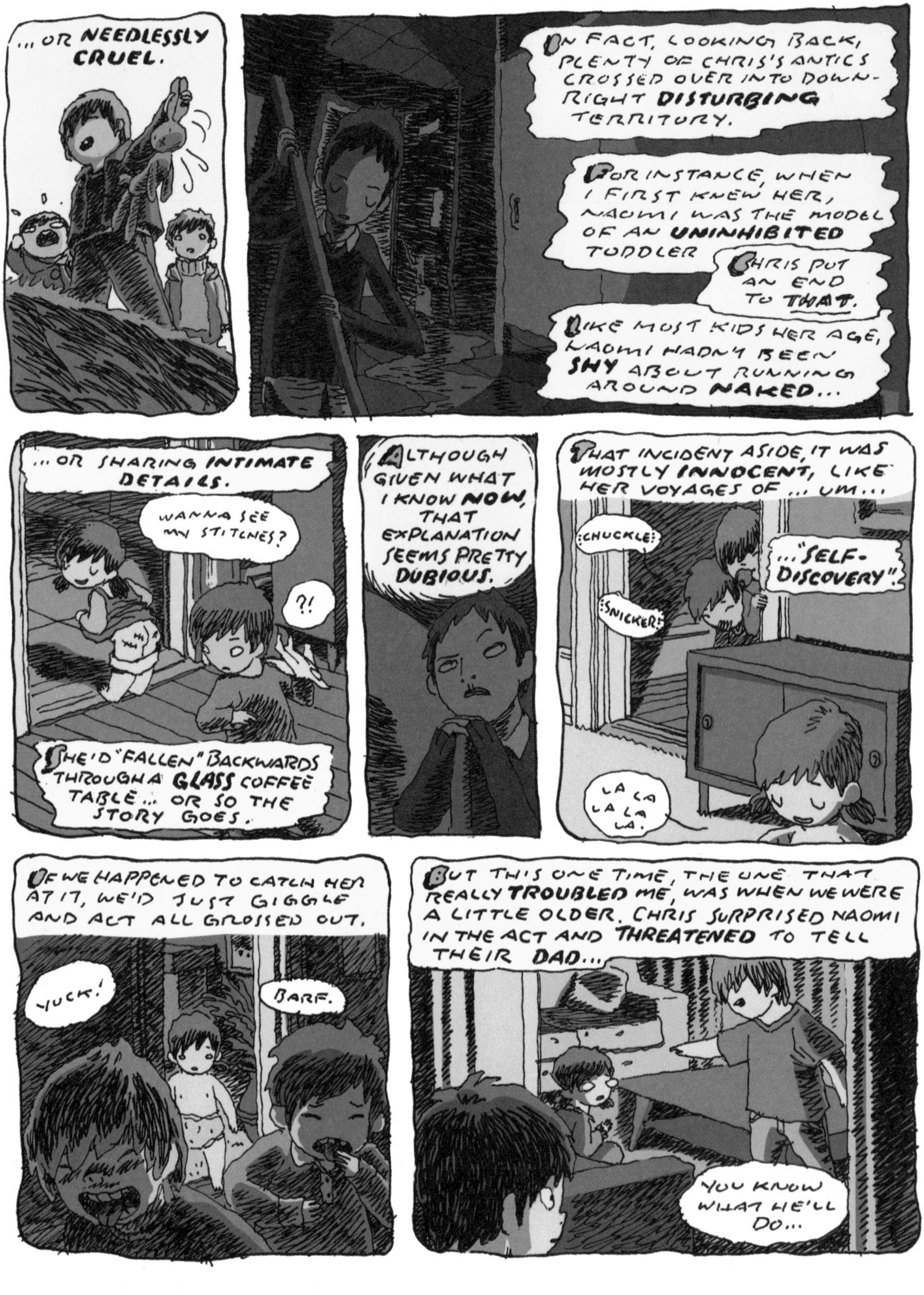

... OR NEEDLESSLY CRUEL.
IN FACT, LOOKING BACK, PLENTY OF CHRIS'S ANTICS CROSSED OVER INTO DOWN-RIGHT DISTURBING TERRITORY.
FOR INSTANCE, WHEN I FIRST KNEW HER, NAOMI WAS THE MODEL OF AN UNINHIBITED TODDLER
CHRIS PUT AN END TO THAT.
LIKE MOST KIDS HER AGE, NAOMI HADN'T BEEN SHY ABOUT RUNNING AROUND NAKED...
... OR SHARING INTIMATE DETAILS.
WANNA SEE MY STITCHES?
?!
SHE'D "FALLEN" BACKWARDS THROUGH A GLASS COFFEE TABLE... OR SO THE STORY GOES.
ALTHOUGH GIVEN WHAT I KNOW NOW, THAT EXPLANATION SEEMS PRETTY DUBIOUS.
THAT INCIDENT ASIDE, IT WAS MOSTLY INNOCENT, LIKE HER VOYAGES OF ... UM...
CHUCKLE
... "SELF-DISCOVERY".
SNICKER
LA LA LA LA LA.
IF WE HAPPENED TO CATCH HER AT IT, WE'D JUST GIGGLE AND ACT ALL GROSSED OUT.
YUCK!
BARF.
BUT THIS ONE TIME, THE ONE THAT REALLY TROUBLED ME, WAS WHEN WE WERE A LITTLE OLDER. CHRIS SURPRISED NAOMI IN THE ACT AND THREATENED TO TELL THEIR DAD...
YOU KNOW WHAT HE'LL DO...

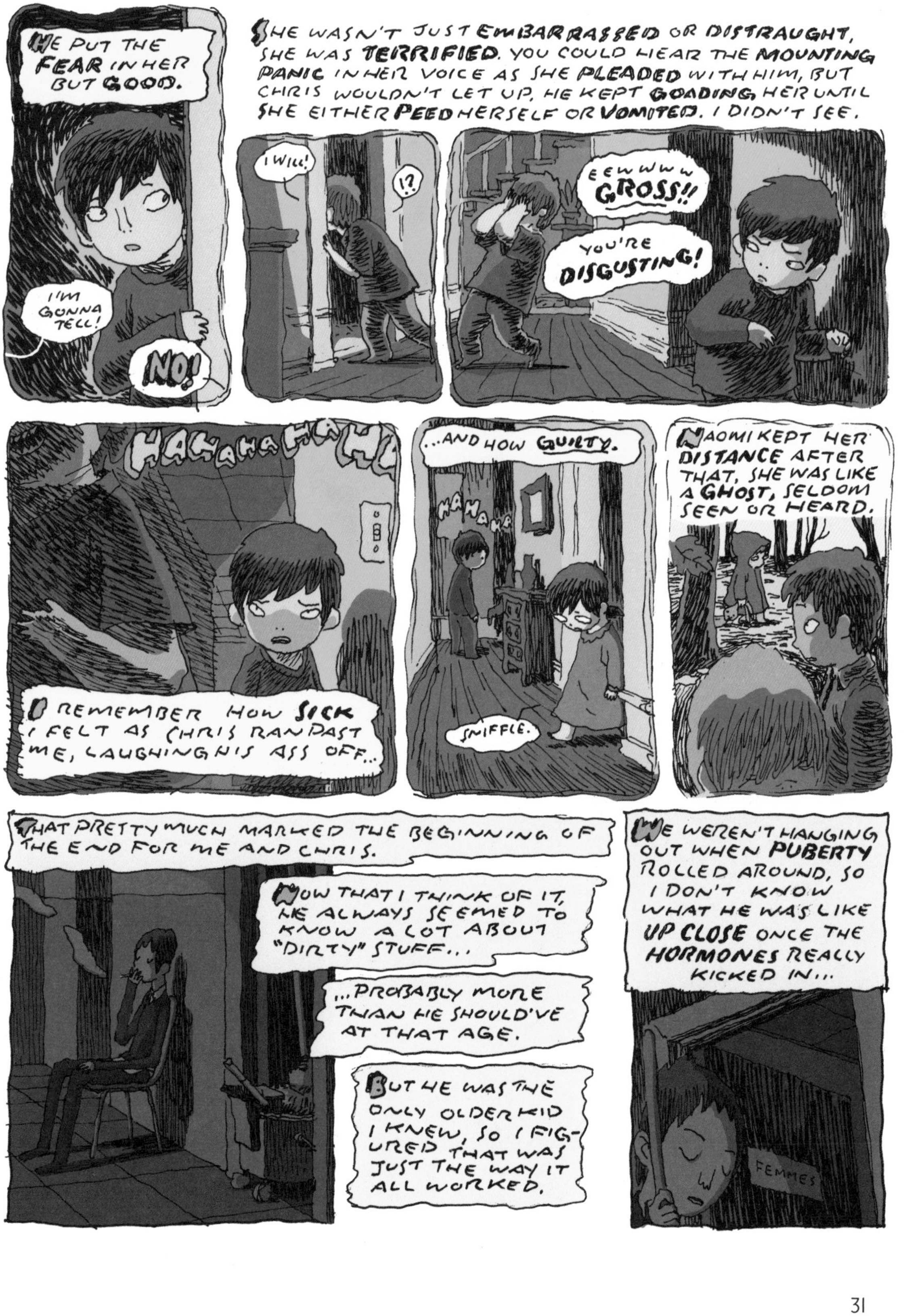

HE PUT THE FEAR IN HER BUT GOOD.
I'M GONNA TELL!
NO!
SHE WASN'T JUST EMBARRASSED OR DISTRAUGHT, SHE WAS TERRIFIED. YOU COULD HEAR THE MOUNTING PANIC IN HER VOICE AS SHE PLEADED WITH HIM, BUT CHRIS WOULDN'T LET UP, HE KEPT GOADING HER UNTIL SHE EITHER PEED HERSELF OR VOMITED. I DIDN'T SEE.
I WILL!
!?
EEWWWW GROSS!!
YOU'RE DISGUSTING!
HAHAHAHAHAH
I REMEMBER HOW SICK I FELT AS CHRIS RAN PAST ME, LAUGHING HIS ASS OFF...
...AND HOW GUILTY.
HAHAHA
SNIFFLE.
NAOMI KEPT HER DISTANCE AFTER THAT, SHE WAS LIKE A GHOST, SELDOM SEEN OR HEARD.
THAT PRETTY MUCH MARKED THE BEGINNING OF THE END FOR ME AND CHRIS.
NOW THAT I THINK OF IT, HE ALWAYS SEEMED TO KNOW A LOT ABOUT "DIRTY" STUFF...
...PROBABLY MORE THAN HE SHOULD'VE AT THAT AGE.
BUT HE WAS THE ONLY OLDER KID I KNEW, SO I FIG-URED THAT WAS JUST THE WAY IT ALL WORKED.
WE WEREN'T HANGING OUT WHEN PUBERTY ROLLED AROUND, SO I DON'T KNOW WHAT HE WAS LIKE UP CLOSE ONCE THE HORMONES REALLY KICKED IN...
FEMMES

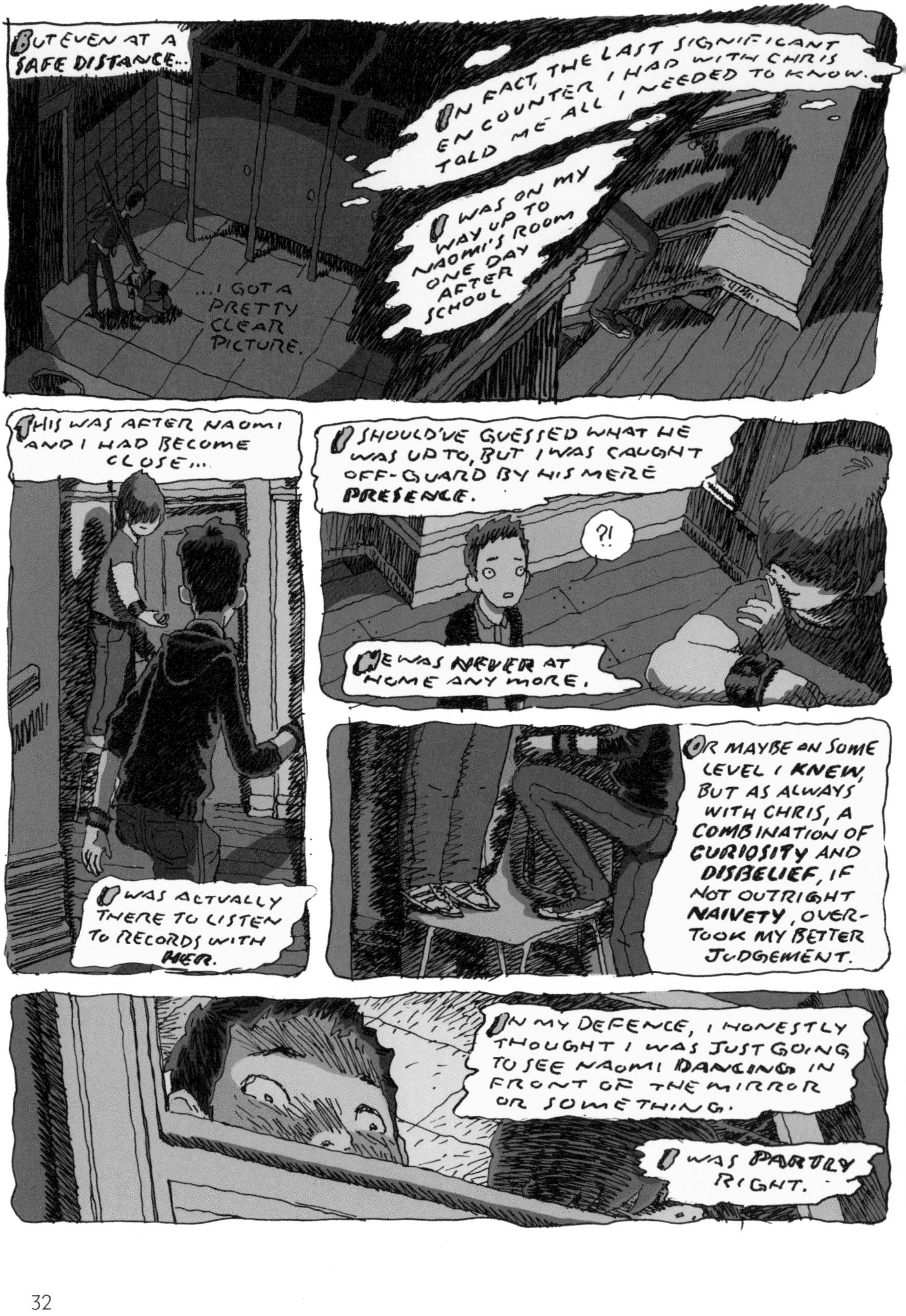
But even at a safe distance...
...I got a pretty clear picture.
In fact, the last significant encounter I had with Chris told me all I needed to know.
I was on my way up to Naomi's room one day after school
This was after Naomi and I had become close...
I was actually there to listen to records with her.
I should've guessed what he was up to, but I was caught off-guard by his mere presence.
?!
He was never at home any more.
Or maybe on some level I knew, but as always with Chris, a combination of curiosity and disbelief, if not outright naivety, overtook my better judgement.
In my defence, I honestly thought I was just going to see Naomi dancing in front of the mirror or something.
I was partly right.

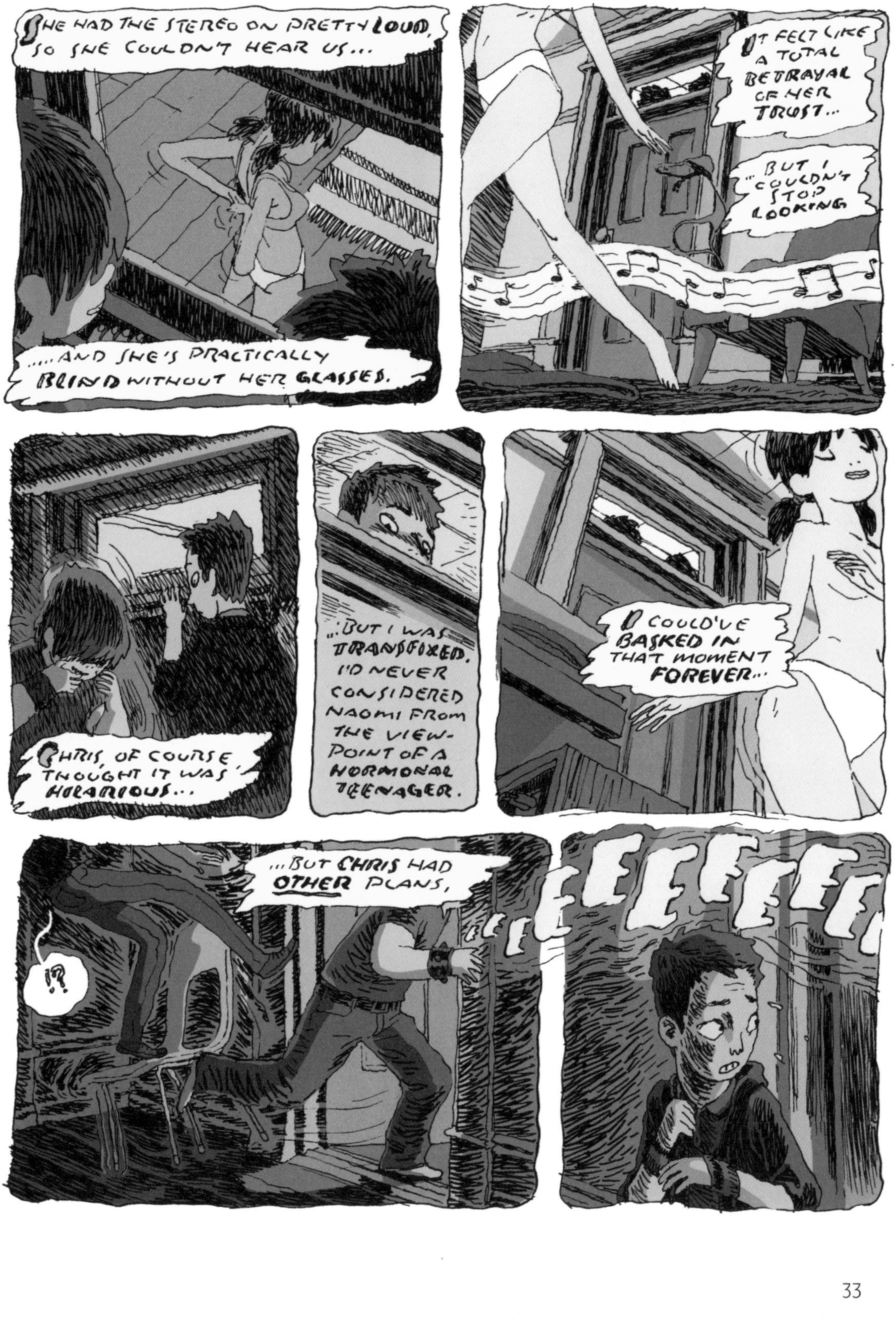
SHE HAD THE STEREO ON PRETTY LOUD, SO SHE COULDN'T HEAR US...
....AND SHE'S PRACTICALLY BLIND WITHOUT HER GLASSES.
IT FELT LIKE A TOTAL BETRAYAL OF HER TRUST...
...BUT I COULDN'T STOP LOOKING
CHRIS, OF COURSE, THOUGHT IT WAS HILARIOUS...
...BUT I WAS TRANSFIXED. I'D NEVER CONSIDERED NAOMI FROM THE VIEW-POINT OF A HORMONAL TEENAGER.
I COULD'VE BASKED IN THAT MOMENT FOREVER...
...BUT CHRIS HAD OTHER PLANS,
!?
EEEEEEEE

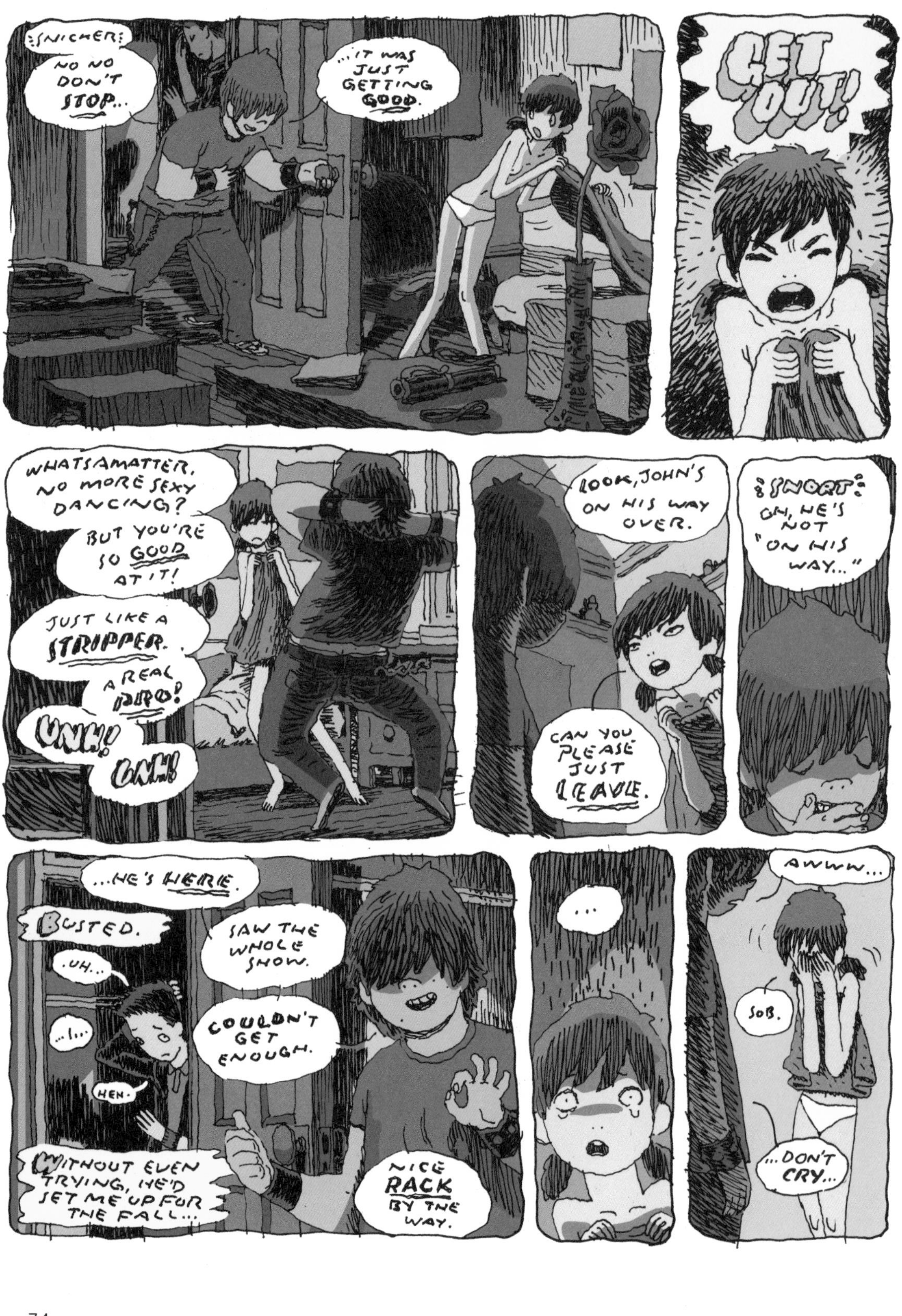
:SNICKER:
NO NO DON'T STOP...
...IT WAS JUST GETTING GOOD.
GET OUT!
WHATSAMATTER, NO MORE SEXY DANCING?
BUT YOU'RE SO GOOD AT IT!
JUST LIKE A STRIPPER.
A REAL PRO!
UNH!
UNH!
LOOK, JOHN'S ON HIS WAY OVER.
CAN YOU PLEASE JUST LEAVE.
:SNORT: OH, HE'S NOT "ON HIS WAY..."
...HE'S HERE.
BUSTED.
.UH...
...I...
HEH.
SAW THE WHOLE SHOW.
COULDN'T GET ENOUGH.
WITHOUT EVEN TRYING, HE'D SET ME UP FOR THE FALL...
NICE RACK BY THE WAY.
...
AWWW...
SOB.
...DON'T CRY...

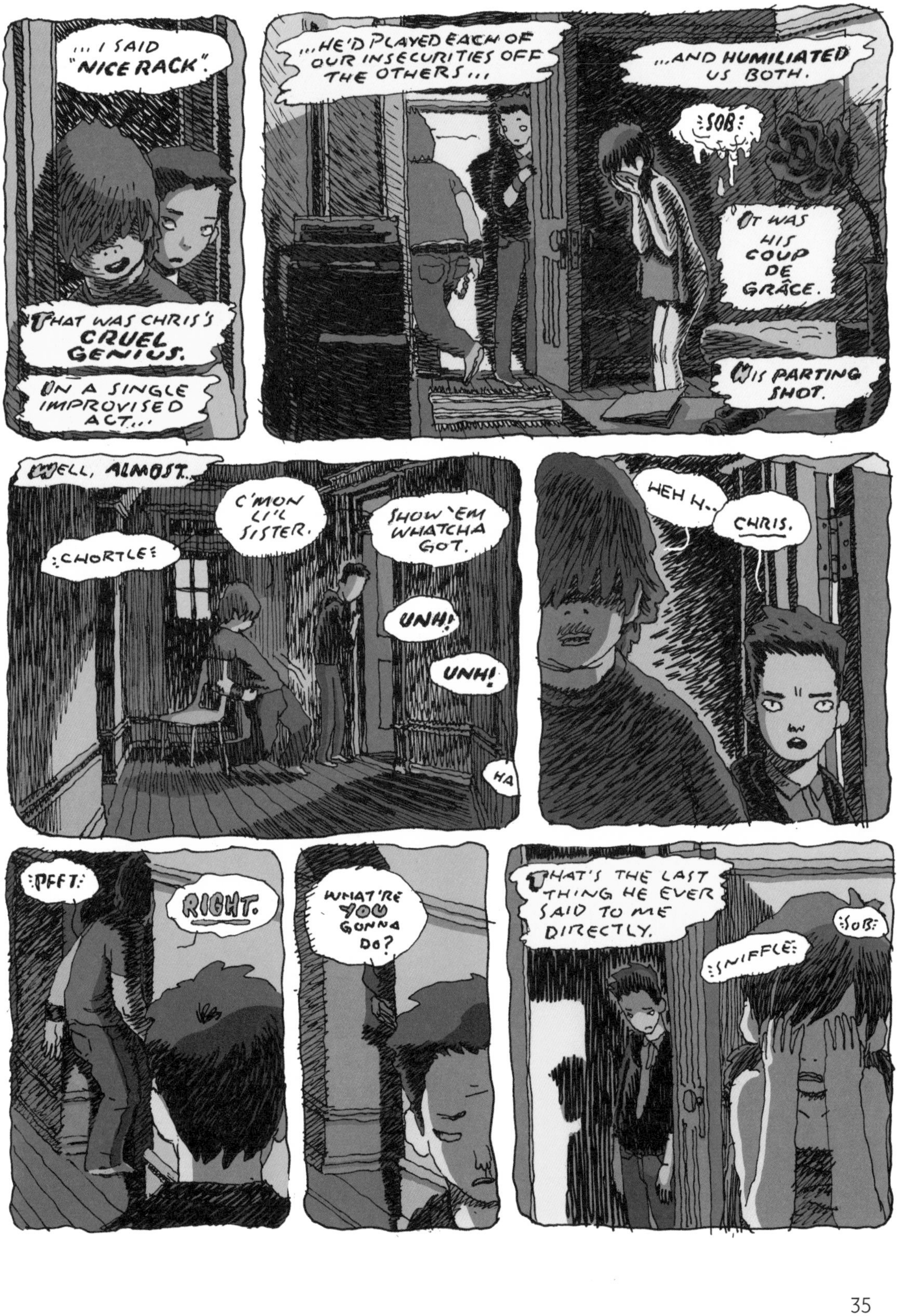
...I SAID "NICE RACK".
THAT WAS CHRIS'S CRUEL GENIUS.
IN A SINGLE IMPROVISED ACT...
...HE'D PLAYED EACH OF OUR INSECURITIES OFF THE OTHERS...
...AND HUMILIATED US BOTH.
SOB
IT WAS HIS COUP DE GRÂCE.
HIS PARTING SHOT.
WELL, ALMOST.
CHORTLE
C'MON LI'L SISTER.
SHOW 'EM WHATCHA GOT.
UNH!
UNH!
HA
HEH H..
CHRIS.
PFFT.
RIGHT.
WHAT'RE YOU GONNA DO?
THAT'S THE LAST THING HE EVER SAID TO ME DIRECTLY.
SOB
SNIFFLE

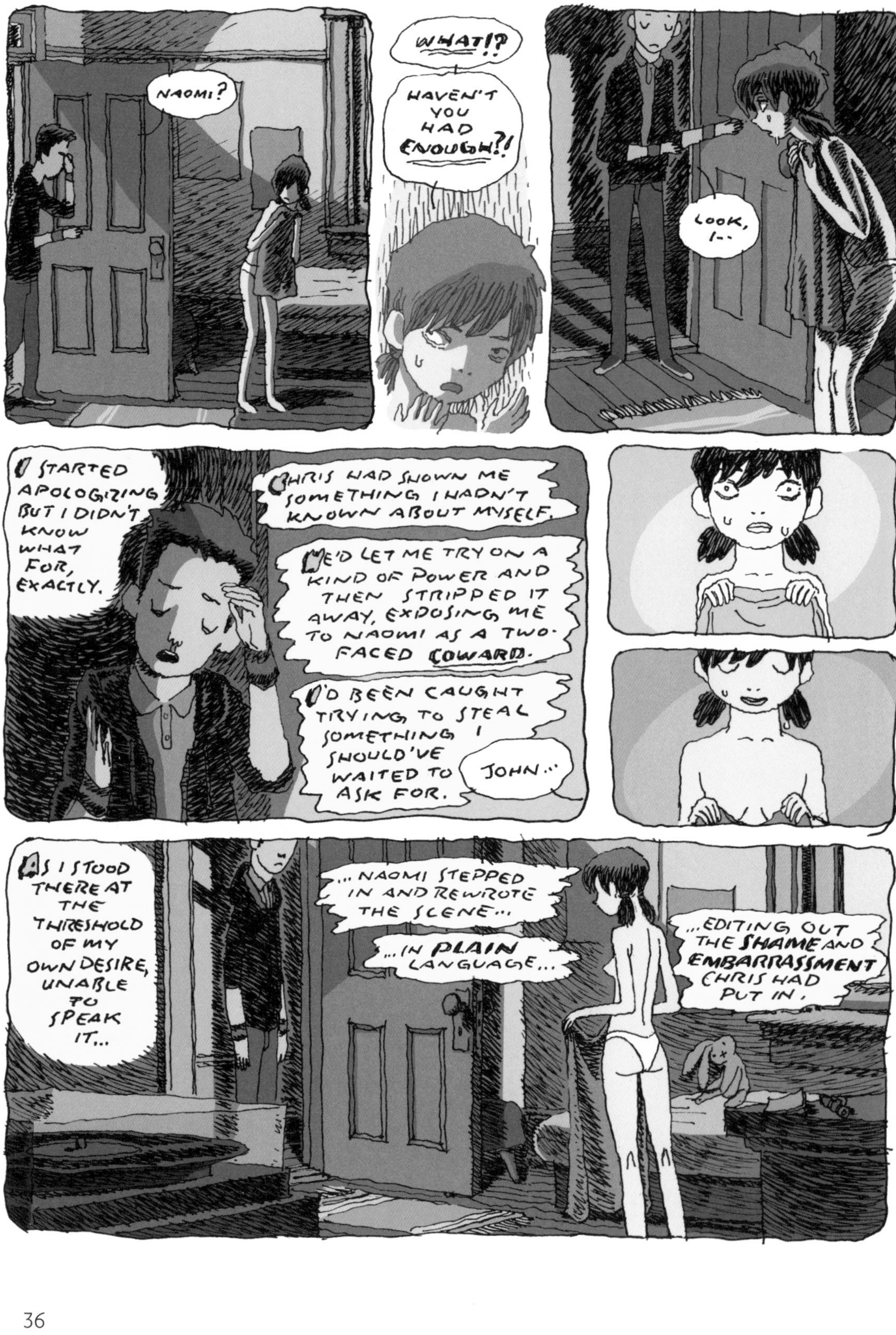
NAOMI?
WHAT!?
HAVEN'T YOU HAD ENOUGH?!
LOOK, I--
I STARTED APOLOGIZING BUT I DIDN'T KNOW WHAT FOR, EXACTLY.
CHRIS HAD SHOWN ME SOMETHING I HADN'T KNOWN ABOUT MYSELF.
HE'D LET ME TRY ON A KIND OF POWER AND THEN STRIPPED IT AWAY, EXPOSING ME TO NAOMI AS A TWO-FACED COWARD.
I'D BEEN CAUGHT TRYING TO STEAL SOMETHING I SHOULD'VE WAITED TO ASK FOR.
JOHN...
AS I STOOD THERE AT THE THRESHOLD OF MY OWN DESIRE, UNABLE TO SPEAK IT...
...NAOMI STEPPED IN AND REWROTE THE SCENE...
...IN PLAIN LANGUAGE...
...EDITING OUT THE SHAME AND EMBARRASSMENT CHRIS HAD PUT IN.

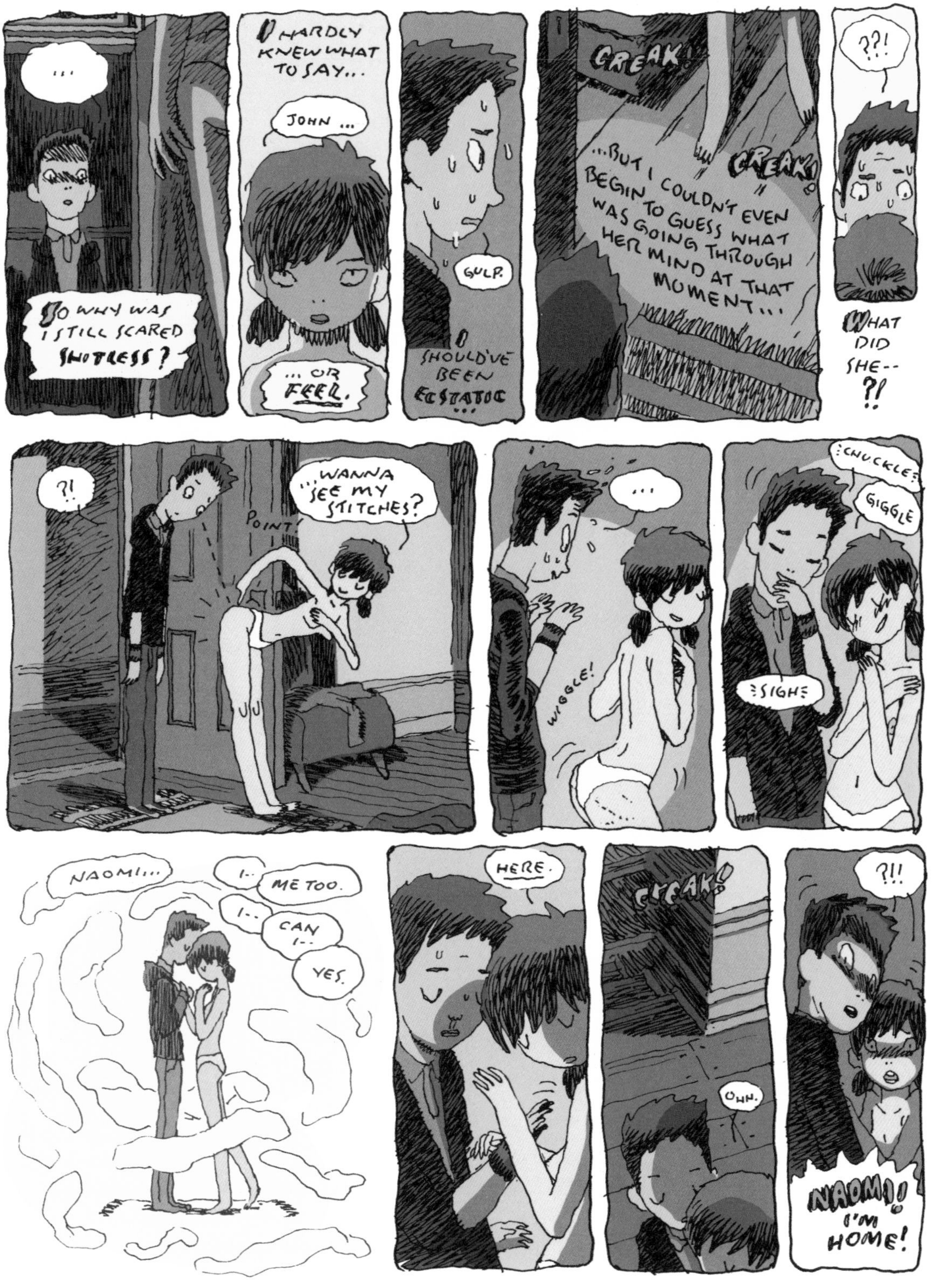
...
SO WHY WAS I STILL SCARED SHOTLESS?
I HARDLY KNEW WHAT TO SAY...
JOHN ...
... OR FEEL.
GULP.
I SHOULD'VE BEEN ECSTATIC...
CREAK!
...BUT I COULDN'T EVEN BEGIN TO GUESS WHAT WAS GOING THROUGH HER MIND AT THAT MOMENT...
CREAK!
??!
WHAT DID SHE-- ?!
?!
...WANNA SEE MY STITCHES?
POINT
...
WIGGLE!
CHUCKLE
GIGGLE
SIGH
NAOMI...
I--
ME TOO.
I--
CAN I--
YES.
HERE.
CREAK!
OHH.
?!!
NAOMI! I'M HOME!

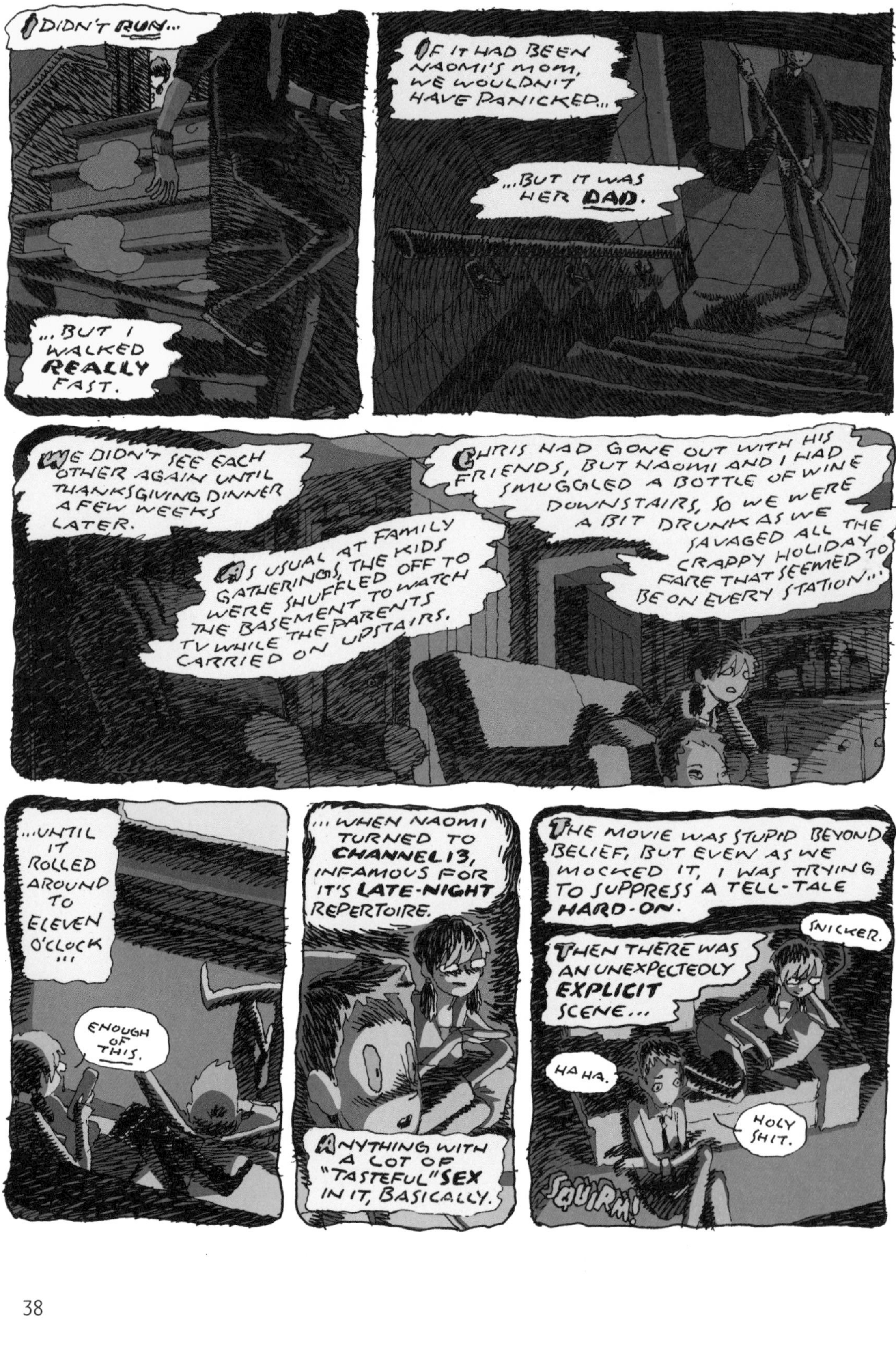
I DIDN'T RUN...
...BUT I WALKED REALLY FAST.
IF IT HAD BEEN NAOMI'S MOM, WE WOULDN'T HAVE PANICKED...
...BUT IT WAS HER DAD.
WE DIDN'T SEE EACH OTHER AGAIN UNTIL THANKSGIVING DINNER A FEW WEEKS LATER.
AS USUAL AT FAMILY GATHERINGS, THE KIDS WERE SHUFFLED OFF TO THE BASEMENT TO WATCH TV WHILE THE PARENTS CARRIED ON UPSTAIRS.
CHRIS HAD GONE OUT WITH HIS FRIENDS, BUT NAOMI AND I HAD SMUGGLED A BOTTLE OF WINE DOWNSTAIRS, SO WE WERE A BIT DRUNK AS WE SAVAGED ALL THE CRAPPY HOLIDAY FARE THAT SEEMED TO BE ON EVERY STATION...
...UNTIL IT ROLLED AROUND TO ELEVEN O'CLOCK...
ENOUGH OF THIS.
...WHEN NAOMI TURNED TO CHANNEL 13, INFAMOUS FOR IT'S LATE-NIGHT REPERTOIRE.
ANYTHING WITH A LOT OF "TASTEFUL" SEX IN IT, BASICALLY.
THE MOVIE WAS STUPID BEYOND BELIEF, BUT EVEN AS WE MOCKED IT, I WAS TRYING TO SUPPRESS A TELL-TALE HARD-ON.
SNICKER.
THEN THERE WAS AN UNEXPECTEDLY EXPLICIT SCENE...
HA HA.
HOLY SHIT.
SQUIRM!

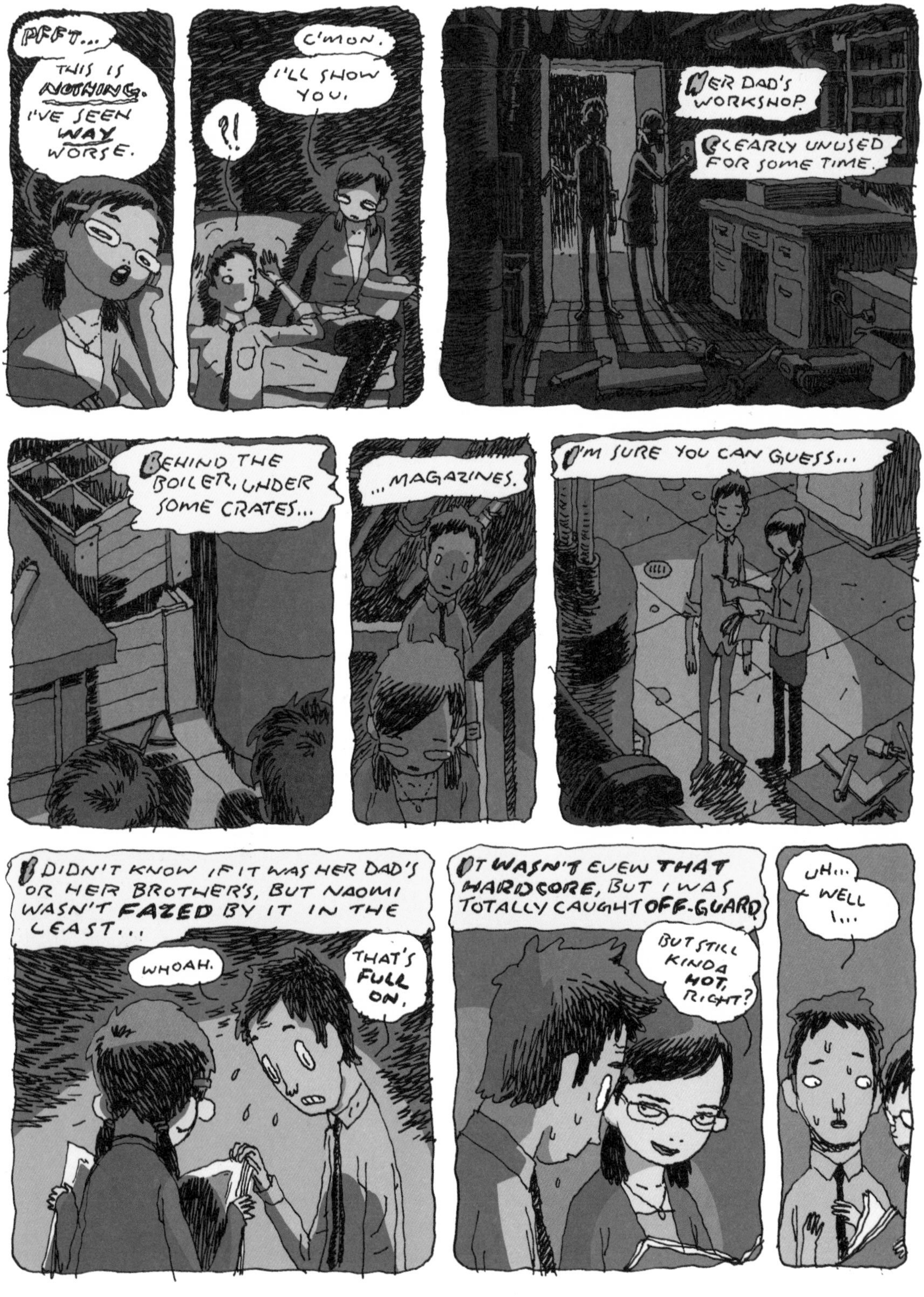
PFFT...
THIS IS NOTHING. I'VE SEEN WAY WORSE.
C'MON.
I'LL SHOW YOU.
?!
HER DAD'S WORKSHOP.
CLEARLY UNUSED FOR SOME TIME.
BEHIND THE BOILER, UNDER SOME CRATES...
...MAGAZINES.
I'M SURE YOU CAN GUESS...
I DIDN'T KNOW IF IT WAS HER DAD'S OR HER BROTHER'S, BUT NAOMI WASN'T FAZED BY IT IN THE LEAST...
WHOAH.
THAT'S FULL ON.
IT WASN'T EVEN THAT HARDCORE, BUT I WAS TOTALLY CAUGHT OFF-GUARD.
BUT STILL KINDA HOT, RIGHT?
UH... WELL I...

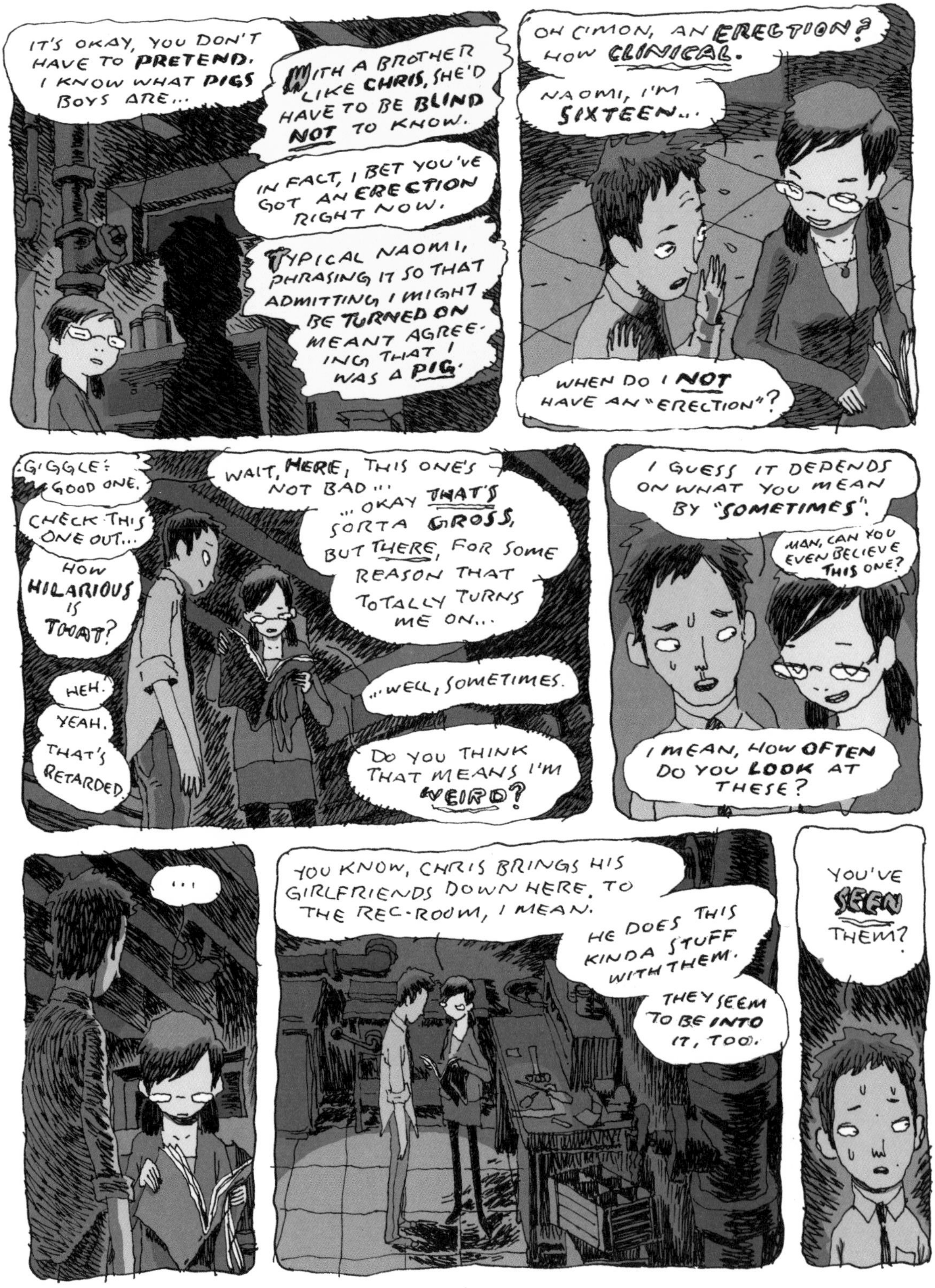

IT'S OKAY, YOU DON'T HAVE TO PRETEND. I KNOW WHAT PIGS BOYS ARE...
WITH A BROTHER LIKE CHRIS, SHE'D HAVE TO BE BLIND NOT TO KNOW.
IN FACT, I BET YOU'VE GOT AN ERECTION RIGHT NOW.
TYPICAL NAOMI, PHRASING IT SO THAT ADMITTING I MIGHT BE TURNED ON MEANT AGREEING THAT I WAS A PIG.
OH C'MON, AN ERECTION? HOW CLINICAL.
NAOMI, I'M SIXTEEN...
WHEN DO I NOT HAVE AN "ERECTION"?
GIGGLE: GOOD ONE.
CHECK THIS ONE OUT...
HOW HILARIOUS IS THAT?
HEH.
YEAH.
THAT'S RETARDED.
WAIT, HERE, THIS ONE'S NOT BAD...
...OKAY THAT'S SORTA GROSS, BUT THERE, FOR SOME REASON THAT TOTALLY TURNS ME ON...
...WELL, SOMETIMES.
DO YOU THINK THAT MEANS I'M WEIRD?
I GUESS IT DEPENDS ON WHAT YOU MEAN BY "SOMETIMES".
MAN, CAN YOU EVEN BELIEVE THIS ONE?
I MEAN, HOW OFTEN DO YOU LOOK AT THESE?
...
YOU KNOW, CHRIS BRINGS HIS GIRLFRIENDS DOWN HERE. TO THE REC-ROOM, I MEAN.
HE DOES THIS KINDA STUFF WITH THEM.
THEY SEEM TO BE INTO IT, TOO.
YOU'VE SEEN THEM?

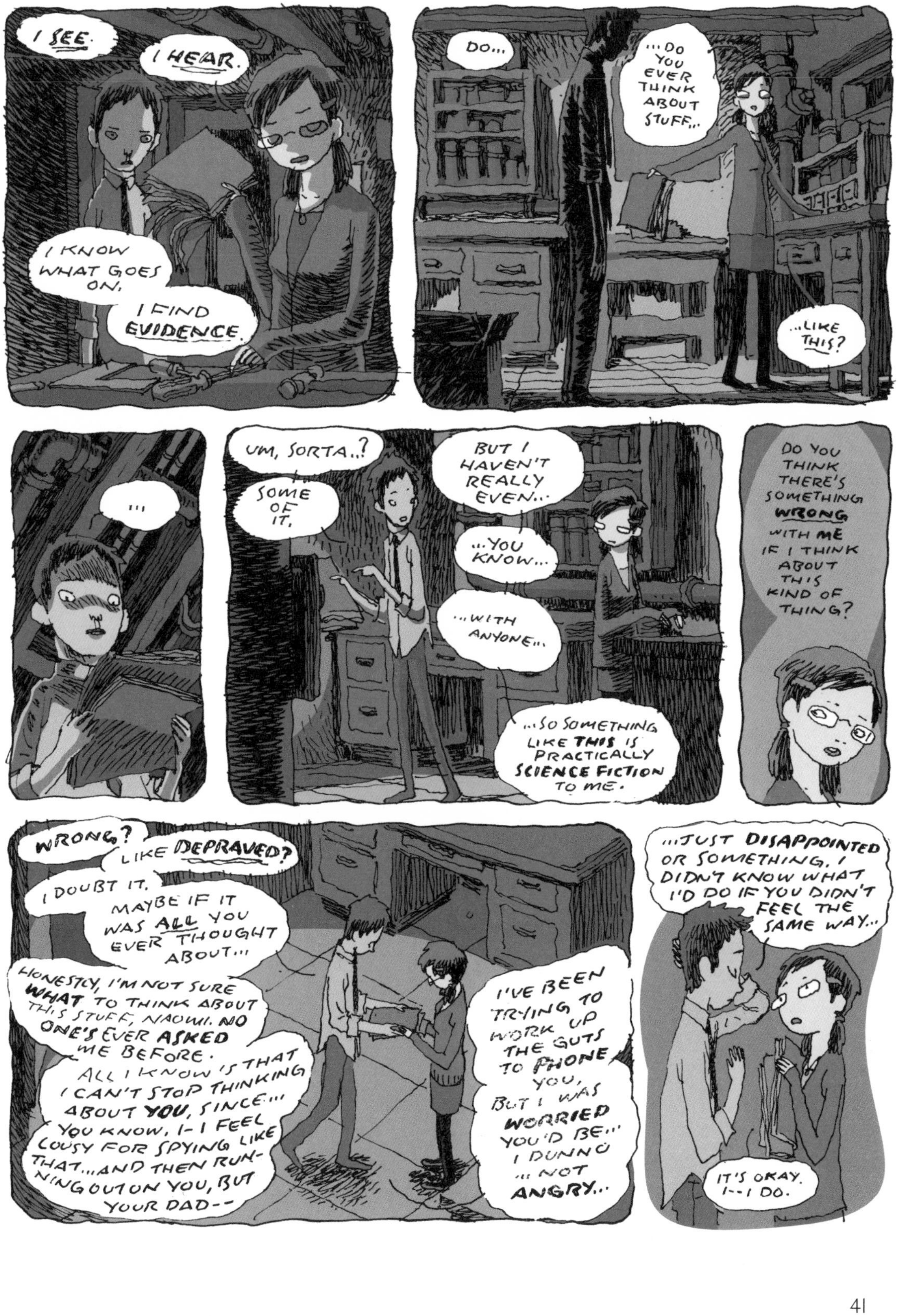
I SEE.
I HEAR.
I KNOW WHAT GOES ON.
I FIND EVIDENCE.
DO...
...DO YOU EVER THINK ABOUT STUFF...
...LIKE THIS?
...
UM, SORTA...?
SOME OF IT.
BUT I HAVEN'T REALLY EVEN...
...YOU KNOW...
...WITH ANYONE...
...SO SOMETHING LIKE THIS IS PRACTICALLY SCIENCE FICTION TO ME.
DO YOU THINK THERE'S SOMETHING WRONG WITH ME IF I THINK ABOUT THIS KIND OF THING?
WRONG?
LIKE DEPRAVED?
I DOUBT IT.
MAYBE IF IT WAS ALL YOU EVER THOUGHT ABOUT...
HONESTLY, I'M NOT SURE WHAT TO THINK ABOUT THIS STUFF, NAOMI. NO ONE'S EVER ASKED ME BEFORE.
ALL I KNOW IS THAT I CAN'T STOP THINKING ABOUT YOU, SINCE... YOU KNOW, I-I FEEL LOUSY FOR SPYING LIKE THAT...AND THEN RUNNING OUT ON YOU, BUT YOUR DAD--
I'VE BEEN TRYING TO WORK UP THE GUTS TO PHONE YOU, BUT I WAS WORRIED YOU'D BE... I DUNNO ...NOT ANGRY...
...JUST DISAPPOINTED OR SOMETHING. I DIDN'T KNOW WHAT I'D DO IF YOU DIDN'T FEEL THE SAME WAY...
IT'S OKAY. I--I DO.

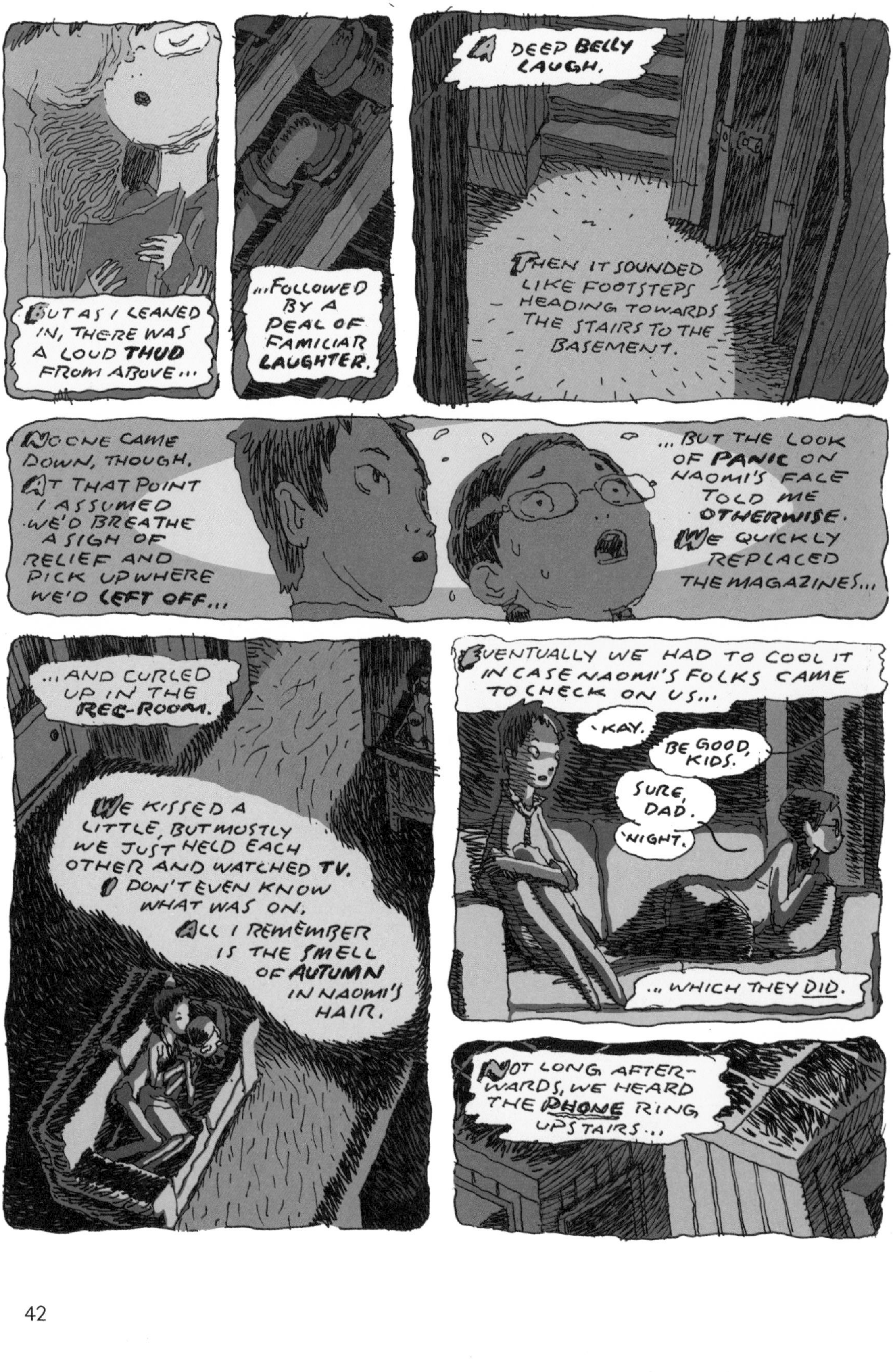
But as I leaned in, there was a loud THUD from above...
...Followed by a peal of familiar LAUGHTER.
A deep BELLY LAUGH.
Then it sounded like footsteps heading towards the stairs to the basement.
No one came down, though.
At that point I assumed we'd breathe a sigh of relief and pick up where we'd LEFT OFF...
...But the look of PANIC on Naomi's face told me OTHERWISE.
We quickly replaced the magazines...
...And curled up in the REC-ROOM.
We kissed a little, but mostly we just held each other and watched TV.
I don't even know what was on.
All I remember is the SMELL of AUTUMN in Naomi's hair.
Eventually we had to cool it in case Naomi's folks came to check on us...
'Kay.
Be good, kids.
Sure, Dad.
'Night.
...Which they DID.
Not long after-wards, we heard the PHONE ring upstairs...

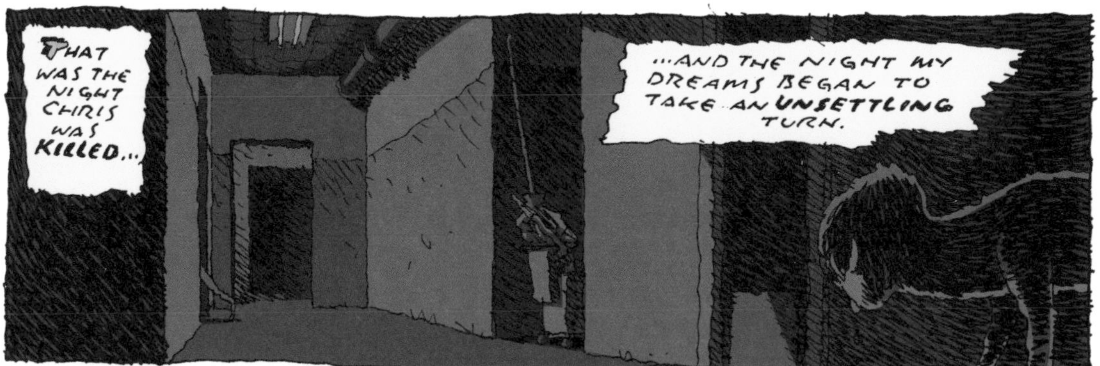

THAT WAS THE NIGHT CHRIS WAS KILLED...
...AND THE NIGHT MY DREAMS BEGAN TO TAKE AN UNSETTLING TURN.

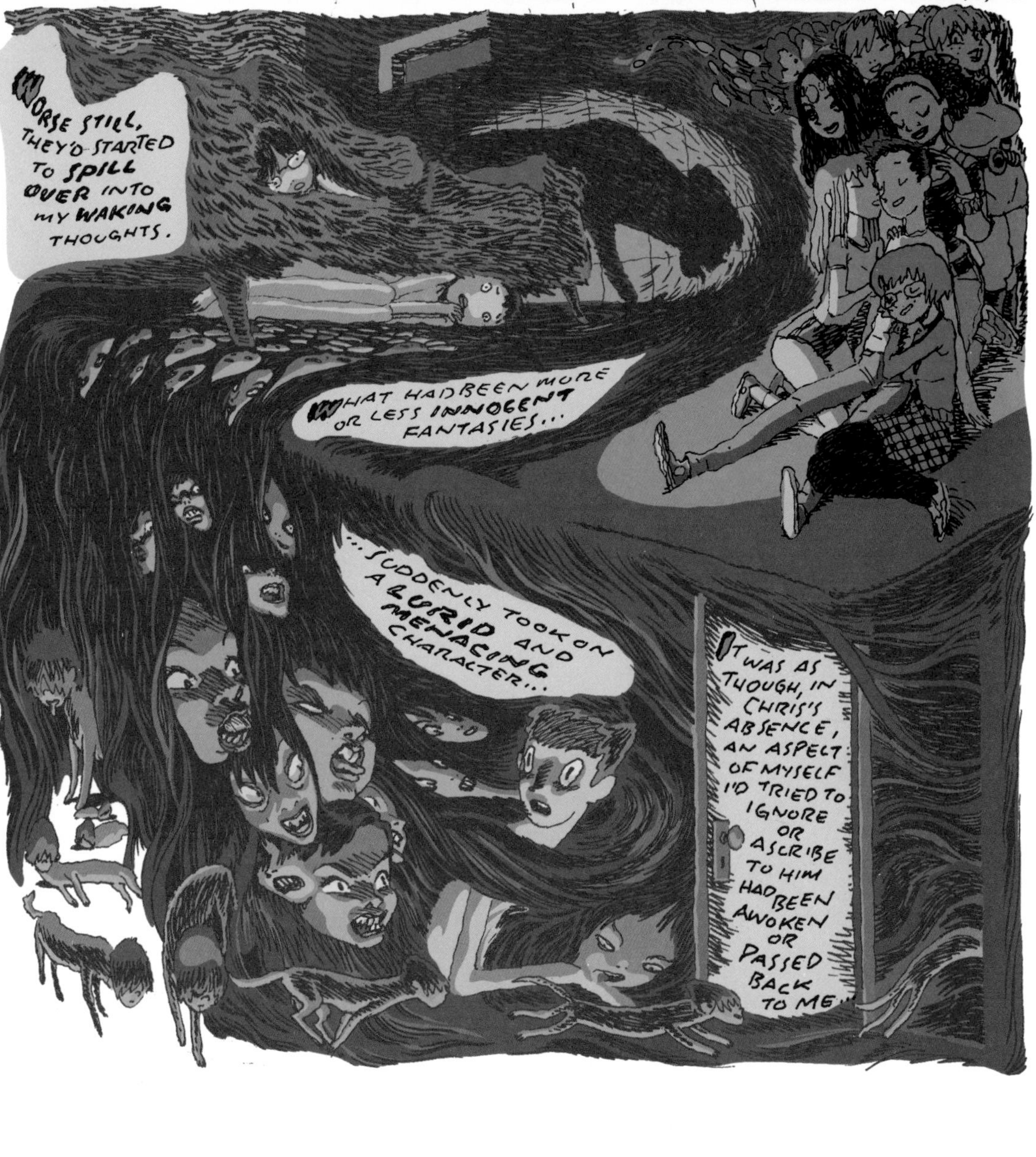

WORSE STILL, THEY'D STARTED TO SPILL OVER INTO MY WAKING THOUGHTS.
WHAT HAD BEEN MORE OR LESS INNOCENT FANTASIES...
...SUDDENLY TOOK ON A LURID AND MENACING CHARACTER...
IT WAS AS THOUGH, IN CHRIS'S ABSENCE, AN ASPECT OF MYSELF I'D TRIED TO IGNORE OR ASCRIBE TO HIM HAD BEEN AWOKEN OR PASSED BACK TO ME...

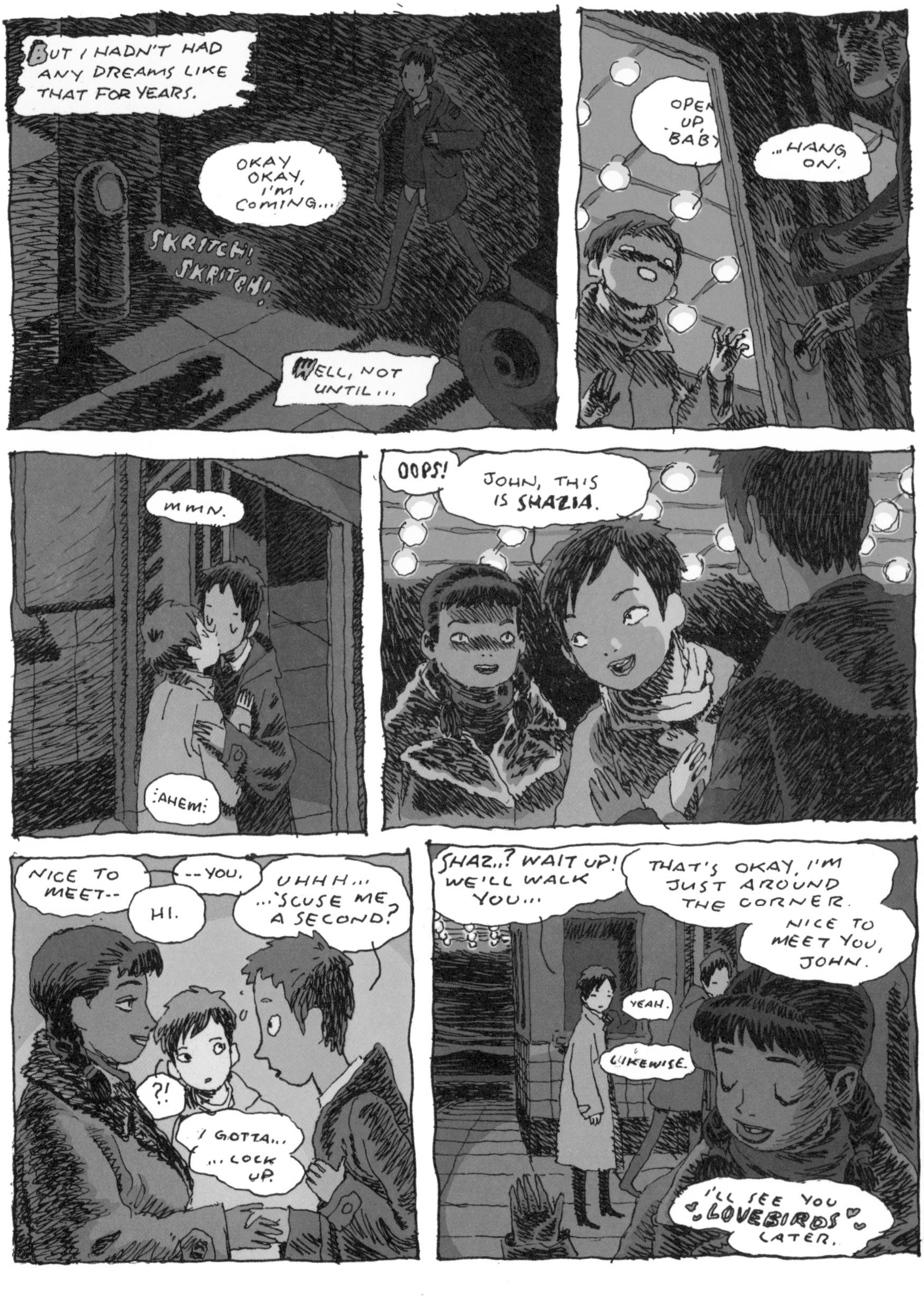

BUT I HADN'T HAD ANY DREAMS LIKE THAT FOR YEARS.
OKAY OKAY, I'M COMING...
SKRITCH! SKRITCH!
WELL, NOT UNTIL...
OPEN UP, BABY
...HANG ON.
MMN.
:AHEM:
OOPS!
JOHN, THIS IS SHAZIA.
NICE TO MEET--
--YOU.
HI.
UHHH... ...'SCUSE ME A SECOND?
?!
I GOTTA... ...LOCK UP.
SHAZ..? WAIT UP! WE'LL WALK YOU...
THAT'S OKAY, I'M JUST AROUND THE CORNER.
NICE TO MEET YOU, JOHN.
YEAH.
LIKEWISE.
I'LL SEE YOU LOVEBIRDS LATER.

SO, HOW WAS CLASS?

GOOD.

SHAZ REALLY LAID INTO THAT POMPOUS JERK IN THE FRONT ROW. HE WAS ALL, "ACCORDING TO BLAH BLAH BLAH..."

SHE TOOK HIM TO THE **MAT**.

TORE HIS ARGUMENT APART POINT BY POINT.

NEH. SOUNDS IMPRESSIVE.

SIGH SHE'S AWESOME.

I DON'T THINK I'D HAVE GOTTEN THROUGH THE PROGRAMME WITHOUT HER.

UM....

..SO WHAT WAS THAT WEIRD MOMENT WHEN I INTRODUCED YOU TWO?

IS EVERYTHING OKAY?

OH! YOU R

YEAH.

SORRY ABOUT THAT.

...SHE LOOKS AN _AWFUL_ LOT LIKE MY EX-**GIRLFRIEND**.

IT CAUGHT ME BY SURPRISE, BUT HONESTLY, IT'S NO BIG DEAL.

THAT'S OKAY, SWEETIE, I UNDERSTAND.

WE ALL HAVE **GHOSTS**.

BESIDES, ONCE YOU GET TO KNOW HER BETTER YOU'LL SEE HOW DIFFERENT

CLIC! CLIC!

CLIC

CLIC CLIC CLIC CLIC CLIC CLIC

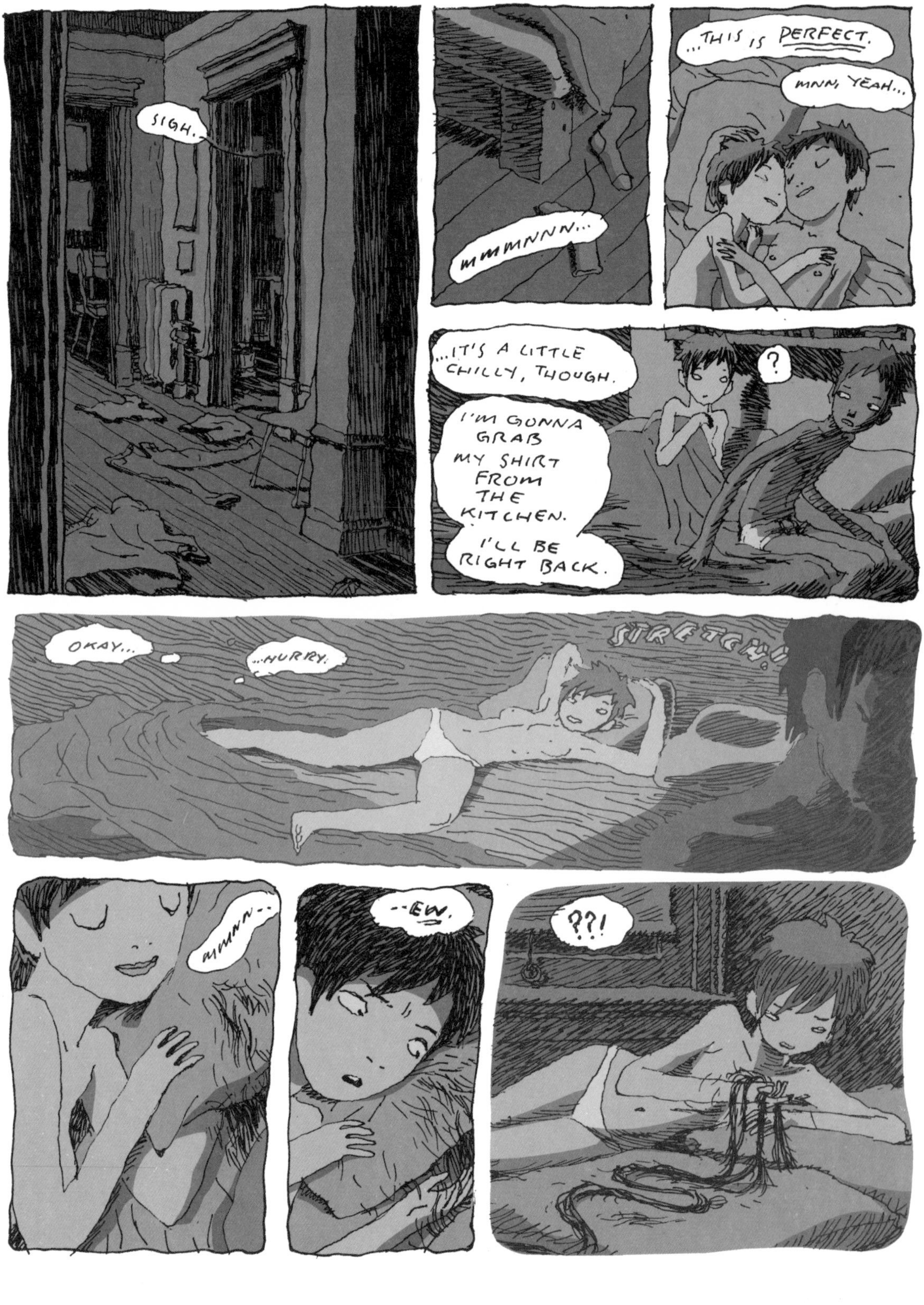
SIGH.
MMMNNN...
...THIS IS PERFECT.
MNN, YEAH...
...IT'S A LITTLE CHILLY, THOUGH.
?
I'M GONNA GRAB MY SHIRT FROM THE KITCHEN.
I'LL BE RIGHT BACK.
OKAY...
...HURRY.
STRETCH!
MMNN...
--EW.
??!

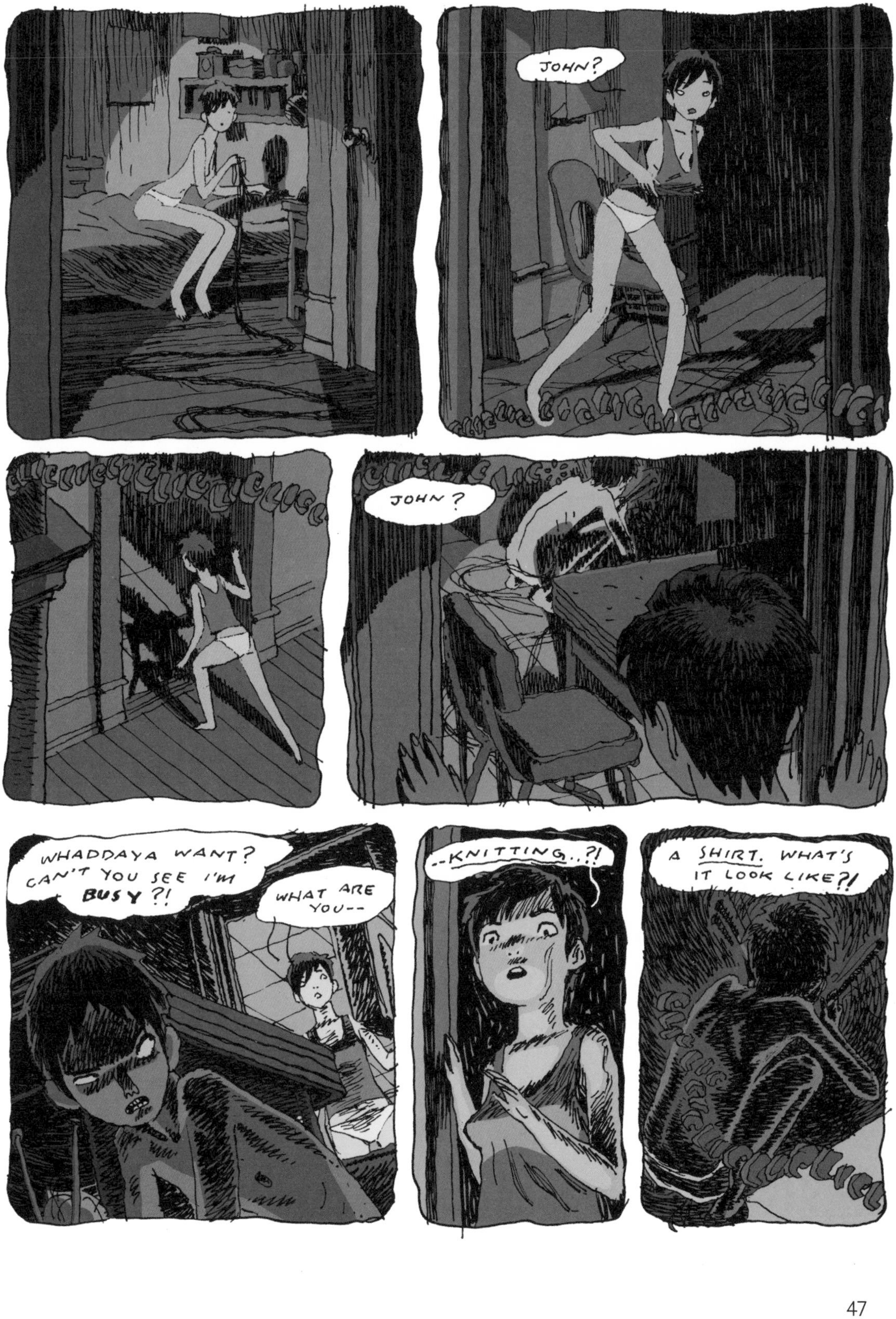
JOHN?
JOHN?
WHADDAYA WANT? CAN'T YOU SEE I'M BUSY?!
WHAT ARE YOU--
..KNITTING..?!
A SHIRT. WHAT'S IT LOOK LIKE?!

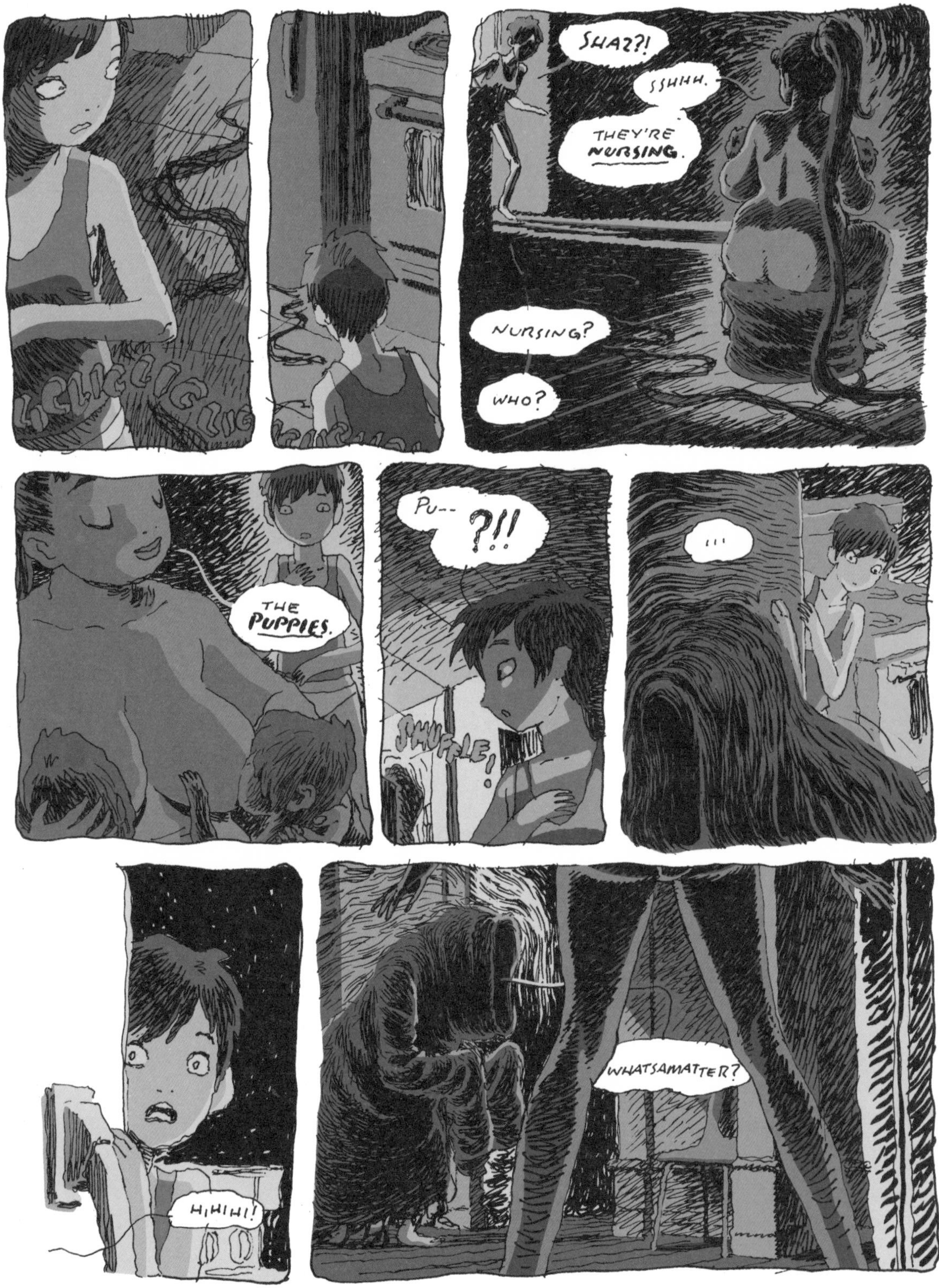
SHAZ?!
SSHHH.
THEY'RE NURSING.
NURSING?
WHO?
THE PUPPIES.
PU-- ?!!
SHUFFLE!
...
HIHIHI!
WHATSAMATTER?

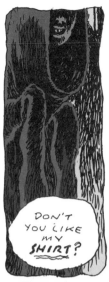

DON'T YOU LIKE MY **SHIRT**?

I MADE IT, MYSELF.

I DON'T LIKE IT!! YOU COME OUT OF THERE!!

HEE HEE, OKAY...

...BUT IT'S SOOOO. **WARM** IN THERE.

YOU SHOULD TRY IT ON...

"!"

:SOB:

OH NO...

:CHOKE:

...NAOMI...

...THE PUPPIES ARE **DEAD.**

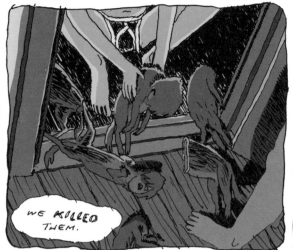

WE **KILLED** THEM.

OH JOHN **NO.**

JOHN?

JOHN?

PUPPIES

..PUPPIES...

DEAD PUP--

...?

ARE YOU OKAY?

HOLY...

JESUS. THAT WAS **INSANE.**

YOU WERE CRYING AND SAYING "PUPPIES" OVER AND OVER.

IT'S OKAY. JUST A **NIGHTMARE.**

:PHEW:

OH MAN, NAOMI, AM I EVER GLAD YOU'RE **HERE...**

ME TOO, BABY...

"...ME TOO."

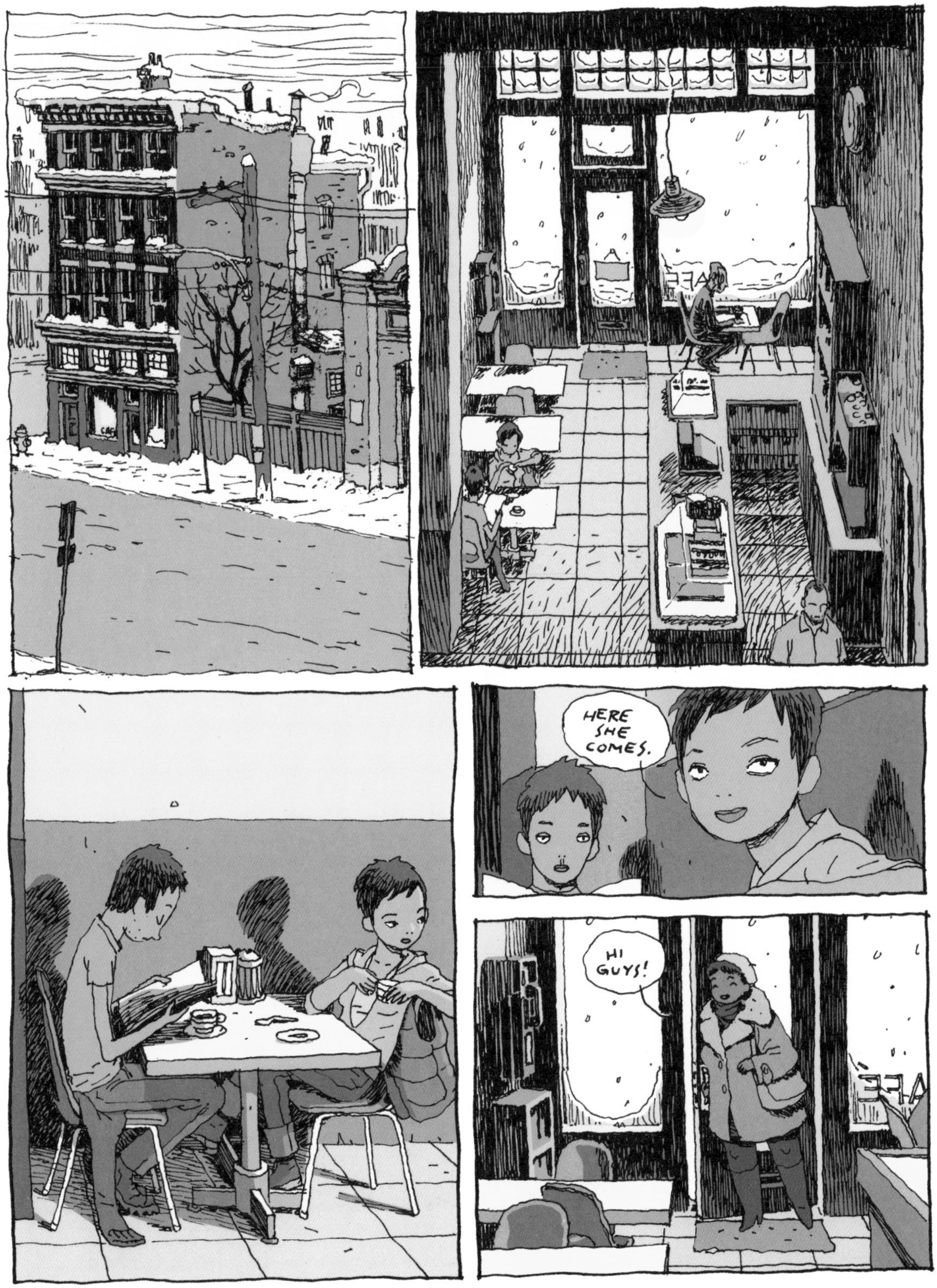
HERE SHE COMES.
HI GUYS!

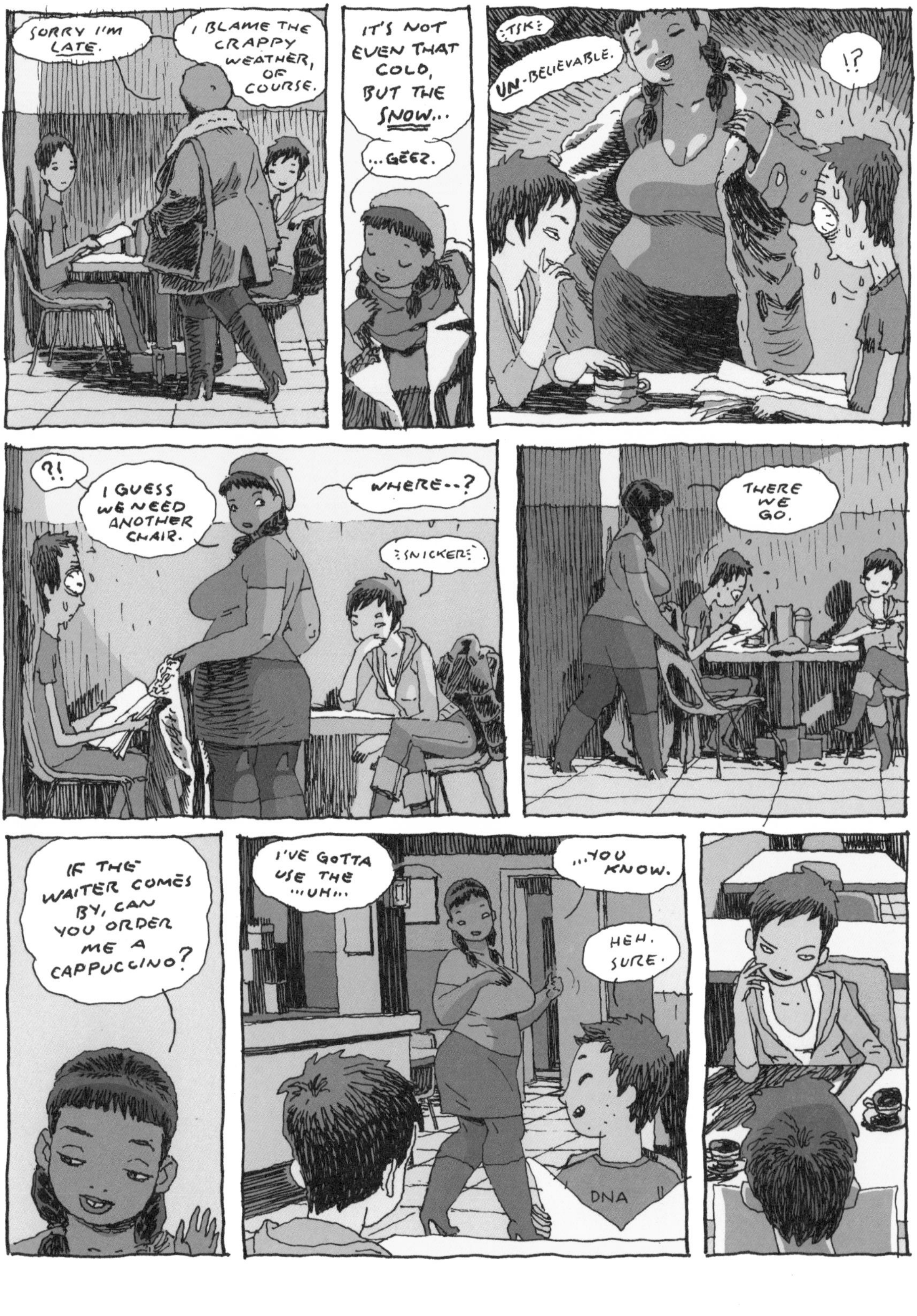
SORRY I'M LATE.
I BLAME THE CRAPPY WEATHER, OF COURSE.
IT'S NOT EVEN THAT COLD, BUT THE SNOW...
...GEEZ.
TSK
UN-BELIEVABLE.
!?
?!
I GUESS WE NEED ANOTHER CHAIR.
WHERE..?
SNICKER
THERE WE GO.
IF THE WAITER COMES BY, CAN YOU ORDER ME A CAPPUCCINO?
I'VE GOTTA USE THE ...UH...
...YOU KNOW.
HEH. SURE.
DNA

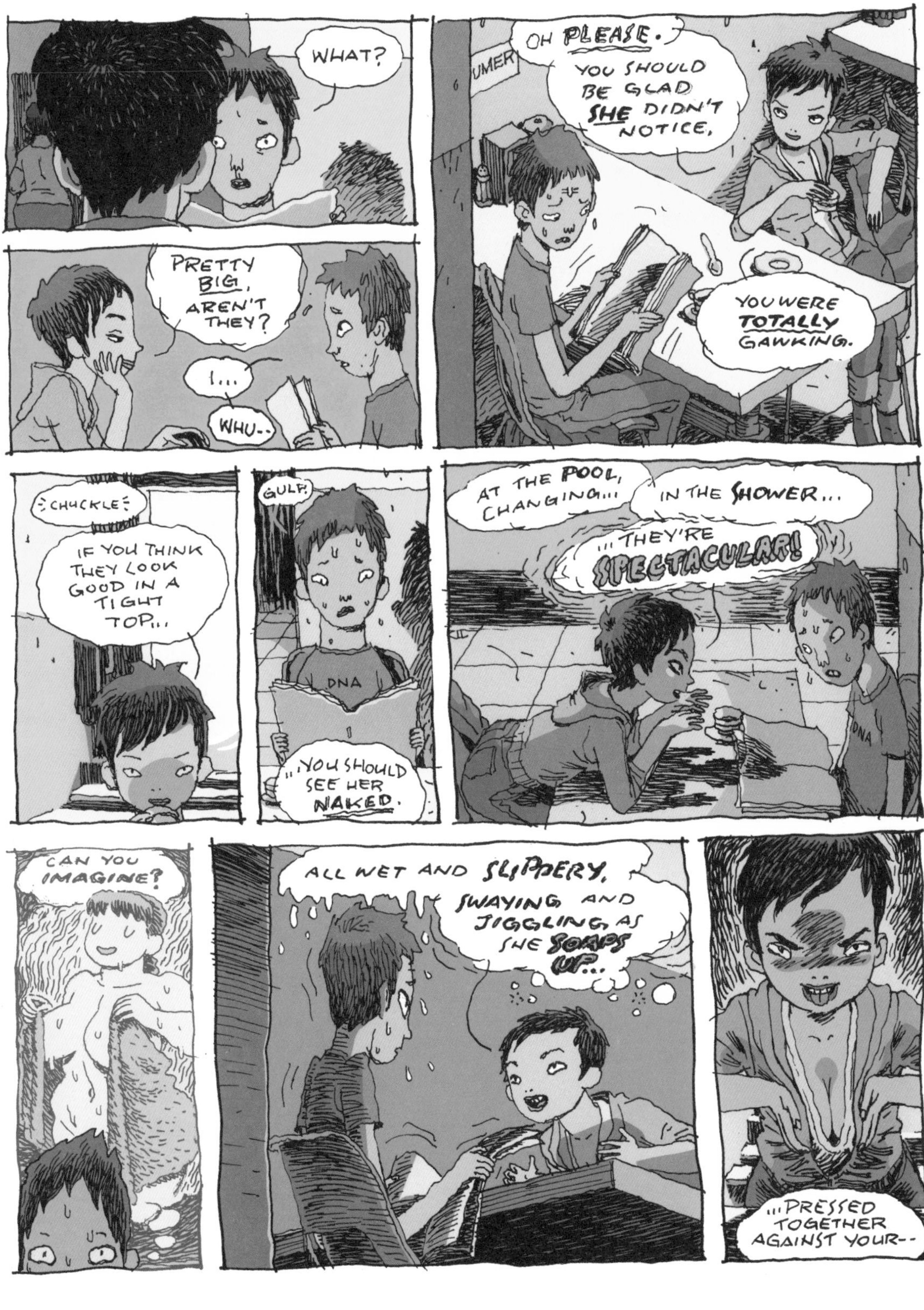
WHAT?
PRETTY BIG, AREN'T THEY?
I...
WHU..
OH PLEASE.
YOU SHOULD BE GLAD SHE DIDN'T NOTICE.
YOU WERE TOTALLY GAWKING.
CHUCKLE
IF YOU THINK THEY LOOK GOOD IN A TIGHT TOP...
GULP!
...YOU SHOULD SEE HER NAKED.
AT THE POOL, CHANGING...
IN THE SHOWER...
...THEY'RE SPECTACULAR!
DNA
CAN YOU IMAGINE?
ALL WET AND SLIPPERY,
SWAYING AND JIGGLING AS SHE SOAPS UP...
...PRESSED TOGETHER AGAINST YOUR--

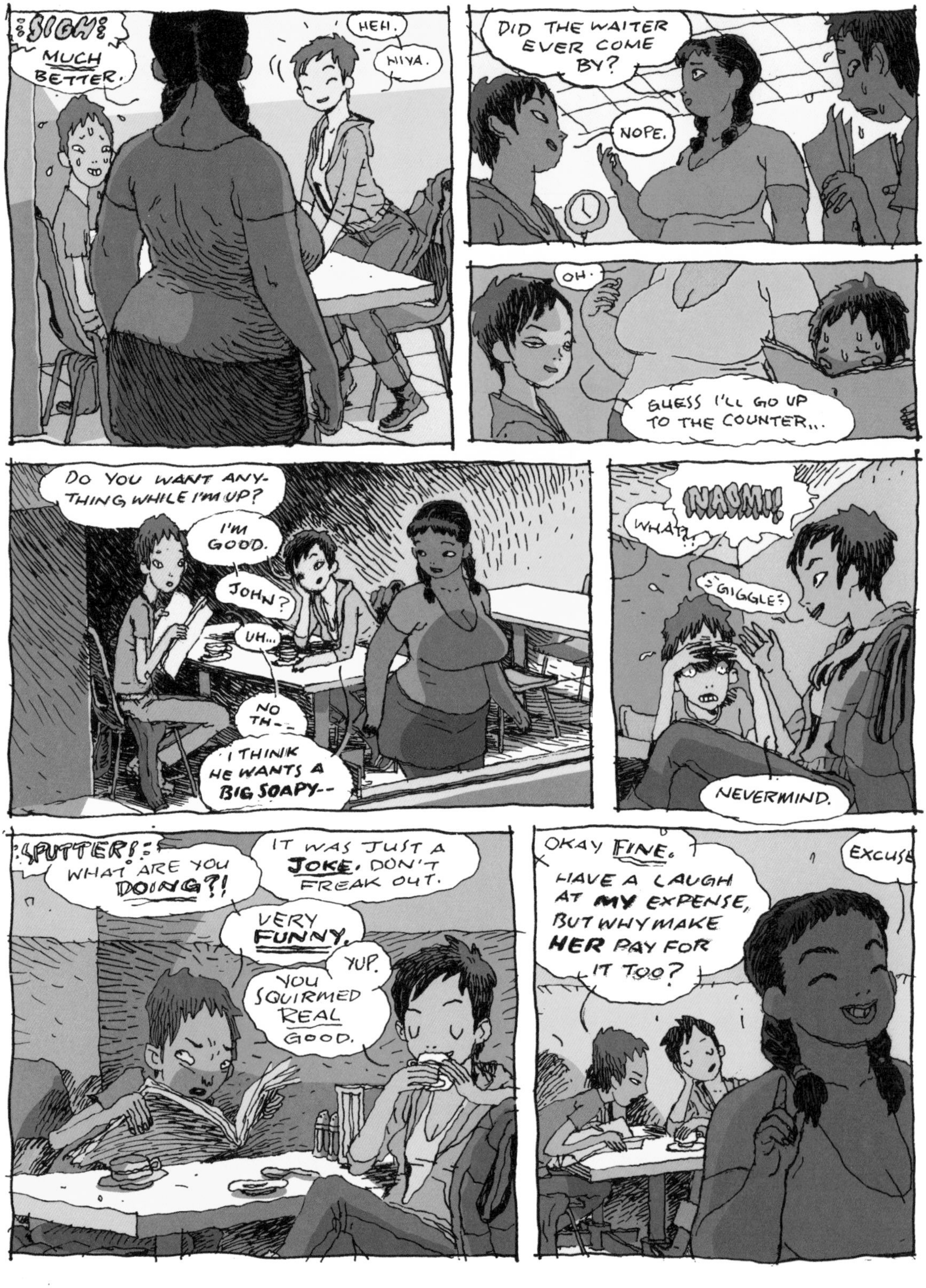
:SIGH:
MUCH BETTER.
HEH.
HIYA.
DID THE WAITER EVER COME BY?
NOPE.
OH.
GUESS I'LL GO UP TO THE COUNTER...
DO YOU WANT ANYTHING WHILE I'M UP?
I'M GOOD.
JOHN?
UH...
NO TH--
I THINK HE WANTS A BIG SOAPY--
NAOMI!
WHAT?!
:GIGGLE:
NEVERMIND.
:SPUTTER!: WHAT ARE YOU DOING?!
IT WAS JUST A JOKE. DON'T FREAK OUT.
VERY FUNNY.
YUP.
YOU SQUIRMED REAL GOOD.
OKAY FINE.
HAVE A LAUGH AT MY EXPENSE, BUT WHY MAKE HER PAY FOR IT TOO?
EXCUSE

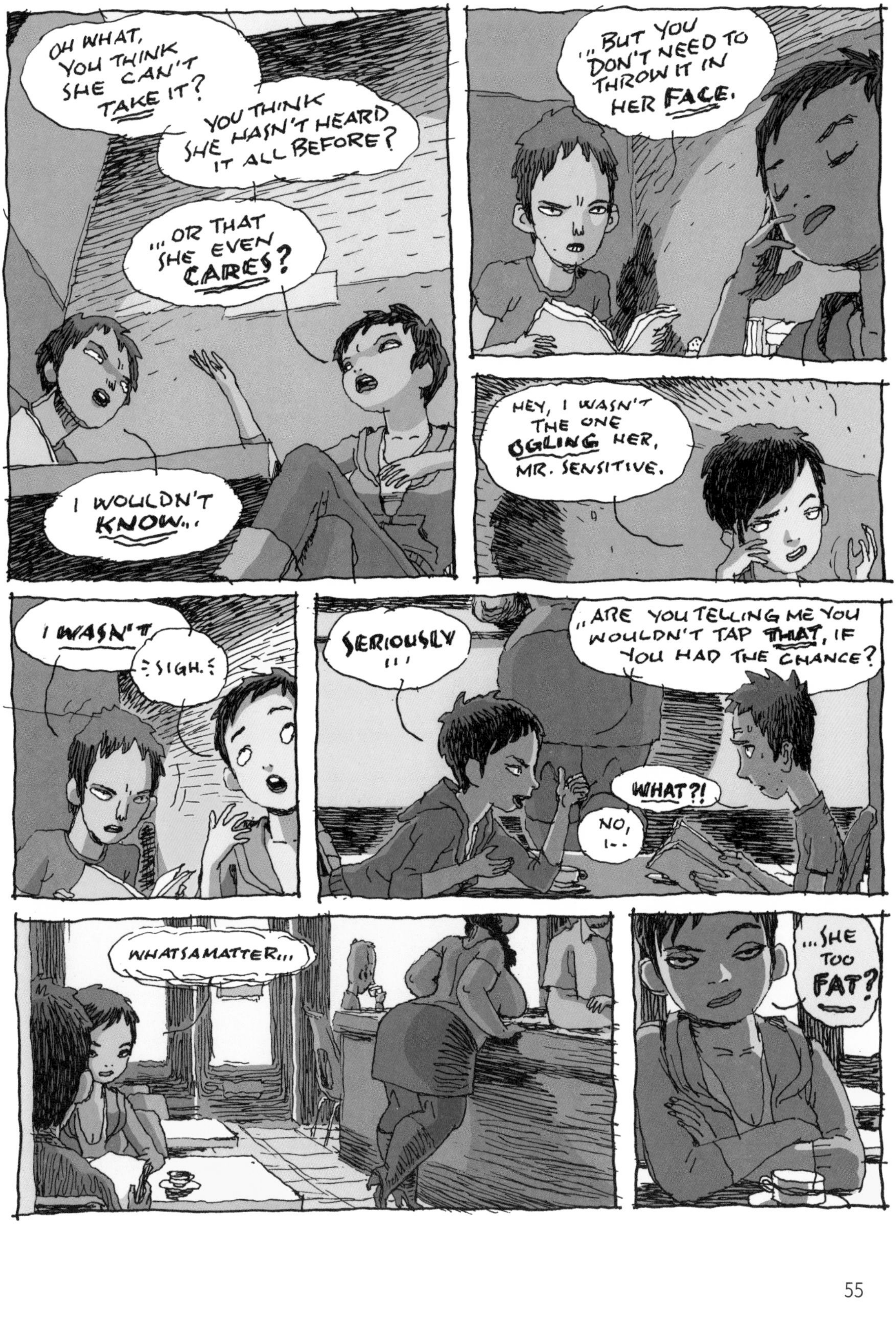
OH WHAT, YOU THINK SHE CAN'T TAKE IT?
YOU THINK SHE HASN'T HEARD IT ALL BEFORE?
... OR THAT SHE EVEN CARES?
I WOULDN'T KNOW...
... BUT YOU DON'T NEED TO THROW IT IN HER FACE.
HEY, I WASN'T THE ONE OGLING HER, MR. SENSITIVE.
I WASN'T
SIGH.
SERIOUSLY ...
... ARE YOU TELLING ME YOU WOULDN'T TAP THAT, IF YOU HAD THE CHANCE?
WHAT?!
NO, I--
WHATSAMATTER...
...SHE TOO FAT?

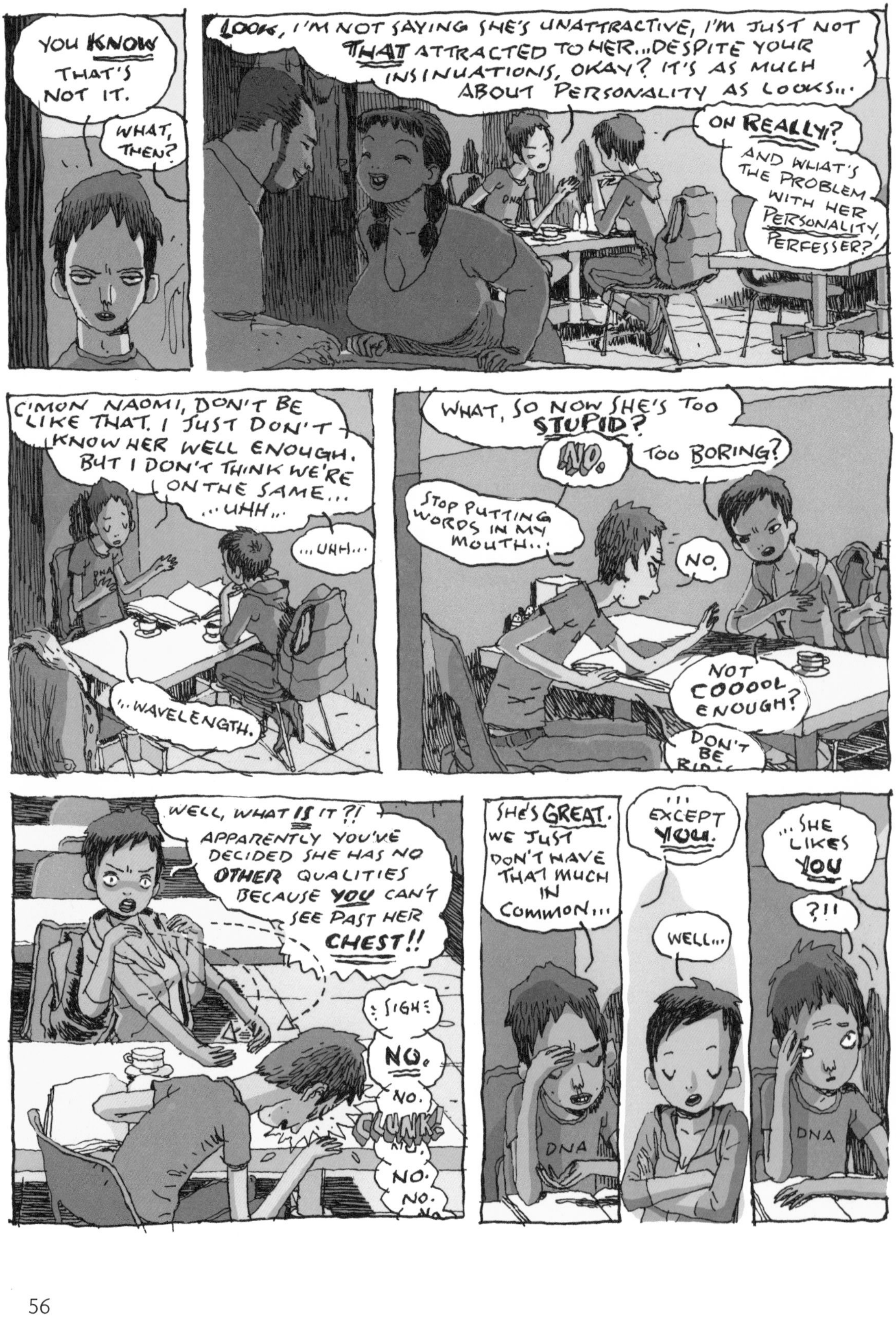
YOU KNOW THAT'S NOT IT.
WHAT, THEN?
LOOK, I'M NOT SAYING SHE'S UNATTRACTIVE, I'M JUST NOT THAT ATTRACTED TO HER... DESPITE YOUR INSINUATIONS, OKAY? IT'S AS MUCH ABOUT PERSONALITY AS LOOKS...
OH REALLY?
AND WHAT'S THE PROBLEM WITH HER PERSONALITY, PERFESSER?
DNA
C'MON NAOMI, DON'T BE LIKE THAT. I JUST DON'T KNOW HER WELL ENOUGH. BUT I DON'T THINK WE'RE ON THE SAME... ...UHH...
...UHH...
...WAVELENGTH.
WHAT, SO NOW SHE'S TOO STUPID?
NO.
TOO BORING?
STOP PUTTING WORDS IN MY MOUTH...
NO.
NOT COOOOL ENOUGH?
DON'T BE
WELL, WHAT IS IT?! APPARENTLY YOU'VE DECIDED SHE HAS NO OTHER QUALITIES BECAUSE YOU CAN'T SEE PAST HER CHEST!!
SIGH
NO.
NO.
CLUNK!
NO.
NO.
NO.
SHE'S GREAT. WE JUST DON'T HAVE THAT MUCH IN COMMON...
DNA
... EXCEPT YOU.
WELL...
...SHE LIKES YOU
?!!
DNA

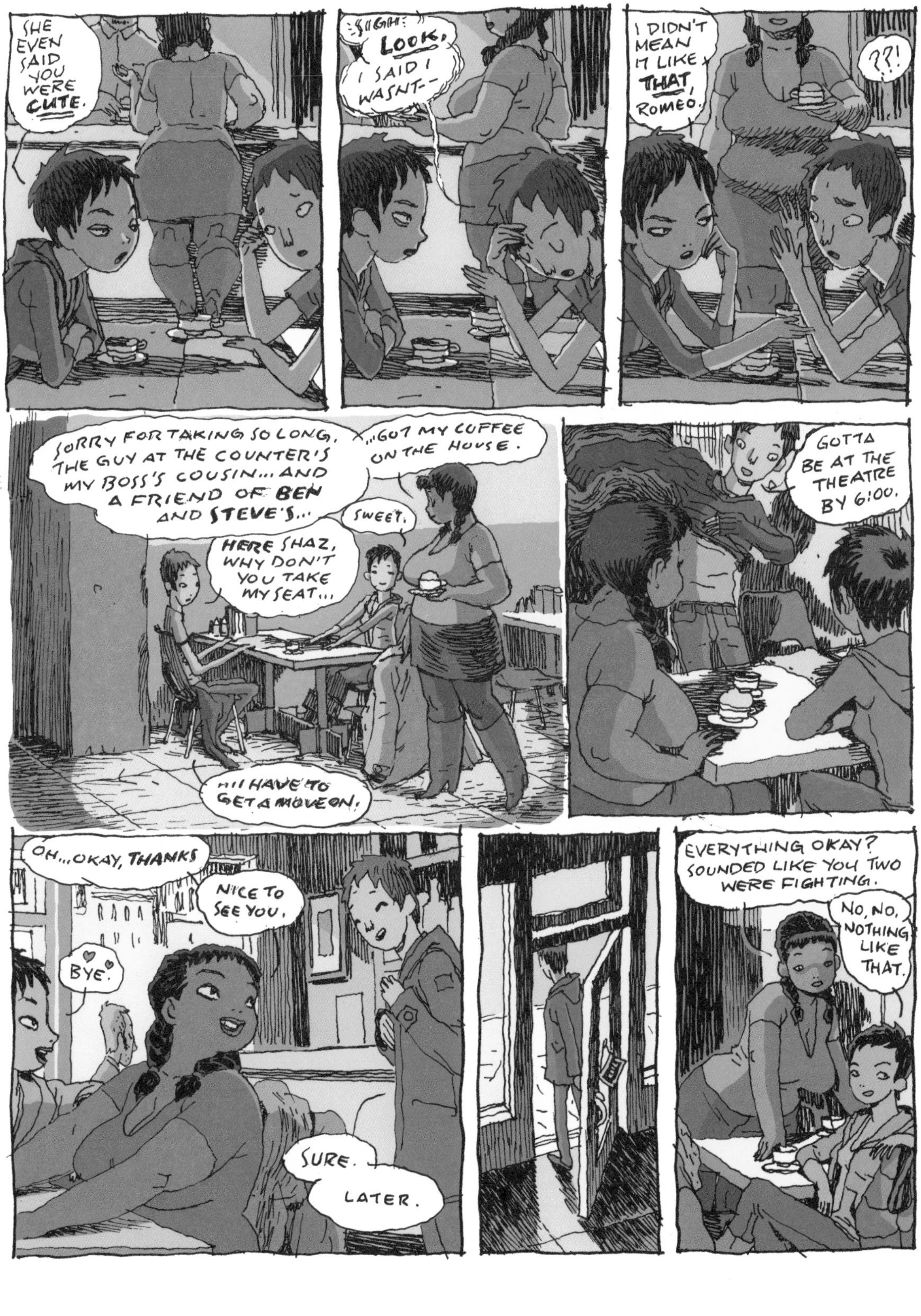
SHE EVEN SAID YOU WERE CUTE.
SIGH
LOOK, I SAID I WASN'T--
I DIDN'T MEAN IT LIKE THAT, ROMEO.
??!
SORRY FOR TAKING SO LONG. THE GUY AT THE COUNTER'S MY BOSS'S COUSIN... AND A FRIEND OF BEN AND STEVE'S...
...GOT MY COFFEE ON THE HOUSE.
SWEET.
HERE SHAZ, WHY DON'T YOU TAKE MY SEAT...
...I HAVE TO GET A MOVE ON.
GOTTA BE AT THE THEATRE BY 6:00.
OH... OKAY, THANKS
NICE TO SEE YOU.
BYE.
SURE.
LATER.
EVERYTHING OKAY? SOUNDED LIKE YOU TWO WERE FIGHTING.
NO, NO, NOTHING LIKE THAT.

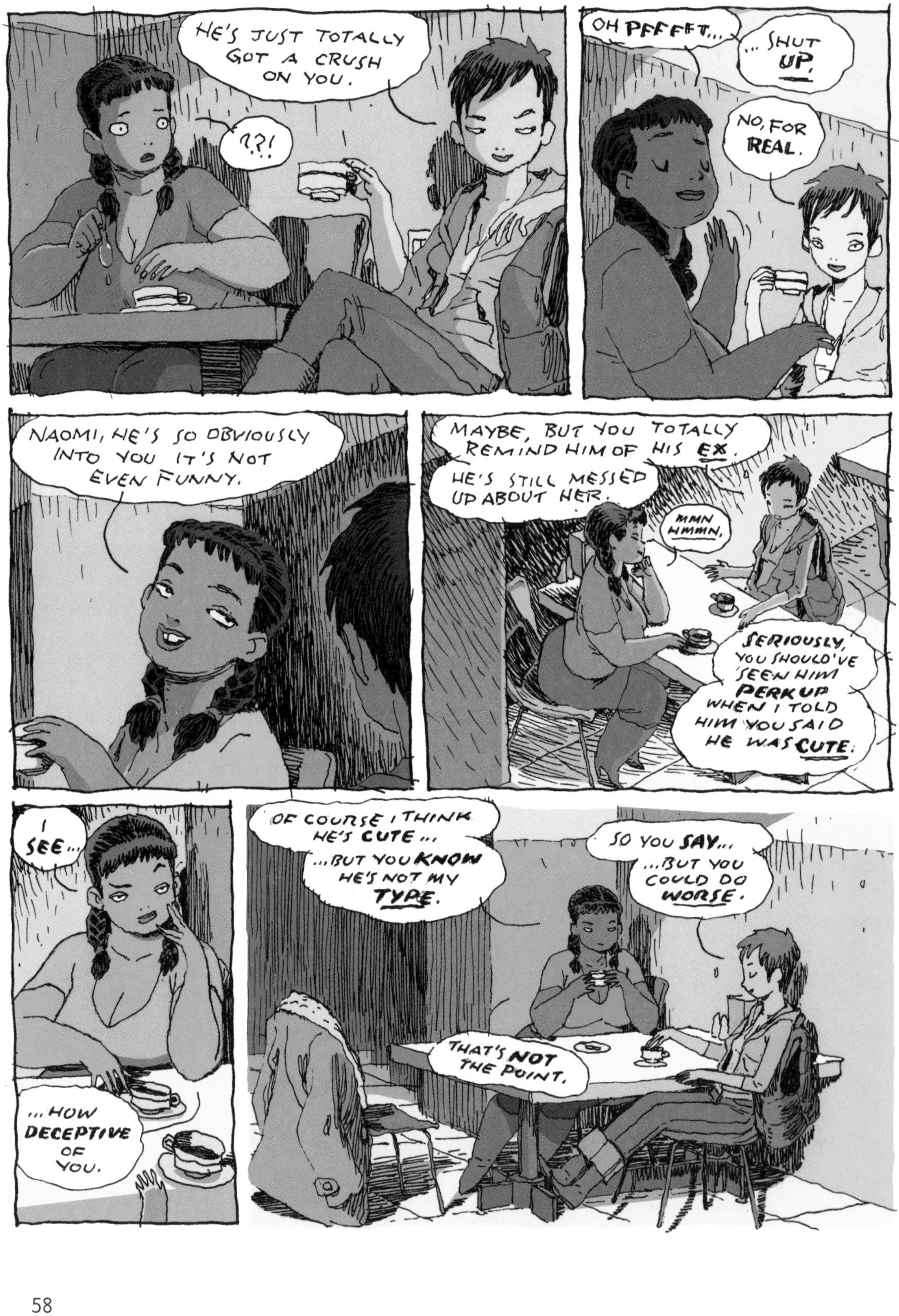
HE'S JUST TOTALLY GOT A CRUSH ON YOU.
??!
OH PFFFFT...
...SHUT UP.
NO, FOR REAL.
NAOMI, HE'S SO OBVIOUSLY INTO YOU IT'S NOT EVEN FUNNY.
MAYBE, BUT YOU TOTALLY REMIND HIM OF HIS EX.
HE'S STILL MESSED UP ABOUT HER.
MMN HMMN.
SERIOUSLY, YOU SHOULD'VE SEEN HIM PERK UP WHEN I TOLD HIM YOU SAID HE WAS CUTE.
I SEE...
...HOW DECEPTIVE OF YOU.
OF COURSE I THINK HE'S CUTE...
...BUT YOU KNOW HE'S NOT MY TYPE.
SO YOU SAY...
...BUT YOU COULD DO WORSE.
THAT'S NOT THE POINT.

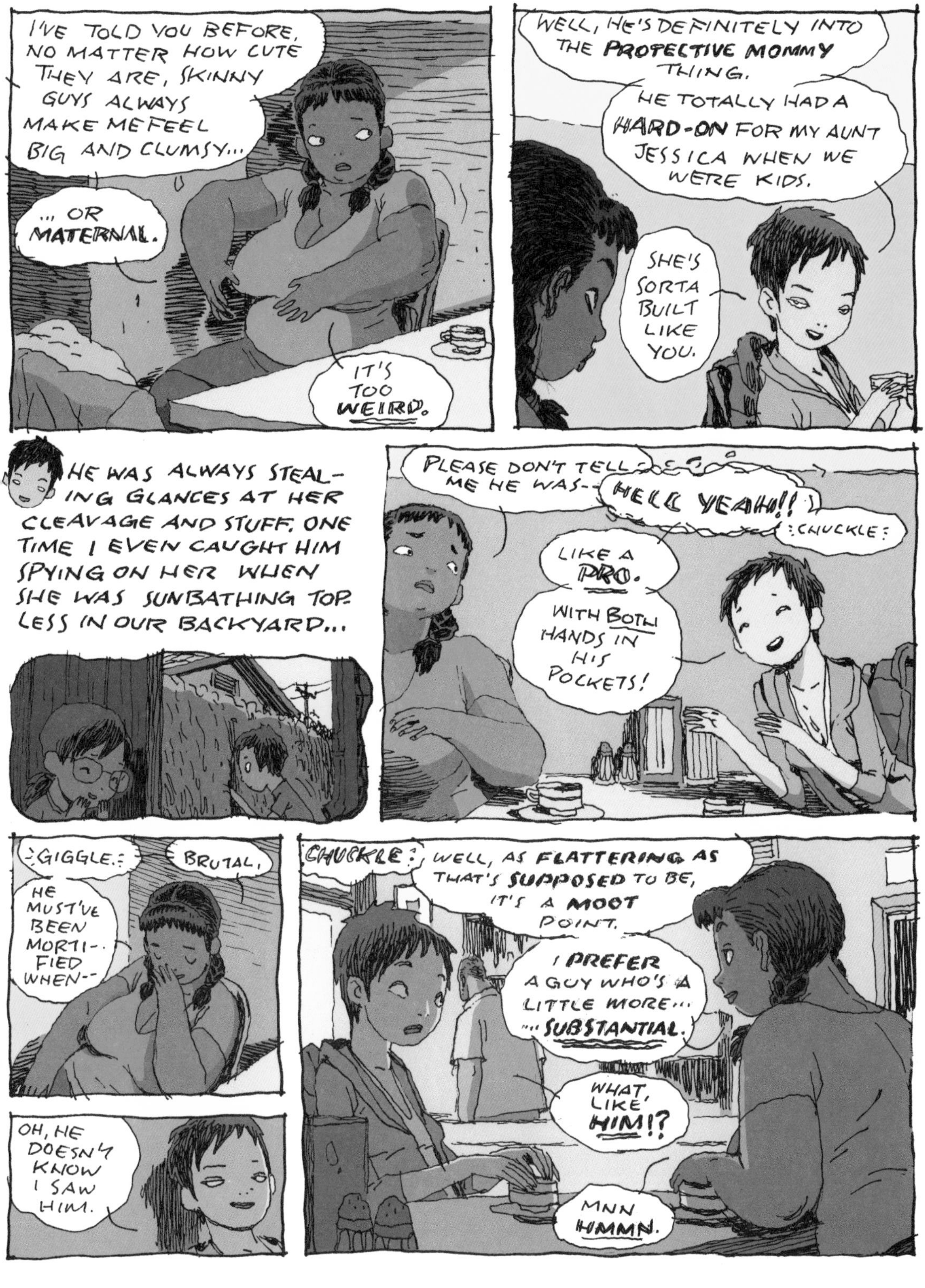

I'VE TOLD YOU BEFORE, NO MATTER HOW CUTE THEY ARE, SKINNY GUYS ALWAYS MAKE ME FEEL BIG AND CLUMSY...
... OR MATERNAL.
IT'S TOO WEIRD.
WELL, HE'S DEFINITELY INTO THE PROTECTIVE MOMMY THING.
HE TOTALLY HAD A HARD-ON FOR MY AUNT JESSICA WHEN WE WERE KIDS.
SHE'S SORTA BUILT LIKE YOU.
HE WAS ALWAYS STEALING GLANCES AT HER CLEAVAGE AND STUFF. ONE TIME I EVEN CAUGHT HIM SPYING ON HER WHEN SHE WAS SUNBATHING TOPLESS IN OUR BACKYARD...
PLEASE DON'T TELL ME HE WAS--
HELL YEAH!!
:CHUCKLE:
LIKE A PRO.
WITH BOTH HANDS IN HIS POCKETS!
:GIGGLE:
BRUTAL.
HE MUST'VE BEEN MORTIFIED WHEN--
OH, HE DOESN'T KNOW I SAW HIM.
:CHUCKLE: WELL, AS FLATTERING AS THAT'S SUPPOSED TO BE, IT'S A MOOT POINT.
I PREFER A GUY WHO'S A LITTLE MORE... ...SUBSTANTIAL.
WHAT, LIKE HIM!?
MNN HMMN.

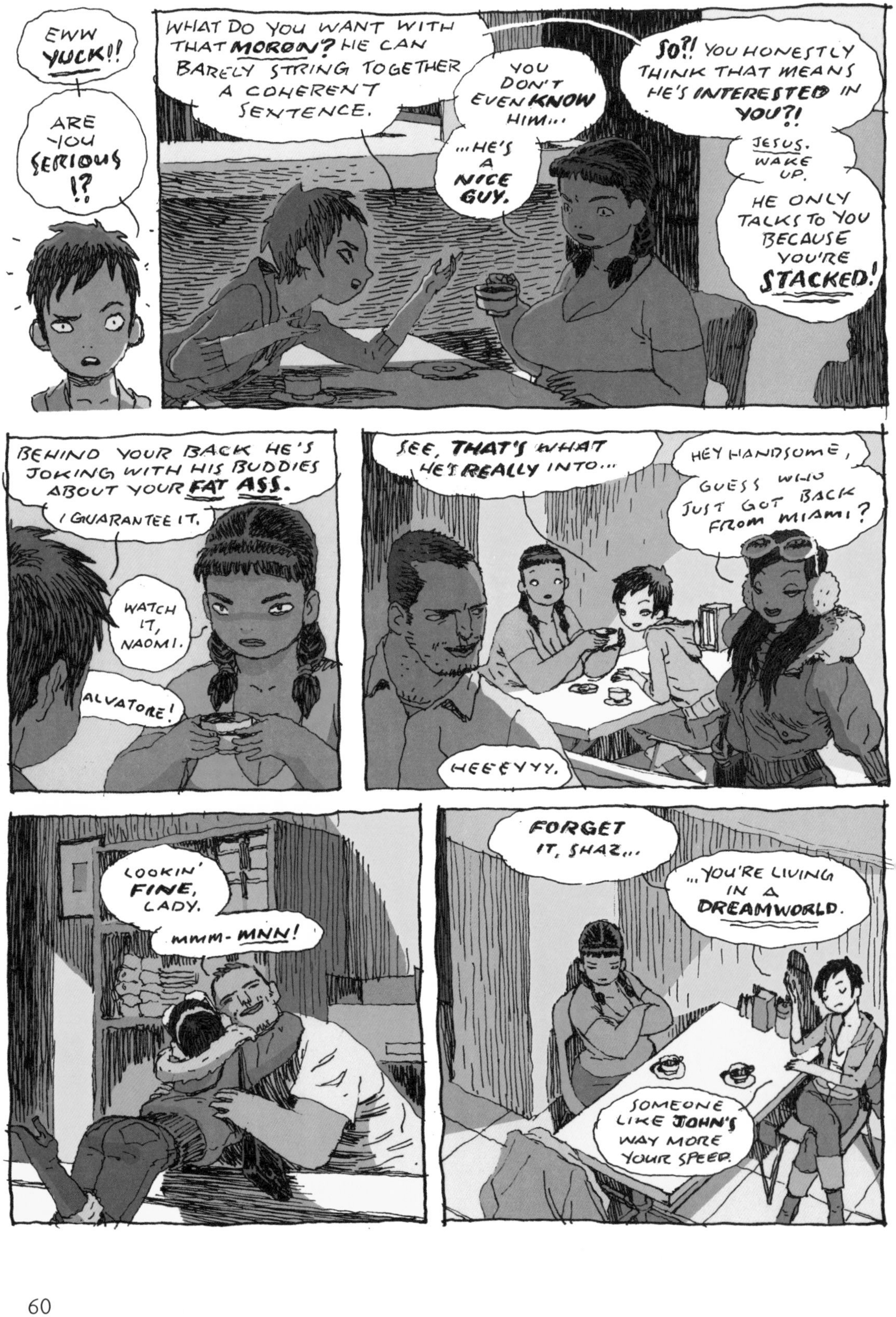
EWW YUCK!!
ARE YOU SERIOUS !?
WHAT DO YOU WANT WITH THAT MORON? HE CAN BARELY STRING TOGETHER A COHERENT SENTENCE.
YOU DON'T EVEN KNOW HIM...
...HE'S A NICE GUY.
SO?! YOU HONESTLY THINK THAT MEANS HE'S INTERESTED IN YOU?!
JESUS. WAKE UP.
HE ONLY TALKS TO YOU BECAUSE YOU'RE STACKED!
BEHIND YOUR BACK HE'S JOKING WITH HIS BUDDIES ABOUT YOUR FAT ASS.
I GUARANTEE IT.
WATCH IT, NAOMI.
ALVATORE!
SEE, THAT'S WHAT HE'S REALLY INTO...
HEY HANDSOME, GUESS WHO JUST GOT BACK FROM MIAMI?
HEEEYYY.
LOOKIN' FINE, LADY.
MMM-MNN!
FORGET IT, SHAZ...
...YOU'RE LIVING IN A DREAMWORLD.
SOMEONE LIKE JOHN'S WAY MORE YOUR SPEED.

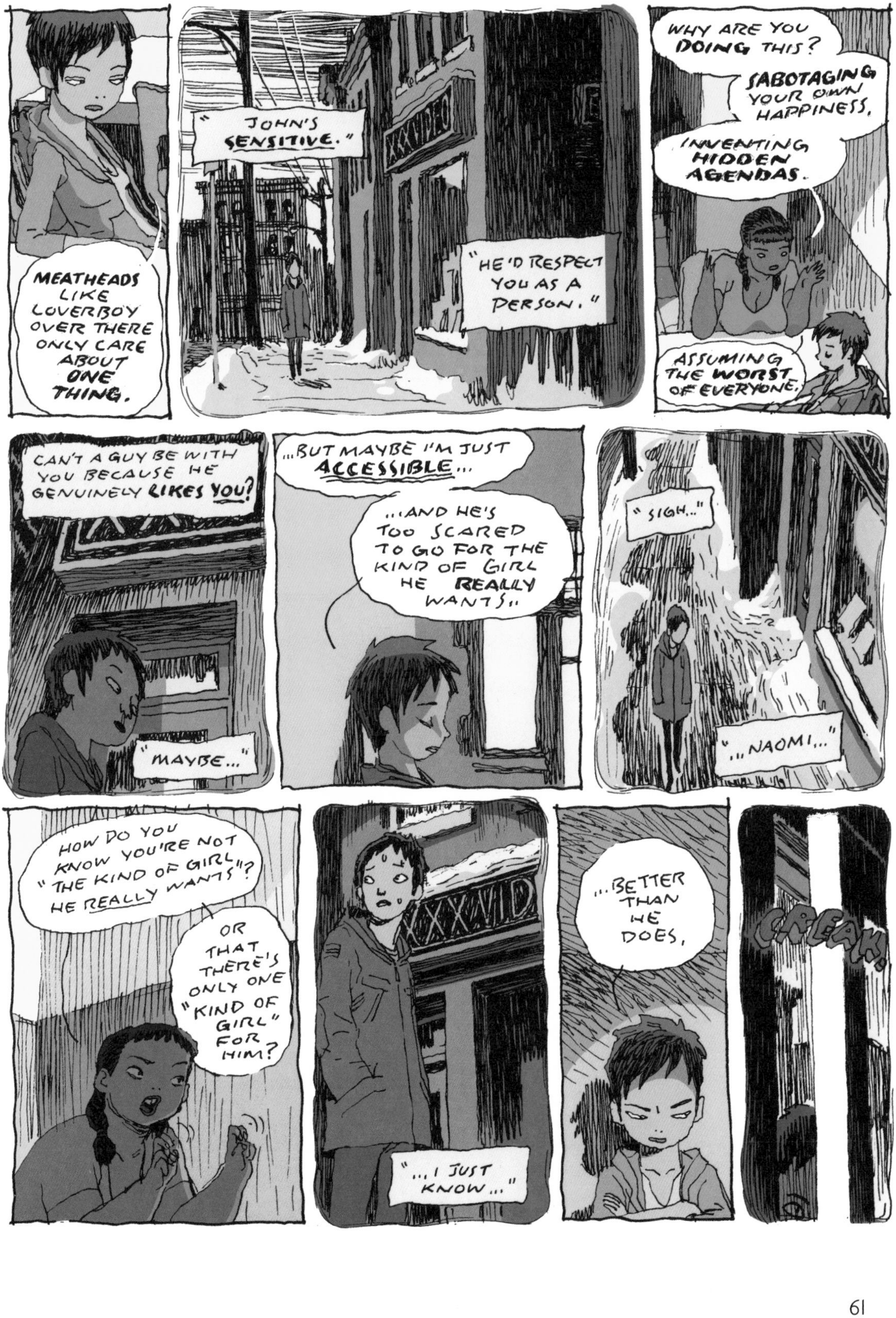
MEATHEADS LIKE LOVERBOY OVER THERE ONLY CARE ABOUT ONE THING.
"JOHN'S SENSITIVE."
XXXVIDEO
"HE'D RESPECT YOU AS A PERSON."
WHY ARE YOU DOING THIS?
SABOTAGING YOUR OWN HAPPINESS,
INVENTING HIDDEN AGENDAS.
ASSUMING THE WORST OF EVERYONE.
CAN'T A GUY BE WITH YOU BECAUSE HE GENUINELY LIKES YOU?
"MAYBE..."
...BUT MAYBE I'M JUST ACCESSIBLE...
...AND HE'S TOO SCARED TO GO FOR THE KIND OF GIRL HE REALLY WANTS..
"SIGH..."
"...NAOMI..."
HOW DO YOU KNOW YOU'RE NOT "THE KIND OF GIRL" HE REALLY WANTS"?
OR THAT THERE'S ONLY ONE "KIND OF GIRL" FOR HIM?
XXXVID
"...I JUST KNOW..."
...BETTER THAN HE DOES.
CREAK!

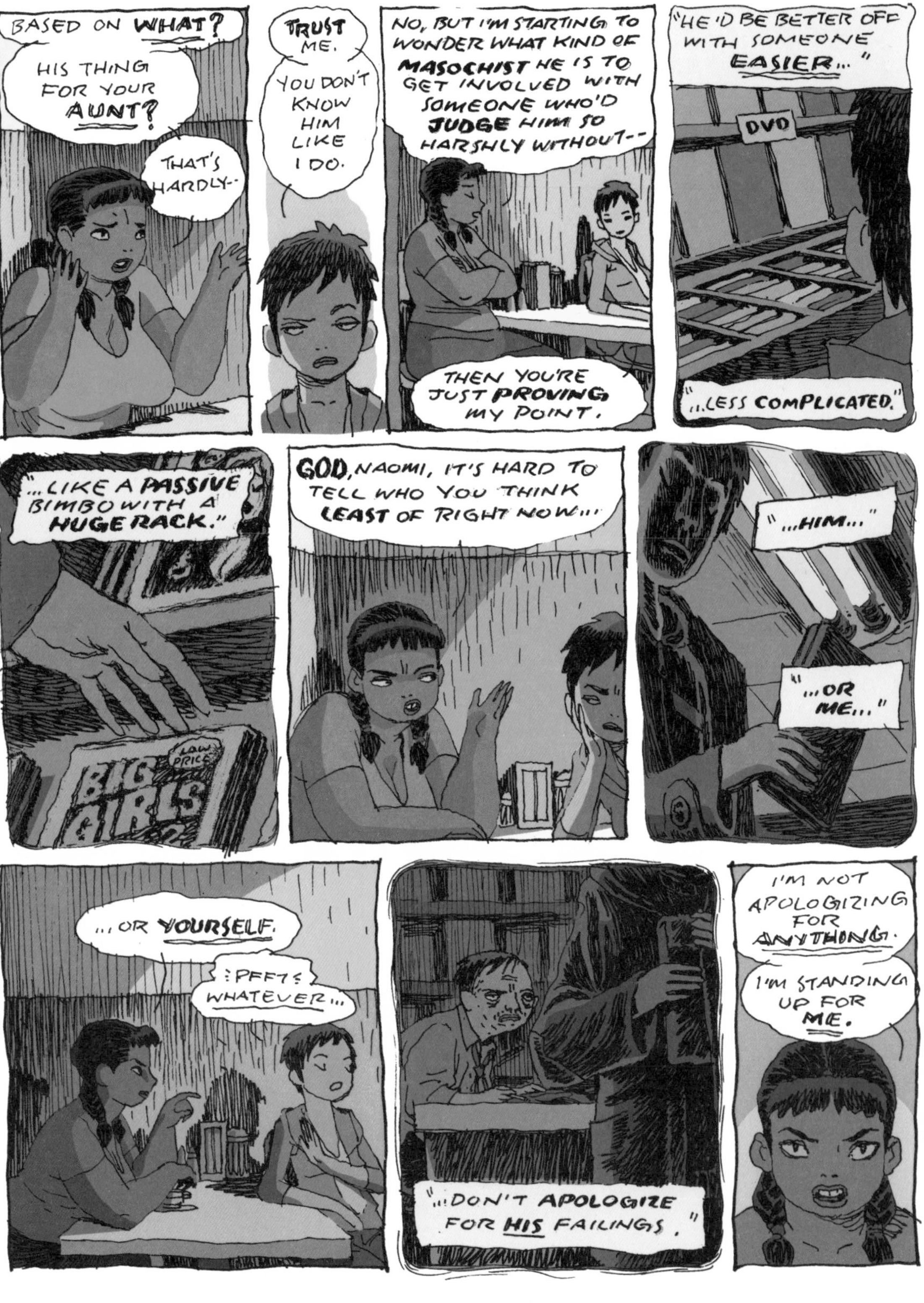
BASED ON WHAT?
HIS THING FOR YOUR AUNT?
THAT'S HARDLY--
TRUST ME.
YOU DON'T KNOW HIM LIKE I DO.
NO, BUT I'M STARTING TO WONDER WHAT KIND OF MASOCHIST HE IS TO GET INVOLVED WITH SOMEONE WHO'D JUDGE HIM SO HARSHLY WITHOUT--
THEN YOU'RE JUST PROVING MY POINT.
"HE'D BE BETTER OFF WITH SOMEONE EASIER..."
DVD
"...LESS COMPLICATED."
"...LIKE A PASSIVE BIMBO WITH A HUGE RACK."
LOW PRICE
BIG GIRLS
GOD, NAOMI, IT'S HARD TO TELL WHO YOU THINK LEAST OF RIGHT NOW...
"...HIM..."
"...OR ME..."
...OR YOURSELF.
:PFFT: WHATEVER...
"...DON'T APOLOGIZE FOR HIS FAILINGS."
I'M NOT APOLOGIZING FOR ANYTHING.
I'M STANDING UP FOR ME.

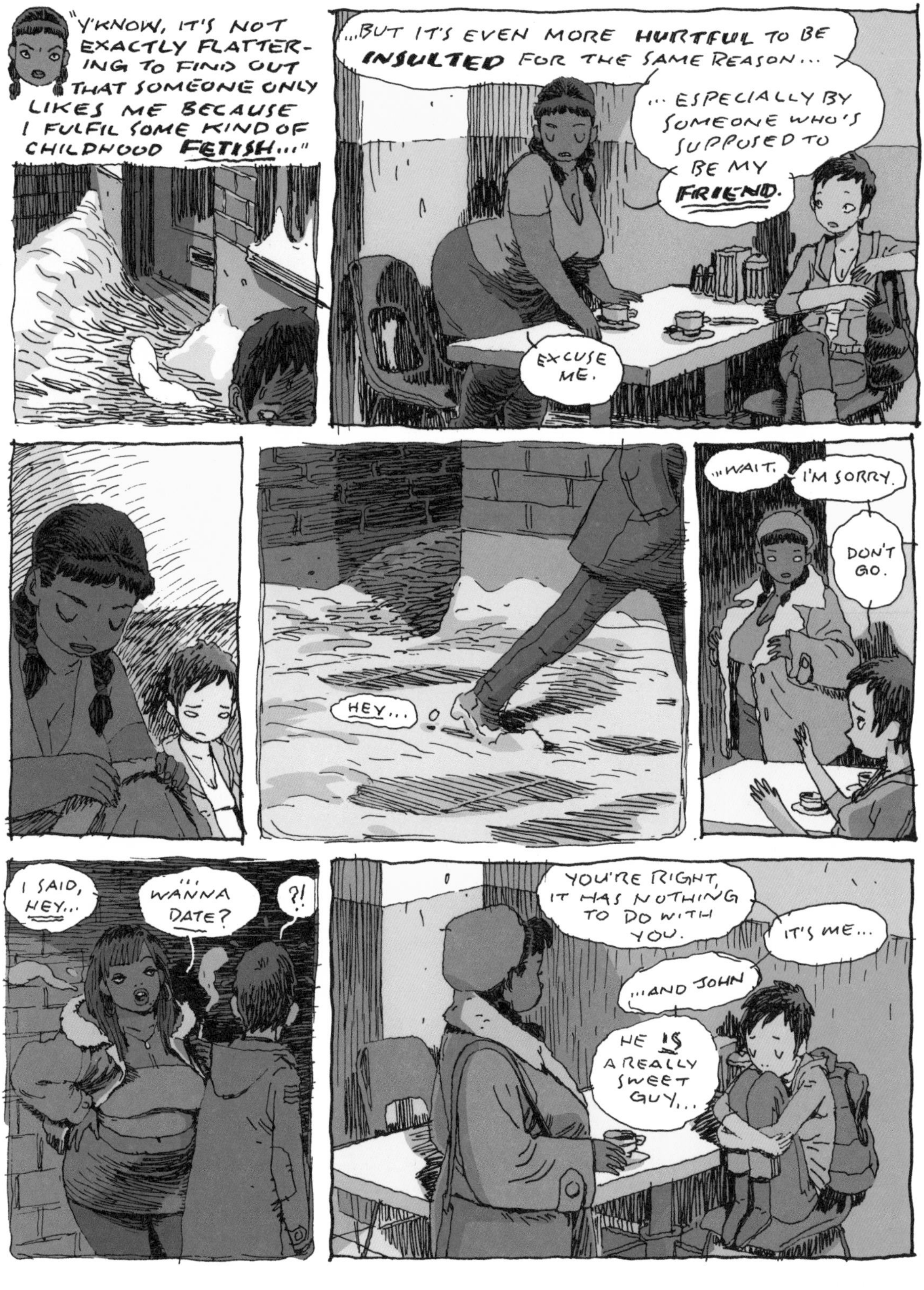
"Y'KNOW, IT'S NOT EXACTLY FLATTERING TO FIND OUT THAT SOMEONE ONLY LIKES ME BECAUSE I FULFIL SOME KIND OF CHILDHOOD FETISH..."
...BUT IT'S EVEN MORE HURTFUL TO BE INSULTED FOR THE SAME REASON...
...ESPECIALLY BY SOMEONE WHO'S SUPPOSED TO BE MY FRIEND.
EXCUSE ME.
HEY...
...WAIT.
I'M SORRY.
DON'T GO.
I SAID, HEY...
...WANNA DATE?
?!
YOU'RE RIGHT, IT HAS NOTHING TO DO WITH YOU.
IT'S ME...
...AND JOHN.
HE IS A REALLY SWEET GUY...

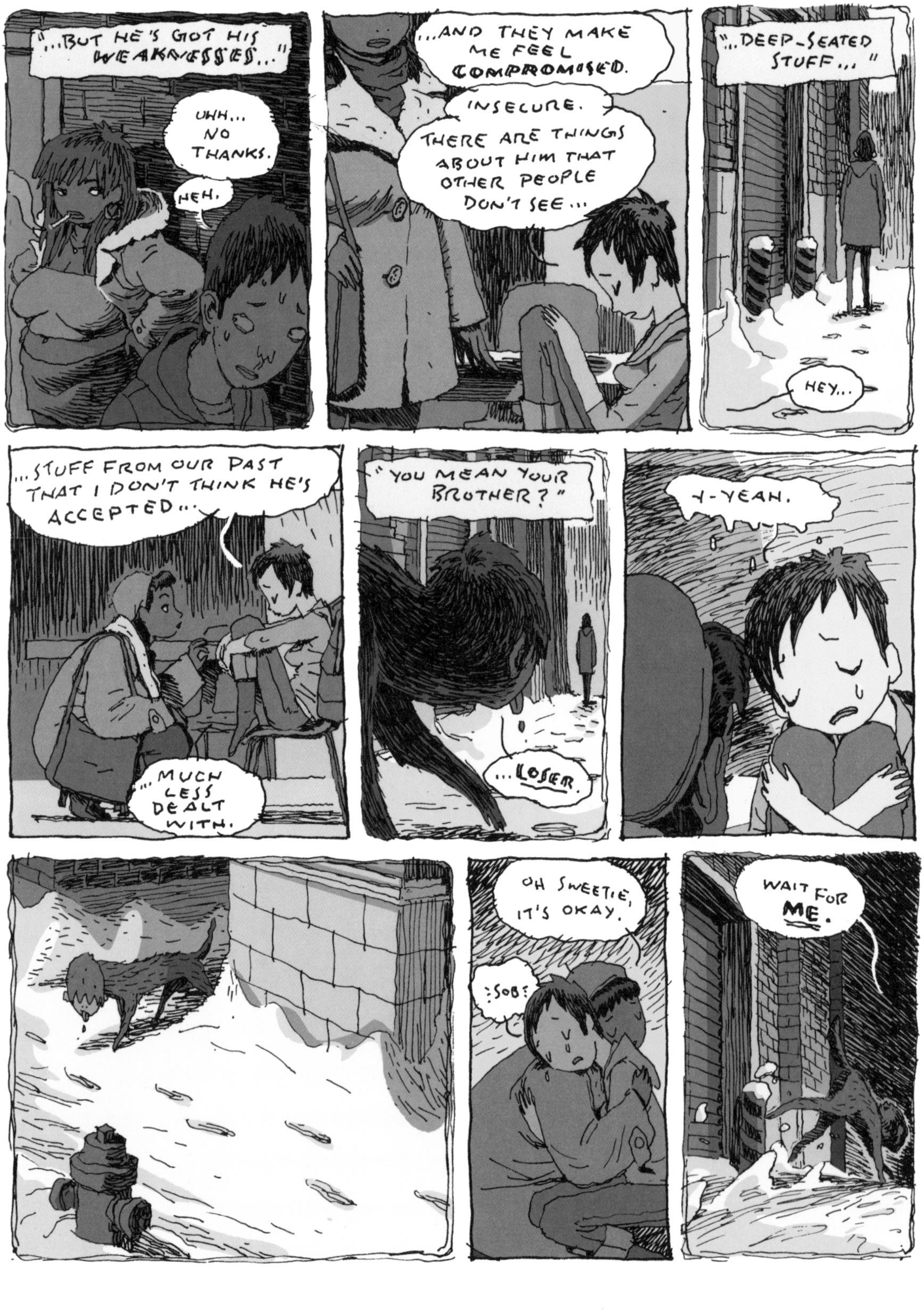
"...BUT HE'S GOT HIS WEAKNESSES..."
UHH... NO THANKS.
HEH.
...AND THEY MAKE ME FEEL COMPROMISED.
INSECURE.
THERE ARE THINGS ABOUT HIM THAT OTHER PEOPLE DON'T SEE...
"...DEEP-SEATED STUFF..."
HEY...
...STUFF FROM OUR PAST THAT I DON'T THINK HE'S ACCEPTED...
...MUCH LESS DEALT WITH.
"YOU MEAN YOUR BROTHER?"
...LOSER.
Y-YEAH.
OH SWEETIE, IT'S OKAY.
:SOB:
WAIT FOR ME.

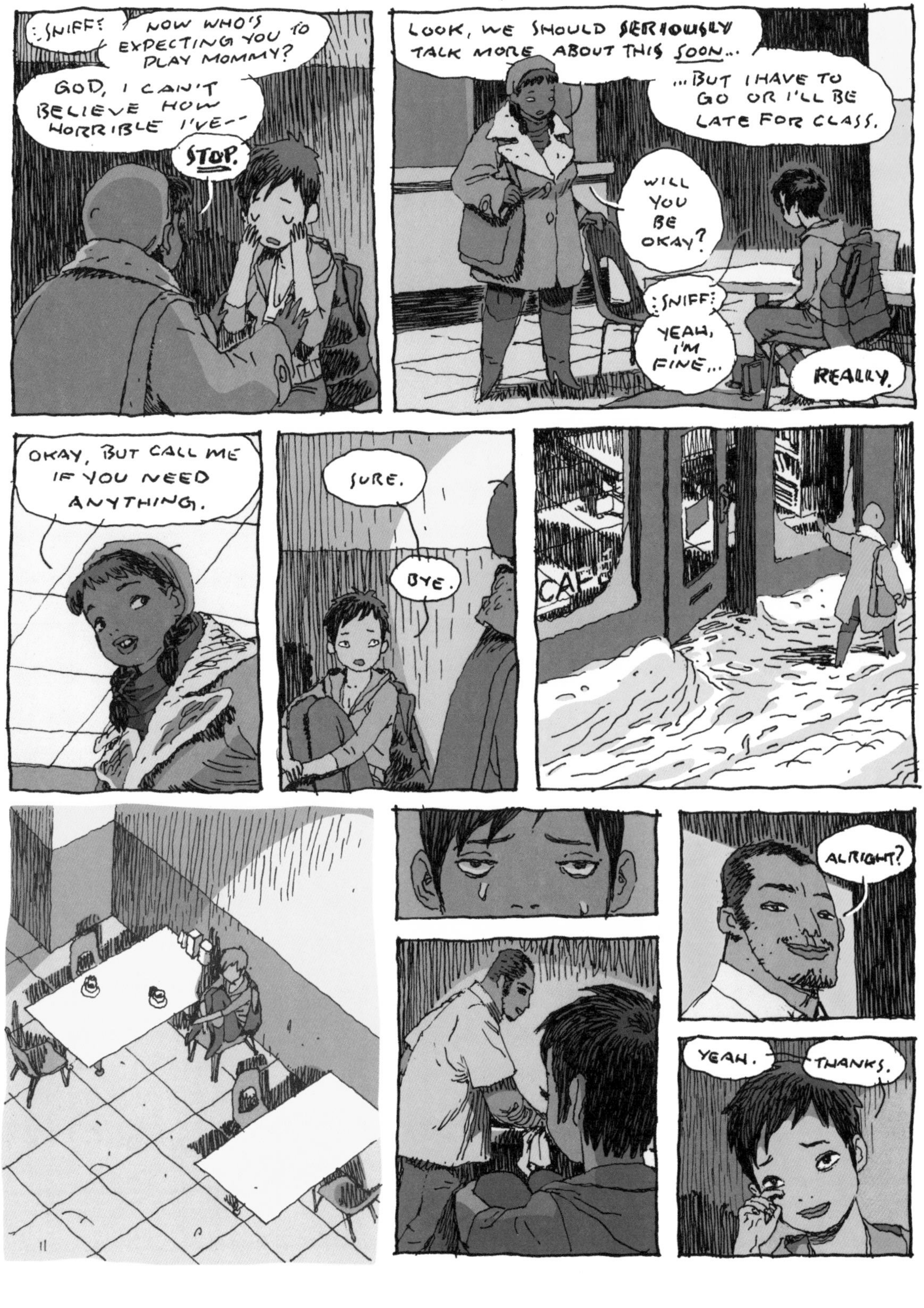
:SNIFF:
NOW WHO'S EXPECTING YOU TO PLAY MOMMY?
GOD, I CAN'T BELIEVE HOW HORRIBLE I'VE--
STOP.
LOOK, WE SHOULD SERIOUSLY TALK MORE ABOUT THIS SOON...
...BUT I HAVE TO GO OR I'LL BE LATE FOR CLASS.
WILL YOU BE OKAY?
:SNIFF:
YEAH, I'M FINE...
REALLY.
OKAY, BUT CALL ME IF YOU NEED ANYTHING.
SURE.
BYE.
CAFE
ALRIGHT?
YEAH.
THANKS.

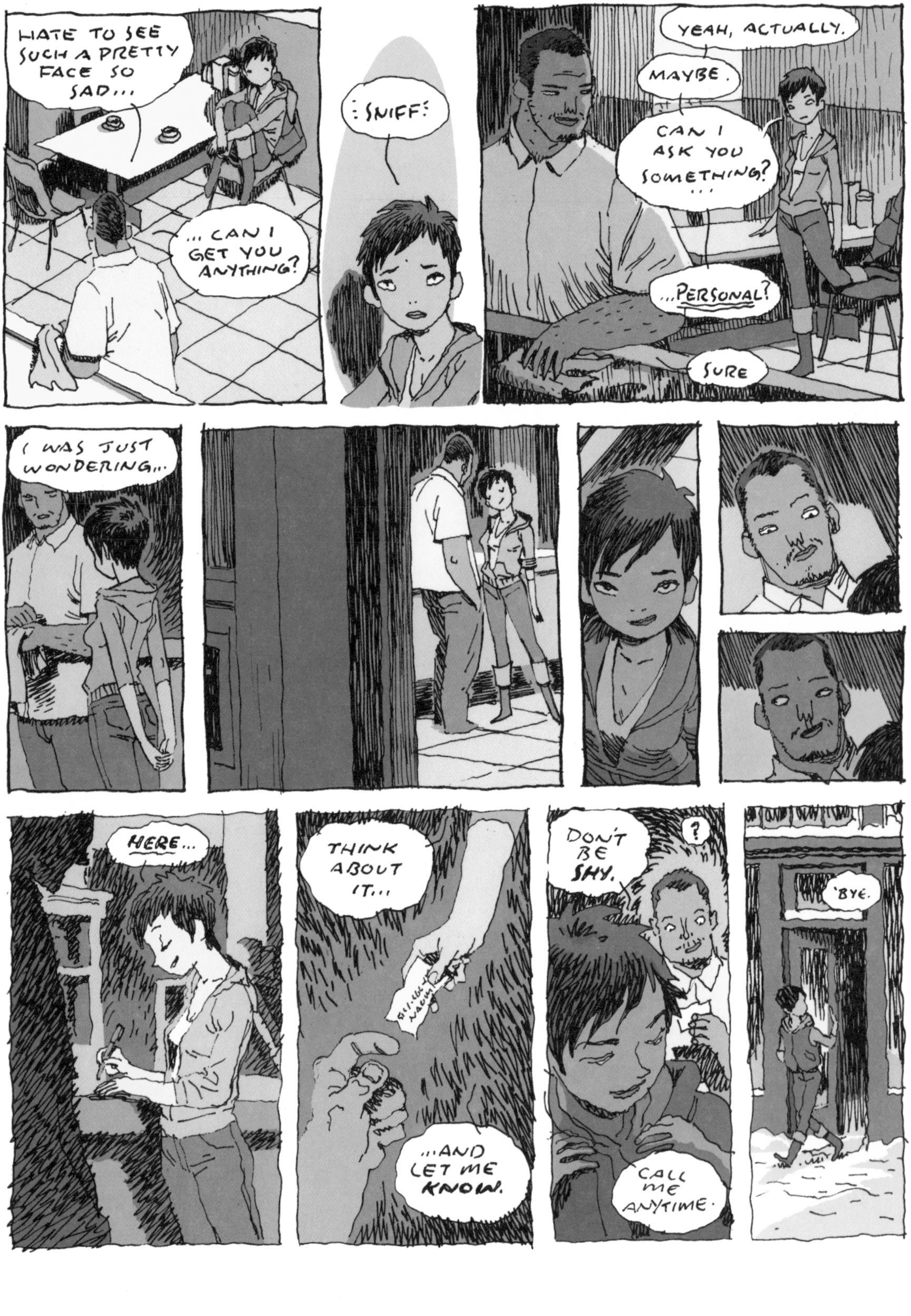
HATE TO SEE SUCH A PRETTY FACE SO SAD...
...CAN I GET YOU ANYTHING?
SNIFF
YEAH, ACTUALLY.
MAYBE.
CAN I ASK YOU SOMETHING? ...
...PERSONAL?
SURE
I WAS JUST WONDERING...
HERE...
THINK ABOUT IT...
...AND LET ME KNOW.
DON'T BE SHY.
?
CALL ME ANYTIME.
'BYE.

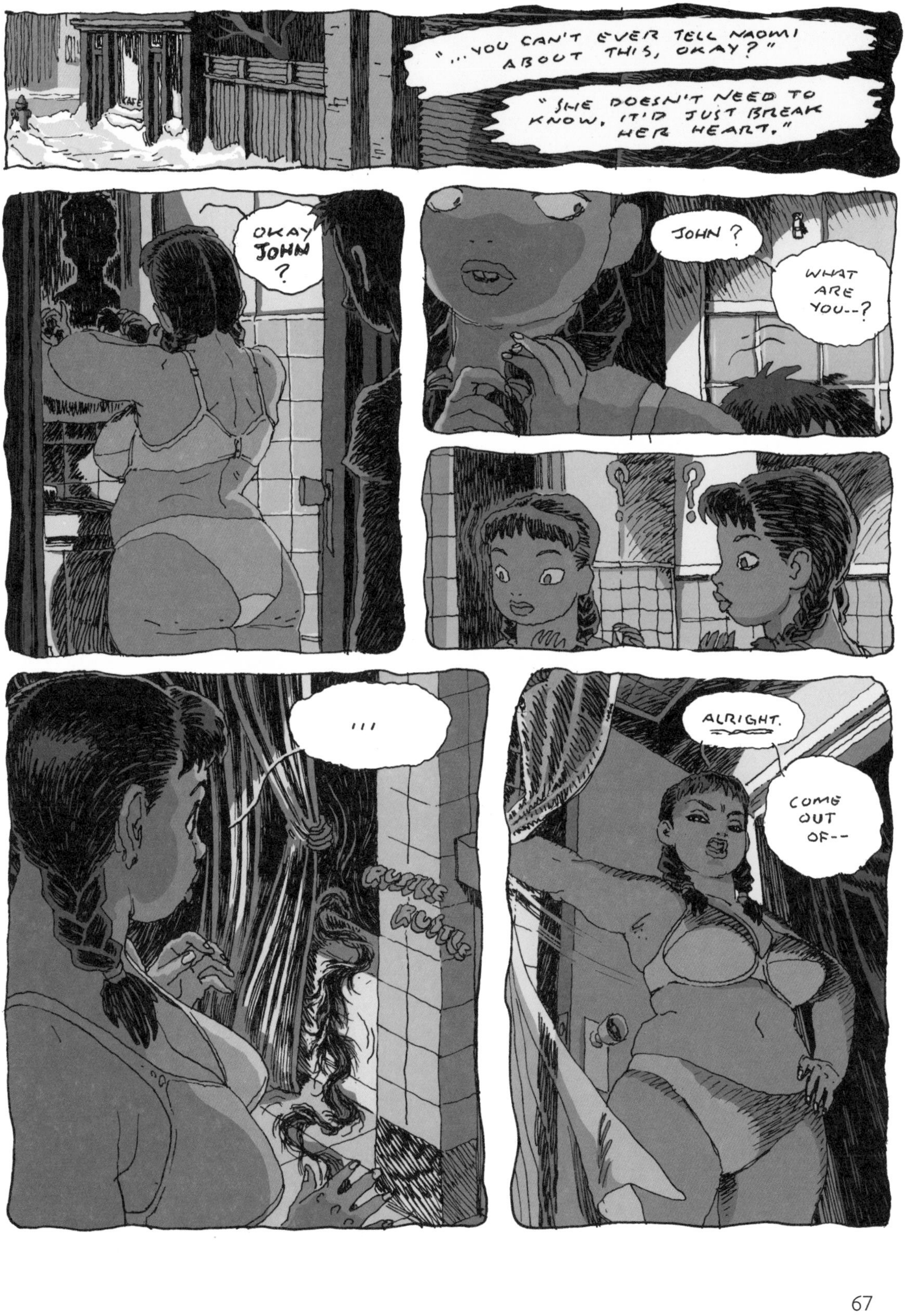
"...YOU CAN'T EVER TELL NAOMI ABOUT THIS, OKAY?"
"SHE DOESN'T NEED TO KNOW. IT'D JUST BREAK HER HEART."
OKAY JOHN ?
JOHN ?
WHAT ARE YOU--?
...
RUSTLE RUSTLE
ALRIGHT.
COME OUT OF--

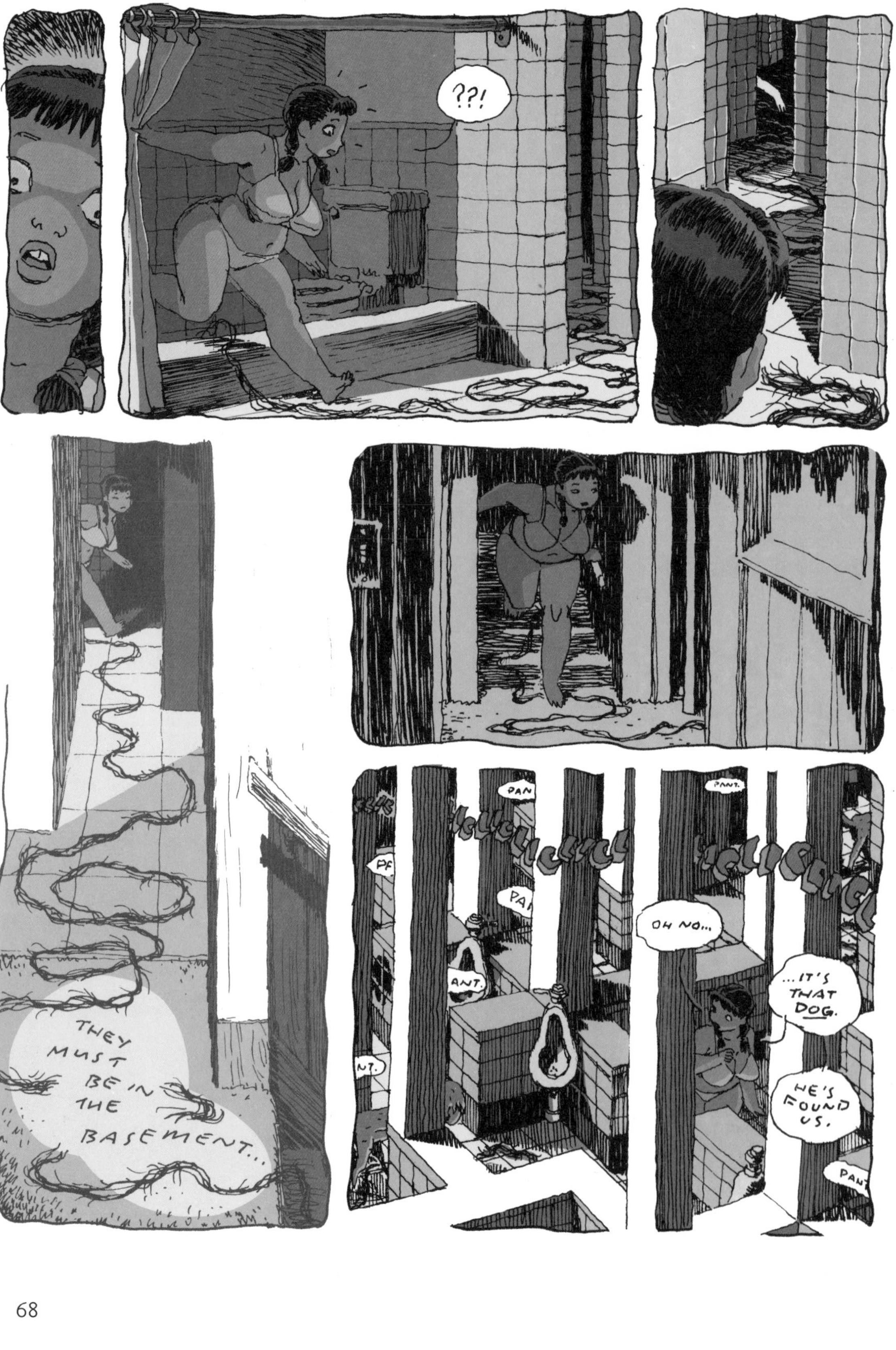
??!
THEY MUST BE IN THE BASEMENT...
PAN
PANT.
PF
PAN
ANT.
NT.
OH NO...
...IT'S THAT DOG.
HE'S FOUND US.
PANT

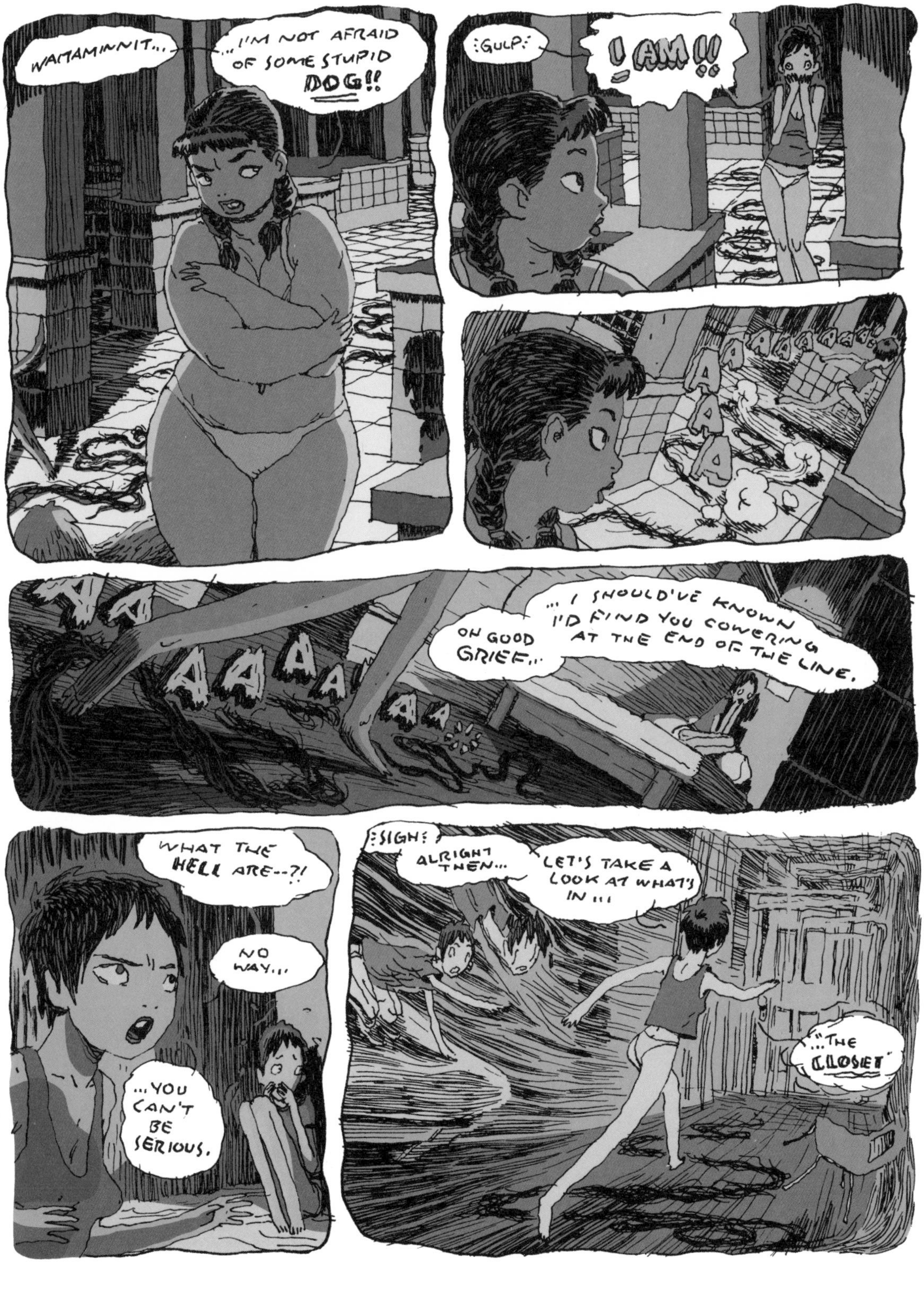
WAITAMINNIT...
...I'M NOT AFRAID OF SOME STUPID DOG!!
:GULP:
I AM!!
AAAAAAAAA
AAAAAAA
OH GOOD GRIEF...
...I SHOULD'VE KNOWN I'D FIND YOU COWERING AT THE END OF THE LINE.
WHAT THE HELL ARE--?!
NO WAY...
...YOU CAN'T BE SERIOUS.
:SIGH:
ALRIGHT THEN...
LET'S TAKE A LOOK AT WHAT'S IN...
...THE CLOSET

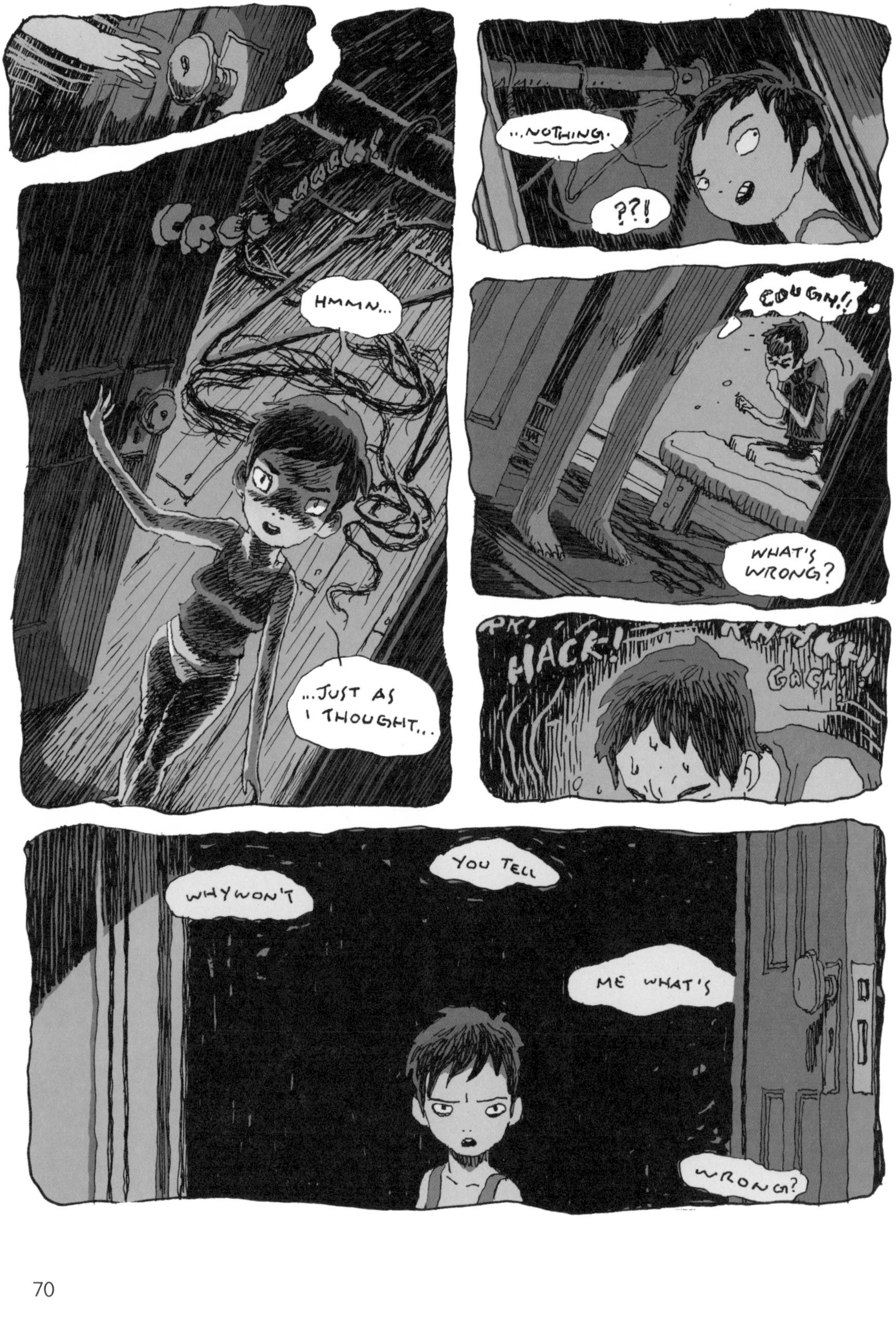
HMMN...
...JUST AS I THOUGHT...
...NOTHING.
??!
COUGH!!
WHAT'S WRONG?
HACK!
GACH!
WHY WON'T
YOU TELL
ME WHAT'S
WRONG?

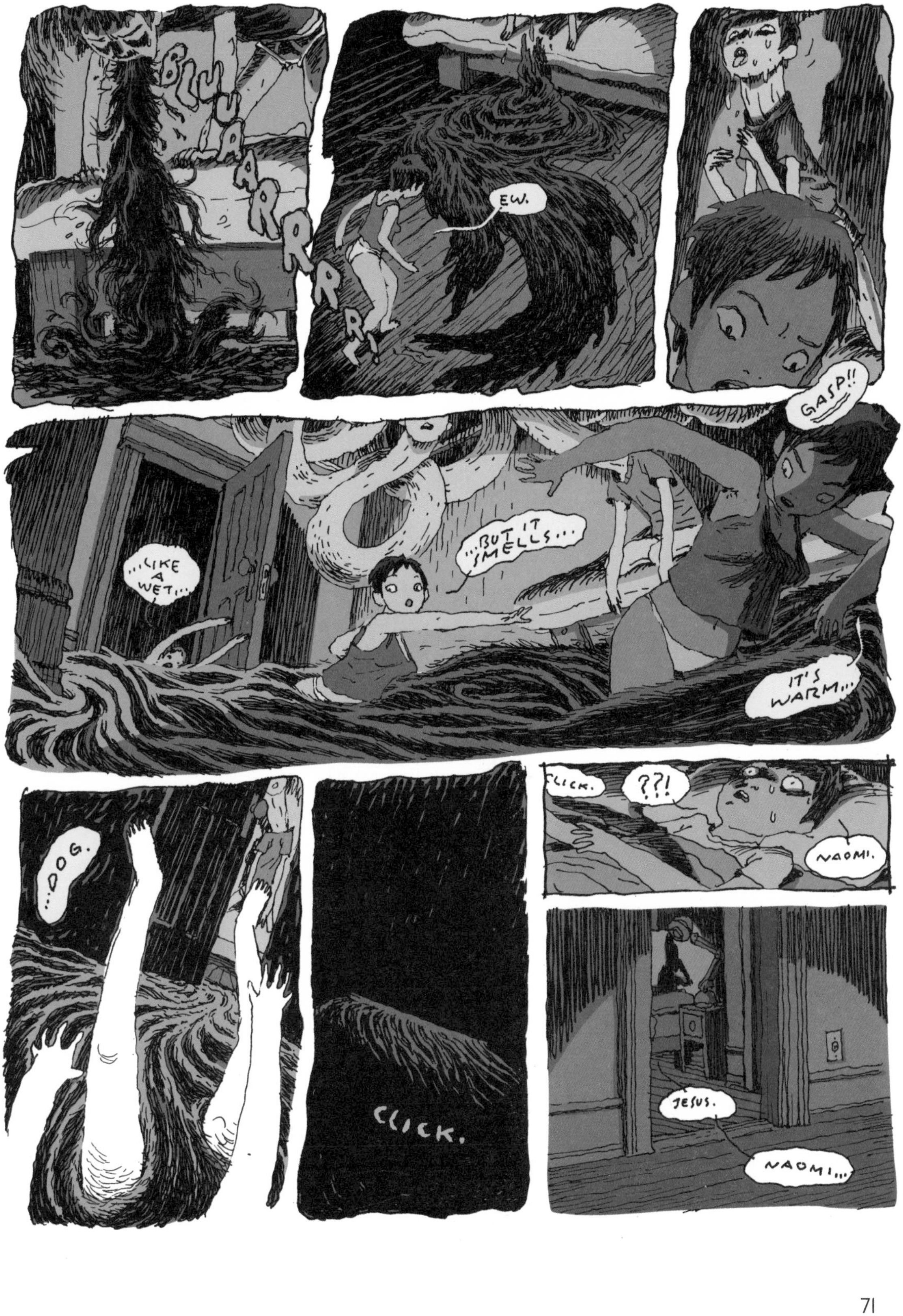
BLUUARRRR!
EW.
GASP!!
...LIKE A WET...
...BUT IT SMELLS...
IT'S WARM...
...DOG.
CLICK.
CLICK.
??!
NAOMI.
JESUS.
NAOMI...

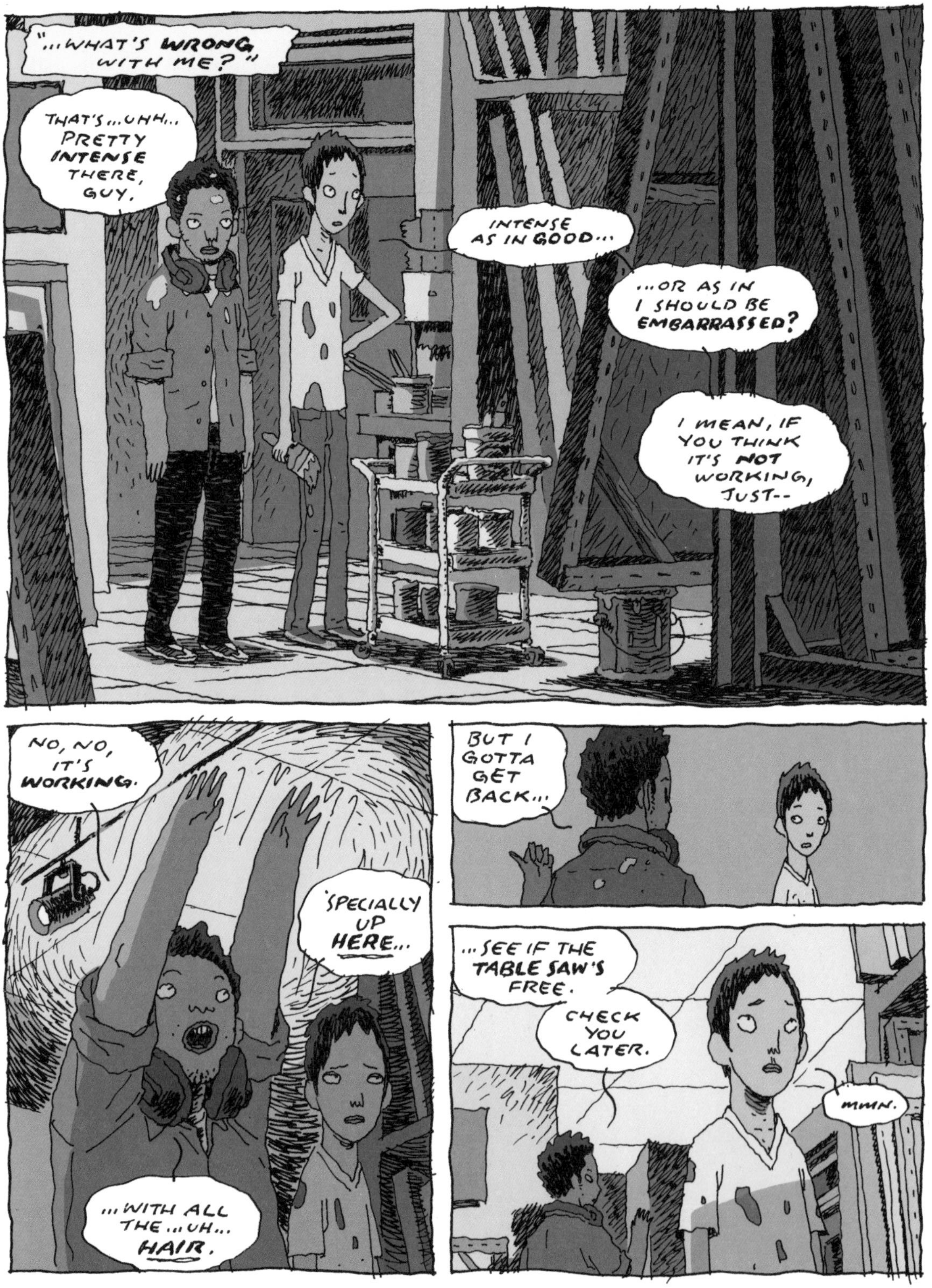
"...WHAT'S WRONG WITH ME?"
THAT'S...UHH... PRETTY INTENSE THERE, GUY.
INTENSE AS IN GOOD...
...OR AS IN I SHOULD BE EMBARRASSED?
I MEAN, IF YOU THINK IT'S NOT WORKING, JUST--
NO, NO, IT'S WORKING.
'SPECIALLY UP HERE...
...WITH ALL THE...UH... HAIR.
BUT I GOTTA GET BACK...
...SEE IF THE TABLE SAW'S FREE.
CHECK YOU LATER.
MMN.

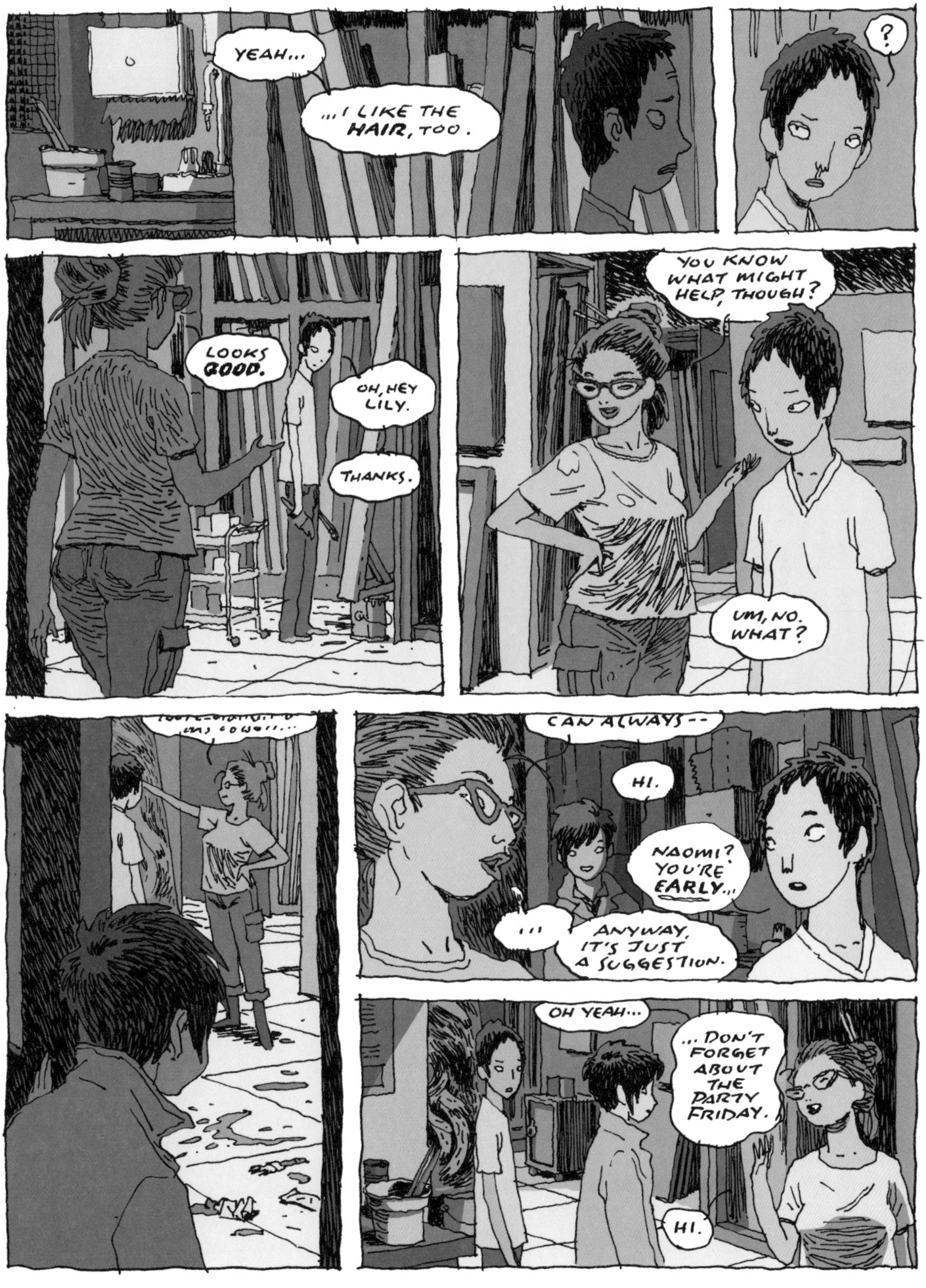
YEAH...
...I LIKE THE HAIR, TOO.
?
LOOKS GOOD.
OH, HEY LILY.
THANKS.
YOU KNOW WHAT MIGHT HELP, THOUGH?
UM, NO. WHAT?
CAN ALWAYS--
HI.
NAOMI? YOU'RE EARLY...
...
ANYWAY, IT'S JUST A SUGGESTION.
OH YEAH...
...DON'T FORGET ABOUT THE PARTY FRIDAY.
HI.

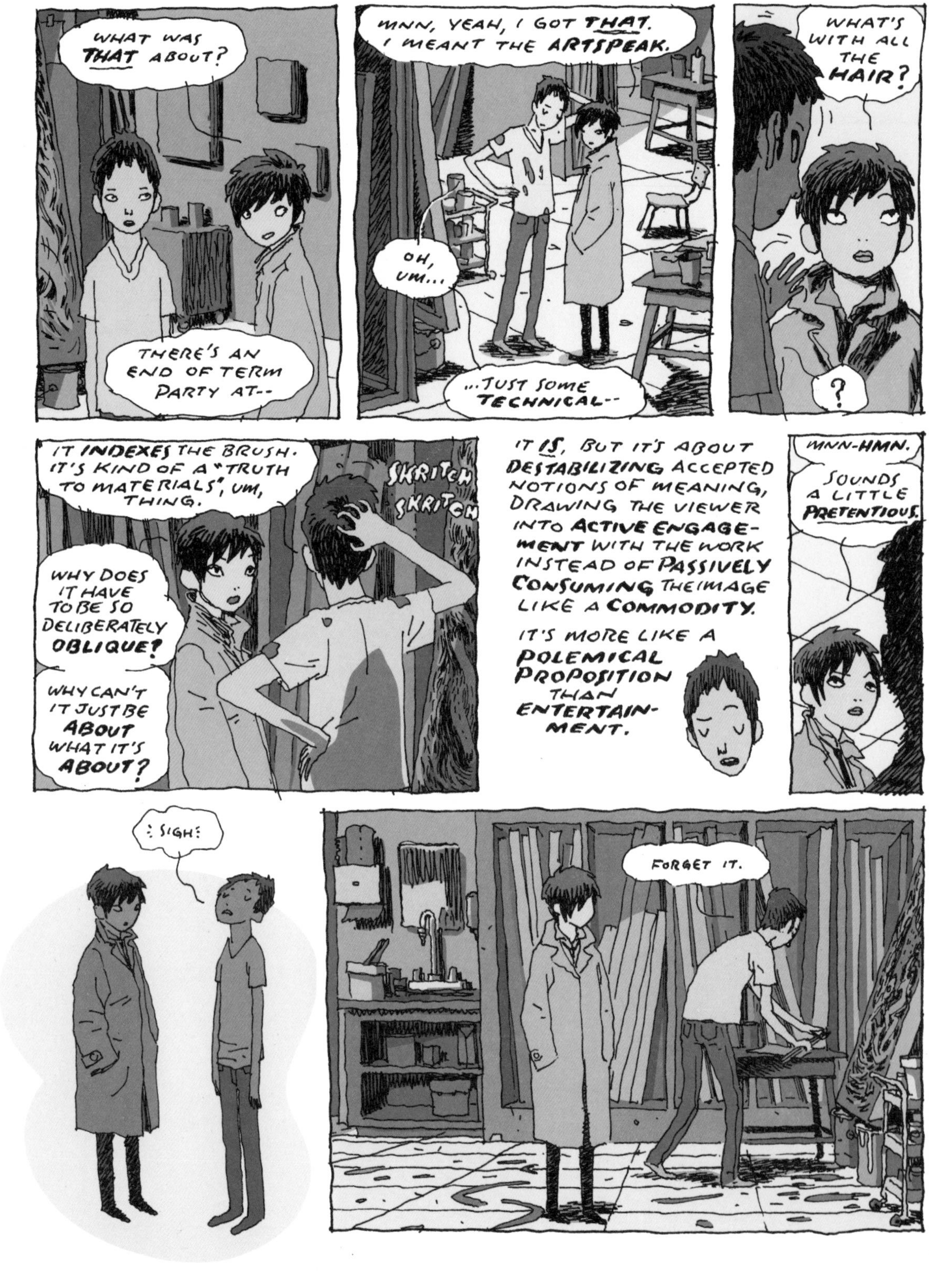
WHAT WAS THAT ABOUT?
THERE'S AN END OF TERM PARTY AT--
MNN, YEAH, I GOT THAT. I MEANT THE ARTSPEAK.
OH, UM...
...JUST SOME TECHNICAL--
WHAT'S WITH ALL THE HAIR?
?
IT INDEXES THE BRUSH. IT'S KIND OF A "TRUTH TO MATERIALS", UM, THING.
SKRITCH
SKRITCH
WHY DOES IT HAVE TO BE SO DELIBERATELY OBLIQUE?
WHY CAN'T IT JUST BE ABOUT WHAT IT'S ABOUT?
IT IS, BUT IT'S ABOUT DESTABILIZING ACCEPTED NOTIONS OF MEANING, DRAWING THE VIEWER INTO ACTIVE ENGAGEMENT WITH THE WORK INSTEAD OF PASSIVELY CONSUMING THE IMAGE LIKE A COMMODITY.
IT'S MORE LIKE A POLEMICAL PROPOSITION THAN ENTERTAINMENT.
MNN-HMN.
SOUNDS A LITTLE PRETENTIOUS.
SIGH
FORGET IT.

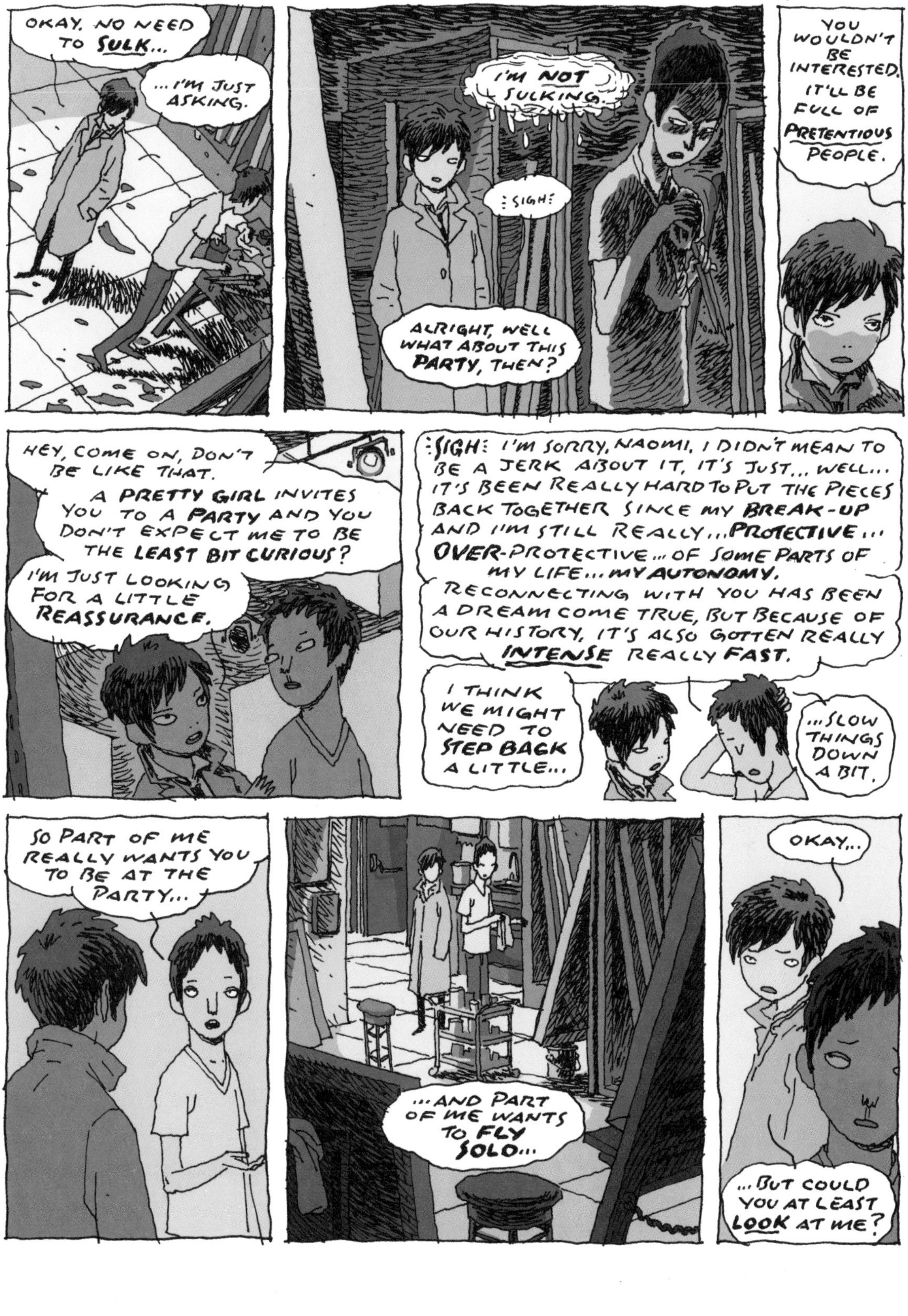
OKAY, NO NEED TO SULK...
...I'M JUST ASKING.
I'M NOT SULKING.
:SIGH:
ALRIGHT, WELL WHAT ABOUT THIS PARTY, THEN?
YOU WOULDN'T BE INTERESTED. IT'LL BE FULL OF PRETENTIOUS PEOPLE.
HEY, COME ON, DON'T BE LIKE THAT. A PRETTY GIRL INVITES YOU TO A PARTY AND YOU DON'T EXPECT ME TO BE THE LEAST BIT CURIOUS?
I'M JUST LOOKING FOR A LITTLE REASSURANCE.
:SIGH: I'M SORRY, NAOMI, I DIDN'T MEAN TO BE A JERK ABOUT IT, IT'S JUST... WELL... IT'S BEEN REALLY HARD TO PUT THE PIECES BACK TOGETHER SINCE MY BREAK-UP AND I'M STILL REALLY... PROTECTIVE... OVER-PROTECTIVE... OF SOME PARTS OF MY LIFE... MY AUTONOMY.
RECONNECTING WITH YOU HAS BEEN A DREAM COME TRUE, BUT BECAUSE OF OUR HISTORY, IT'S ALSO GOTTEN REALLY INTENSE REALLY FAST.
I THINK WE MIGHT NEED TO STEP BACK A LITTLE...
...SLOW THINGS DOWN A BIT.
SO PART OF ME REALLY WANTS YOU TO BE AT THE PARTY...
...AND PART OF ME WANTS TO FLY SOLO...
OKAY...
...BUT COULD YOU AT LEAST LOOK AT ME?

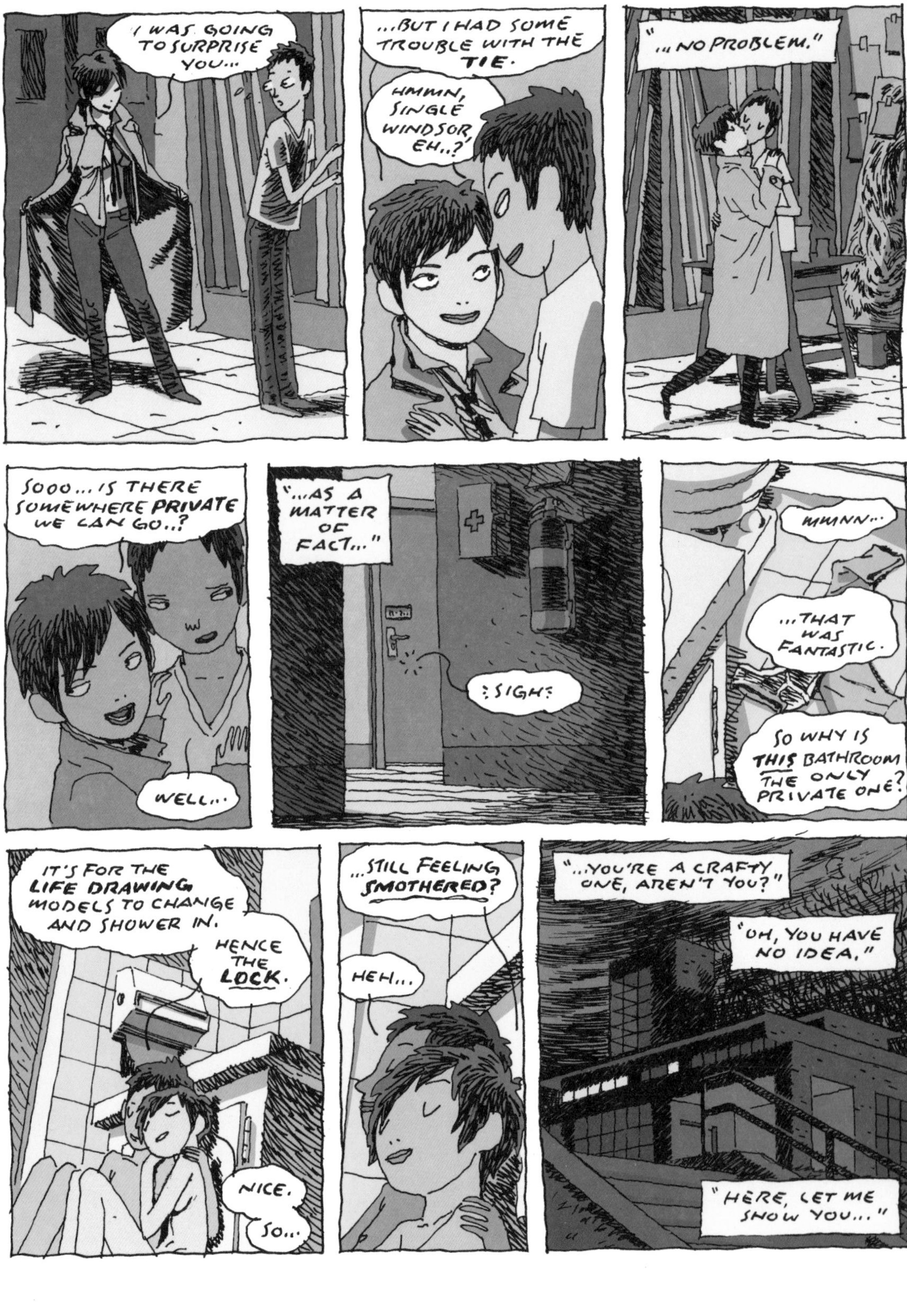
I WAS GOING TO SURPRISE YOU...
...BUT I HAD SOME TROUBLE WITH THE TIE.
HMMN, SINGLE WINDSOR, EH..?
"...NO PROBLEM."
SOOO... IS THERE SOMEWHERE PRIVATE WE CAN GO..?
WELL...
"...AS A MATTER OF FACT..."
:SIGH:
MMNN...
...THAT WAS FANTASTIC.
SO WHY IS THIS BATHROOM THE ONLY PRIVATE ONE?
IT'S FOR THE LIFE DRAWING MODELS TO CHANGE AND SHOWER IN.
HENCE THE LOCK.
NICE.
SO...
...STILL FEELING SMOTHERED?
HEH...
"...YOU'RE A CRAFTY ONE, AREN'T YOU?"
"OH, YOU HAVE NO IDEA."
"HERE, LET ME SHOW YOU..."

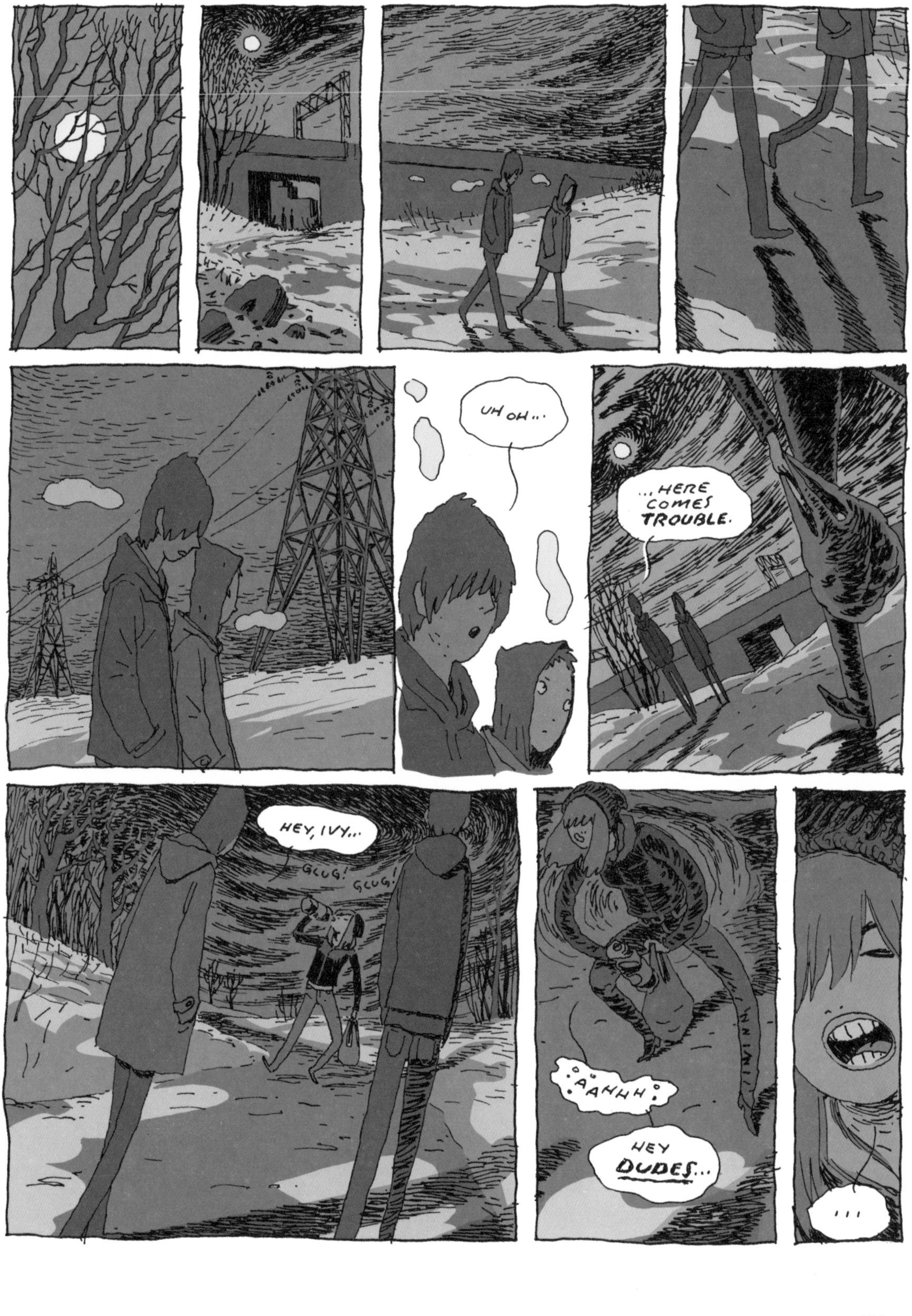
UH OH...
...HERE COMES TROUBLE.
HEY, IVY...
GLUG!
GLUG!
AAHHH
HEY DUDES...
...

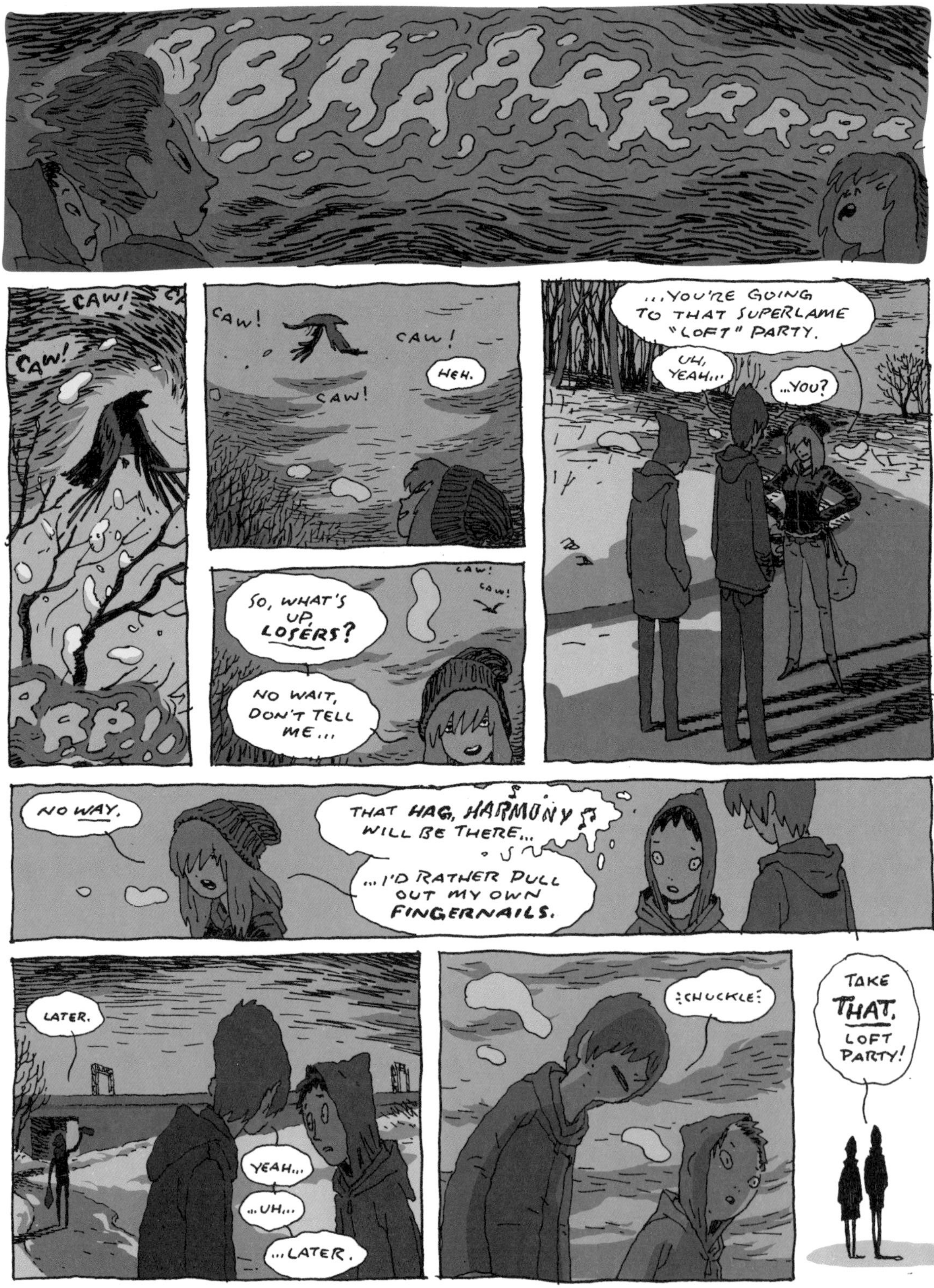
BAARRRRRR
CAW!
CAW!
RRP!
CAW!
CAW!
CAW!
HEH.
CAW!
CAW!
SO, WHAT'S UP, LOSERS?
NO WAIT, DON'T TELL ME...
...YOU'RE GOING TO THAT SUPERLAME "LOFT" PARTY.
UH, YEAH...
...YOU?
NO WAY.
THAT HAG, HARMONY WILL BE THERE...
...I'D RATHER PULL OUT MY OWN FINGERNAILS.
LATER.
YEAH...
...UH...
...LATER.
CHUCKLE
TAKE THAT, LOFT PARTY!

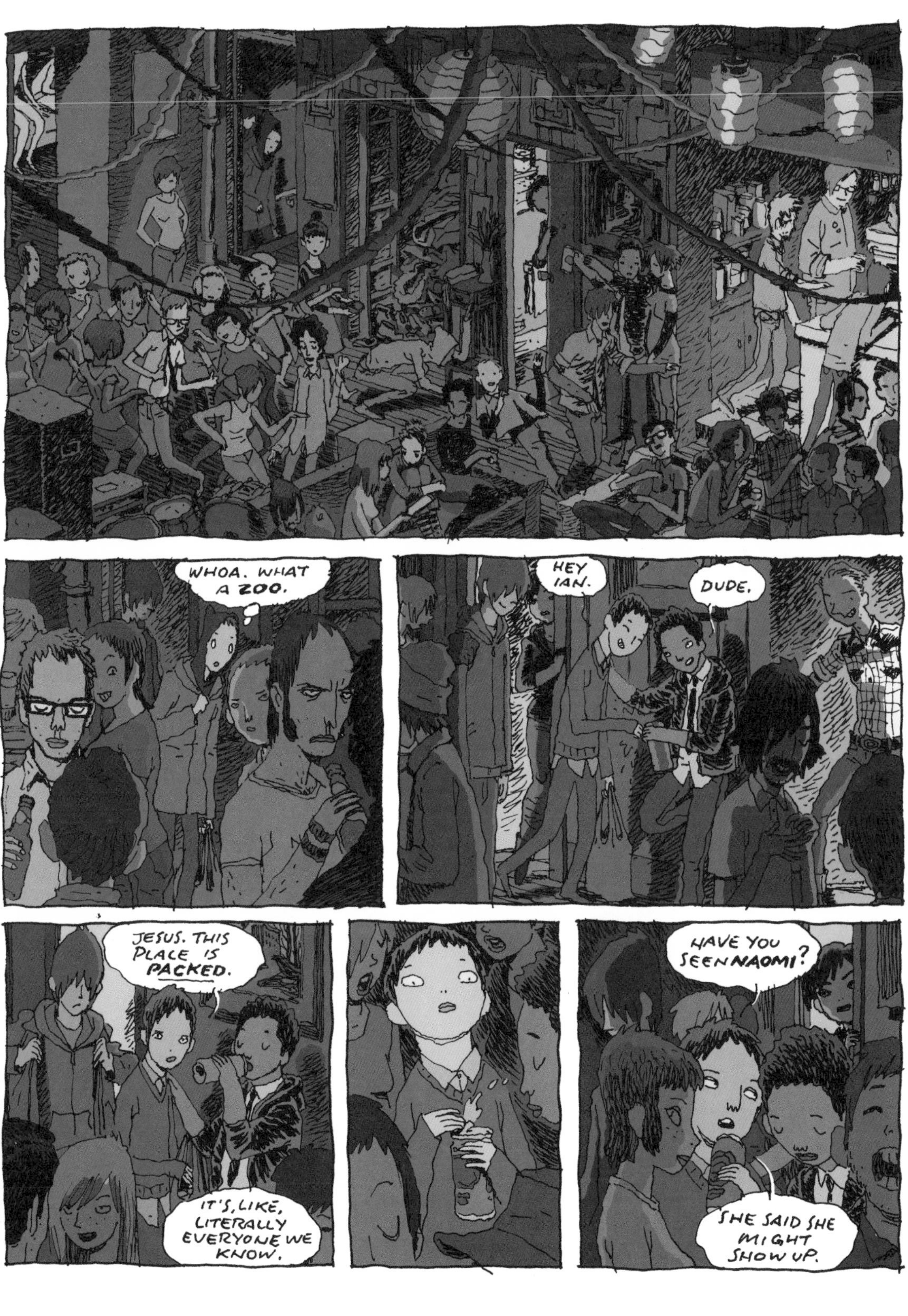
WHOA. WHAT A ZOO.
HEY IAN.
DUDE.
JESUS. THIS PLACE IS PACKED.
IT'S, LIKE, LITERALLY EVERYONE WE KNOW.
HAVE YOU SEEN NAOMI?
SHE SAID SHE MIGHT SHOW UP.

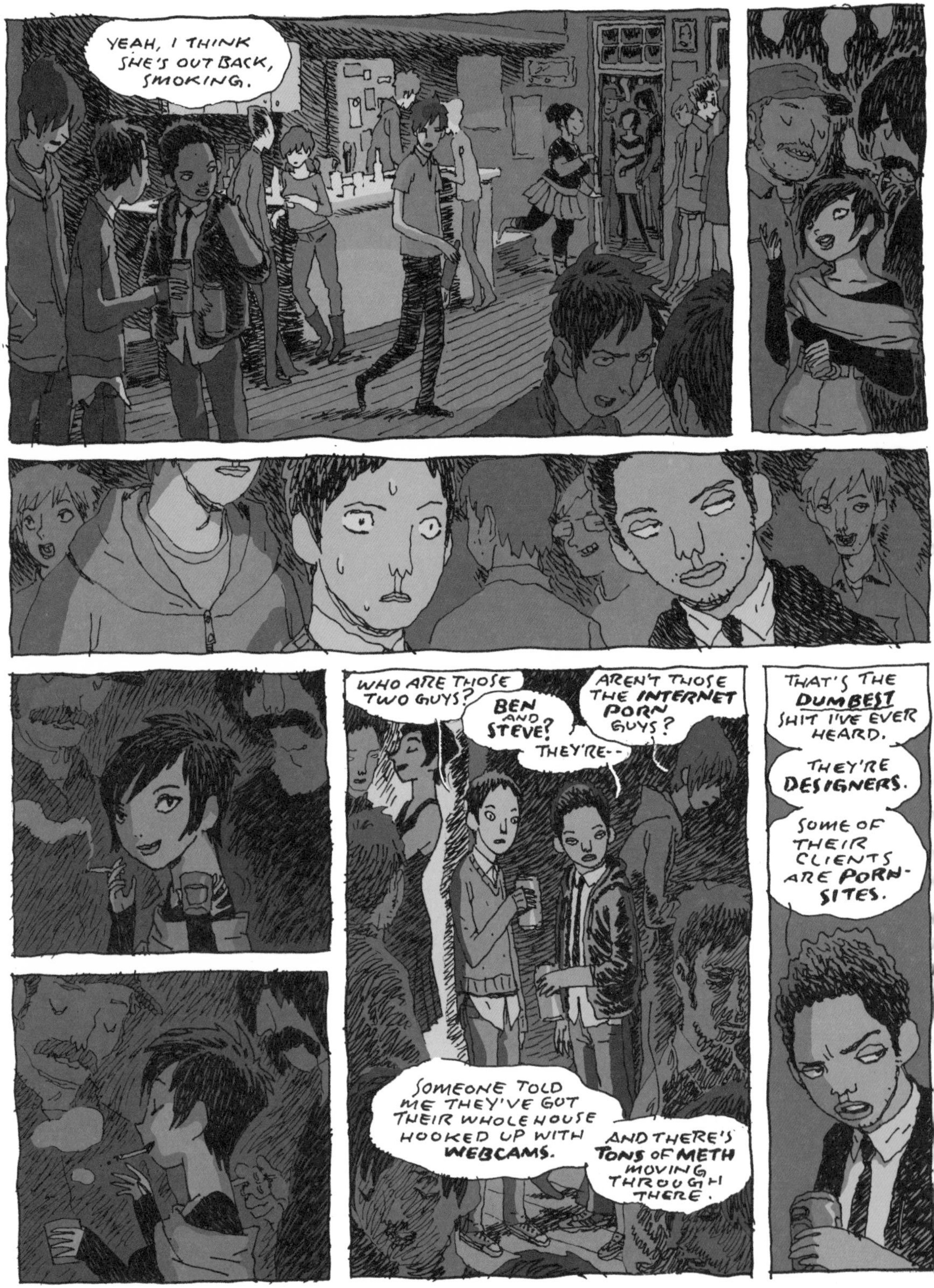
YEAH, I THINK SHE'S OUT BACK, SMOKING.
WHO ARE THOSE TWO GUYS?
BEN AND STEVE?
AREN'T THOSE THE INTERNET PORN GUYS?
THEY'RE--
SOMEONE TOLD ME THEY'VE GOT THEIR WHOLE HOUSE HOOKED UP WITH WEBCAMS.
AND THERE'S TONS OF METH MOVING THROUGH THERE.
THAT'S THE DUMBEST SHIT I'VE EVER HEARD.
THEY'RE DESIGNERS.
SOME OF THEIR CLIENTS ARE PORN-SITES.

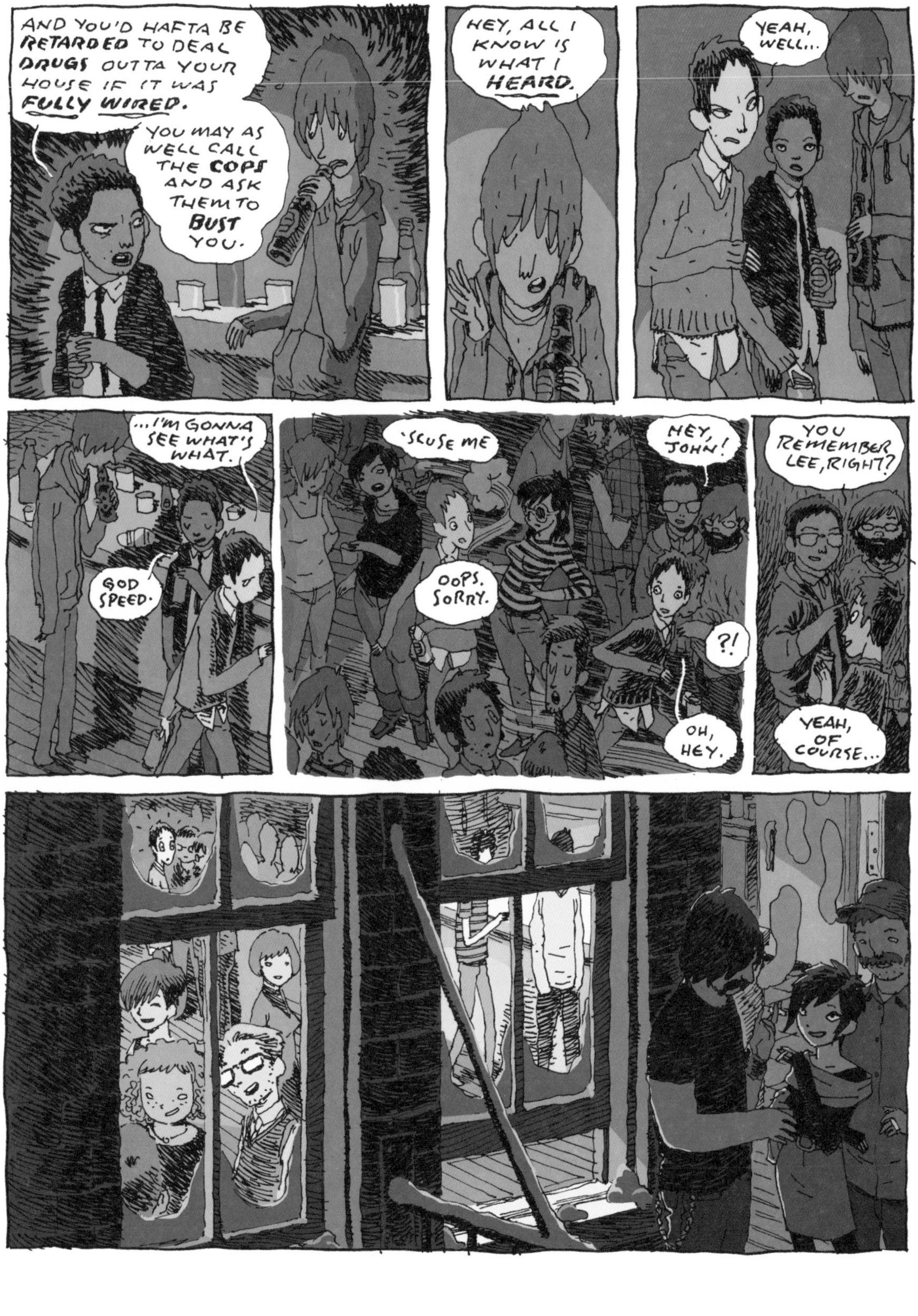
AND YOU'D HAFTA BE RETARDED TO DEAL DRUGS OUTTA YOUR HOUSE IF IT WAS FULLY WIRED.
YOU MAY AS WELL CALL THE COPS AND ASK THEM TO BUST YOU.
HEY, ALL I KNOW IS WHAT I HEARD.
YEAH, WELL...
...I'M GONNA SEE WHAT'S WHAT.
GOD SPEED.
'SCUSE ME
OOPS. SORRY.
HEY, JOHN!
?!
OH, HEY.
YOU REMEMBER LEE, RIGHT?
YEAH, OF COURSE...

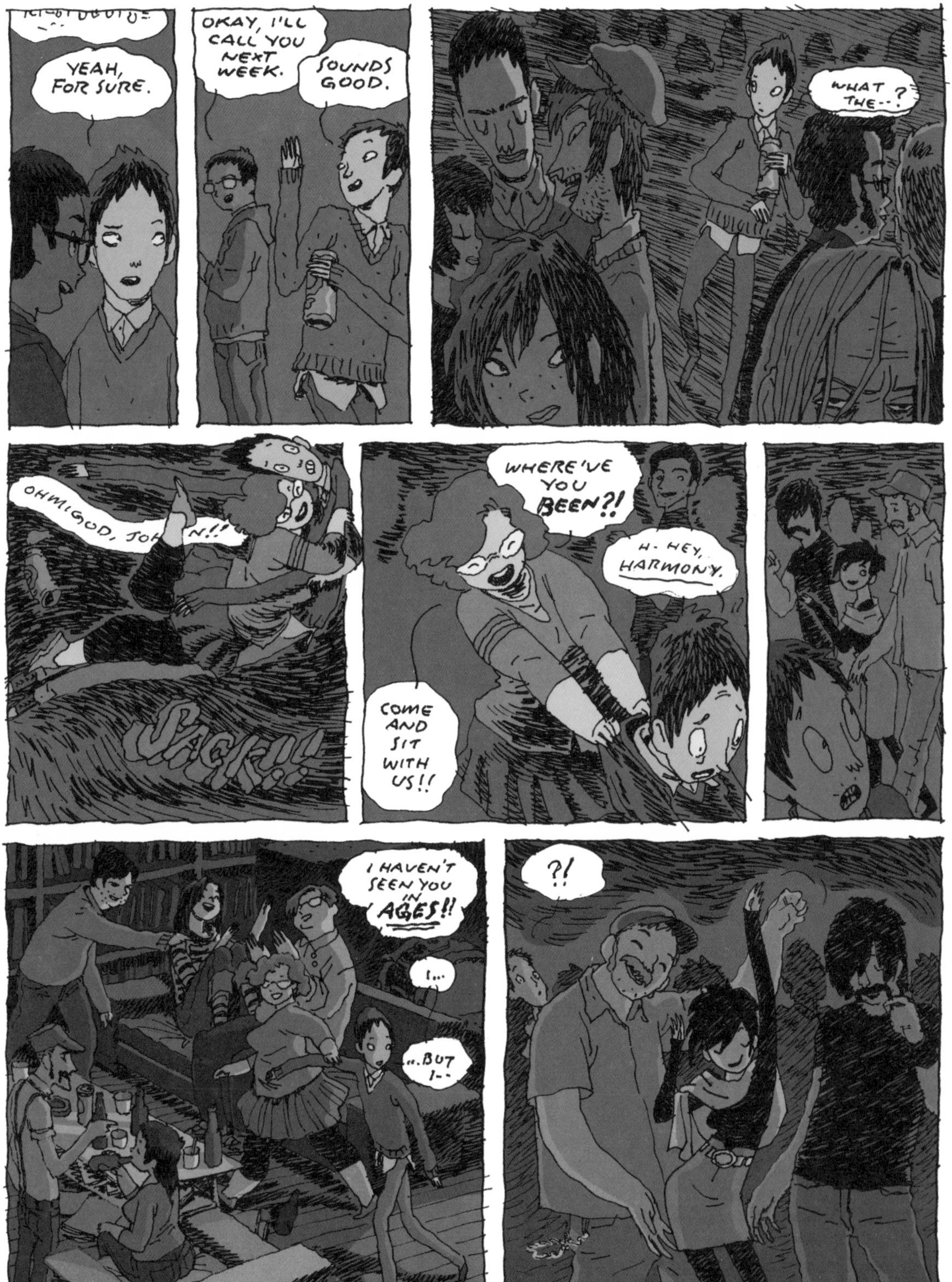
YEAH, FOR SURE.
OKAY, I'LL CALL YOU NEXT WEEK.
SOUNDS GOOD.
WHAT THE--?
OHMIGOD, JO N!!
SACK!!
WHERE'VE YOU BEEN?!
H- HEY, HARMONY.
COME AND SIT WITH US!!
I HAVEN'T SEEN YOU IN AGES!!
I...
...BUT I--
?!

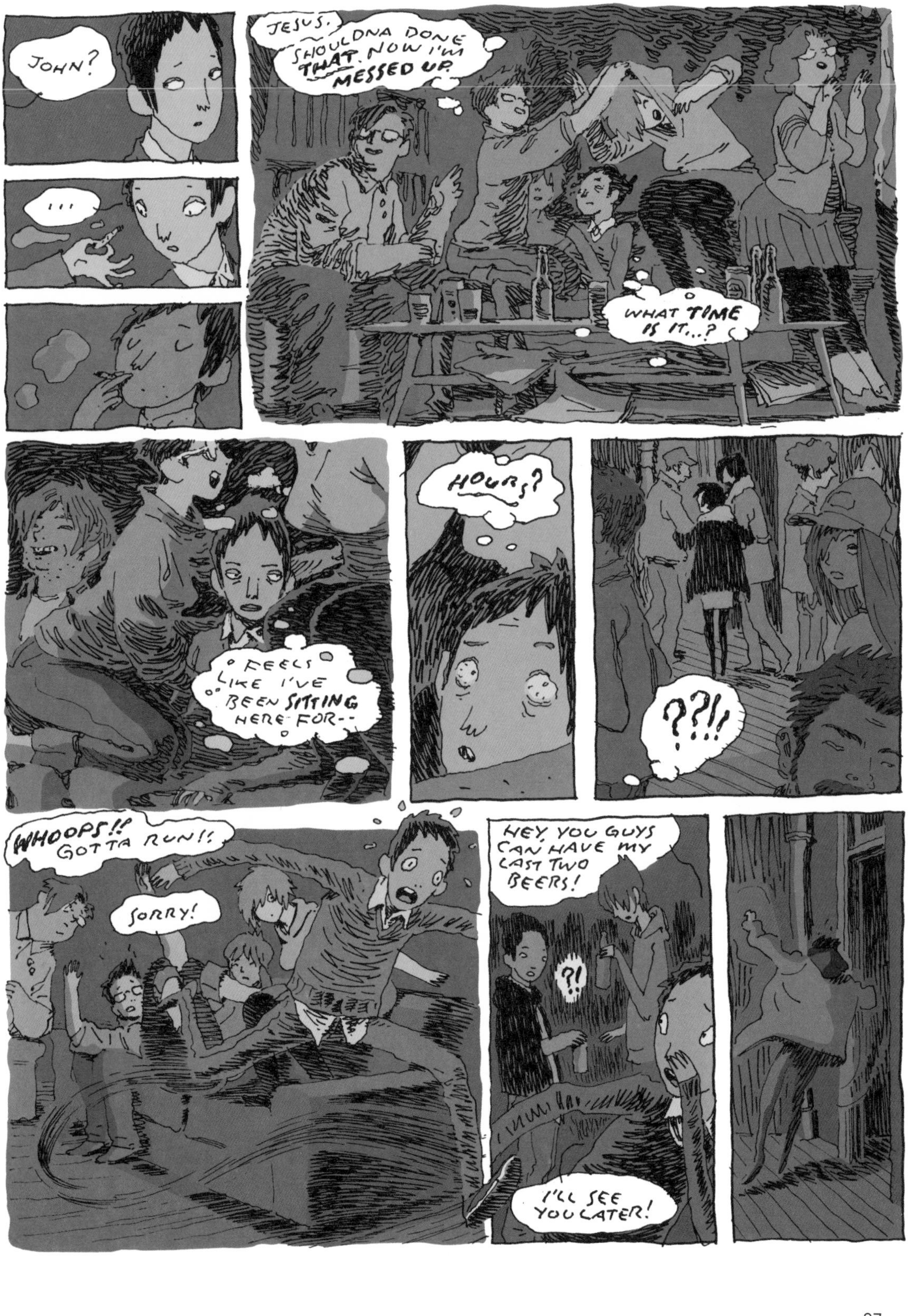
JOHN?
...
JESUS. SHOULDNA DONE THAT. NOW I'M MESSED UP.
WHAT TIME IS IT...?
FEELS LIKE I'VE BEEN SITTING HERE FOR--
HOURS?
??!!
WHOOPS!! GOTTA RUN!!
SORRY!
HEY, YOU GUYS CAN HAVE MY LAST TWO BEERS!
?!
I'LL SEE YOU LATER!

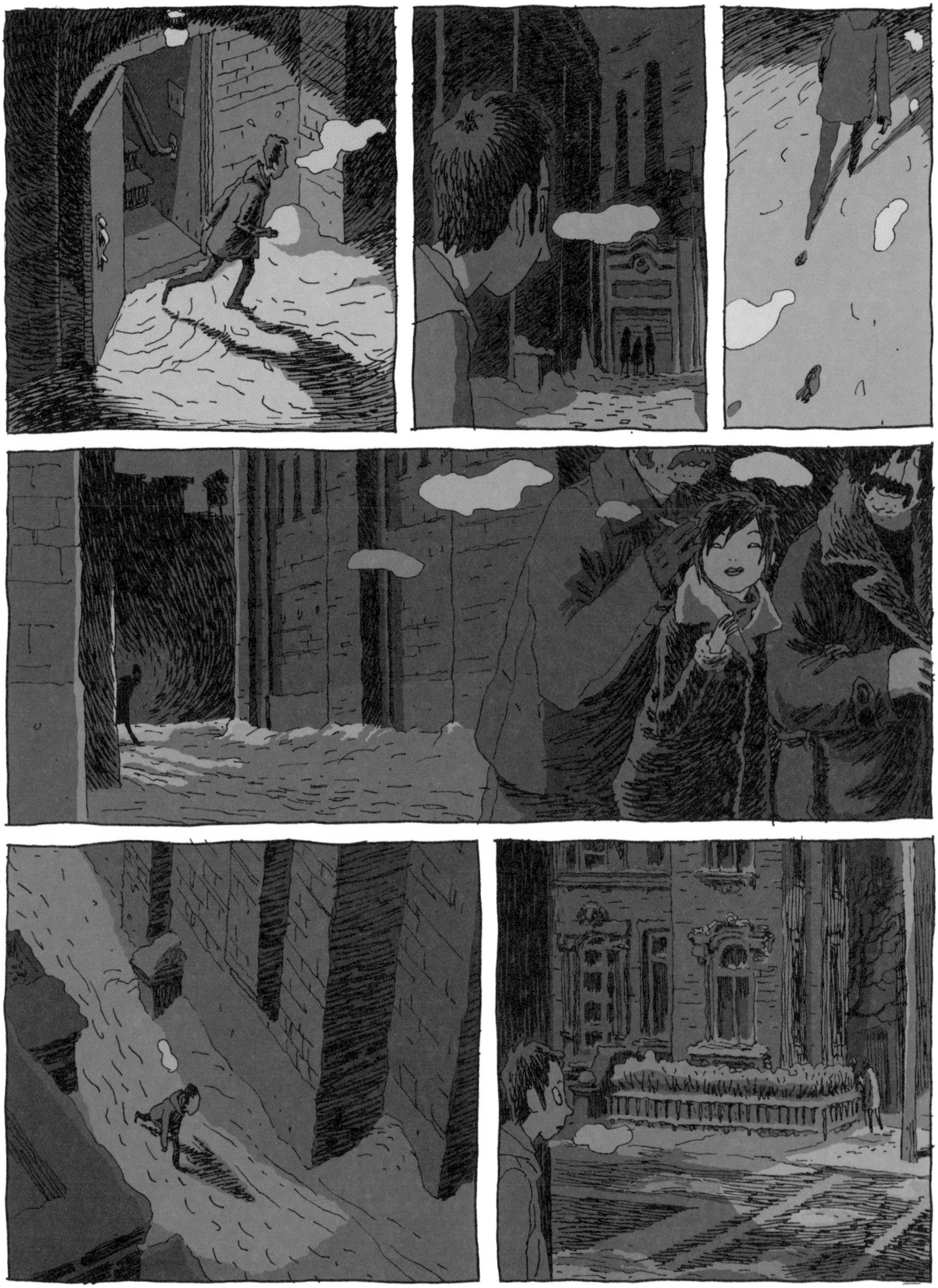

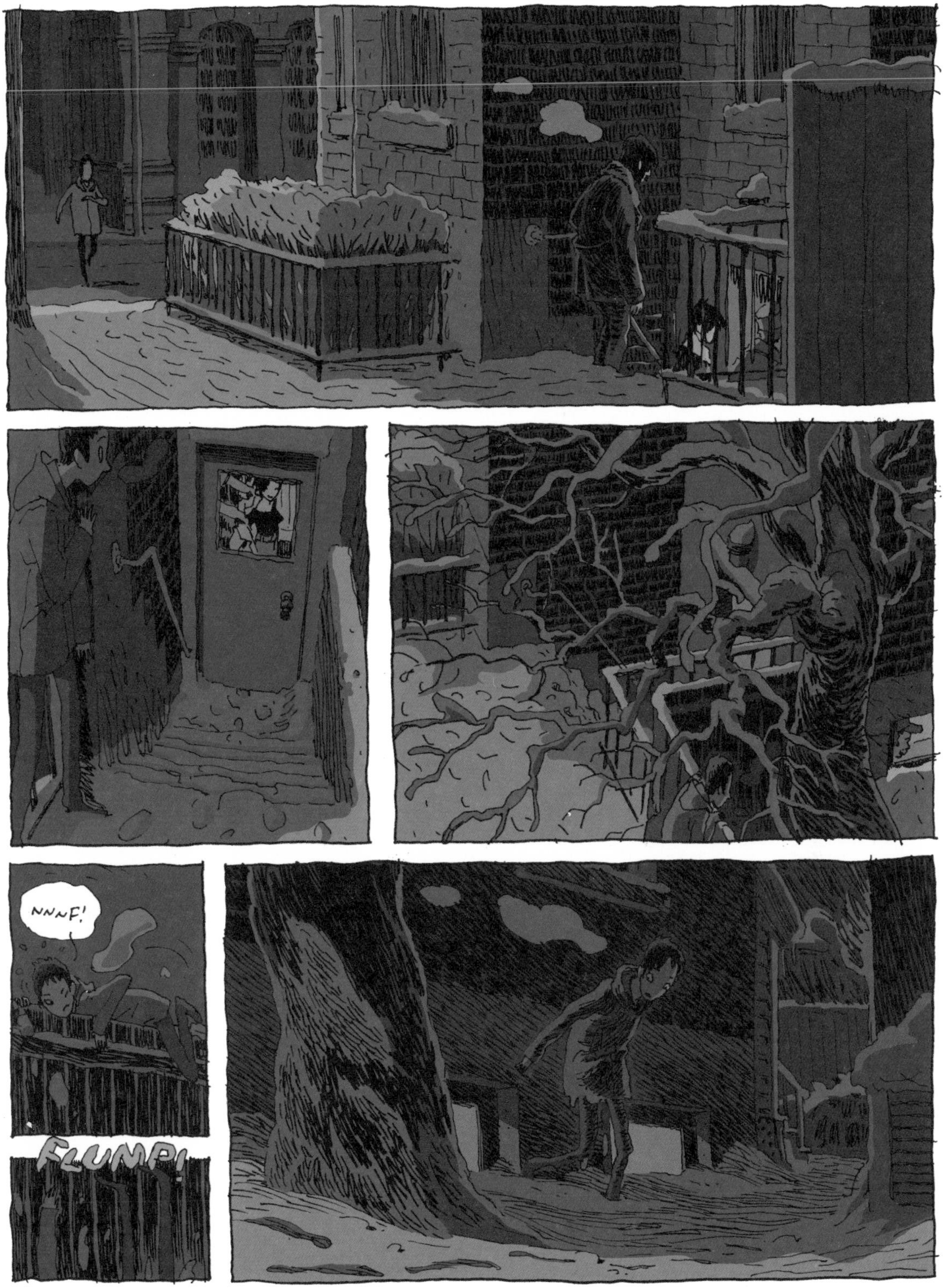
NNNF!
FLUMP!

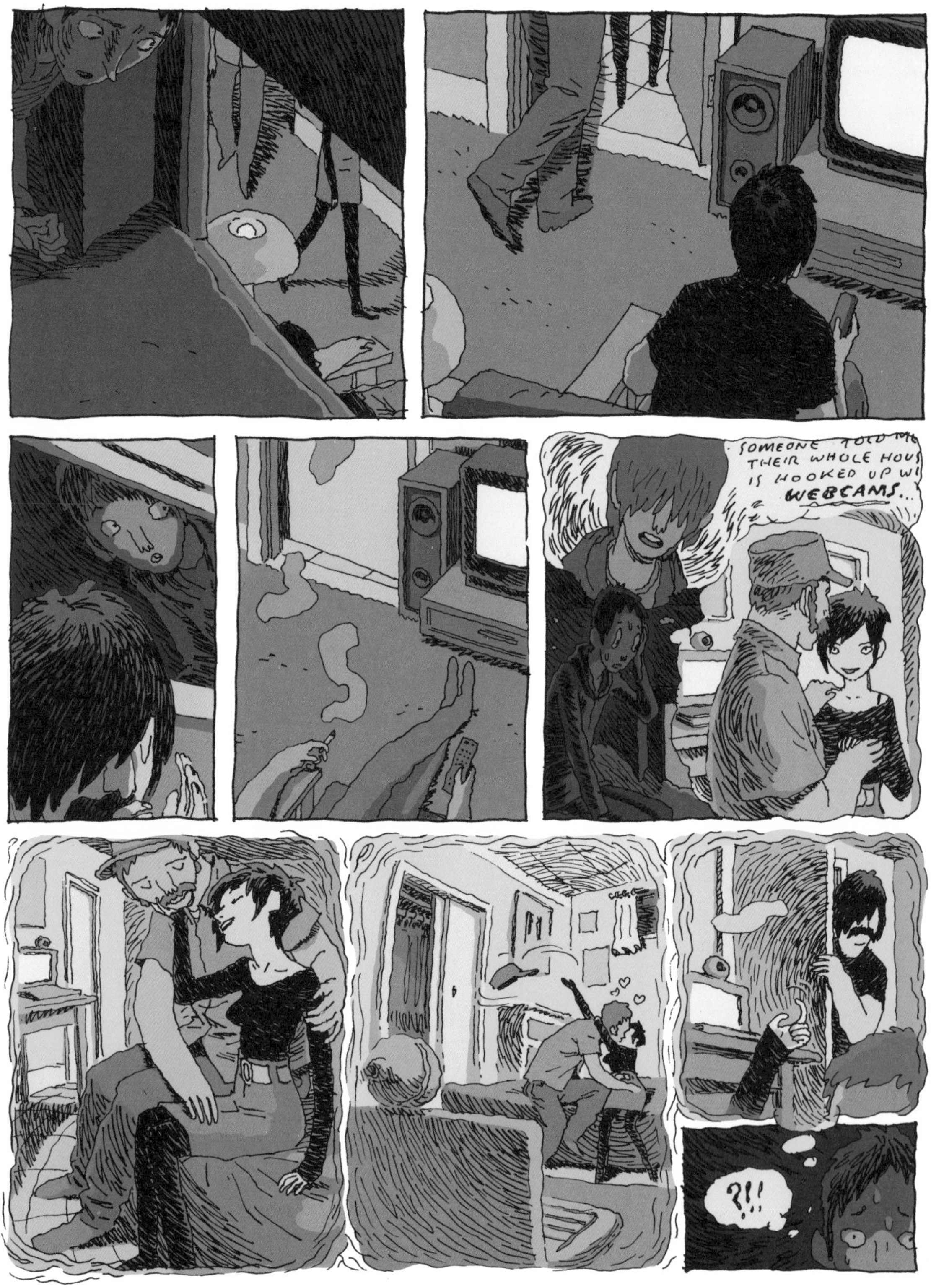
SOMEONE TOLD ME THEIR WHOLE HOUS IS HOOKED UP WI WEBCAMS...
?!!

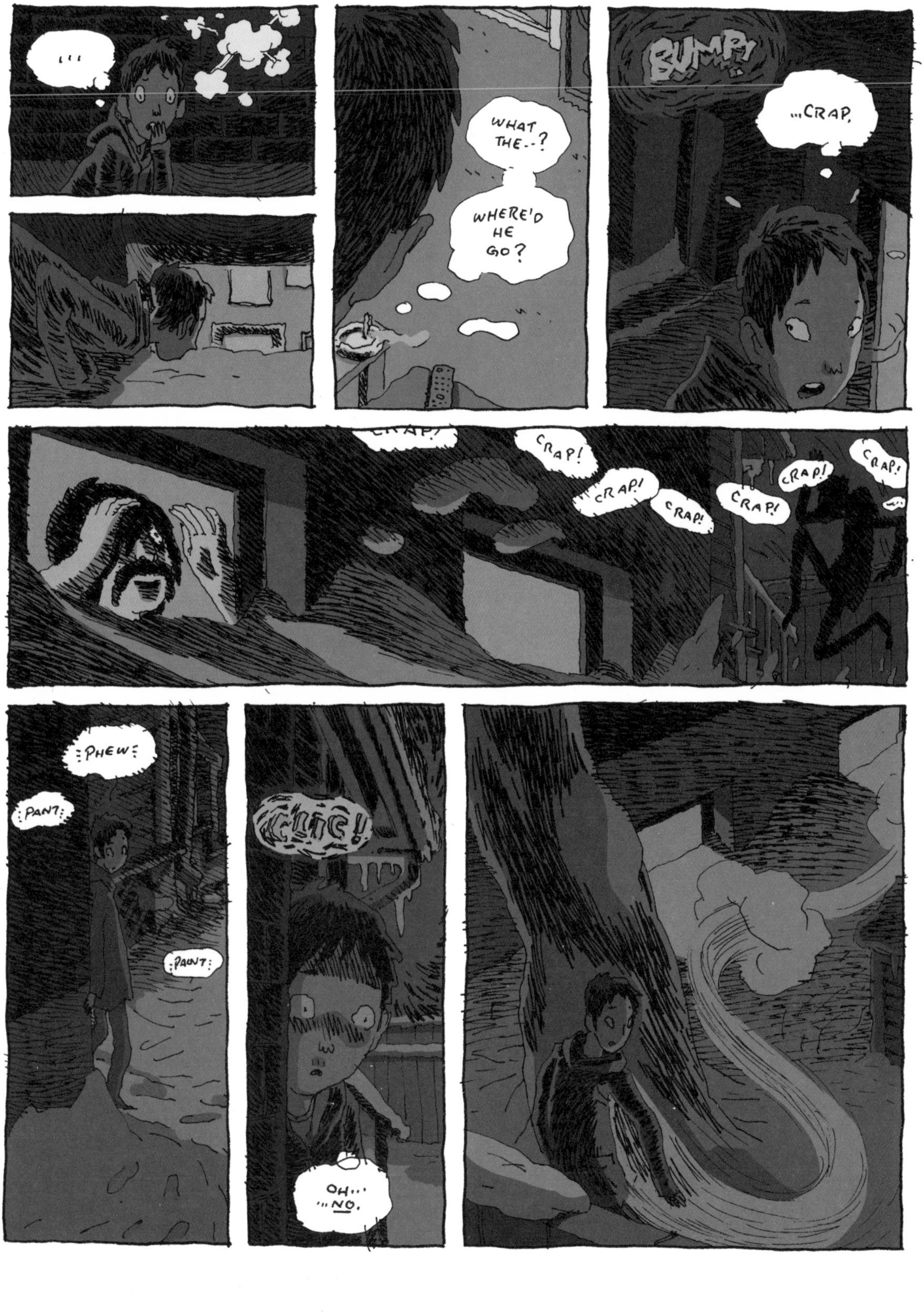
...
WHAT THE--?
WHERE'D HE GO?
BUMP!
...CRAP.
CRAP!
CRAP!
CRAP!
CRAP!
CRAP!
CRAP!
CRAP!
PHEW
PANT
PANT
CHIC!
OH...
...NO.

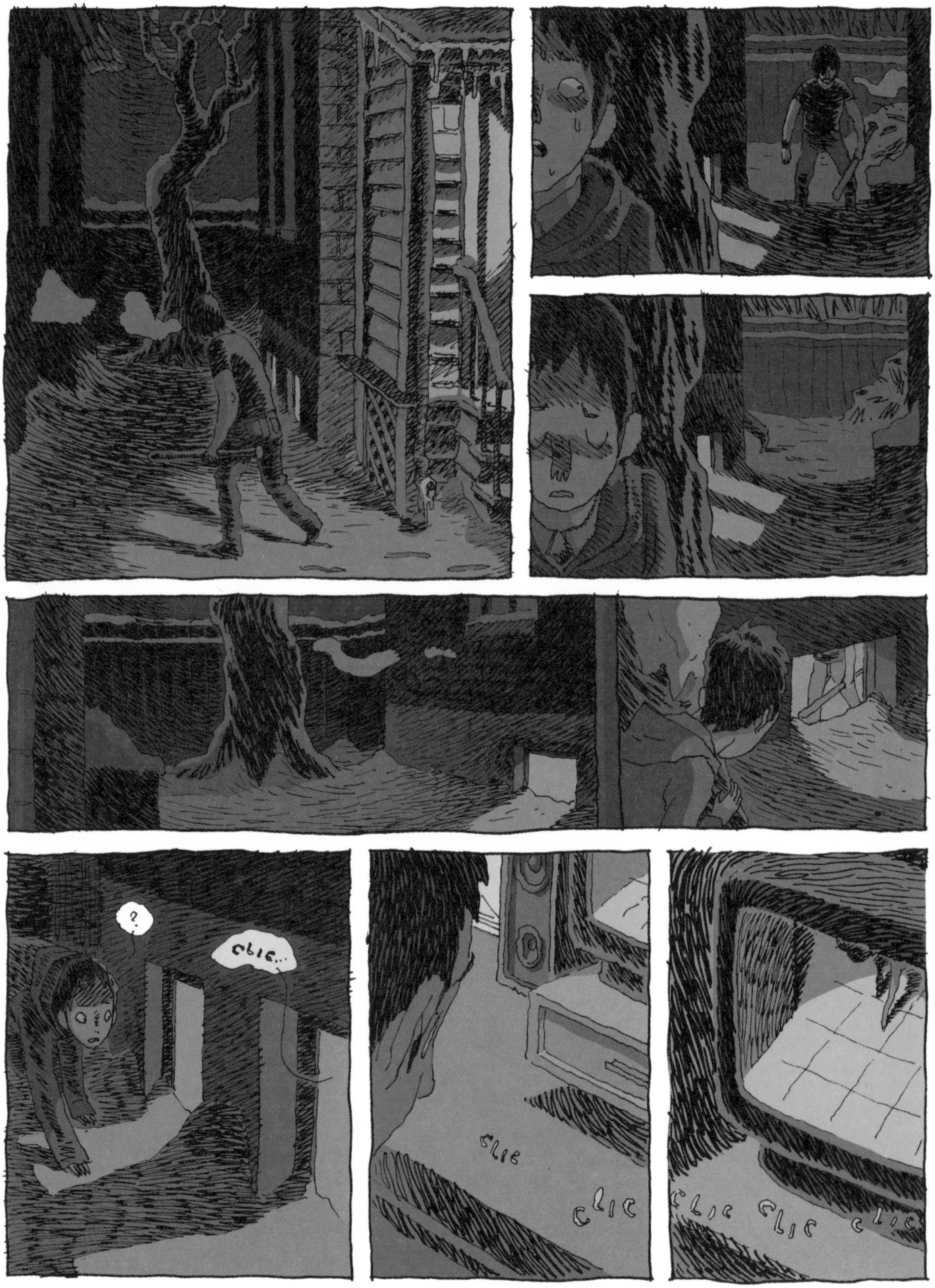
?
clic...
clic
clic
clic
clic
clic

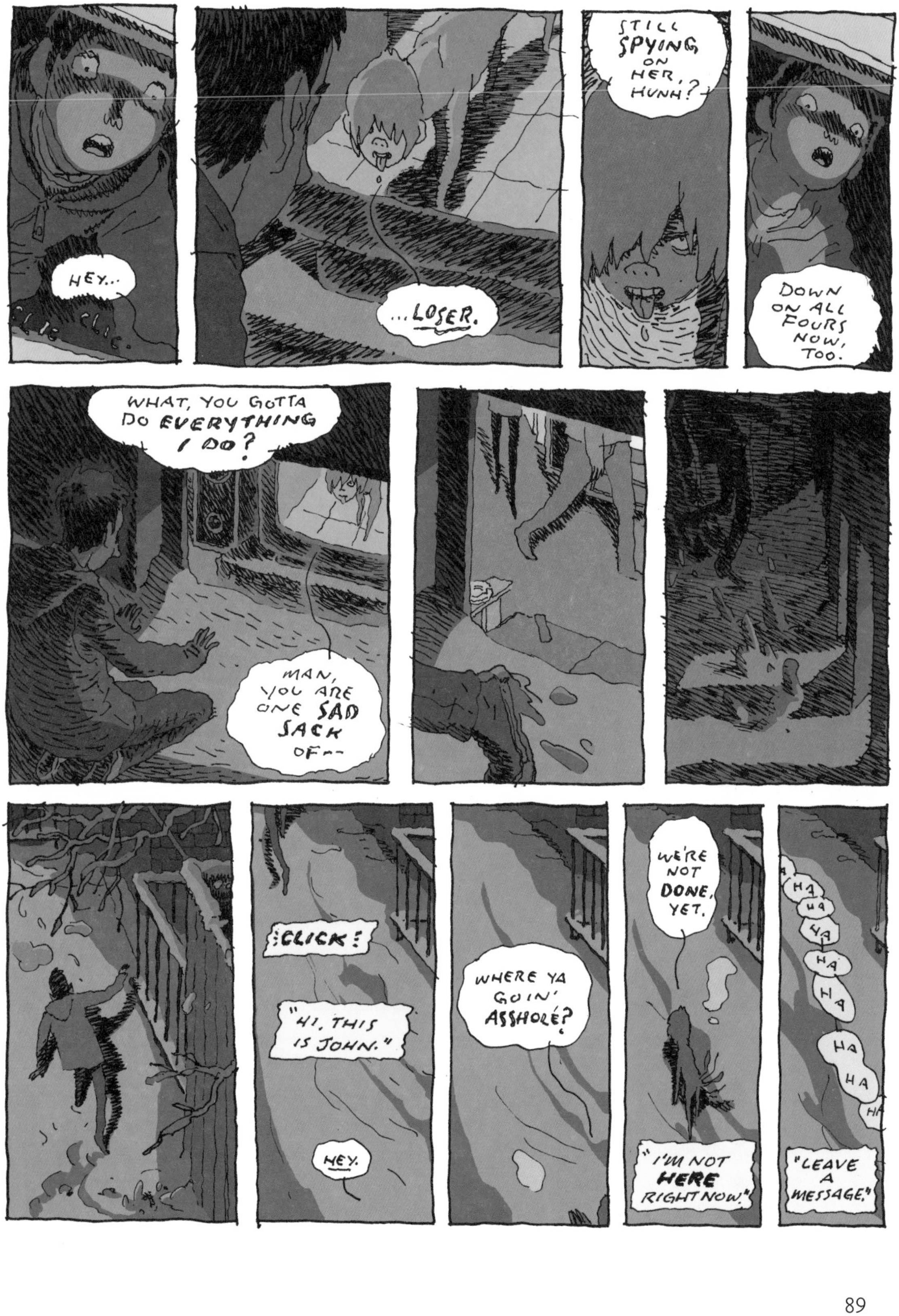
HEY...
CLIC CLIC.
...LOSER.
STILL SPYING ON HER, HUNH?
DOWN ON ALL FOURS NOW, TOO.
WHAT, YOU GOTTA DO EVERYTHING I DO?
MAN, YOU ARE ONE SAD SACK OF--
CLICK!
"HI, THIS IS JOHN."
HEY.
WHERE YA GOIN' ASSHOLE?
WE'RE NOT DONE, YET.
"I'M NOT HERE RIGHT NOW."
HA HA HA HA HA HA HA HA HA HA
"LEAVE A MESSAGE."

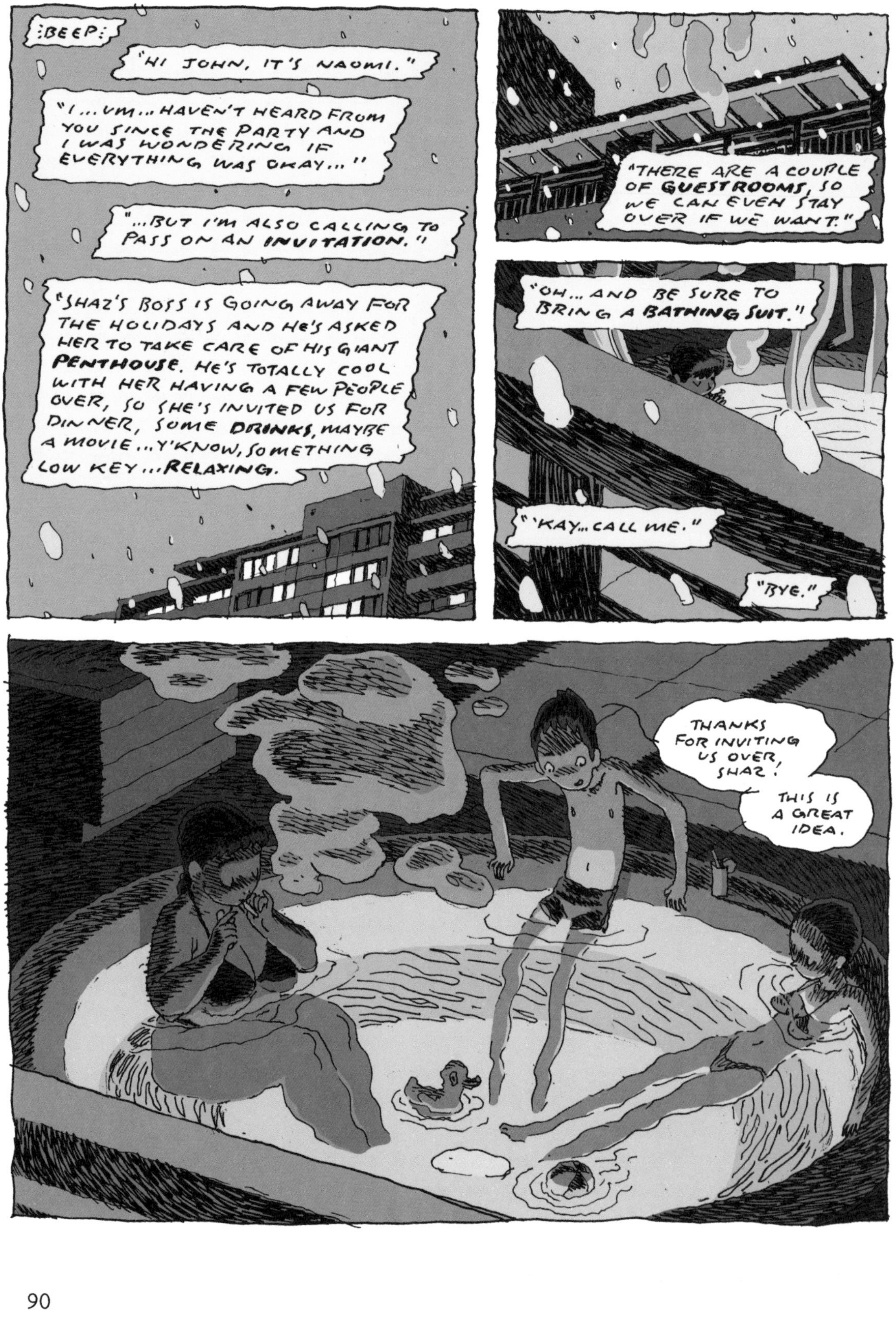
:BEEP:
"HI JOHN, IT'S NAOMI."
"I... UM... HAVEN'T HEARD FROM YOU SINCE THE PARTY AND I WAS WONDERING IF EVERYTHING WAS OKAY..."
"...BUT I'M ALSO CALLING TO PASS ON AN INVITATION."
"SHAZ'S BOSS IS GOING AWAY FOR THE HOLIDAYS AND HE'S ASKED HER TO TAKE CARE OF HIS GIANT PENTHOUSE. HE'S TOTALLY COOL WITH HER HAVING A FEW PEOPLE OVER, SO SHE'S INVITED US FOR DINNER, SOME DRINKS, MAYBE A MOVIE... Y'KNOW, SOMETHING LOW KEY... RELAXING.
"THERE ARE A COUPLE OF GUESTROOMS, SO WE CAN EVEN STAY OVER IF WE WANT."
"OH... AND BE SURE TO BRING A BATHING SUIT."
"'KAY... CALL ME."
"BYE."
THANKS FOR INVITING US OVER, SHAZ!
THIS IS A GREAT IDEA.

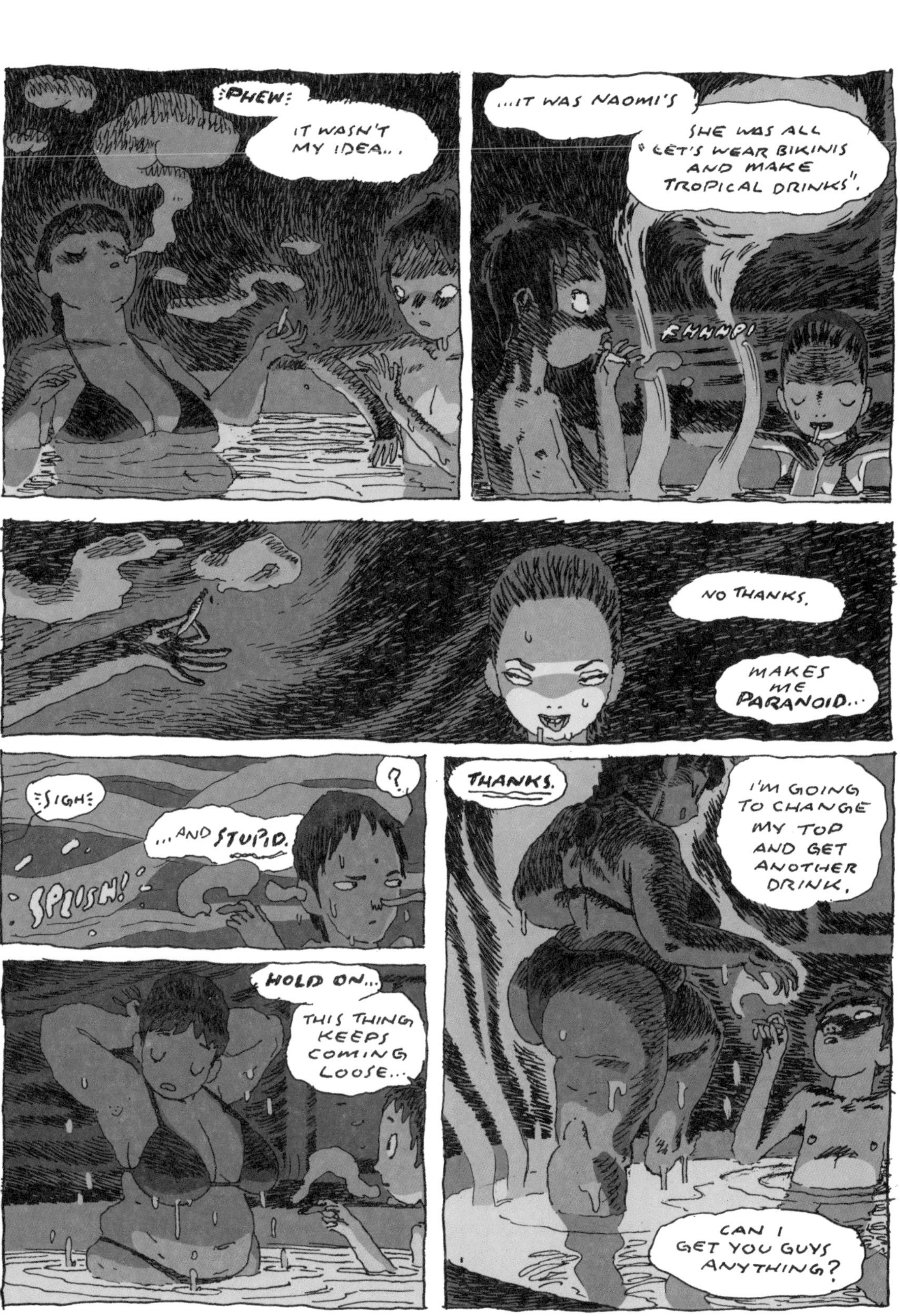
PHEW
IT WASN'T MY IDEA...
...IT WAS NAOMI'S
SHE WAS ALL "LET'S WEAR BIKINIS AND MAKE TROPICAL DRINKS".
FHHHP!
NO THANKS.
MAKES ME PARANOID...
SIGH
...AND STUPID.
SPLISH!
?
THANKS.
I'M GOING TO CHANGE MY TOP AND GET ANOTHER DRINK.
HOLD ON...
THIS THING KEEPS COMING LOOSE...
CAN I GET YOU GUYS ANYTHING?

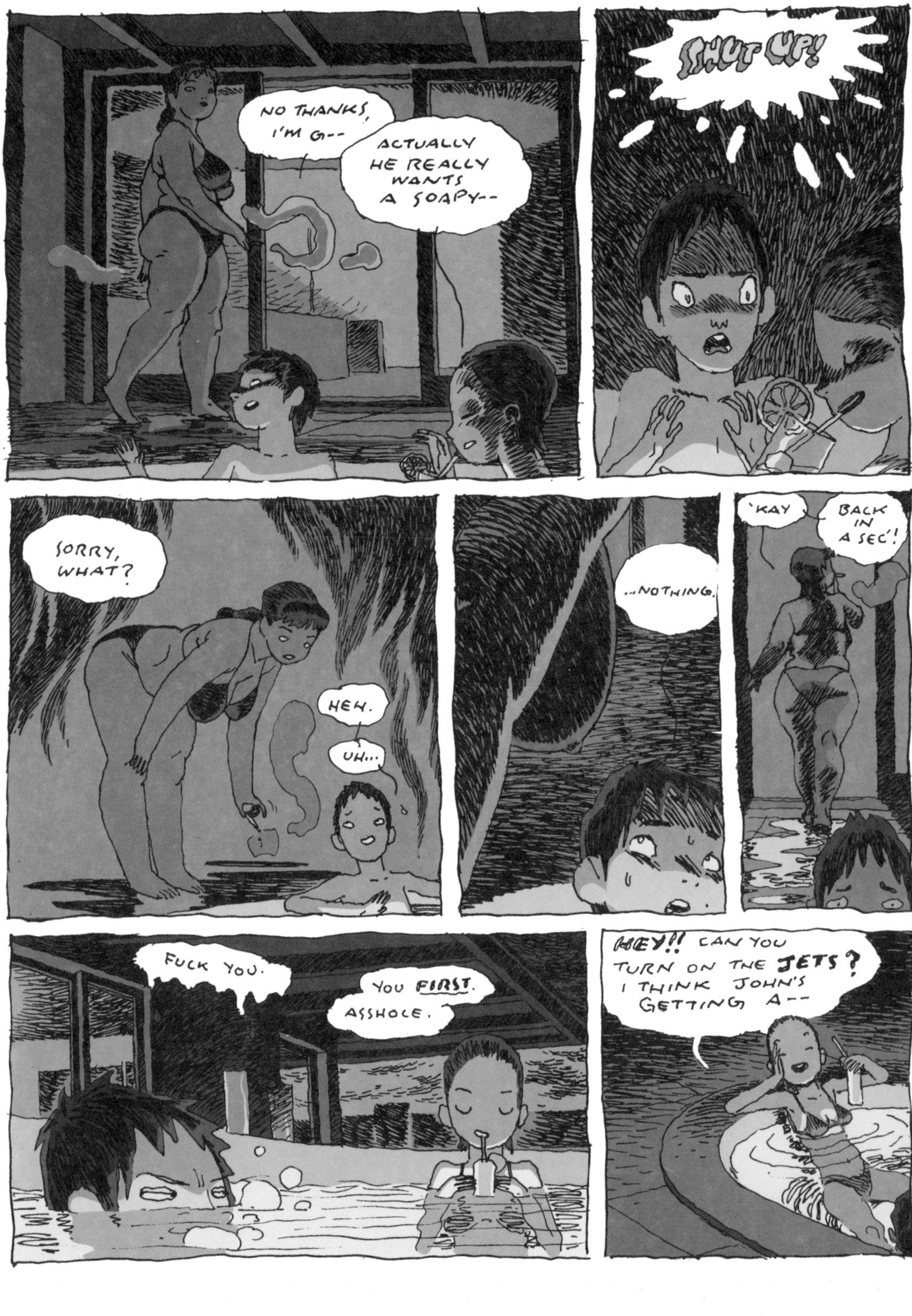
NO THANKS, I'M G--
ACTUALLY HE REALLY WANTS A SOAPY--
SHUT UP!
SORRY, WHAT?
HEH.
UH...
...NOTHING.
'KAY
BACK IN A SEC'!
FUCK YOU.
YOU FIRST. ASSHOLE.
HEY!! CAN YOU TURN ON THE JETS? I THINK JOHN'S GETTING A--

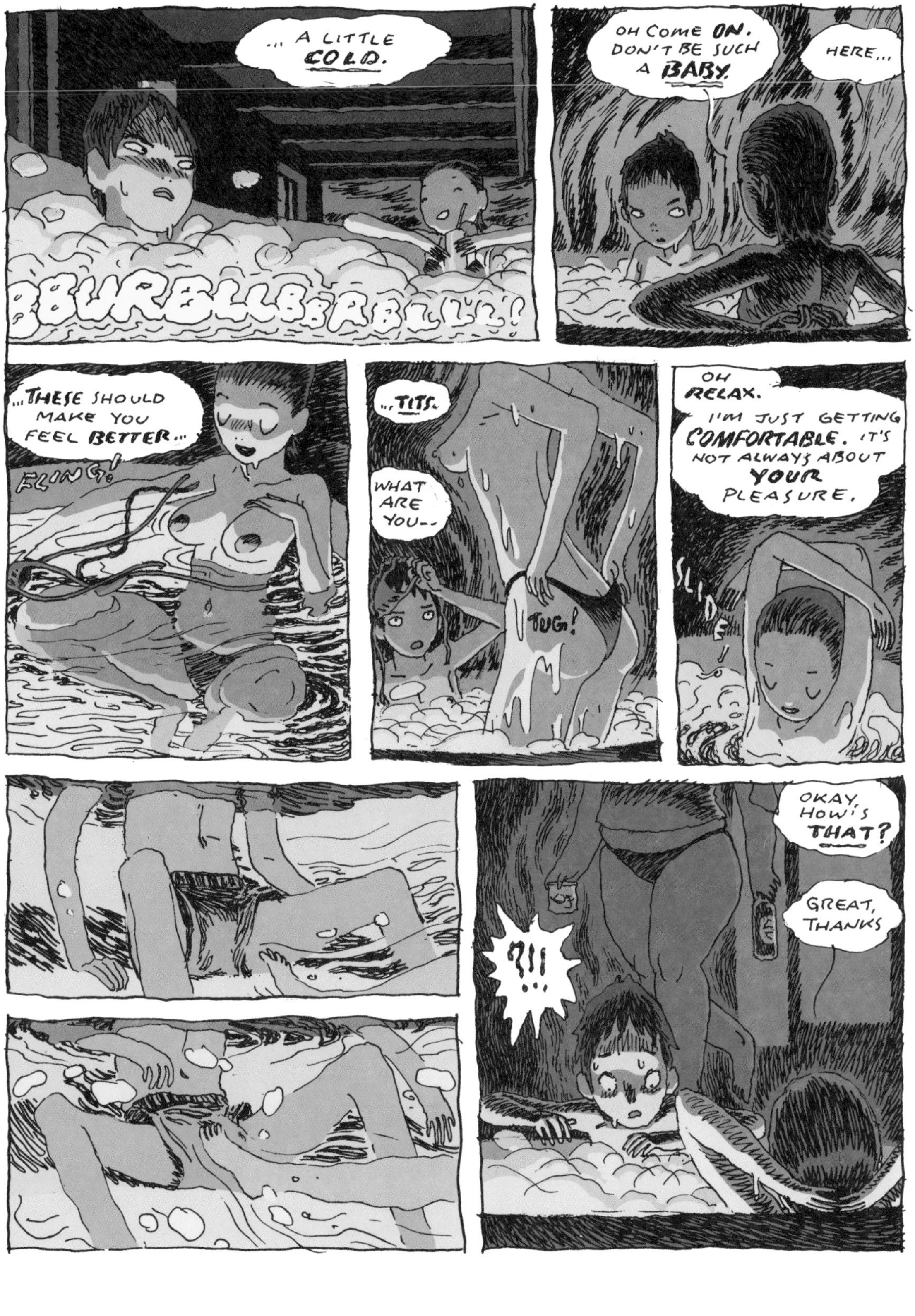

... A LITTLE COLD.
BBURBLLBBRABLLLL!
OH COME ON. DON'T BE SUCH A BABY.
HERE...
...THESE SHOULD MAKE YOU FEEL BETTER...
FLING!
...TITS.
WHAT ARE YOU--
TUG!
OH RELAX.
I'M JUST GETTING COMFORTABLE. IT'S NOT ALWAYS ABOUT YOUR PLEASURE.
SLIDE!
OKAY, HOW'S THAT?
GREAT, THANKS
?!!

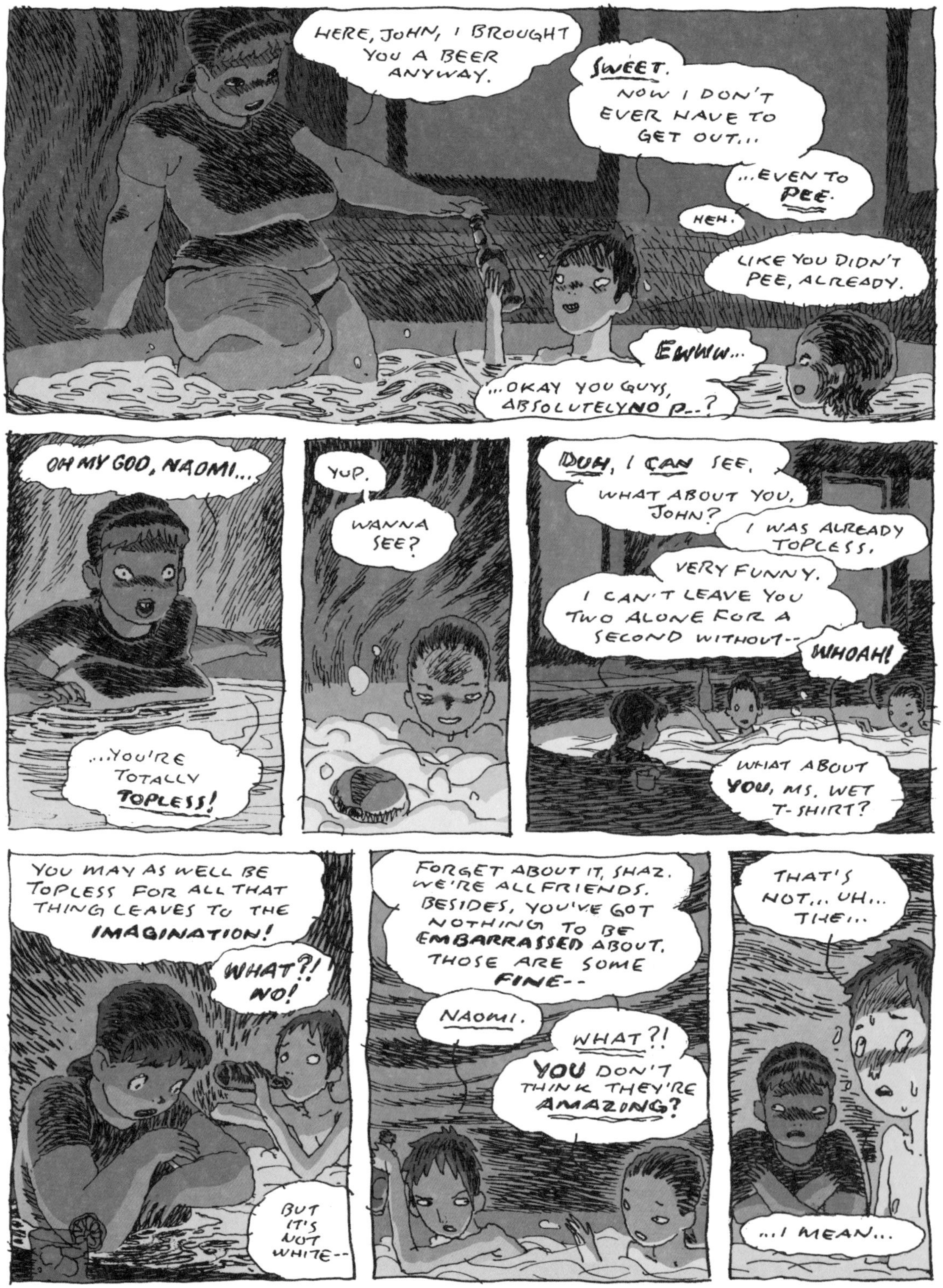
HERE, JOHN, I BROUGHT YOU A BEER ANYWAY.
SWEET. NOW I DON'T EVER HAVE TO GET OUT...
...EVEN TO PEE.
HEH.
LIKE YOU DIDN'T PEE, ALREADY.
EWWW...
...OKAY YOU GUYS, ABSOLUTELY NO P...?
OH MY GOD, NAOMI...
...YOU'RE TOTALLY TOPLESS!
YUP.
WANNA SEE?
DUH, I CAN SEE.
WHAT ABOUT YOU, JOHN?
I WAS ALREADY TOPLESS.
VERY FUNNY.
I CAN'T LEAVE YOU TWO ALONE FOR A SECOND WITHOUT--
WHOAH!
WHAT ABOUT YOU, MS. WET T-SHIRT?
YOU MAY AS WELL BE TOPLESS FOR ALL THAT THING LEAVES TO THE IMAGINATION!
WHAT?! NO!
BUT IT'S NOT WHITE--
FORGET ABOUT IT, SHAZ. WE'RE ALL FRIENDS. BESIDES, YOU'VE GOT NOTHING TO BE EMBARRASSED ABOUT. THOSE ARE SOME FINE--
NAOMI.
WHAT?!
YOU DON'T THINK THEY'RE AMAZING?
THAT'S NOT... UH... THE...
...I MEAN...

DON'T TELL ME YOU HADN'T **NOTICED.**

ALRIGHT, NAOMI, KNOCK IT OFF.

DON'T MIND **HER**, JOHN.

THERE'S ONLY ONE WAY TO DEAL WITH THIS LITTLE **MINDFUCKER**...

OW!

HEE HEE

...**BRUTE FORCE.**

MOMMY TO THE RESCUE.

BLAP!

BUT I THINK FOR EVERYONE'S SAFETY, I'M GONNA SUBMERGE THE **BIG GUNS**

APPARENTLY, THEY'RE TOO **DANGEROUS** TO BE LEFT OUT IN THE **OPEN.**

ESPECIALLY WITH **CHILDREN** AROUND.

:PHEW:

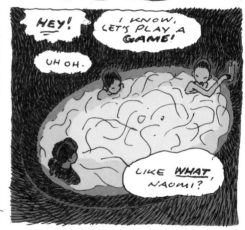

HEY!

I KNOW, LET'S PLAY A **GAME!**

UH OH.

LIKE **WHAT**, NAOMI?

TRUTH OR **DARE!!**

MNNN....

I DON'T KNOW...

OH COME **ON**, YOU **LOSERS**, I'LL EVEN GO FIRST. ASK ME **ANYTHING.**

DON'T BE SO **UPTIGHT.** THIS'S SUPPOSED TO BE **FUN**, REMEMBER?

ALRIGHT. BUT YOU BETTER **SMARTEN UP** AND **PLAY NICE**, LITTLE MISSY... ...OR I'LL FUCK YOUR SHIT **UP.**

:SIGH:

OKAY, NAOMI, WHAT'S IT GONNA BE, TRUTH, DARE OR **DOUBLE DARE.**

TRUTH!!

LET'S SEE...

...I THINK WE'LL GO WITH THE USUAL OPENER...

...IF YOU COULD HAVE SEX WITH ANY...

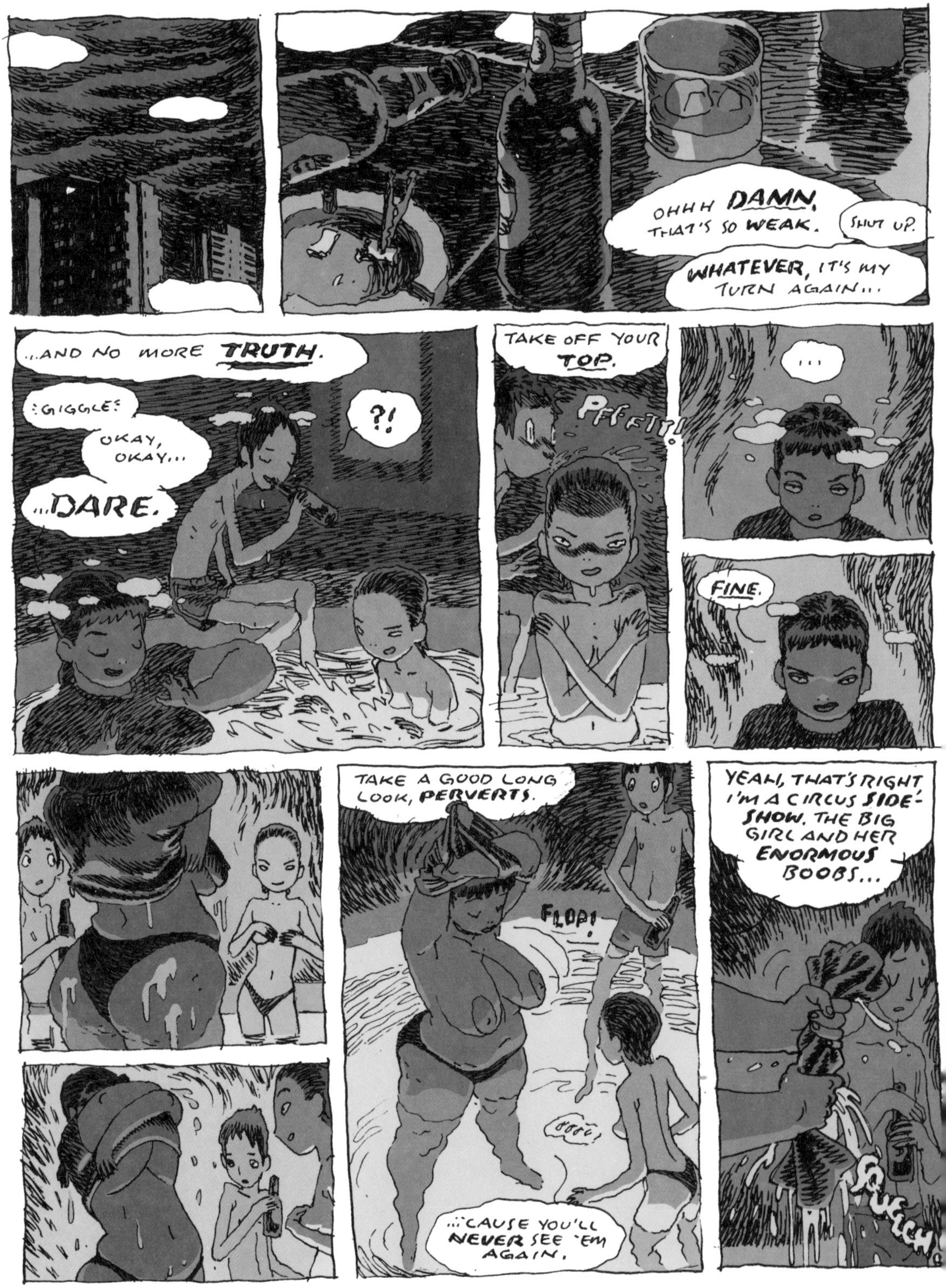
OHHH DAMN. THAT'S SO WEAK.
SHUT UP.
WHATEVER, IT'S MY TURN AGAIN...
...AND NO MORE TRUTH.
:GIGGLE:
OKAY, OKAY...
...DARE.
?!
TAKE OFF YOUR TOP.
PFFFTT!
...
FINE.
TAKE A GOOD LONG LOOK, PERVERTS.
FLOP!
OOOO!
...'CAUSE YOU'LL NEVER SEE 'EM AGAIN.
YEAH, THAT'S RIGHT I'M A CIRCUS SIDE-SHOW. THE BIG GIRL AND HER ENORMOUS BOOBS...
SQUELCH!

HAPPY NOW?

HERE, THIS MUST BE FOR **YOUR** BENEFIT, JOHN...

...NAOMI'S SEEN 'EM **PLENTY** OF TIMES SHAME ON YOU **BOTH**...

STUPENDOUS! ...ASSHOLES.

NOW IT'S **YOUR** TURN AND IT HAS TO BE A **DARE**.

WHAT?! NO WAY! BESIDES, IT'S SHAZ'S TURN TO **ASK**.

SHE'S TOO **BAKED**. SO I DARE **YOU** TO **FEEL** HER UP.

THAT'D BE **ANOTHER** DARE FOR HER, TOO, **FORGET IT**.

YES, DO IT. **HLKKK!**

BLAAAAH!

OH DEAR... **HHUUARRRLLFP!**

...WE BETTER MAKE SURE SHE'S OKAY.

97

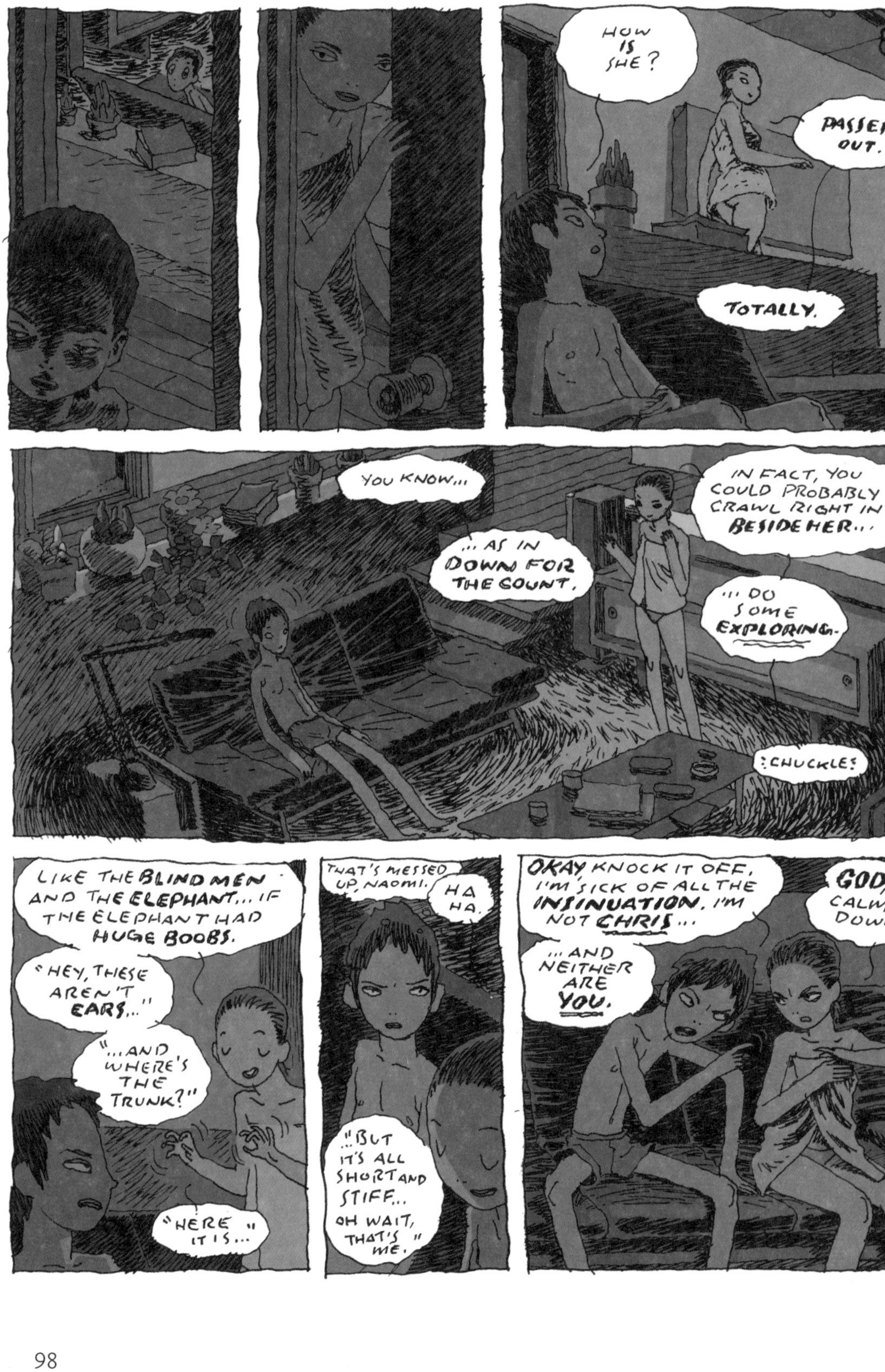
HOW IS SHE?
PASSED OUT.
TOTALLY.
YOU KNOW...
...AS IN DOWN FOR THE COUNT.
IN FACT, YOU COULD PROBABLY CRAWL RIGHT IN BESIDE HER...
...DO SOME EXPLORING.
CHUCKLE
LIKE THE BLIND MEN AND THE ELEPHANT... IF THE ELEPHANT HAD HUGE BOOBS.
"HEY, THESE AREN'T EARS..."
"...AND WHERE'S THE TRUNK?"
"HERE IT IS..."
THAT'S MESSED UP, NAOMI.
HA HA.
"...BUT IT'S ALL SHORT AND STIFF... OH WAIT, THAT'S ME."
OKAY KNOCK IT OFF. I'M SICK OF ALL THE INSINUATION. I'M NOT CHRIS...
...AND NEITHER ARE YOU.
GOD, CALM DOWN.

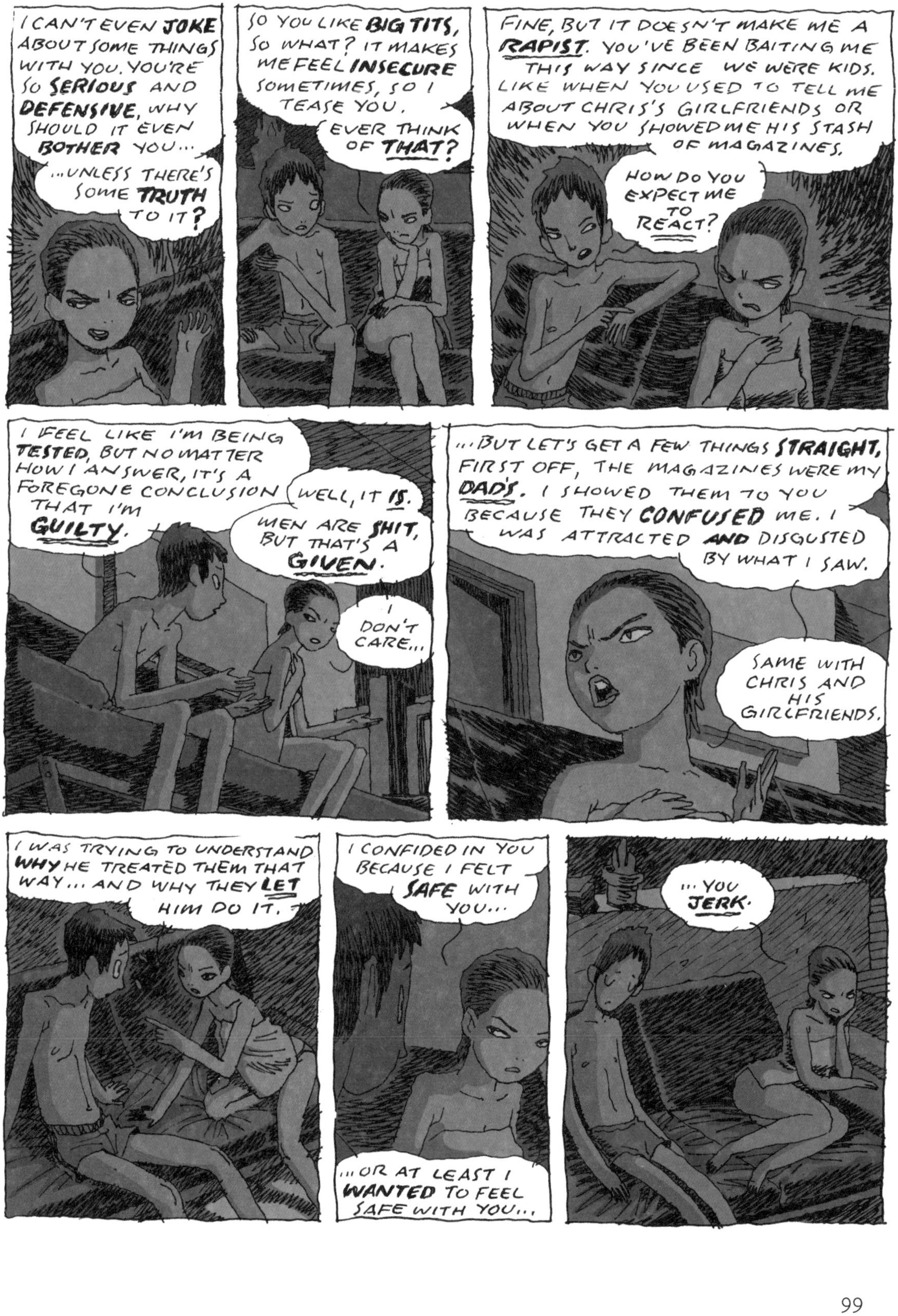
I CAN'T EVEN JOKE ABOUT SOME THINGS WITH YOU. YOU'RE SO SERIOUS AND DEFENSIVE, WHY SHOULD IT EVEN BOTHER YOU...
...UNLESS THERE'S SOME TRUTH TO IT?
SO YOU LIKE BIG TITS, SO WHAT? IT MAKES ME FEEL INSECURE SOMETIMES, SO I TEASE YOU.
EVER THINK OF THAT?
FINE, BUT IT DOESN'T MAKE ME A RAPIST. YOU'VE BEEN BAITING ME THIS WAY SINCE WE WERE KIDS. LIKE WHEN YOU USED TO TELL ME ABOUT CHRIS'S GIRLFRIENDS OR WHEN YOU SHOWED ME HIS STASH OF MAGAZINES.
HOW DO YOU EXPECT ME TO REACT?
I FEEL LIKE I'M BEING TESTED, BUT NO MATTER HOW I ANSWER, IT'S A FOREGONE CONCLUSION THAT I'M GUILTY.
WELL, IT IS.
MEN ARE SHIT, BUT THAT'S A GIVEN.
I DON'T CARE...
...BUT LET'S GET A FEW THINGS STRAIGHT, FIRST OFF, THE MAGAZINES WERE MY DAD'S. I SHOWED THEM TO YOU BECAUSE THEY CONFUSED ME. I WAS ATTRACTED AND DISGUSTED BY WHAT I SAW.
SAME WITH CHRIS AND HIS GIRLFRIENDS.
I WAS TRYING TO UNDERSTAND WHY HE TREATED THEM THAT WAY... AND WHY THEY LET HIM DO IT.
I CONFIDED IN YOU BECAUSE I FELT SAFE WITH YOU...
...OR AT LEAST I WANTED TO FEEL SAFE WITH YOU...
...YOU JERK.

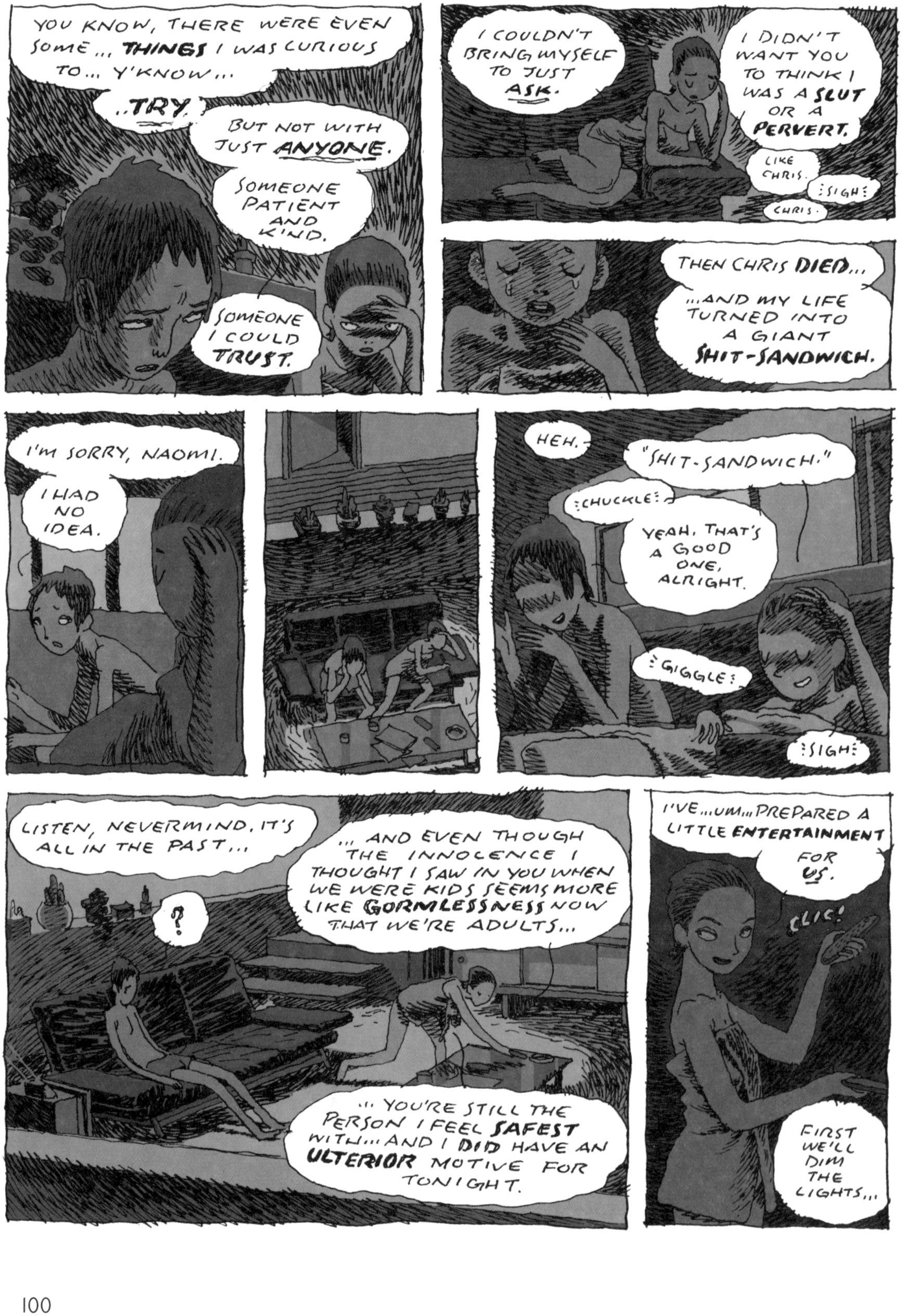
YOU KNOW, THERE WERE EVEN SOME... THINGS I WAS CURIOUS TO... Y'KNOW...
..TRY.
BUT NOT WITH JUST ANYONE.
SOMEONE PATIENT AND KIND.
SOMEONE I COULD TRUST.
I COULDN'T BRING MYSELF TO JUST ASK.
I DIDN'T WANT YOU TO THINK I WAS A SLUT OR A PERVERT.
LIKE CHRIS.
SIGH
CHRIS.
THEN CHRIS DIED...
...AND MY LIFE TURNED INTO A GIANT SHIT-SANDWICH.
I'M SORRY, NAOMI.
I HAD NO IDEA.
HEH.
"SHIT-SANDWICH."
CHUCKLE
YEAH, THAT'S A GOOD ONE, ALRIGHT.
GIGGLE
SIGH
LISTEN, NEVERMIND, IT'S ALL IN THE PAST...
?
... AND EVEN THOUGH THE INNOCENCE I THOUGHT I SAW IN YOU WHEN WE WERE KIDS SEEMS MORE LIKE GORMLESSNESS NOW THAT WE'RE ADULTS...
... YOU'RE STILL THE PERSON I FEEL SAFEST WITH... AND I DID HAVE AN ULTERIOR MOTIVE FOR TONIGHT.
I'VE...UM...PREPARED A LITTLE ENTERTAINMENT FOR US.
CLIC!
FIRST WE'LL DIM THE LIGHTS...

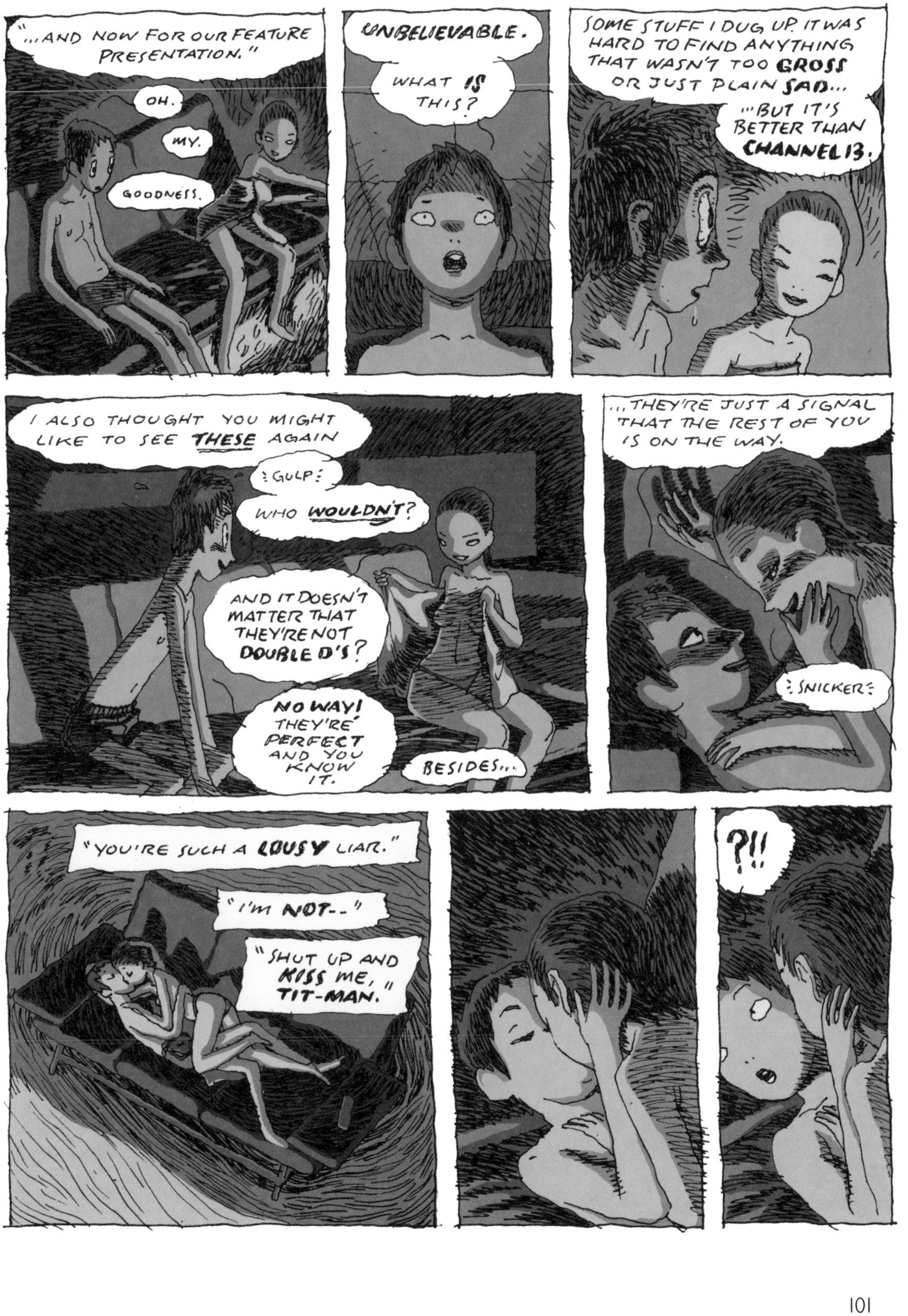
"...AND NOW FOR OUR FEATURE PRESENTATION."
OH.
MY.
GOODNESS.
UNBELIEVABLE.
WHAT IS THIS?
SOME STUFF I DUG UP. IT WAS HARD TO FIND ANYTHING THAT WASN'T TOO GROSS OR JUST PLAIN SAD...
...BUT IT'S BETTER THAN CHANNEL 13.
I ALSO THOUGHT YOU MIGHT LIKE TO SEE THESE AGAIN
:GULP:
WHO WOULDN'T?
AND IT DOESN'T MATTER THAT THEY'RE NOT DOUBLE D'S?
NO WAY! THEY'RE PERFECT AND YOU KNOW IT.
BESIDES...
...THEY'RE JUST A SIGNAL THAT THE REST OF YOU IS ON THE WAY.
:SNICKER:
"YOU'RE SUCH A LOUSY LIAR."
"I'M NOT--"
"SHUT UP AND KISS ME, TIT-MAN."
?!!

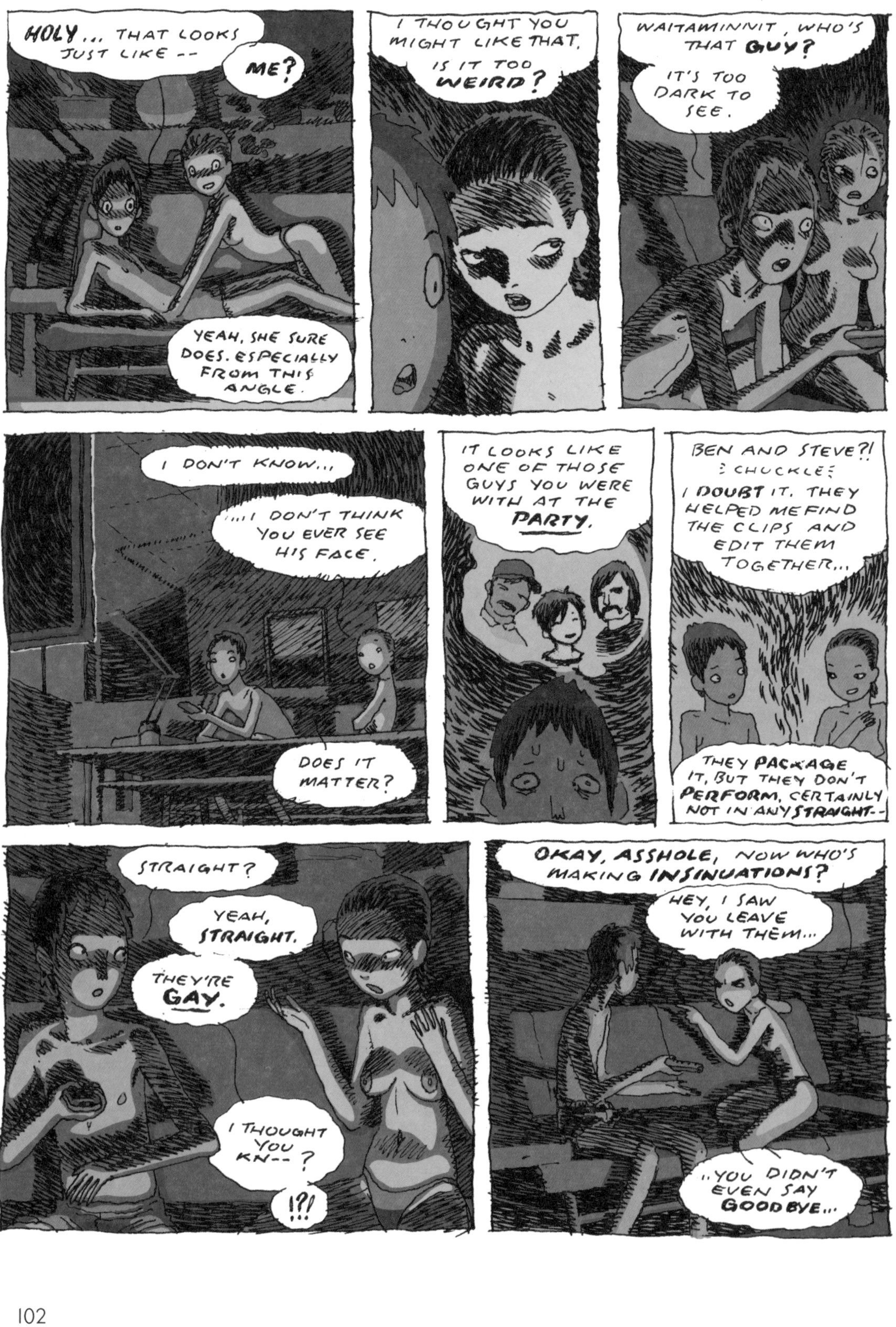
HOLY... THAT LOOKS JUST LIKE --
ME?
YEAH, SHE SURE DOES. ESPECIALLY FROM THIS ANGLE.
I THOUGHT YOU MIGHT LIKE THAT. IS IT TOO WEIRD?
WAITAMINNIT, WHO'S THAT GUY?
IT'S TOO DARK TO SEE.
I DON'T KNOW...
...I DON'T THINK YOU EVER SEE HIS FACE.
DOES IT MATTER?
IT LOOKS LIKE ONE OF THOSE GUYS YOU WERE WITH AT THE PARTY.
BEN AND STEVE?! :CHUCKLE: I DOUBT IT. THEY HELPED ME FIND THE CLIPS AND EDIT THEM TOGETHER...
THEY PACKAGE IT, BUT THEY DON'T PERFORM, CERTAINLY NOT IN ANY STRAIGHT--
STRAIGHT?
YEAH, STRAIGHT.
THEY'RE GAY.
I THOUGHT YOU KN--?
!?!
OKAY, ASSHOLE, NOW WHO'S MAKING INSINUATIONS?
HEY, I SAW YOU LEAVE WITH THEM...
...YOU DIDN'T EVEN SAY GOODBYE...

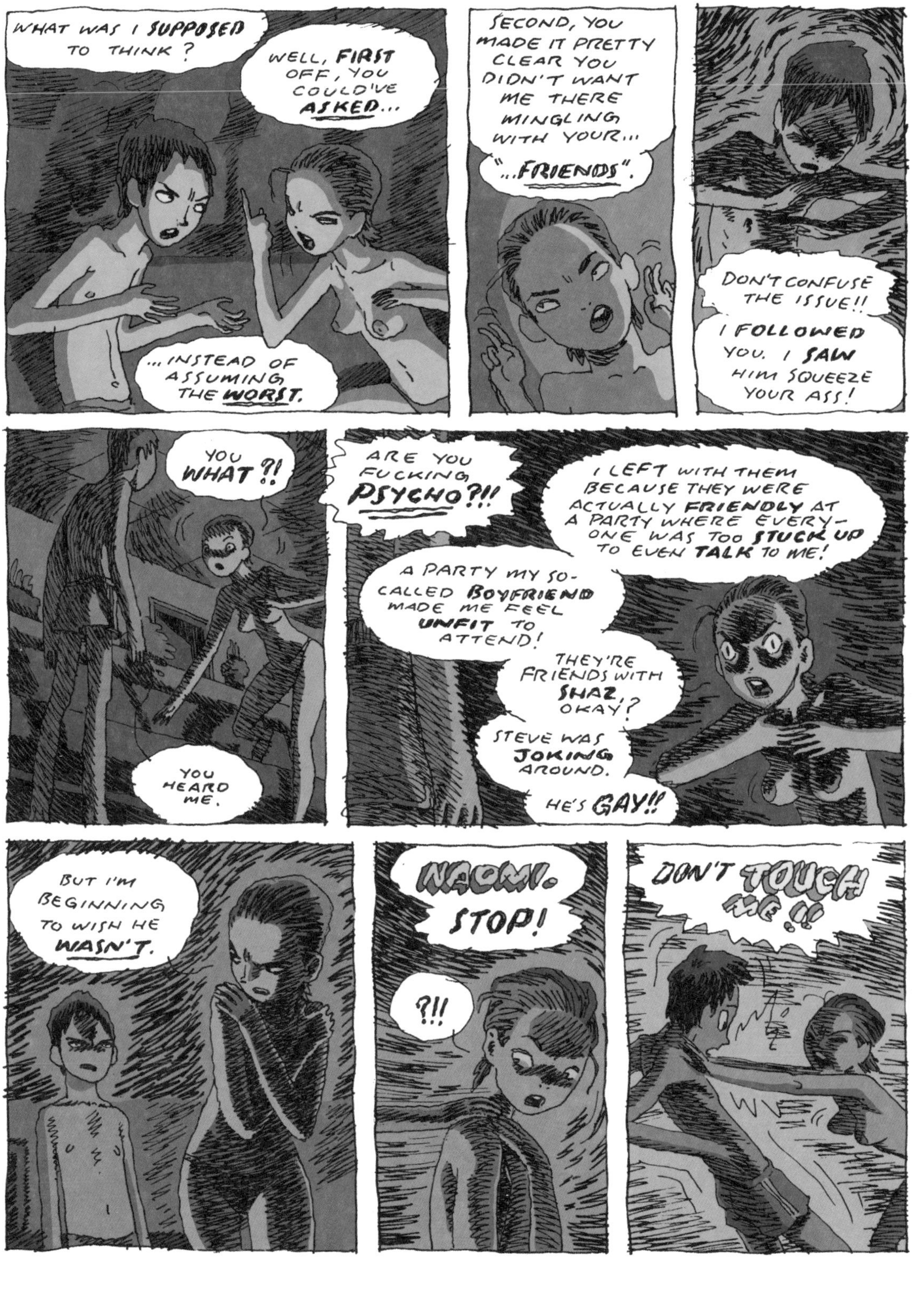
WHAT WAS I SUPPOSED TO THINK?
WELL, FIRST OFF, YOU COULD'VE ASKED...
...INSTEAD OF ASSUMING THE WORST.
SECOND, YOU MADE IT PRETTY CLEAR YOU DIDN'T WANT ME THERE MINGLING WITH YOUR...
"...FRIENDS".
DON'T CONFUSE THE ISSUE!!
I FOLLOWED YOU. I SAW HIM SQUEEZE YOUR ASS!
YOU WHAT?!
YOU HEARD ME.
ARE YOU FUCKING PSYCHO?!!
I LEFT WITH THEM BECAUSE THEY WERE ACTUALLY FRIENDLY AT A PARTY WHERE EVERYONE WAS TOO STUCK UP TO EVEN TALK TO ME!
A PARTY MY SO-CALLED BOYFRIEND MADE ME FEEL UNFIT TO ATTEND!
THEY'RE FRIENDS WITH SHAZ, OKAY?
STEVE WAS JOKING AROUND.
HE'S GAY!!
BUT I'M BEGINNING TO WISH HE WASN'T.
NAOMI.
STOP!
?!!
DON'T TOUCH ME!!

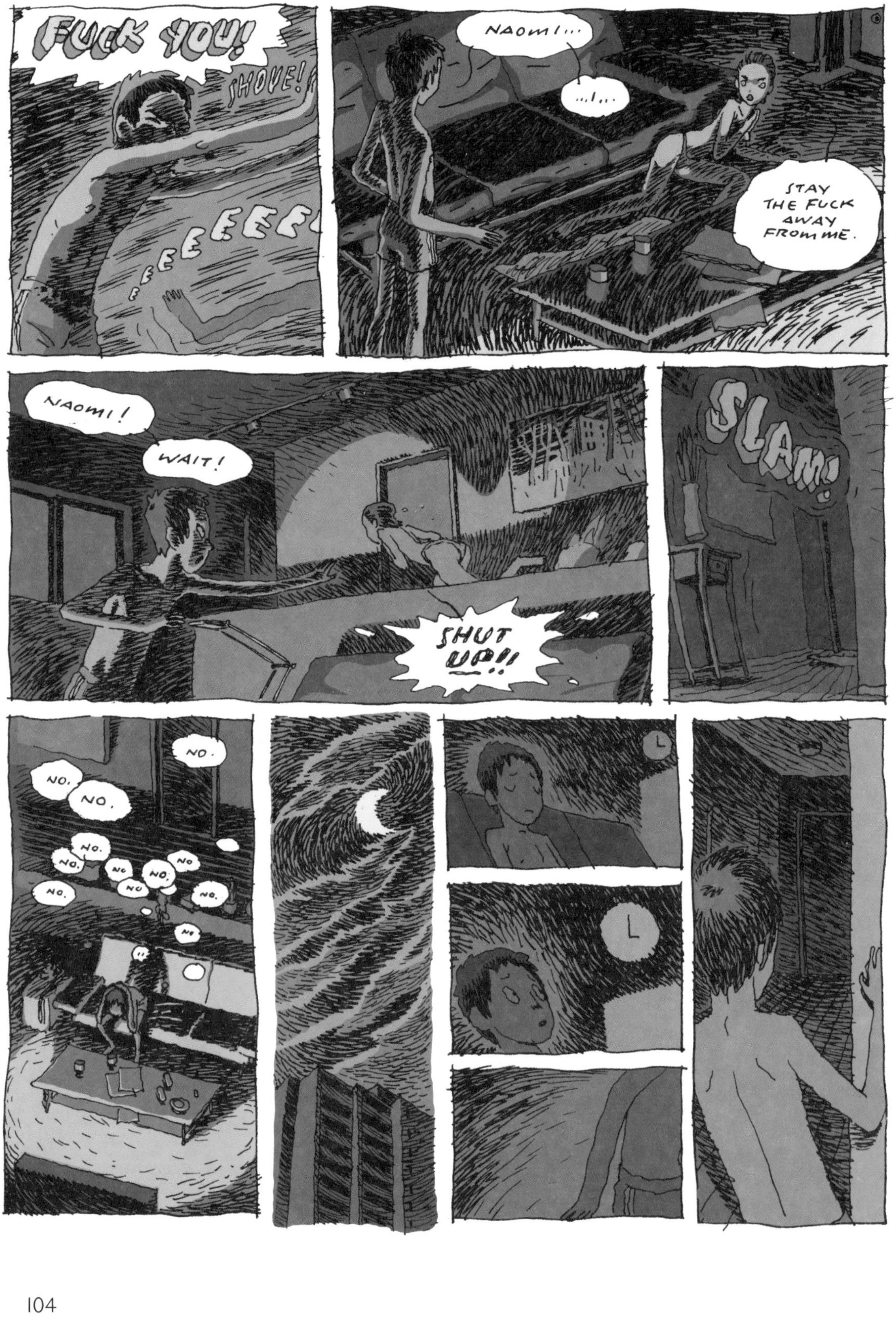
FUCK YOU!
SHOVE!
EEEEEEE
NAOMI...
...!...
STAY THE FUCK AWAY FROM ME.
NAOMI!
WAIT!
SHUT UP!!
SLAM!
NO.
NO.
NO.
NO.
NO.
NO
NO.
NO
NO.
NO.
NO
!!

:SOB:

:SNIFFLE:

KNOCK! KNOCK!

NAOMI?

:SNIFF:

PLEASE...

...GO TO HELL.

ZZZZZZ.

ZZZZZ ZZ

?

ZZZZZZZZZ

WOW.

SHE SURE SNORES LOUD.

ZZZZZZ

105

ZZZZZZ

SHE **SEEMS** OKAY.

BARFED A FEW MORE TIMES.

WH--?

ZZZZZ ZZZZ ZZ

SWEET MOTHER OF **JESUS.**

ZZZZZ

IN FACT, YOU COULD PROBABLY CRAWL RIGHT IN.

"BESIDE HER...

"DO SOME **EXPLORING.**"

"YOU KNOW..."

"...AS IN DOWN FOR THE COUNT."

"PASSED OUT."

JOHN?   "TOTALLY."

OHHH MY HEAD.

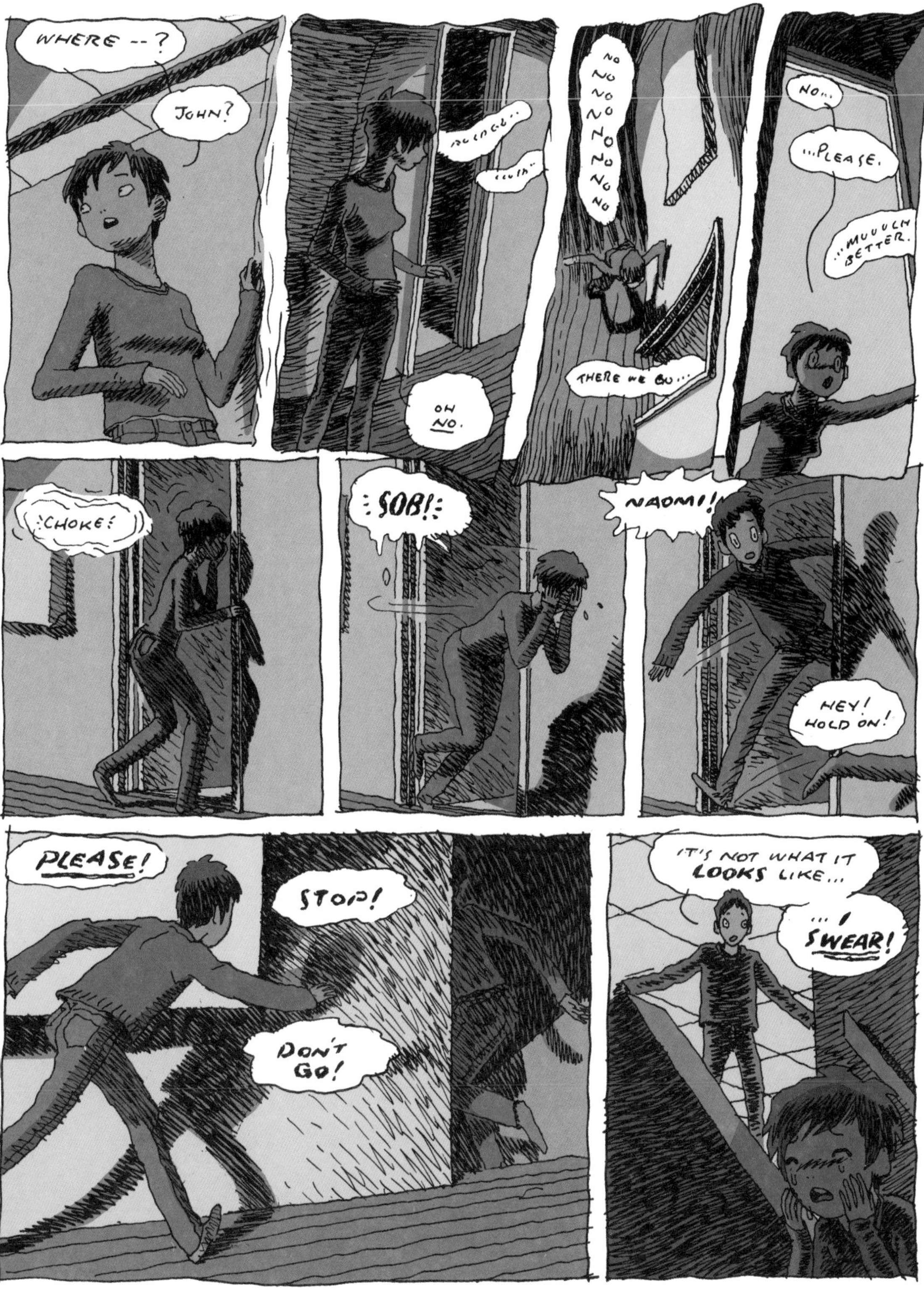
WHERE --?
JOHN?
OH NO.
NO NO NO NO NO NO NO NO NO NO
THERE WE GO...
NO...
...PLEASE.
...MUUULH BETTER.
:CHOKE:
SOB!
NAOMI!
HEY! HOLD ON!
PLEASE!
STOP!
DON'T GO!
IT'S NOT WHAT IT LOOKS LIKE...
... I SWEAR!

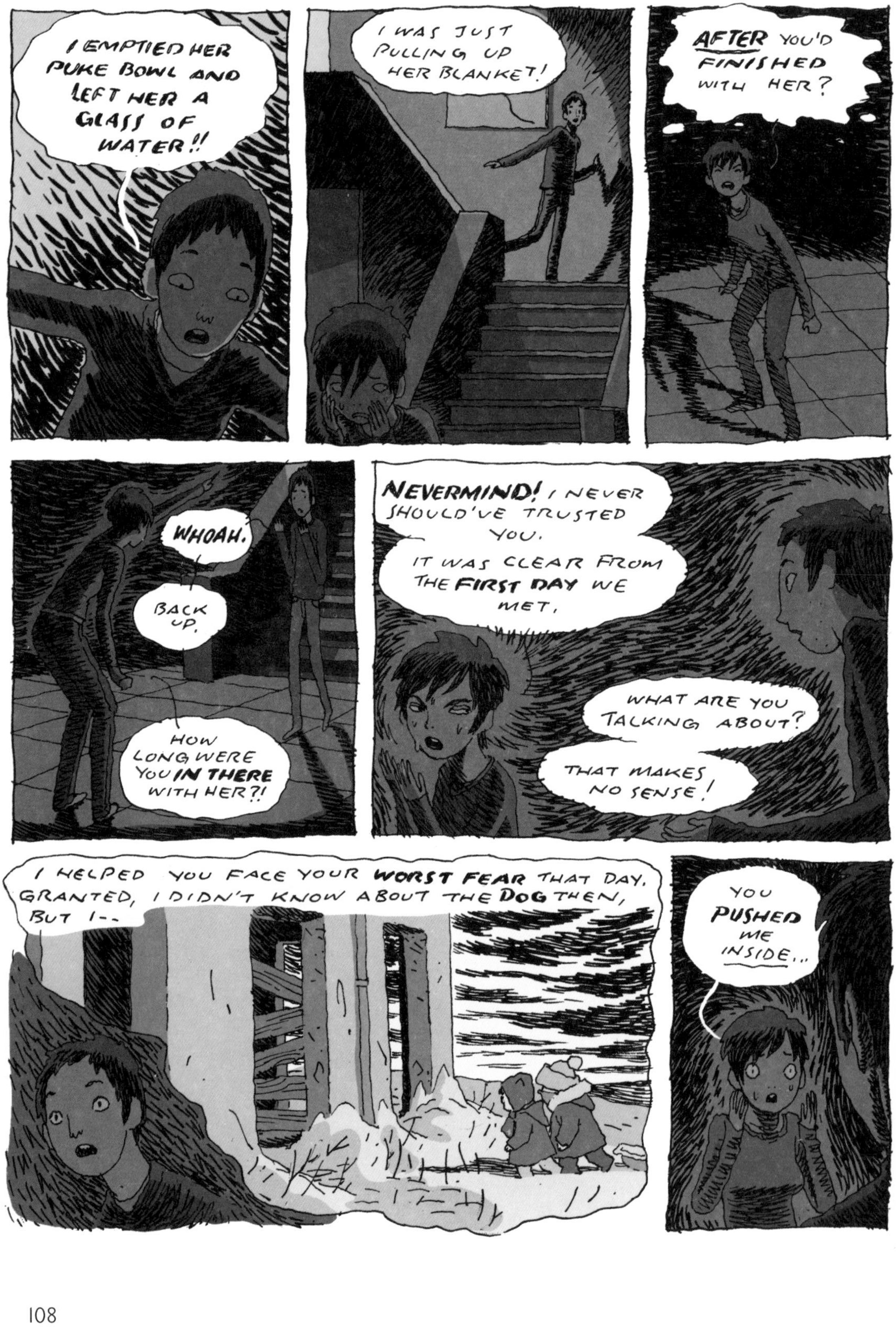
I EMPTIED HER PUKE BOWL AND LEFT HER A GLASS OF WATER!!
I WAS JUST PULLING UP HER BLANKET!
AFTER YOU'D FINISHED WITH HER?
WHOAH.
BACK UP.
HOW LONG WERE YOU IN THERE WITH HER?!
NEVERMIND! I NEVER SHOULD'VE TRUSTED YOU.
IT WAS CLEAR FROM THE FIRST DAY WE MET.
WHAT ARE YOU TALKING ABOUT?
THAT MAKES NO SENSE!
I HELPED YOU FACE YOUR WORST FEAR THAT DAY. GRANTED, I DIDN'T KNOW ABOUT THE DOG THEN, BUT I--
YOU PUSHED ME INSIDE...

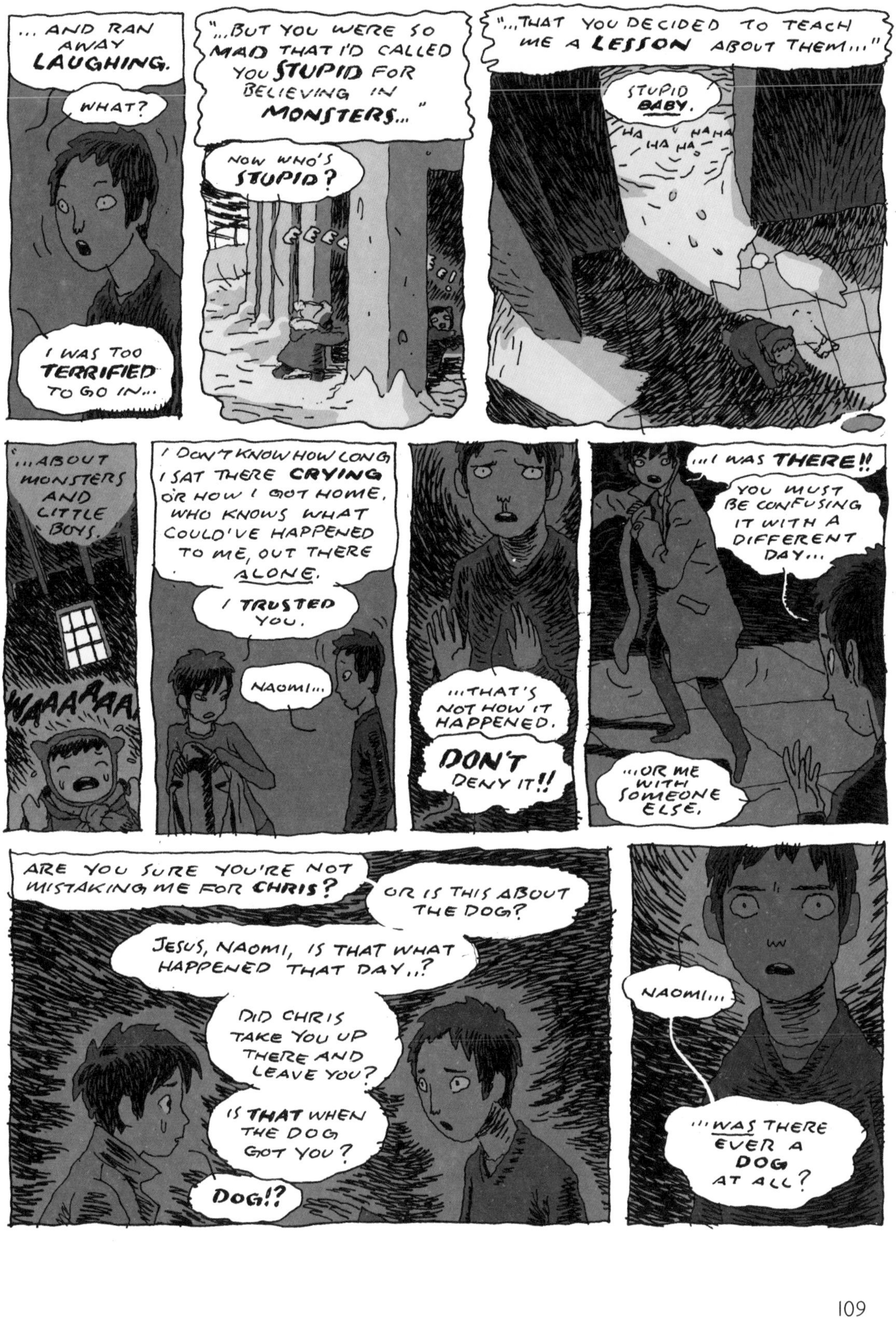

...AND RAN AWAY LAUGHING.
WHAT?
I WAS TOO TERRIFIED TO GO IN...
"...BUT YOU WERE SO MAD THAT I'D CALLED YOU STUPID FOR BELIEVING IN MONSTERS..."
NOW WHO'S STUPID?
EEEE
EE!
"...THAT YOU DECIDED TO TEACH ME A LESSON ABOUT THEM..."
STUPID BABY.
HA HA HA HA HAHA
"...ABOUT MONSTERS AND LITTLE BOYS."
WAAAAAAA
I DON'T KNOW HOW LONG I SAT THERE CRYING OR HOW I GOT HOME. WHO KNOWS WHAT COULD'VE HAPPENED TO ME, OUT THERE ALONE.
I TRUSTED YOU.
NAOMI...
...THAT'S NOT HOW IT HAPPENED.
DON'T DENY IT!!
...I WAS THERE!!
YOU MUST BE CONFUSING IT WITH A DIFFERENT DAY...
...OR ME WITH SOMEONE ELSE.
ARE YOU SURE YOU'RE NOT MISTAKING ME FOR CHRIS?
OR IS THIS ABOUT THE DOG?
JESUS, NAOMI, IS THAT WHAT HAPPENED THAT DAY..?
DID CHRIS TAKE YOU UP THERE AND LEAVE YOU?
IS THAT WHEN THE DOG GOT YOU?
DOG!?
NAOMI...
...WAS THERE EVER A DOG AT ALL?

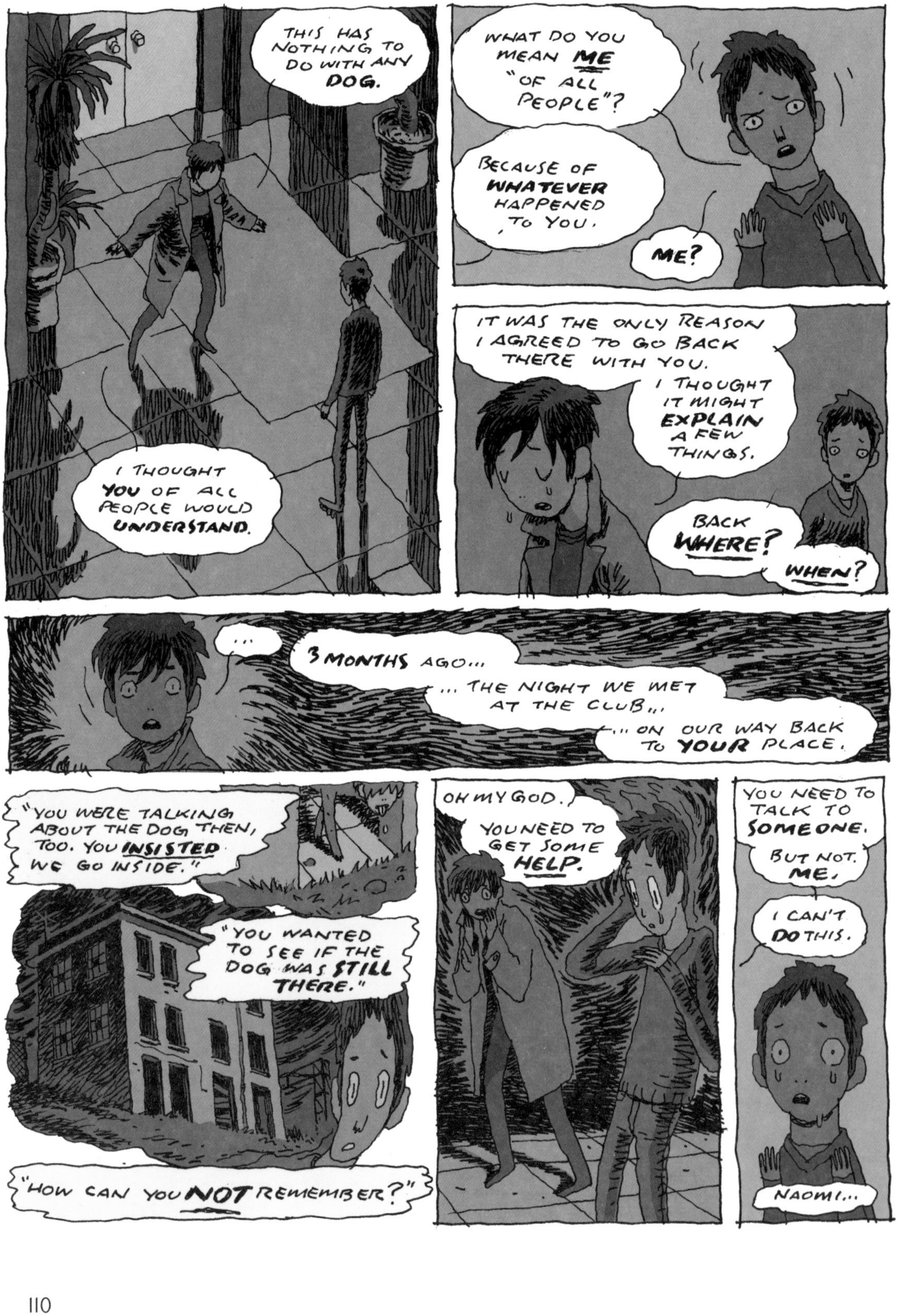
THIS HAS NOTHING TO DO WITH ANY DOG.
I THOUGHT YOU OF ALL PEOPLE WOULD UNDERSTAND.
WHAT DO YOU MEAN ME "OF ALL PEOPLE"?
BECAUSE OF WHATEVER HAPPENED TO YOU.
ME?
IT WAS THE ONLY REASON I AGREED TO GO BACK THERE WITH YOU.
I THOUGHT IT MIGHT EXPLAIN A FEW THINGS.
BACK WHERE?
WHEN?
...
3 MONTHS AGO...
... THE NIGHT WE MET AT THE CLUB...
... ON OUR WAY BACK TO YOUR PLACE.
"YOU WERE TALKING ABOUT THE DOG THEN, TOO. YOU INSISTED WE GO INSIDE."
"YOU WANTED TO SEE IF THE DOG WAS STILL THERE."
"HOW CAN YOU NOT REMEMBER?"
OH MY GOD.
YOU NEED TO GET SOME HELP.
YOU NEED TO TALK TO SOMEONE.
BUT NOT ME.
I CAN'T DO THIS.
NAOMI...

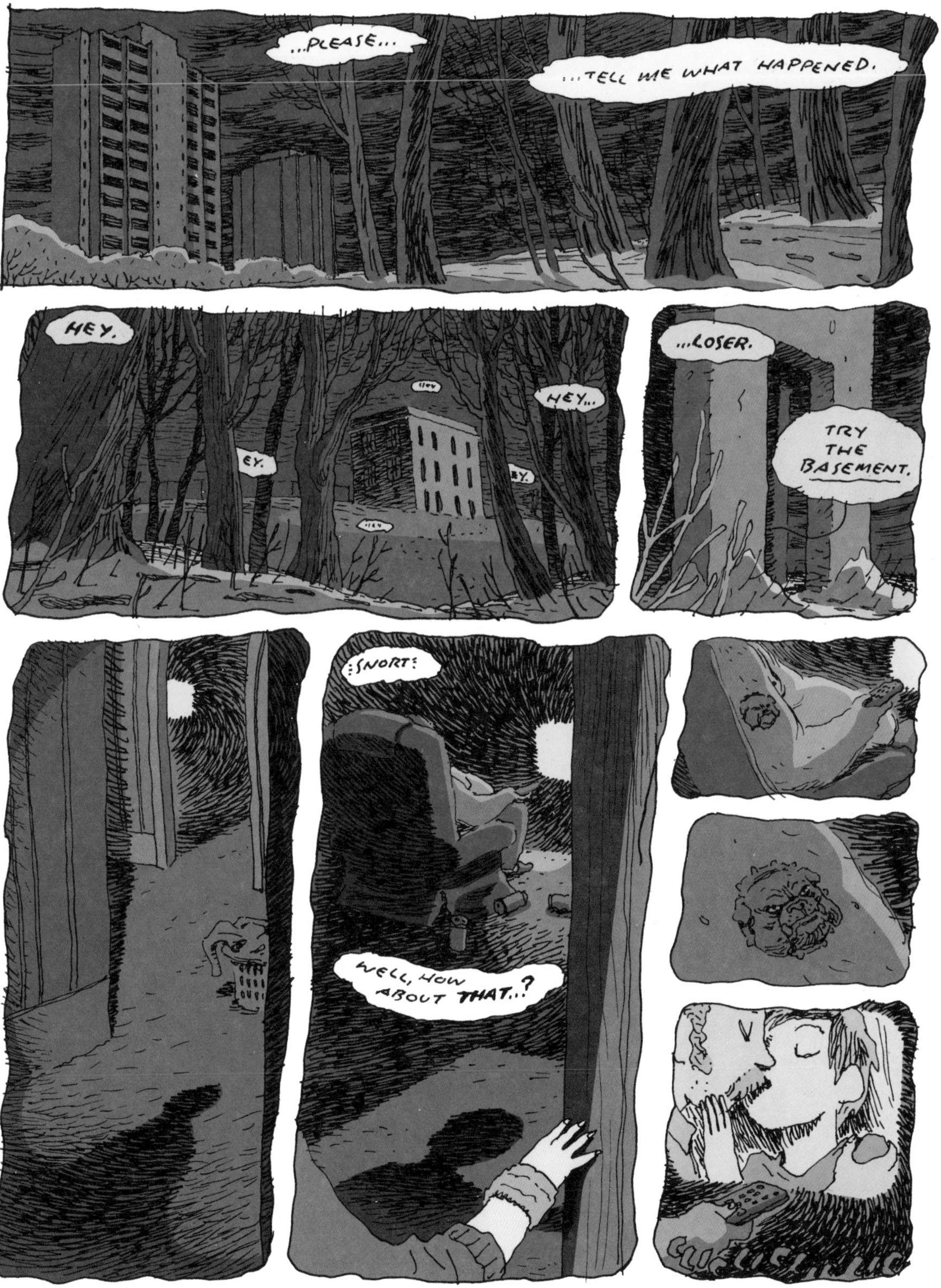
...PLEASE...
...TELL ME WHAT HAPPENED.
HEY.
HEY...
EY.
EY.
...LOSER.
TRY THE BASEMENT.
SNORT
WELL, HOW ABOUT THAT..?

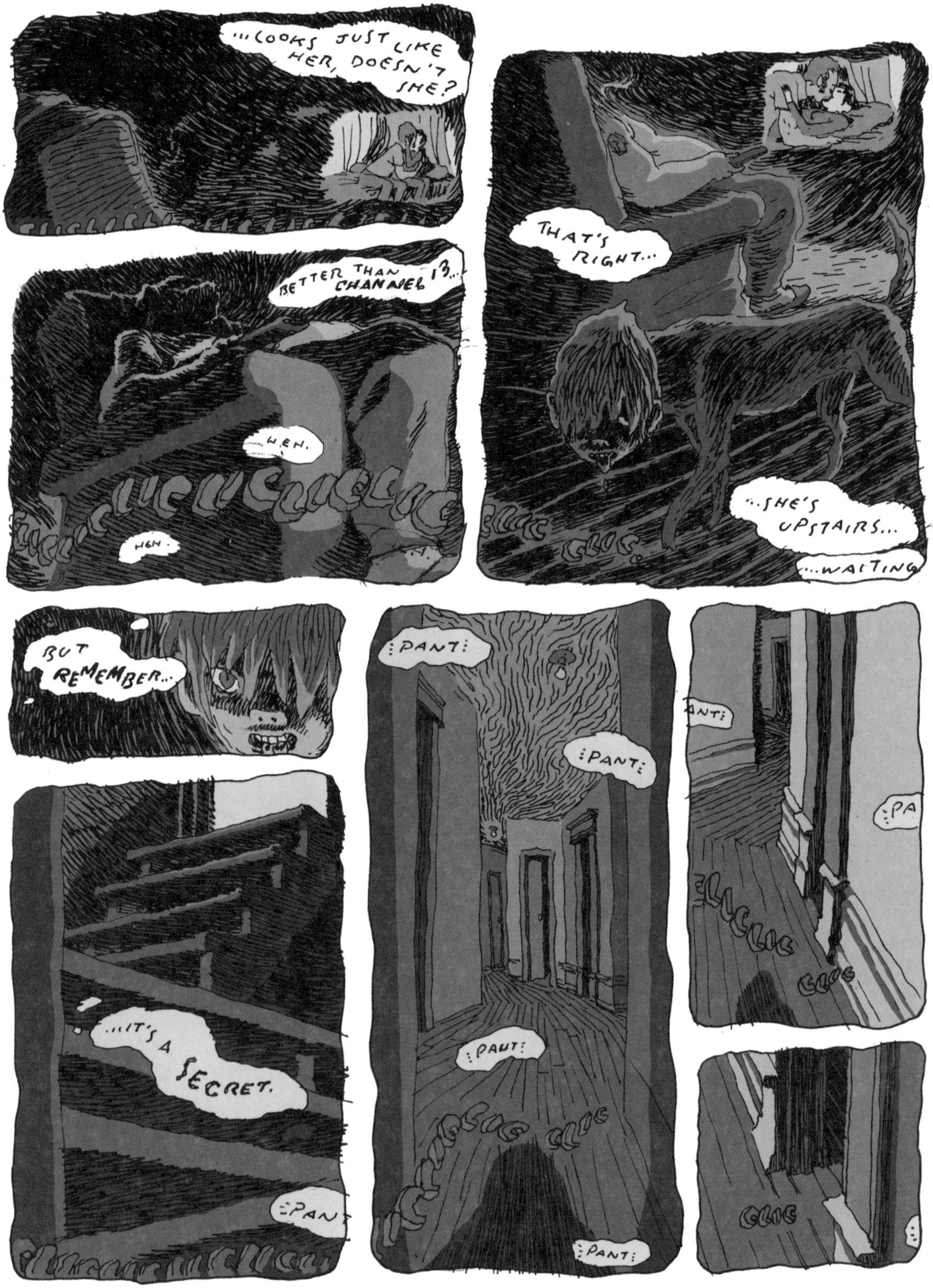
...LOOKS JUST LIKE HER, DOESN'T SHE?
BETTER THAN CHANNEL 13...
HEH.
HEH.
THAT'S RIGHT...
...SHE'S UPSTAIRS...
...WAITING
BUT REMEMBER...
...IT'S A SECRET.
PANT
PANT
PANT
PANT
PANT
PANT
PA

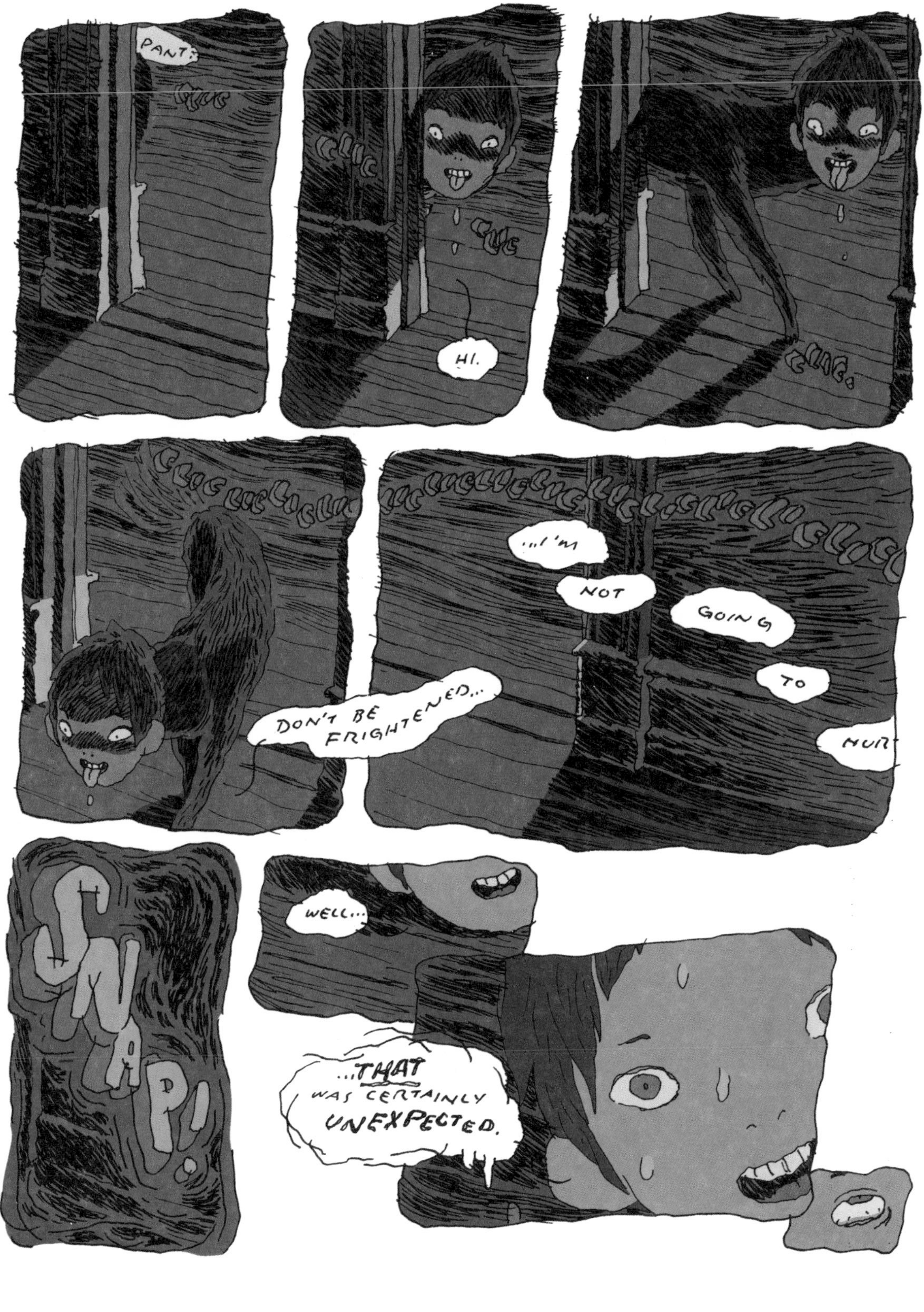
PANT.
HI.
DON'T BE FRIGHTENED...
...I'M
NOT
GOING
TO
HURT
SNAP!
WELL...
...THAT was certainly UNEXPECTED.

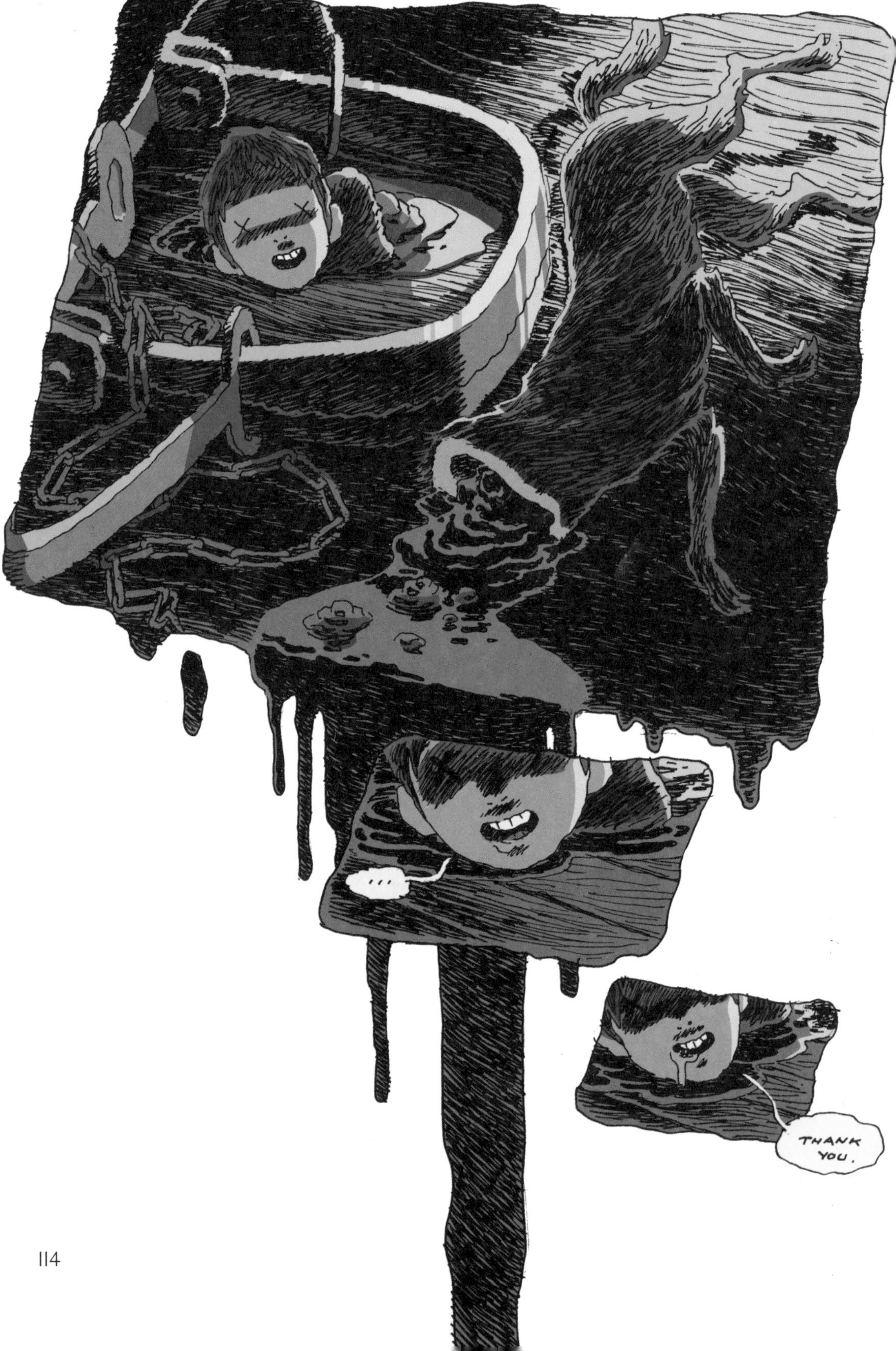
...
THANK YOU.

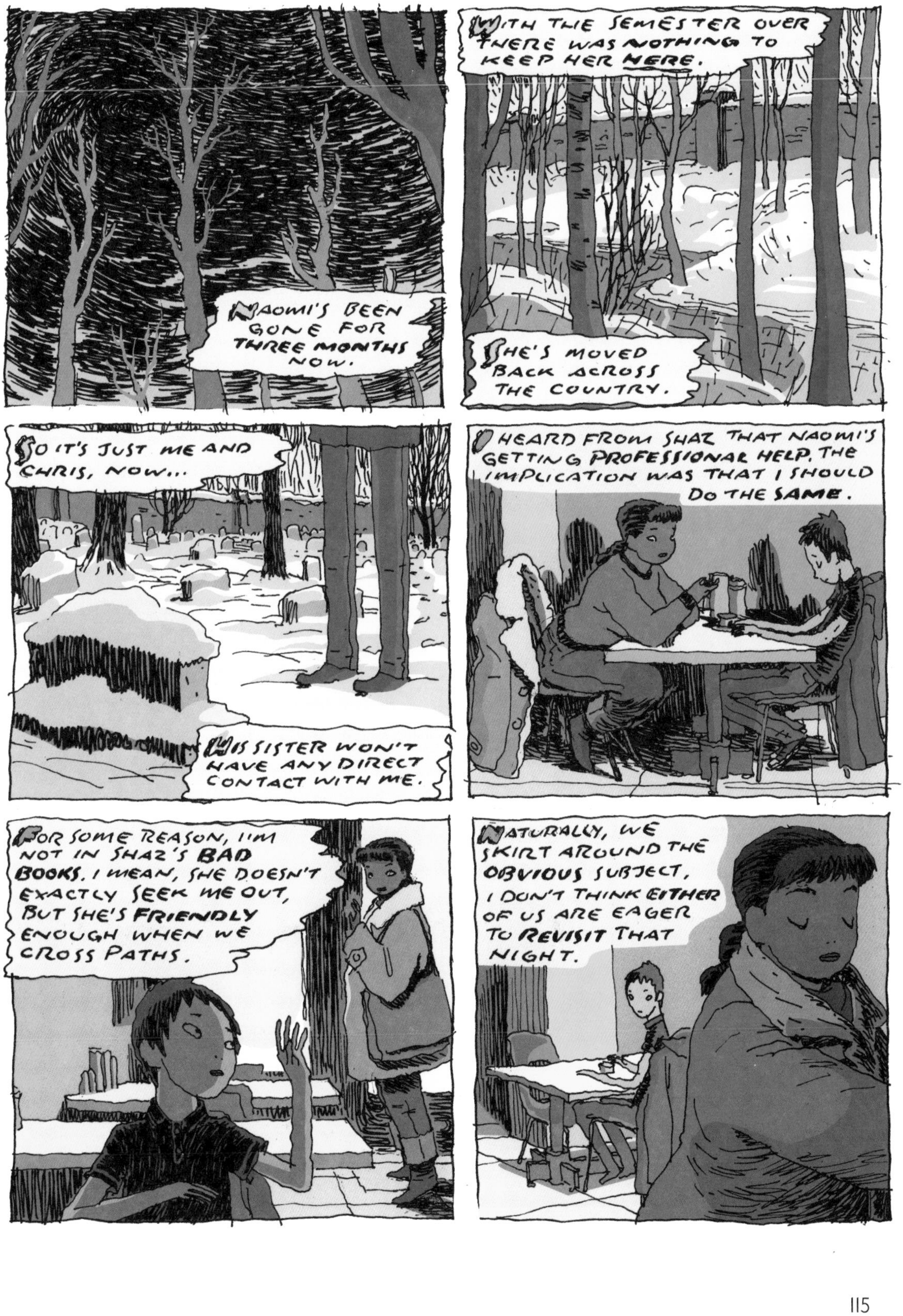

NAOMI'S BEEN GONE FOR THREE MONTHS NOW.
WITH THE SEMESTER OVER THERE WAS NOTHING TO KEEP HER HERE.
SHE'S MOVED BACK ACROSS THE COUNTRY.
SO IT'S JUST ME AND CHRIS, NOW...
HIS SISTER WON'T HAVE ANY DIRECT CONTACT WITH ME.
I HEARD FROM SHAZ THAT NAOMI'S GETTING PROFESSIONAL HELP. THE IMPLICATION WAS THAT I SHOULD DO THE SAME.
FOR SOME REASON, I'M NOT IN SHAZ'S BAD BOOKS. I MEAN, SHE DOESN'T EXACTLY SEEK ME OUT, BUT SHE'S FRIENDLY ENOUGH WHEN WE CROSS PATHS.
NATURALLY, WE SKIRT AROUND THE OBVIOUS SUBJECT, I DON'T THINK EITHER OF US ARE EAGER TO REVISIT THAT NIGHT.

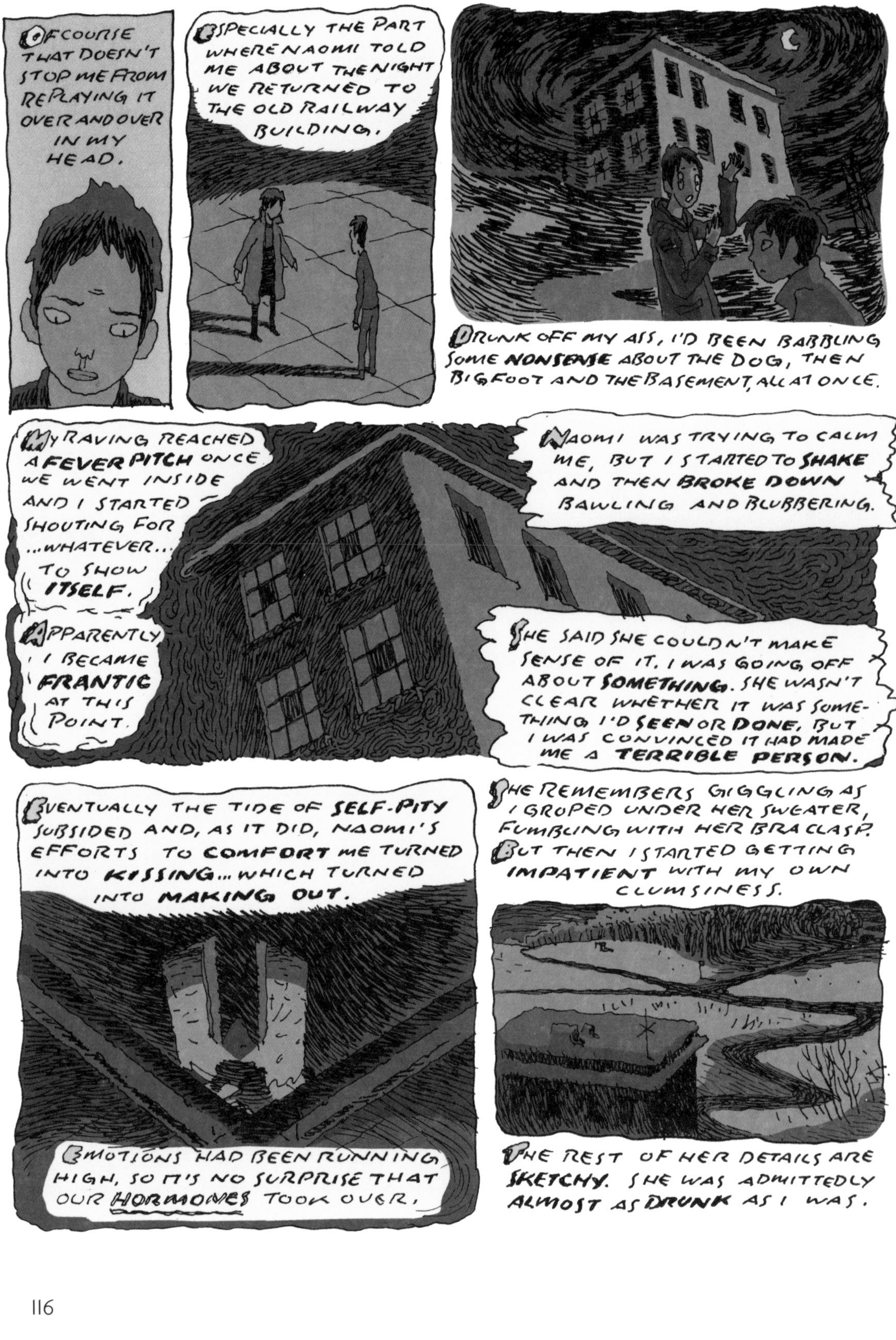
Of course that doesn't stop me from replaying it over and over in my head.
Especially the part where Naomi told me about the night we returned to the old railway building.
Drunk off my ass, I'd been babbling some NONSENSE about the dog, then Bigfoot and the basement, all at once.
My raving reached a FEVER PITCH once we went inside and I started shouting for ...whatever... to show ITSELF.
Apparently I became FRANTIC at this point.
Naomi was trying to calm me, but I started to SHAKE and then BROKE DOWN bawling and blubbering.
She said she couldn't make sense of it. I was going off about SOMETHING. She wasn't clear whether it was something I'd SEEN or DONE, but I was convinced it had made me a TERRIBLE PERSON.
Eventually the tide of SELF-PITY subsided and, as it did, Naomi's efforts to COMFORT me turned into KISSING... which turned into MAKING OUT.
Emotions had been running high, so it's no surprise that our HORMONES took over.
She remembers giggling as I groped under her sweater, fumbling with her bra clasp.
But then I started getting IMPATIENT with my own clumsiness.
The rest of her details are SKETCHY. She was admittedly ALMOST as DRUNK as I was.

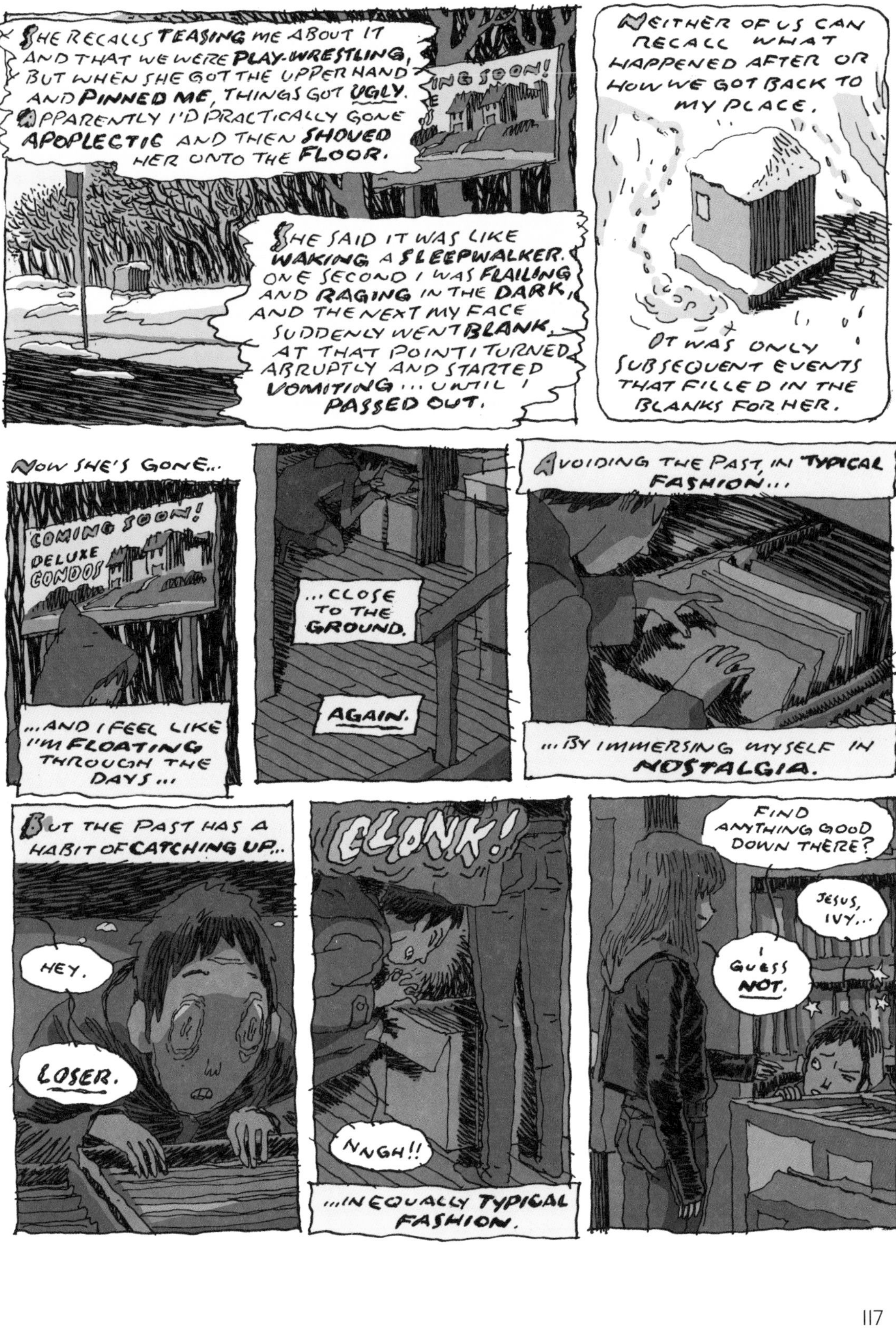
SHE RECALLS TEASING ME ABOUT IT AND THAT WE WERE PLAY-WRESTLING, BUT WHEN SHE GOT THE UPPER HAND AND PINNED ME, THINGS GOT UGLY. APPARENTLY I'D PRACTICALLY GONE APOPLECTIC AND THEN SHOVED HER ONTO THE FLOOR.
SHE SAID IT WAS LIKE WAKING A SLEEPWALKER. ONE SECOND I WAS FLAILING AND RAGING IN THE DARK, AND THE NEXT MY FACE SUDDENLY WENT BLANK. AT THAT POINT I TURNED ABRUPTLY AND STARTED VOMITING ... UNTIL I PASSED OUT.
NEITHER OF US CAN RECALL WHAT HAPPENED AFTER OR HOW WE GOT BACK TO MY PLACE.
IT WAS ONLY SUBSEQUENT EVENTS THAT FILLED IN THE BLANKS FOR HER.
NOW SHE'S GONE...
COMING SOON! DELUXE CONDOS
...AND I FEEL LIKE I'M FLOATING THROUGH THE DAYS...
...CLOSE TO THE GROUND.
AGAIN.
AVOIDING THE PAST, IN TYPICAL FASHION...
...BY IMMERSING MYSELF IN NOSTALGIA.
BUT THE PAST HAS A HABIT OF CATCHING UP...
HEY.
LOSER.
CLONK!
NNGH!!
...IN EQUALLY TYPICAL FASHION.
FIND ANYTHING GOOD DOWN THERE?
JESUS, IVY...
I GUESS NOT.

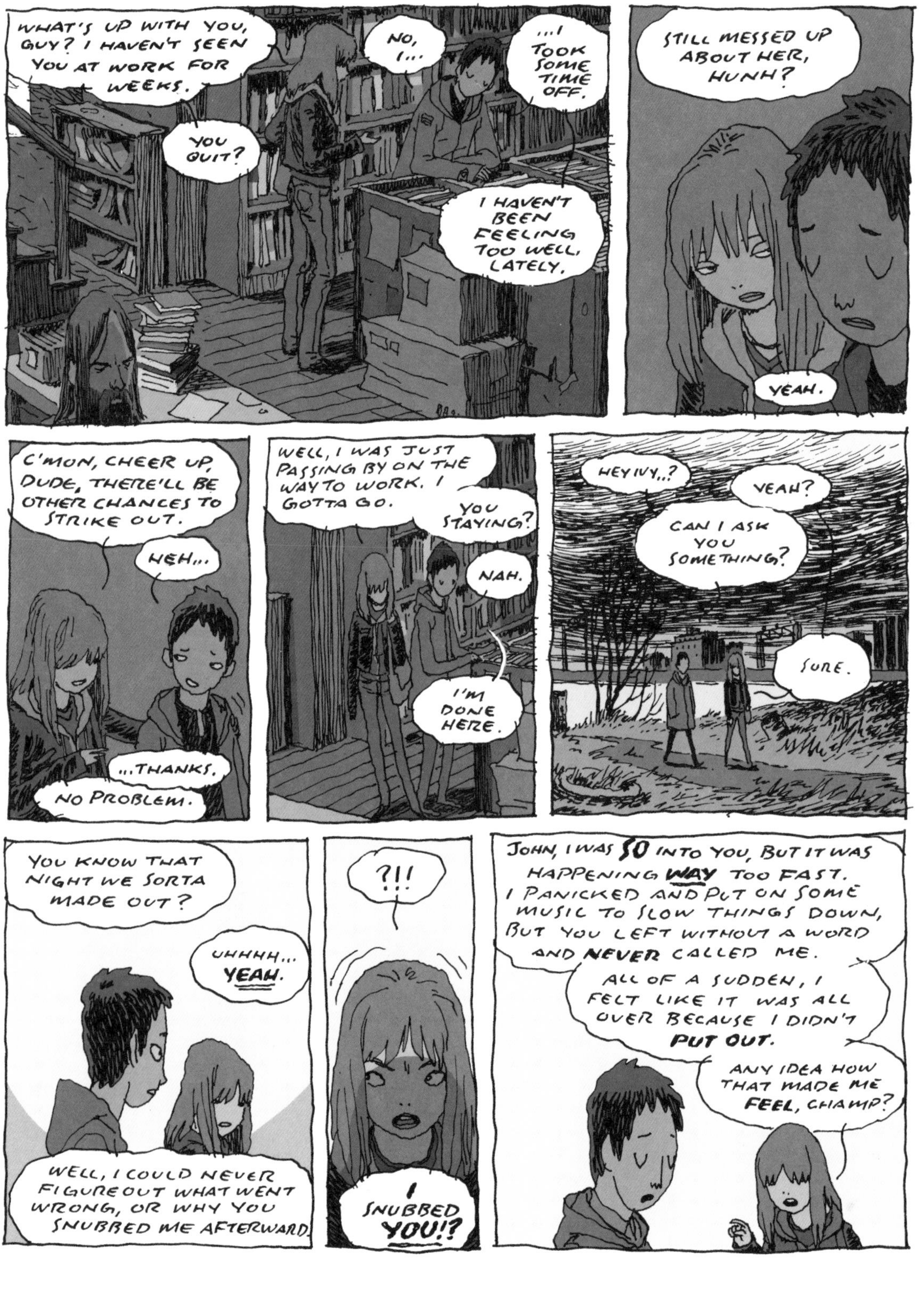
WHAT'S UP WITH YOU, GUY? I HAVEN'T SEEN YOU AT WORK FOR WEEKS.
NO, I...
...I TOOK SOME TIME OFF.
YOU QUIT?
I HAVEN'T BEEN FEELING TOO WELL, LATELY.
STILL MESSED UP ABOUT HER, HUNH?
YEAH.
C'MON, CHEER UP, DUDE, THERE'LL BE OTHER CHANCES TO STRIKE OUT.
HEH...
...THANKS.
NO PROBLEM.
WELL, I WAS JUST PASSING BY ON THE WAY TO WORK. I GOTTA GO.
YOU STAYING?
NAH.
I'M DONE HERE.
HEY IVY...?
YEAH?
CAN I ASK YOU SOMETHING?
SURE.
YOU KNOW THAT NIGHT WE SORTA MADE OUT?
UHHHH... YEAH.
WELL, I COULD NEVER FIGURE OUT WHAT WENT WRONG, OR WHY YOU SNUBBED ME AFTERWARD.
?!!
I SNUBBED YOU!?
JOHN, I WAS SO INTO YOU, BUT IT WAS HAPPENING WAY TOO FAST. I PANICKED AND PUT ON SOME MUSIC TO SLOW THINGS DOWN, BUT YOU LEFT WITHOUT A WORD AND NEVER CALLED ME.
ALL OF A SUDDEN, I FELT LIKE IT WAS ALL OVER BECAUSE I DIDN'T PUT OUT.
ANY IDEA HOW THAT MADE ME FEEL, CHAMP?

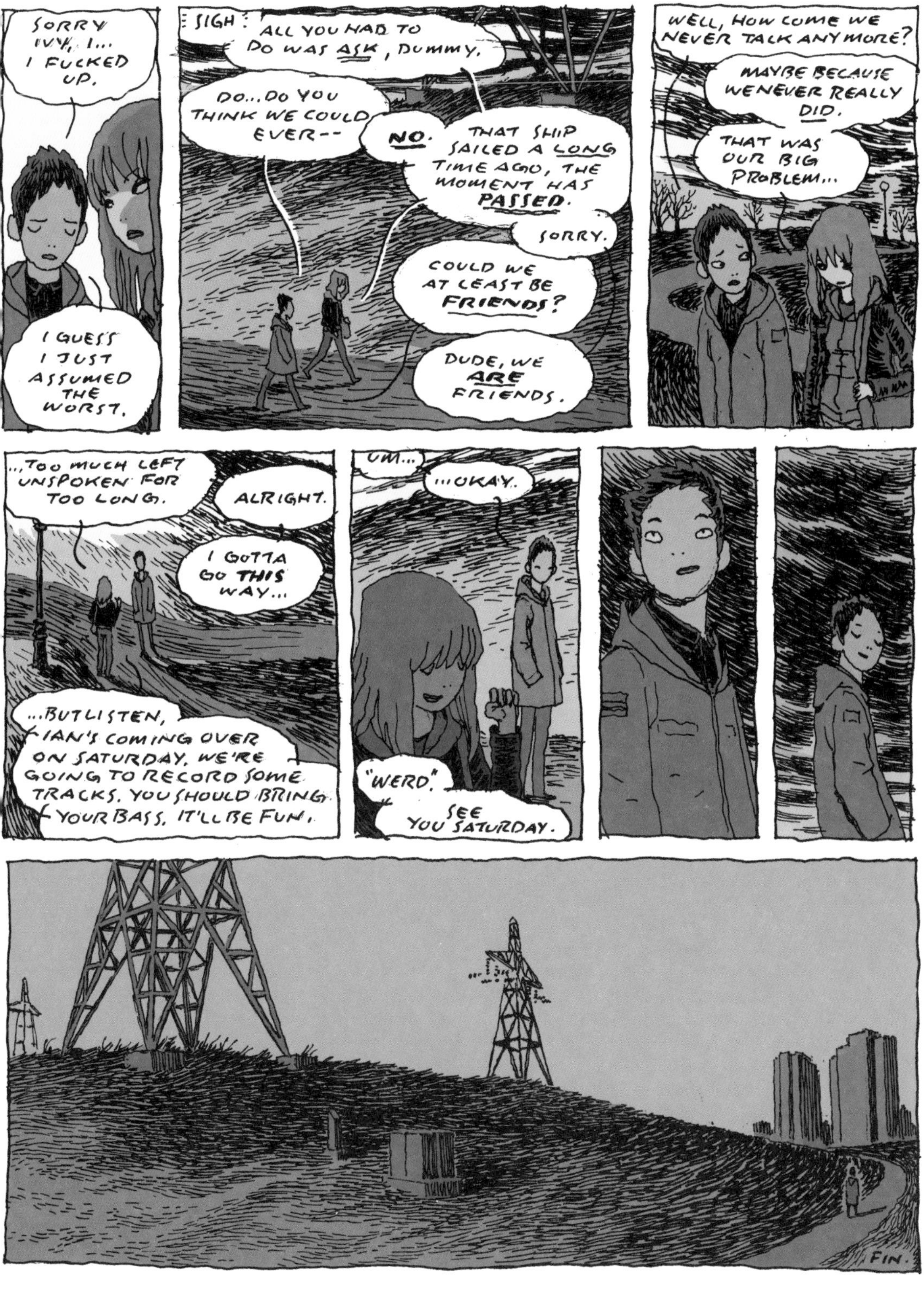
SORRY IVY, I... I FUCKED UP.
I GUESS I JUST ASSUMED THE WORST.
SIGH
ALL YOU HAD TO DO WAS ASK, DUMMY.
DO... DO YOU THINK WE COULD EVER--
NO.
THAT SHIP SAILED A LONG TIME AGO, THE MOMENT HAS PASSED.
SORRY.
COULD WE AT LEAST BE FRIENDS?
DUDE, WE ARE FRIENDS.
WELL, HOW COME WE NEVER TALK ANYMORE?
MAYBE BECAUSE WE NEVER REALLY DID.
THAT WAS OUR BIG PROBLEM...
...TOO MUCH LEFT UNSPOKEN FOR TOO LONG.
ALRIGHT.
I GOTTA GO THIS WAY...
...BUT LISTEN, IAN'S COMING OVER ON SATURDAY, WE'RE GOING TO RECORD SOME TRACKS. YOU SHOULD BRING YOUR BASS, IT'LL BE FUN.
UM...
...OKAY.
"WERD".
SEE YOU SATURDAY.
FIN.

About the author

Patrick McEown was born in Ottawa, Canada, in 1968 and began drawing at an early age. Along with a steady diet of Marvel Comics and science fiction paperbacks inherited from his older siblings, two of his formative childhood influences were Tove Jansson's *Finn Family Moomintroll* and Edward Gorey's illustrations for John Bellairs's *The House with a Clock in its Walls*. While he has maintained a lifelong admiration for both authors, it would be several years before their work would leave a visible mark on his own.

With the '80s – and adolescence – came the agitated strains of post-punk and the independent comics of the Hernandez brothers, Chester Brown, Charles Burns and Gary Panter, following in the wake of '60s pioneers like Robert Crumb. Swept up in this D.I.Y. zeitgeist, Patrick left high school to strike out on his own as a cartoonist and illustrator. However, largely self-taught and relatively inexperienced, he spent these early years honing his craft as a hired gun on other people's projects, rather than authoring his own.

The '90s found him freelancing for just about every reputable comic book publisher in North America and "moving around a lot", dividing his time between Canada's west coast and New York City. During this period, he contributed a significant chapter to Matt Wagner's Eisner Award-winning *Grendel* saga for Dark Horse Comics. A collaboration with Mike Mignola on *Zombie World: Champion of the Worms* followed soon afterwards, but Patrick's own voice as a creator would only begin to develop in the latter part of the decade through shorter, more personal works, encouraged by friends like Dave Cooper, Bob Fingerman, Gavin McInnes, and a remarkably supportive community of Seattle-based cartoonists.

His ambitions for comics and illustration would take a brief hiatus at the turn of the millennium when he shifted into animation work as a storyboard artist for the Warner Bros. series *Batman Beyond*, and began a Bachelor's Degree in Fine Arts at the University of Victoria. It was at this point that he made some pivotal trips to France, where he rediscovered in European comics a sensibility he'd long identified with.

Hair Shirt was written and drawn while completing his Master's Degree in Studio Arts at Concordia University in Montreal, Quebec, where he now teaches drawing. He also continues to work as a storyboard artist, most recently on the Cartoon Network's cult-hit series, *The Venture Bros.* He doesn't read as many comics as he used to, but he's greatly impressed by the breadth and depth of innovation in the medium these days – mostly in independent comics – and he's glad to still be part of it.

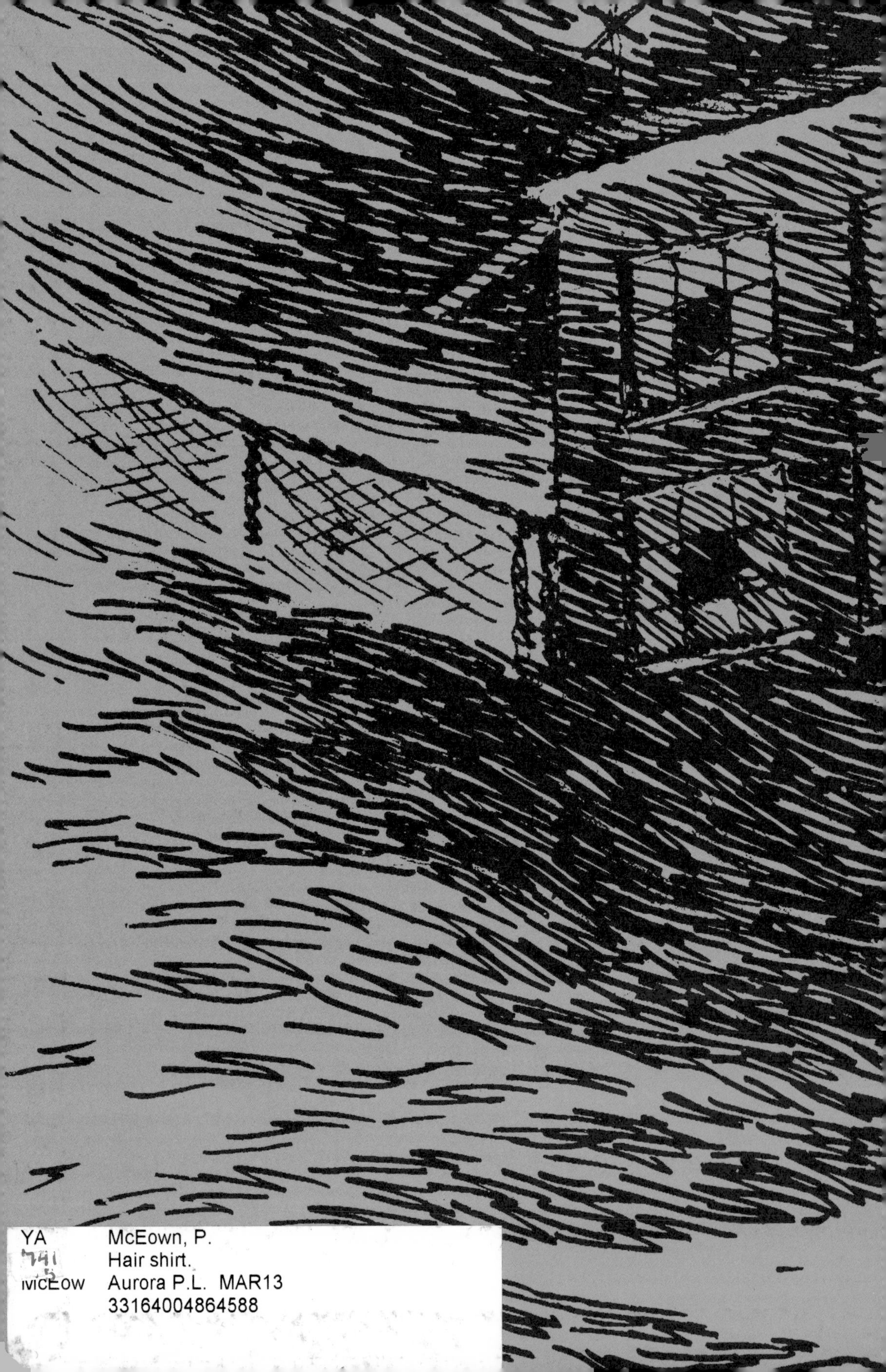